THE LIES THAT SHATTER

THE LIES THAT SHATTER

TRUTH & LIES DUET, BOOK TWO

A.V. ASHER

WINTER ZEPHYR PRESS

Ebook ISBN: 978-1-7365439-2-4
Paperback ISBN: 978-1-7365439-4-8
Hardcover: 978-1-7365439-5-5

Cover design: Damonza.com
Editing: My Brother's Editor

NOTE FROM THE AUTHOR

The Lies That Shatter is the second book in my Truth & Lies duet. This series is best enjoyed in order as it is the continuation of Alec and Sadie's story. Please read *The Truth Keeps Silent* before enjoying this novel.

Content warning: This book is intended for a mature audience and contains strong language, explicit sex and graphic descriptions of violence which some readers may find disturbing. Reader discretion is advised.

But to see her, was to love her;
   Love but her, and love for ever.--

   — ROBERT BURNS, *AE FOND KISS*

PART I

CHAPTER ONE

F ire ripped through Alec McKinley's body, his muscles quivering with the effort. He inhaled deeply. Sweat and metal hung in the air. On the exhale, he pushed the weights up, willing his pecs to fucking cooperate. Rock music thrummed along with the clank of weights hitting the floor.

"Go, man. Go," Mason's voice rang out.

"Aye, one more. You got this," Declan said, above him, one hand on the bar. Alec pressed up, his biceps trembling. He brought the bar back to his chest.

One more.

Fighting the tearing pain racing up his side, he forced the bar up for the last rep. Declan took the bar and hooked it on the frame. Relief washed through Alec's arms, but the ache of his injury persisted.

"Fuck." He sat up, wiping his brow in annoyance. "It's not even that damn heavy."

Mason handed him his water. "It's only your second workout since the doctor cleared you, man. Give yourself some time."

He was right, but that didn't keep Alec's frustration at bay. Almost three months had passed since the bullet pierced through his body, damaging his liver and nearly catching his spine. Alec was damned lucky to be alive.

It took months of painful physical therapy before the doctor finally cleared him for the gym and here he sat, sweating like a pig at less than half the weight he was used to working with.

Alec had time. The trial wouldn't begin for another eleven months. He had nearly a year to get himself back in working condition. He needed to be in top form before Mercedes came home to him.

Letting her leave hurt more than the bullet he'd taken to save her life. They had spent far too much of their lives separated, as it was. But knowing that she loved him was enough to keep him moving forward until they could be together.

Christ, eleven more months without her will be hell.

Declan seemed to read his thoughts. "What time are you supposed to talk to her?"

Alec checked his watch. "At eight o'clock, at least that's what they said. They'll be on their lunch break. I need to get home and clean up."

In a few hours he'd get to talk to Mercedes again. She was coming out of hiding to give testimony during an evidentiary hearing in San Francisco. Alec had barely slept since finding out the prosecutors had allowed them a fifteen-minute video call during her break. It would never be enough, but he'd take what he could get.

"Are you going to tell her?" Declan's blue eyes sparked with amusement.

"Nah, it's not ready yet," Alec said, throwing his towel into his bag.

Mason scoffed. "She might want some time to plan."

"Aye, but it's too soon. I don't want to get her hopes up if it doesn't play out."

"I don't think you could disappoint her with this," Declan

said with a chuckle. "You're giving her a literal world of options."

"Aye. Only if I make it work."

Mason and Declan shared a look, and Mason rolled his eyes. "You'll make it work, man."

Alec's phone buzzed and his pulse kicked up a notch. He hoped to hell they weren't messaging him to cancel the call. It was from his friend and computer tech, Cressida Bennett.

Check this out.

Alec opened the link to the video. Declan and Mason peered over his shoulder to watch as an American reporter stood in the courtyard of the federal building, a microphone in his hand.

Thanks, Mary. Depositions are set to begin today in the case of billionaire and CEO Marcus Cooper. Cooper was arrested two months ago on bribery and conspiracy to commit fraud charges, in a case that has shaken the pharmaceutical industry. Brenden Whitley, recently appointed US Attorney for the Northern District of California, alleges Cooper falsified data to conceal how addictive and deadly the popular prescription pain medication Sutanyl was and then bribed several FDA officials to obtain approval to sell the drug on the open market.

The camera panned wide to show a group of professionals climbing the stairs into the building. While the reporter spoke, the camera zoomed in, and Alec stopped breathing.

There she was.

How could someone blend in and stand out at the same time? Her clothes were the same as the others in the group. Business sophisticate with a black blazer, skirt, and heels that accentuated her curves. The wide sunglasses covered a good portion of her face. But Alec would know her anywhere.

Fucking gorgeous.

We expect several witnesses to give testimony in this case. One source within the prosecutor's office told us at least one witness has a significant security detail. Our source would not disclose to us why the government felt this level of security was necessary. We do believe that what he or she has to say is incredibly damning to Cooper Pharma, and possibly, to Cooper himself.

Alec scoffed. Damning was a serious understatement. Mercedes had handed the FBI a blueprint of Cooper's criminal enterprise. Not to mention she'd been held captive in Marcus Cooper's home, her blood was all over the penthouse, and she'd heard him giving orders to his thugs.

A man came into the camera view and Alec's stomach clenched.

Fuck.

What the ever-loving hell was Jason Hollis doing there?

Mercedes's abusive ex shouldn't be anywhere near her. And yet, he'd walked through the same doors she had.

A ball of ice worked through Alec's gut. Jason was a pro at manipulation and head games. Who knew what kind of shit he was pulling with her.

This fucking injury.

Without it, Alec would be there, keeping her safe and making sure that fucker didn't even look at her.

Mason put his hand on Alec's shoulder. "She has an armed escort, and it's broad daylight. He isn't getting to her."

Thousands of things could go wrong and there'd be nothing he could do. Anxious energy pulsed through him, pooling in his fingertips. Helplessness was not an emotion Alec had much experience with. These last few months had given him his fill.

The reporter on scene ended his feed. The two anchors in the studio droned on and on, making wilder guesses into the potential outcomes of the trial. These people had already admitted they'd been told next to nothing. That wouldn't stop them from trying this case with theories and conjectures for the next few months.

He dropped his phone into his gym bag and flung it over his shoulder. Then he followed Declan and Mason out of the gym and onto the buzzing London sidewalk. His mind was lost in planning for the future, when this hell was over.

———

ALEC PACED HIS FLAT, THE SILENCE BRINGING THE WALLS IN ON him. He'd tried turning on the telly, but the adverts grated on his nerves, so he switched it off. Being alone in his own home never used to be so lonely.

Alec checked his watch for the third time in as many minutes. She was late.

What if the prosecutor changed his mind and wouldn't let her call? Or maybe the internet went down? He checked and then rechecked that his Wi-Fi still had a signal.

It was too damn quiet.

His eye caught the glossy wood of her violin, propped against the wall, and the ache in his chest took another stab at him. The day he'd come home from the hospital and found it lying against his pillow was when it hit him. She was really gone.

The chimes of an incoming video call rang out through the room, making him jump. Alec clicked the answer button and waited impatiently for the screen to change.

When Mercedes came on the screen, his heart leaped into his throat. She'd always been able to take his breath away.

"Oh Christ, you're beautiful," he blurted out.

A grin broke out on her face, and she bit her lip.

"Sorry. Not a proper greeting. Hello, darling."

"Hi. I thought it was perfect." Mercedes's voice trembled when she spoke. "God, you look amazing. Are you feeling okay? I've worried about you every day."

"Aye, I'm doing well. Physical therapy has helped and I'm working on getting my strength back. It's coming along."

"You promise? You're not just saying that so I won't worry?"

"I promise, I'm getting better. I swear." Seeing the distress in her eyes was killing him. "How are you? Are they keeping you safe?"

Her shoulder came up in a shrug. "It's fine. I can't tell you much about it, but it's comfortable and it feels pretty secure." Her brow furrowed. "I did have to move once."

Alarm rang through him. "What? When?"

"About a month ago. They didn't go into the details, but they heard we were compromised. So, I had to start over."

"Jesus, Sadie . . ."

"I'm fine, everything's fine." She cleared her throat. "How is everyone?"

She was changing the subject for the same reason he hadn't told her how hard his recovery was going. "Aye, all is well. I talked to your sister yesterday. She wanted me to share some news with you." He gave an expectant pause. Mercedes's brows lifted and she tilted her head. "She and Luke are going to start trying for a baby."

"Oh, my god! Really?" Mercedes's hazel eyes welled with tears. She brought her fingers to the bridge of her nose.

"Hey, don't cry, darling. Charlotte will be okay."

"I know. It's the best news. I couldn't be more excited for them," Mercedes said tearfully. "It's just . . . I probably won't be there for her. I always thought I'd host her baby shower and pamper her with spa days." She dabbed at her lashes with her finger. "Now, I don't think they'll even let her tell me when she's pregnant. Sometimes I have to remind myself why I'm doing this."

"They didn't give you a choice. But they pulled that shit drug from the market because of you. You're already helping save thousands of lives."

"I know. That's one reason I keep going."

"I just wish you didn't need to be around Jason."

Her eyes widened. "How did you know he's here?"

"I know everything." Alec shot her a smug look.

Mercedes let out a laugh and arched her brow.

"I'm kidding, I caught sight of you on a news report a few hours ago."

Mercedes laughed. "Oh, yeah, that makes sense. He's out on bail but I have a protective order against him. I don't think he'll risk anything right here in the open. Plus, I have my security detail who will keep him from me. I can avoid him for the most part."

Jealousy curled in Alec's gut. That piece of shit didn't deserve to breathe the same air as Mercedes. "I'd feel a hell of a lot better if I could be there."

Her expression softened. "Well, there was only one way that was going to happen, and the cards didn't line up."

"Aye, we can still make it happen." Alec held her gaze.

Mercedes pressed her lips together and looked down, a smile playing on her lips. "Someday."

Marriage was the only way he could have joined Mercedes in the program, but he'd been too injured to be anything but a liability for her. But goddamn, he wanted it. He wondered what she might say if he were to ask. It wasn't the way he wanted to marry her, but if it meant they could be together, he'd do it in a heartbeat. They belonged together. The taste of the future they'd had in Scotland had been far too brief.

This woman was his world. She deserved better than a hurried proposal over a video chat.

Alec swallowed the lump in his throat. "Are you still in love with me?"

Mercedes eyes flashed with a longing that cut into him. "More than ever. You?"

An ache hit him so hard in the chest. "Aye, so much it hurts." He wanted to touch her, to feel her body under his. Loving him the way only she could.

He heard a knock on her end, and she spoke to someone in the room with her. She looked back to Alec, her expression crestfallen. "They're telling me my time is up."

Alec's heart fell, but he pulled up his mouth in a smile. "Okay. You be careful and come home to me."

"You too. I worry about you so much."

Alec smiled. "I'll be fine. I love you, Sadie."

"I love you too, Alec. I always will."

The video blinked away, leaving the screen washed in a powder blue. She was gone. Alec inhaled deeply, letting the fissure erupt in him. It was one more goodbye, but it wasn't forever.

CHAPTER TWO

Mercedes stared at the screen, the lump in her throat aching painfully.

Alec looked so damned amazing. She hadn't seen him since she'd left him in his hospital room three months ago. Then, he'd been pale and broken. But now, the healthy glow had returned to his cheeks and his voice was strong. The ribbon of fear that had been running through her since she'd left him loosened enough to let her breathe. He was in his own home, looking comfortable and whole. That's all that mattered.

Mercedes wiped at her lashes, thankful her mascara was waterproof. God, she missed him so damn much. These months without him had taken a toll, especially since she had little to do but think about him.

Today, she was especially grateful they'd been allowed to talk. Coming out of hiding to show up for a hearing against your abuser and one of the most powerful men in the world wasn't an everyday occurrence. Alec was her anchor. A touch of sanity in the insane world she was in.

Mercedes left the office and joined Federal Marshal Larissa King in the hall.

"How'd it go?" Larissa asked, her smile stiff and formal.

"Good. He looked so strong."

An intern from the US attorney's office click-clacked down the marble corridor toward them. "Ms. Elliott, Mr. Whitley asked me to escort you back to the courtroom. We're getting started soon."

Mercedes gave the intern a tight smile. "Wouldn't want to keep the man himself waiting."

The intern didn't respond, instead turning to lead the way. Mercedes followed until the two women paused in the wide reception area. The chatter from the gathered attorneys and court employees reverberated off the stone walls.

The sensation of being exposed and vulnerable clenched Mercedes's insides. They shouldn't be out here, they had private witness rooms set aside to keep her hidden. She ducked behind a large column where fewer people were gathered. Larissa and the intern were only steps away and engrossed in their conversation.

Mercedes leaned against the column, taking the weight off her aching feet. She hadn't worn heels in a while, and they were certainly making it known.

It was easy to tune out the world and let her mind drift back to Alec. She wanted one more small moment where she could savor the glow of their talk. What she wouldn't give to be back in his arms.

"You look as incredible as ever."

The tender tone sent a shiver of fear running down her back. She turned to find Jason's ice-blue eyes scorching through her. He'd slipped around the column without her even aware he was nearby.

What the hell? Where was the team dedicated to keeping this man away from her?

Jason's face, still handsome and angled, was thinner than the last time she'd seen him. He wore a tailored suit, and his blond hair was neatly styled. A soft smile played on his lips and the longing in his expression hadn't changed.

Memories of his voice, screaming at her to choose between Alec's life or a bullet in the brain, came flooding in her mind. She searched around the room. Larissa was gone.

Where the hell was she?

Jason stepped closer to her, and she scrambled back. Too late. He had deftly separated her from anyone else who would care.

"Walk away, Jason. Or I'll scream," she rasped, hating how much her voice shook.

His smile widened and his gaze dragged up her body. "Oh, but I might like that." The sex coating his words sent revulsion spiraling through her. "But how do you think *they'll* take it?" He gestured over his shoulder.

A gaggle of journalists had entered the foyer crowding around the US attorney, Brenden Whitley, as he strode through the corridor. Whitley was barking answers as he went.

Shit.

Up to this point, Mercedes had remained anonymous to the press. One peep of drama and they would swarm, feasting on every nugget until they tore her life and every ounce of safety apart.

Jason's tone was gentle. "I only wanted to say hello, and to see for myself how you've been."

How can he look so sincere?

He stepped toward her. "The last time we saw each other was pretty . . . tense."

"Tense?" she snapped. "You kidnapped me, beat me and held a gun to my head and told me you'd kill me if I didn't choose you. That goes beyond tense."

"But you chose me."

Anger flared in her. "Uh, yeah. Because of the gun." She scowled and lifted her chin. "Even in your delusions, you know Alec is all I want."

His eyes hardened and the warning bells she'd long since dismantled reared to life, screaming at her. She glanced around the room again, vulnerability increasing by the second.

You can not afford to piss him off.

But it was too late. The fake gentleness dropped, and a familiar rage took its place. "But you're *nothing* to him," he growled. "While you're gone, he's having all the pussy he wants. It only took Mariah batting her fucking eyes at him, and he was all over it. Probably fucking some skinny little whore right now, not giving a shit about you."

Mercedes's stomach turned at the vision, his words implanted in her brain.

No, no, no.

Mercedes made a dash to get past him, but he stepped in front of her. Her heart thundered, and the room tilted.

Jason's lips twisted up. "That would make him just like all the others, right? They say they love you and then they fuck someone else." He tilted his head and laughed. "You really think he's going to wait for you? No one else would. No one but me."

The truth peppered in his words sank her further. But she lifted her chin up and tried once more to go around him. This time, his hand snaked out and snatched her arm and jerked her into him. He pressed her against him, his breath grazing her cheek.

Fear froze her muscles. This man should have never been able to touch her again. And yet, she was powerless to stop him.

Jason groaned and he caressed her chin. "God, I've missed you so much."

"Let me go," she whispered. Full-on panic was shredding her resolve apart. The room spun sickeningly, stealing her ability to think.

"What the fuck?" A deep male shout cut through the air.

Suddenly, Jason's grasp released. Mercedes tottered backward on her heels, her back smacking against the column. Relief surged through her veins, and she focused on counting out the seconds between each shaky exhale.

A large man stood between them, hand on the gun holstered to his hip. There was shouting and footsteps on the marble floors as other men came and escorted Jason away.

"Are you okay? Sadie?" Warm brown eyes came into focus. Federal Marshal Noah Ramirez leaned down to study her face.

Mercedes swallowed hard and nodded. "I'm okay, Noah."

"I am so sorry. He never should have gotten so close to you."

Mercedes pressed her back against the column, letting it cool her heated skin. A cold sweat had broken out on her brow. The US attorney was gone, as was the horde of journalists. She didn't know how much of the encounter they'd caught, if any.

"Where's Larissa?" Noah's gaze swept the room. "Let's get you out of here. You shouldn't even be out in the open like this." Annoyance tinged his words.

Straightening her shoulders, she smoothed the fabric of her blouse and ran her shaking fingers through her hair to tame any flyaway pieces. She still had a job to do. They'd worked too damn hard and given up too damn much to let Jason throw her off balance now.

Noah guided her gently, eyeing the members of the press as they skirted past them. He led her around a few corners to a room designated for witnesses.

"What did he say to you?"

Mercedes shook her head. "It's not important." She pulled in a deeper breath, trying to bring her focus on the testimony she needed to give.

"It *is* important. He violated the protection order. That bastard's about to land his ass back in jail."

That she hadn't been the one to realize this showed how

much Jason had rattled her. Her thoughts were so fractured that she couldn't hold on to the good. Only seeing the bad. Jason's taunting words were echoing in her head.

They say they love you and then they fuck someone else. You really think he's going to wait for you? No one else would. No one but me.

"You're right. I'll give a full statement when I'm done." Mercedes's fingers tingled with the anxious energy pulsing in her veins. Bach's *Cello Suite Number One* came into her head and her fingers worked the strings in her mind. Why a cello piece was anyone's guess, but the tone and rhythm were perfect to soothe her fractured spirit.

She did her best to put Jason out of her head, to focus on Alec and the way he loved her.

WHILE MERCEDES WAITED FOR HER CAR, SHE ROLLED HER shoulders, attempting to ease the strain on her muscles. It had been a long day, and she was ready for a hot shower and sleep. Unfortunately, neither were in the cards for her immediately. The supervisor on her case hadn't wanted her in the city any longer than necessary, so they would have to drive back to her safe house tonight.

The first time she'd been whisked away to a safe house, Alec let her lean against him while she slept. It'd been much more comfortable than leaning against the window would have been, but really, it had been an excuse to snuggle up with him. He'd wrapped his arms around her and held her for hours. It was the first time she'd felt safe in years. She wished more than anything to go back to that.

A black car with tinted windows pulled up, and Noah opened the glass door to escort her into the parking garage. He'd been sticking closer to her since the run in with Jason. She was grateful he was there for her. Sometimes Larissa was a little inattentive. Her wandering off was proof of that.

Noah came around the car and slid in next to her, flashing her a smile. "That went well today, don't you think?" He was a big man, nearly as big as Alec, with warm brown skin and dark brown eyes. All he had to do was flash his dimpled grin and the ladies at the courthouse melted. Mercedes was pretty sure he wasn't there for the ladies, but she didn't know him well enough to jump into his business.

"Better than expected. With any luck, we gave them enough to take that asshole down."

Larissa peered back at Mercedes through the rearview mirror.

"Ms. Elliott," she said stiffly. "I wanted to apologize to you for leaving you alone this afternoon. The intern from the prosecutor's office asked for a rundown of our protocol, and I got distracted. I should never have let Jason Hollis get so close to you."

Mercedes shot a quick look at Noah. His face was impassive, but she wondered if he and Larissa had gotten into it. They couldn't afford for these kinds of mistakes to happen. But it was done. "It's alright. He likely would have figured out another way to talk to me. Hopefully, he'll be locked away after this."

Larissa gave her a tight smile and a nod. Then she maneuvered the car out of the garage, passing by the throng of press as they went. They must be nearly ready for the evening news cycle. Some noted the car, snapping a few pictures as they drove by. Mercedes had to hope her anonymity held.

The sun had set behind the buildings, casting an evening glow on the city. They had a few hours' drive to the safe house outside of Sacramento. She kicked her heels off and laid her head back against the rest.

The car hit the ramp onto the Bay Bridge, and the traffic was flowing steadily. Mercedes looked back at the city she'd lived in most of her life. She shouldn't miss this place. It was here every insecurity had been forged. Where she was let down time and time again by a mother who didn't want her. Where the closest person in her world had loved and betrayed her. Where a man who said he loved her had beaten and torn her down. Pain was interwoven throughout the streets.

She shouldn't miss it, but she did.

The sparks of city lights hitting the water stretched out all the way to the Golden Gate. The last sight of the western sun, long since set, cast a deep blue glow all around. She would always treasure the person she was now from the lessons she'd learned.

Jason was wrong. Alec wasn't like the others. He loved her the way no one ever had. He'd bled for her. He'd killed for her.

When this was over, they'd be together. And then she'd get to go home.

CHAPTER THREE

The smell of urine and garbage filled Adam Wilson's nostrils, making him huff out the air and hold his breath. Even in the pretentious Nob Hill neighborhood, the back entrances smelled like shit.

He climbed the stoop and stopped at the metal door to enter the code on the keypad. Once it beeped, he pulled it open and stepped into the hallway.

Adam doubted the FBI knew Marcus Cooper was here tonight, but he could never be too sure. Marcus wasn't known for his subtlety. Trying to keep that man's fucking ego under control since his arrest had become its own challenge.

Not only that, but Adam was taking a hell of a risk marching his ass through this place. The FBI had a target on him, especially since he'd offed one of their agents in London a few months ago.

Fucking London.

Their once flourishing operation had taken a big hit after that shit show. Patrick was dead, Mariah was in the wind and Jason was in jail. The biggest blow came when Marcus himself was indicted.

It was insane for Adam to be coming in for a face-to-face

meeting with so much heat on them, but if Marcus wanted him to take the risk, he'd do it. He didn't have a choice.

Adam made his way up to the top floor. One of their security team met him at the elevator door.

"Have you swept the room and hallways?" Adam asked.

"Yes, sir. Finished up ten minutes ago. Mr. Cooper is . . . entertaining a guest. I'll do a sweep again after she leaves."

Adam pulled the card out of his pocket and opened the door. Music played throughout the penthouse. A breeze moved through the rooms and a killer view of the San Francisco skyline appeared through the open door. Adam kept himself out of the doorframe. They had swept the penthouse for bugs, but he wouldn't put it past the FBI to rent out nearby spaces to observe Marcus's visitor list.

A noise from outside drew his attention, and Adam walked to one of the other windows. He peered through the sheer curtains enough to take in the sight on the balcony.

For fuck's sake.

Marcus was standing on the patio, his pants around his knees, his cock in the mouth of a naked woman. His hips were thrusting, ramming her throat hard. Grunts carried into the suite. She was certainly eager. Based on her blonde hair and toned ass, she wasn't Mrs. Cooper.

Only a rich fuck like Marcus would get a blow job on a balcony to piss off the FBI.

Adam walked to the fully stocked bar and mixed a gin martini, making sure he made a lot of noise when he shook the drink. Marcus wouldn't hurry things up on his account, but he might for a drink.

"Fuck," Marcus shouted. "Suck me, fuck! God yeah, right there."

Oh good, he's nearly done.

Adam poured himself a shot of tequila and sat on the barstool. A minute later, Marcus came in from the balcony, followed by the busty blonde, her tits on full display for him. He slid up the zipper of his pants.

"You're certainly punctual, Adam. I've always appreciated that about you." Marcus slapped the girl's ass. She giggled, shooting a lusty stare at Adam.

Adam curled his mouth up and pushed the stem of the martini toward his boss.

"You want a turn?" Marcus said, gesturing to the girl with his head.

"You offering?" He raked his gaze over the woman. Rich brown eyes fluttered back at him and his cock hardened a bit more. She had the look that turned him on, but the eyes were all wrong. If only they were a blue gray. He'd fuck her all night, for sure.

"Should I wait in the guest room, Mr. Cooper?" Her hand played with the collar of Marcus's shirt.

Marcus's gaze scanned Adam. "Perhaps. Why don't you get comfortable? Mr. Wilson might join you. We'll see how our meeting goes."

Once she had left the room, Marcus picked up the martini glass, swirling the olives on the glass pick. "I pay a significant fee for your services, do I not?"

Adam's gut churned. "You have always been generous."

"In fact, some might say, out of all my employees, you've benefited the most?"

A shiver crawled down Adam's spine. "Yes, sir."

The saccharine smile dropped from Marcus's face. "So, do you mind explaining to me how Mercedes Elliott is still alive?"

"We had a hit scheduled, but they got word we had compromised her safe house and moved her."

"How did they know?"

"We're still working out the details of that. We recently turned a new asset. They've provided her location, but I'm waiting for visual confirmation she's actually there." Adam sipped, letting the tequila burn down his throat. "Once we know for sure, I have a pro on standby ready to strike."

"That's admirable work. But she's already given testimony. The hearing yesterday was a disaster for us. She got Whitley almost everything he asked for."

"Jason got a few things removed. And he'll be instrumental in tearing her credibility apart if we have to go to trial."

"Yes, but enough got through to fuck us. And forgive me if I don't think Jason Hollis was the best person to be providing evidence on my behalf. It's because of him I lost a decent man and had to have brains cleaned up off my marble floor."

Marcus wasn't wrong. Jason was a volatile mess.

"Jason's aware of his position with us. His fate is not only tied to ours, but at our mercy. He won't testify against you, and he is in the unique position of making Mercedes seem crazy. Dead or alive, we're going to need to discredit the hell out of her."

Marcus stirred his drink with the pick of olives. "I want him gone. He's a fucking liability when it comes to that woman."

Jason had been taken to a federal facility and Adam's diminished network was struggling to support the primary targets. He was going to need to be creative if he was going to get to Jason.

Marcus smirked. "Too many mistakes, Adam. The last three years have been one clusterfuck after another. It's been quite exhausting."

"I know I let you down. It won't happen again."

Marcus sipped his drink. "Any word on Mara?"

Adam stiffened. Mara Donovan, Marcus's longtime assistant, had been the catalyst for all this chaos. Everything the feds had on Marcus had been because of Mara.

"Not yet. They never found her body, so it's likely she's alive."

Marcus inhaled deeply and let it out. "I should have left my fucking wife. If I had, Mara never would've spoken to that damn lawyer. Then she'd be the one sucking me off and not some slut with fake tits."

Adam's jaw tightened. "I have eyes in the UK working to find her. Unlike Mercedes Elliott, Mara doesn't have someone like Alec McKinley to keep her off the grid. I doubt she can stay hidden much longer."

Marcus turned an icy stare on him. "She's evaded us now for over a year. Are we sure she doesn't have help?"

Adam grimaced at the implication in his boss's words. "Not that we can see. But we're doing what we can."

Marcus sighed. "Fine. Take care of Mercedes and Jason first. She can't be allowed to testify at any more of these hearings. The evidence they're allowing in is fucking killing us."

"Yes, sir." Adam finished his drink and set it on the counter.

"Good." Marcus stood up and held out a hand to Adam. "Now get your ass in there and fuck that girl. Consider it a bonus. You're one of the few who managed to keep himself out of jail so far."

An hour later, Adam slipped out of the building and made his way down the steep hill where his car waited. Shooting a load into a pouty little mouth was usually a decent stress reliever, but somehow, he still walked away unsatisfied. There were only a few women who had ever been enough to pull him away from the day's worries. High priced hookers didn't do it for him anymore.

His phone buzzed, and he answered with his earpiece.

"This is Citadel."

"Good evening, this is Prodigy," a deep male voice came through the line. "We have confirmation."

Adam stopped walking, his heart leaping in his chest. "You sure?"

"Positive. Our asset is on site."

Fuck.

There was too much at stake. He had made his deal and sold his soul. The time to turn back had come and gone years ago. He was either all in, or he was going to lose everything.

"Do I have instructions or what?" Annoyance coated Prodigy's tone.

Adam closed his eyes. "Affirmative. Take her out."

"Copy."

Adam pressed the end button, regret hollowing him. This wasn't the man he was supposed to be, but it was the man he was.

CHAPTER FOUR

D irt plumed above the truck as it pulled down the dirt road. Mercedes squinted through the dusty screen, trying to identify the vehicle making its way to the house.

"I'm pretty sure it's Noah," she called to Larissa.

Larissa, who had been peeking through another window, grunted in agreement. "What's he doing here?"

Mercedes shrugged. "Maybe he forgot something."

Larissa frowned but didn't respond. Mercedes was a bit surprised as well. He'd only left for his home in Sacramento this morning. They didn't expect him back for three days.

As soon as Noah walked through the door, Mercedes could see something was wrong. His eyes were red-rimmed, and his smile was forced.

"What're you doing back?" Larissa said, annoyance filling her tone.

Mercedes wasn't sure what the big deal was. He had his own room here, so it wasn't as if it was an imposition. Besides, Noah was much better company. She'd been expecting three days of near silence.

Noah cleared his throat. "I'd rather crash here tonight."

Mercedes's heart went out to him. Whatever had brought him back to the house was clearly killing him.

Larissa's brows pinched together. "You have the next few days off."

Mercedes shook her head. *What a freakin' robot.*

"I did, but they were vacation days. I'm canceling them." Noah brushed past her and headed to his room. Larissa's gaze followed him, the frown never leaving her face.

Larissa wasn't the warmest of women. Even in the fading light of evening, she still had her ash blonde hair tightened back into a severe bun. Mercedes often wondered if she'd ever let her hair down. Literally.

Noah was an absolute teddy bear, though. They had gotten along right from the start.

Mercedes walked down the hall to Noah's door and knocked gently. At his soft call, she turned the knob. He was sitting on the bed, his phone clutched in his hand. When he saw it was her, he straightened up.

"Are you okay?" she asked, hoping he wouldn't mind her crossing the line into personal.

"Yeah, I'm good." He gave her a broad smile, but his eyes told her everything. This man was in a hell of a lot of pain. Mercedes tilted her head and waited.

Noah's smile faded, and he looked away. "My fiancée and I have been struggling lately. He hasn't been open to my being away from home so much. So, I took the time off to surprise him. You know, a little romantic staycation." The phone in front of him lit up with a text. He read it and tossed it on the bed without responding. "But I guess he wasn't as lonely as I thought."

"Oh, damn, Noah. I'm sorry." A pang of sadness clenched her chest.

Noah nodded his thanks and gave her a tight smile. "I hope you don't mind me crashing your night."

Mercedes scoffed. "Are you kidding? Larissa and I were

talking about all the wild parties we were going to throw while you were gone. Now what'll we do?"

Noah chuckled softly.

She walked to him and put her hand on his shoulder. "Can I get you anything? A shot of whisky? A vat of ice cream?"

"Nah, I'm good. Thank you, though." His grin was a little less forced. "I'm going to turn in for the night."

She gave his shoulder a squeeze. "Okay, you know where I am if you need to talk. I've got lots of time." Mercedes walked to the door. "A bit of advice from someone who's been in your shoes; block his number and try to get some rest. Nothing he says tonight's going to fix anything."

"Yeah, that's probably a good idea. Thank you."

Mercedes gave him one last sympathetic smile. "Anytime."

She padded to her own room and closed the door behind her. Leaning on the wall, she took in a deep breath.

Noah didn't deserve to be hurt that way. She knew how much damage that sort of betrayal could do.

They say they love you and then they fuck someone else.

What if Jason was right?

What if, months from now, Alec changed his mind? How would she even know he was with someone else? He could be like Noah's fiancé. Too selfish to let her go, but not willing to stay faithful.

She'd offered Alec an out, and it had ripped her heart apart to do it. But Alec had been the one to hold on to what they had. Even now, her pulse raced at his words.

Stay in love with me. Tell me you'll be mine through it all. And when it's over, come home.

Alec would wait. She had to have faith in him.

Fucking Jason.

Abandonment, cheating, never being enough. He'd needled his way right into her head, knowing exactly how to cut the deepest. Her painful past was his to play with.

She pushed his words out of her head. She'd be damned if she'd let him steal another ounce of happiness or security from her.

Mercedes changed and washed her face. It was still early in the evening, but it wasn't like time mattered here. She could spend the entire day in her pajamas if she felt like it. It was just a different kind of prison.

Glancing out her window, she took in the dark fields that surrounded the house. The distant lights of Sacramento reflected across the clouds. She pulled the cord to close the blinds and climbed into the full-size bed.

As she drifted off to sleep, she recalled the perfect tone of Alec's voice and that delicious accent. Mercedes couldn't wait to return to their sweet little river haven in Scotland and get lost in the bliss of his body.

"MERCEDES!" LARISSA HISSED, GIVING HER SHOULDER A shake. "Sadie, wake up. We have to move now!"

"What?" Mercedes sat up, the fog of sleep disorienting her.

The acrid scent of smoke wafted through the air. *What the hell?*

"We need to go," Larissa said.

Mercedes scrambled from the bed and slipped on her shoes. "What's happening?"

"We don't know. Noah's looking for the cause, but there's a fire. Let's go."

Two gunshots rang through the night and Mercedes froze, her heart jumping. She met Larissa's eyes and saw a glimmer of remorse there.

"Oh, god. Noah," Mercedes whispered.

"We have to move!"

Mercedes hurried through the kitchen after Larissa.

Smoke was billowing through the living room as flames licked up the curtains.

The small hall to the garage hadn't shown signs of the fire, so Mercedes ran to it. She touched the handle. It was cold.

"Larissa!" she called. "The garage is okay! We can get to the car."

"No!" Larissa said between coughs. "We need to go this way! Come on!" She dashed through the smoke to the front door.

Mercedes stopped midway through the living room. This made no sense. They didn't know who or what was out there.

Smoke was coating the living room, burning her lungs. She coughed and covered her mouth and nose with her arm. Tears filled her eyes, and she rubbed them to ease the sting.

"Mercedes! Now!" Larissa threw open the front door and stepped onto the porch.

Mercedes had no more time to deliberate. As soon as she stepped onto the porch, she saw him.

Tactical gear.

Glowing green goggles.

And a fucking rifle aimed right at her.

Mercedes tried to dive back into the flaming house as a flash erupted from the shadowed man.

Thwack.

The impact reverberated through every bone in her body, tearing through her thigh. She cried out as her leg gave way and she landed hard on the floor. Smoke seared her lungs as she breathed through the agony.

Scrambling, she tried to push herself up onto her feet. Her injured leg wouldn't hold her weight.

She had to move.

The garage.

Mercedes crawled through the kitchen. The smoke wasn't as dense as the living room. She latched onto a kitchen chair and pulled herself up. Then she slid the chair along the floor to support her.

Where the hell was Larissa?

Five distant shots pierced through the chaos. She froze.

Fuck! He was still outside.

Keep going. Don't stop.

She reached the little hall and grabbed the door handle and shrieked. It seared into her fingertips as if it had been baked.

"No! Damn it!" she cried out, the tears making it hard to see.

That was it. Her only way out was where the assassin waited. Mercedes wasn't even sure she could get back through the living room.

No hope for it. She moved the chair and took a few steps. Her good leg slid out on the wet linoleum, and she toppled to the floor. Her palms landed in a sticky pool. She'd slipped on her own blood.

Pressing herself up, she made to stand again when Larissa came into her line of vision. Tears made trails down Larissa's soot smeared face.

Relief washed through Mercedes. "Larissa, help." She reached her hand out to the agent. "Help me up, I can't walk."

Larissa's arm came up and Mercedes froze.

A shouted command came from somewhere in the distance, but all Mercedes could see was the barrel of the gun aimed at her head.

"Larissa?"

"This isn't personal, Sadie," Larissa said, her voice calm and detached.

Oh, Alec. I'm so sorry.

Mercedes lifted her chin and waited for the sharp pain that would end it.

Without warning, Larissa's head came apart above her.

Blood and bone blew out of her forehead, pieces splattering across Mercedes's face. Larissa fell forward, collapsing on top of Mercedes's ravaged leg.

Screaming filled Mercedes's ears. Screams of agony. Screams of terror.

Then she realized it was her own.

"Christ, Sadie!" a strained voice was calling to her. "Talk to me!"

"Alec?"

She could swear it was him. Was he here, or was she losing her mind?

It was so cold.

The pain had lessened, and she knew what she was feeling. She'd been here before. The sting of dying would ease the closer she got to the end. Her eyes closed and she imagined one last time what her life could have been.

CHAPTER FIVE

Alec had been on the phone for a good portion of the morning. The American client he'd cultivated a month ago was already netting him a decent referral business. West Coast operations in the United States were well on track for a physical office within the next year.

When Alec told Mercedes he had a plan to expand his company into California, he wasn't kidding. After he thought Mercedes had fallen in love with someone else, he'd shelved the idea of expanding into America, tackling the European market instead. Financially, it had worked out.

Now he was making plans again. He didn't want to make her choose between her homeland or his. She could go home, to the city she'd grown up in, and see her sister whenever she liked. Or they could live in London. He could live in either and work in both.

Alec organized his notes and added reminders of what they needed to secure the clients' building when he heard the squeaky shoes of Mrs. Downey coming down the hallway.

"Sorry to disturb, Alec. You said to let Ms. Elliott's sister through anytime she rang?"

"Aye, thank you." Alec's heart leaped. Charlotte didn't call him often. He checked his mobile, noticing he'd missed a few calls from her.

He picked up the office phone and hit the line. "Charlie, is everything okay?"

"Alec," she said in a choked sob. Alec's pulse instantly shot up.

No, no, no.

"What's happened?"

"I just had a visit from the marshals . . ."

No. This isn't happening.

"They got her. She's gone."

"Charlotte . . ." The words were stuck and he could barely speak. "How?"

"They didn't tell me anything, other than there was an attack on the safe house. By the time backup arrived, Sadie and the two agents guarding her were dead and the house had been burned to the ground. I think the suspect is dead too, but I don't know." She sobbed. "I'm sorry. I didn't understand much after they said she was dead."

Dead. Sadie was dead.

A cry ripped from his throat, and he dropped the phone. The pain in his chest made the room swirl, and he stumbled from the desk and sank to the floor.

This isn't happening. This isn't real.

"Alec? Alec, what's going on?" Cressida's broke through the chaos of his mind. The tunnel of pain wouldn't let him focus. He could only shake his head, tears burning behind his eyes.

"Mrs. Downey! Get Declan, please."

Alarm echoed through the office, and within seconds, Declan's blue eyes were peering into his.

"Oy, Alec, talk to me, mate."

Alec gestured to the phone on the floor, words catching painfully. "Charlotte," he managed.

"He got a call from Ms. Elliott's sister," Mrs. Downey supplied.

Declan snatched up the phone. "Charlie? It's Dec, what's going on?" Then he spun to look at Alec. His face changed as he listened.

Alec shook his head. "No." was all he could manage.

It can't be true. It can't be. She was going to come home to be with him. They were going to have another chance to be together.

Declan spoke quietly to Charlotte, but none of it made sense to Alec.

Cressida's arm wrapped around his shoulder, and she held him tight to her. Tears were spilling freely down his face.

"Confirm it. Please," he whispered to her.

"I will Alec, but right now, Dec and I are going to take care of you. I want you to breathe, okay? Just focus on breathing."

Alec put his head in his hands and tried to do as Cressida said, but he could only manage shallow sobs. Nothing was right. His heart had been destroyed. Shattered into a million pieces, and nothing would ever be right again.

CHAPTER SIX

"It's been a damn good week, Adam."

Adam grunted his response and slid the offered glass toward him. Marcus Cooper's smile hadn't faded since Adam had delivered the news that Mercedes Elliott was out of the picture.

While it was always good to see the boss happy, Adam took no pleasure in killing like this. There was still a small part of him that wanted things to be different. But his guilt only extended so far. It's not as if they had given him a choice. At least not one he could live with.

Adam sipped and hid his grimace at the taste of gin. Cooper was obsessed with this damn cocktail and always made them for everyone. *It's like drinking a fucking tree.*

Cooper swirled his drink. "The lawyers think it'll force Whitley to drop the federal corruption charges. He has nothing to tie anything to me anymore."

"Well, that's good news."

"We still aren't out of the woods, though. The negative press coverage is killing us and most of my investors are getting skittish."

"That should die down once the press coverage eases."

"I've seen nothing about Mercedes Elliott anywhere. If I were Whitley, I'd broadcast the shit out of the fact that a witness and two marshals are dead." Cooper turned to Adam. "Why hasn't he announced her death yet?"

Adam waved his hand dismissively. "Who knows why that fucker does anything. It's not like anyone knew who she was. They kept her identity pretty locked down."

Cooper nodded. "Still, I'm going to have to protect my assets in the company. With Sutanyl off the market, I can't afford to have all my loans called in if my backers decide to run for it."

"So, what's the plan?" Adam set the drink on the counter. Cooper would probably scoop it up in a few minutes for himself.

"Unfortunately, I'm going to have to withdraw from the company, at least on paper. Hopefully, it will improve our image."

"If you step back, who will take over?"

Cooper lifted his shoulder. "My son, Tyler, of course. He'll start joining us for these little meetings."

Ah, fuck.

Tyler Cooper was the epitome of the rich white kid, an entitled pervert who thought the world revolved around him. The fucker had gotten out of a slew of criminal charges without blinking his eye. Adam had helped to cover them up when needed, making sure Tyler's indiscretions were never even whispered about.

The last thing he wanted was to have to report to that little dickhead.

Cooper seemed to read his thoughts. "I want to make sure the chain of command is certain here. Tyler will answer to me, and you will answer to both of us. Your obligations to me are inheritable."

Adam's jaw clenched tight. "Understood. I hope Tyler is open to coaching. Not like the incident with the girl."

Cooper's lips pursed. "Yes, that was an unfortunate event, and he almost fucked everything up. But it won't be like that this time. He'll keep his dick in his pants and his eye focused on the company. I'm sure he'll do well."

Not fucking likely. Little fuckheads like Tyler Cooper didn't take direction from anyone.

"I'm sure we can keep an eye on him, sir. Teach him the ropes."

Cooper leaned over and picked up Adam's martini and gulped down the last bit. "Good, I'm glad we worked all that out."

JASON WALKED THE LENGTH OF THE YARD, ENJOYING THE SUN on his face. He didn't get a lot of time to be outside. Now that he was back in jail, they were keeping him on a tight leash.

Cooper thought he was being a loyal soldier. But Jason wanted the chance to see Mercedes as often as possible and staying up on the case was the only way to do that.

He could still hear the echo of her words, making the choice. Mercedes loved him. She could have picked McKinley, but she hadn't. McKinley didn't stand a chance against what he and Mercedes shared.

Getting to talk to her at the hearing last week was as close to heaven as he was likely to get for a while. But it had cost him his freedom.

Worth it.

She was so fucking beautiful in that outfit, with her makeup in place and that gorgeous hair flowing down her back. It made him so hot thinking of her. If anything, that hearing had given him fresh memories to use when he jerked off to her.

Jason jogged another lap, letting his heart rate increase before he hit the weight yard. This place wasn't great, but at least they had a decent circuit. His doctor had ordered him to take it easy and let his wounds heal. But fuck that. He craved the adrenaline rush that came with lifting.

A guard came toward him.

What does this asshole want?

"Hollis, you have a meeting. Your lawyer is here, along with the US attorney and an FBI agent."

Jason frowned. "What? I thought that was next week?"

"I don't make the schedule. They're here now. Move your ass."

Jason wiped his brow on his sleeve and followed behind the guard back to the admin building. Brenden Whitley had been trying to get a plea deal out of him for months. He could take a dick.

The lawyers he had were pretty much useless. Cooper bought and paid for them. Jason was getting free representation and Cooper was getting to keep his finger on him. Jason let them act as his lawyers so he could stay in the loop. Eventually, he would need to sever his ties with the pompous shit bags.

The guard led him to the private rooms where inmates met with their attorneys. The US attorney and the FBI agent both stood when Jason came in, but his own lawyer barely looked up.

Jason didn't return the tight smile Brenden Whitley gave him, instead flopping into the seat across from them. The guard cuffed him to the iron table between them and stepped out of the room.

"Mr. Hollis, you remember Special Agent Nick Kessler?"

The Black man offered a tight nod.

"I do." Jason sent Whitley a smug smile. "This sure is an honor, *Brenden*. It's nice to see you taking such a hands-on approach."

"Thank you," Whitley said tightly. "We think you might have a reason to take our deal now."

Jason's lawyer sighed and put his phone down, his bored stare aimed at the prosecutor.

"Why would I do that?"

"Because, two nights ago, Marcus Cooper had Mercedes Elliott executed in her safe house."

Blood rushed to Jason's head. He couldn't have heard that right. "You'd better not be fucking with me."

"We're not fucking with you, Mr. Hollis. Mercedes, along with both of her security detail were killed. Do you know a man named Thomas Martin, otherwise known as Prodigy?" Kessler slipped a photo out of his folder. Jason stared at it. The bullet opening up the man's head didn't detract from his features.

Yeah, he fucking knew Prodigy.

They used that fucker for assassinations and nothing more. Jason's breath became shallow, and a numbness washed over him.

This can't be true. She can't be gone.

He glared up at Whitley. "Why aren't you showing me Sadie? If she's dead, why wouldn't you show me her too?"

Cooper's lawyer suddenly joined in. "Mr. Hollis, you shouldn't speak until we . . ."

"Shut the fuck up." Jason growled at the lawyer. He turned back to Whitley and Kessler. "Show me."

Whitley and Kessler exchanged a look, and Kessler pulled out another picture and slid it across the table.

Jason turned away to breathe through the bile working its way up his chest. The image of the burned-out corpse seared into his mind. Her sweet face charred and ruined. That beautiful hair, nothing but scorched pieces. The gaping hole that cracked open her forehead told him they'd executed her from behind. The same way they did in most of their targets.

His throat was threatening to close. "How did they get to her?"

"Jason," his lawyer tried to intervene.

Whitley ignored the lawyer. "The investigation is ongoing. But she had one of the highest levels of security the government could offer. Somehow they still managed."

"Did either of the agents with her have debt? Or maybe a few secrets they couldn't afford to let out?"

Whitley and Kessler shared a look. "It's possible."

Those motherfuckers had infiltrated her security and betrayed her.

He'd always known it was possible, but fuck.

"That's how Cooper gets us. He finds something we need and exploits it. You want to watch their families to see if someone benefited from this . . . assassination."

Agent Kessler leaned forward. "You know, with Sadie gone, we don't have as strong of a case."

Anger clawed through him. "Why is that my problem? You fuckers are the ones who were supposed to protect her. What were you doing while these people tricked her into thinking she was safe and then slaughtered her? Hmm?"

"He's going to get away with *all of* it, Jason." Whitley's words rang in his head. "Not just the case, but her murder too."

"What do you mean? You have the assassin's body. The fuck else do you need?"

"Proof," Whitley snapped. "We know damn well he ordered the hit. But we have jack shit when it comes to proving it."

That asshole Cooper would get away with her murder, only because he'd been rich enough to cover his crimes.

Not this time.

"What do you want from me?"

"Jason," his lawyer tried again. "We need to end this conversation now. I need a moment with my client."

"Fuck off," Jason growled, rage coursing through him. "You're fired. Get out."

"But . . ."

"You don't represent me. Tell Cooper to get ready. Now, get the fuck out!"

The rushing of Jason's pulse in his ears drowned out the lawyer's complaints as he left the room.

How was she gone? This couldn't be real. She was going to come around. Jason had been so damn sure.

"Do you want to consult a different attorney?" Whitley broke through his grief.

"No, I don't give a fuck. What do I need to do?"

"Write up a statement telling us everything Marcus Cooper has ever done and then testify. Make sure that fucker pays."

Laughter burst from Jason's chest. *Fuck it.* "All right. I do have a few requirements for my testimony."

Whitley took out a pen, poising it above the paper expectantly.

"I want to be free and under protection while I await trial."

Whitley tapped his finger on the table. "I can't just make that happen. We have to . . ."

"I don't give a shit." Jason snapped. "I'm not going to rot in this fucking place. Make it happen."

Whitley sighed. "What else?"

"Full immunity. Not even a hint of a charge."

Whitley jotted that down. "I'll see what I can do."

"When is her funeral?"

"In a week."

"I'd want to be there."

Kessler shifted in his seat. "That might be tough. We don't know where they're holding it. It might be in London. If it is, there is no way you're going."

Jason's head popped up. "Why would Sadie's funeral be in London?"

"She was planning to return there when the trial ended."

Jason's heart faltered. There was only one reason she

would want to live in that city again. Mercedes had planned to be with Alec McKinley, after all. After everything Jason had done for her, she would have still picked McKinley.

It didn't matter anymore. She was dead.

Jason wanted to die too. But not before he fucked Marcus Cooper over.

CHAPTER SEVEN

A week and a half had gone by in a blur. Alec hadn't been able to think straight since Charlotte's call. Every normal part of life was a challenge. He didn't want to leave his bed, even though sleep was impossible. Food lodged in his throat and more than once, he'd thrown up. He hadn't shaved since the morning his life ended.

Declan had taken to sleeping in Alec's guest room. Alec was pretty sure his cousin thought he was going to eat a bullet. Not that Alec hadn't thought of it. It would be so much easier to live without this constant haunting pain.

It wasn't just the torment of knowing he would have to live without her.

It was the guilt.

Alec had convinced her to go into the program. Mercedes had resisted, wanting to stay by his side as he recovered. She was adamant about it.

It didn't matter that Alec hadn't been in any shape to protect her. He had the training, the knowledge to take her underground where they would never find her. But he'd been weak. Unable to do more than kiss her goodbye. If he'd have been stronger, she'd be alive today.

He'd never be able to forgive himself for that.

Alec walked to the curtains and drew them back. He winced at the light, the sun teetering on the edge of the horizon past the Golden Gate Bridge. It wasn't his first visit here, but it was the one that was going to haunt him his entire life.

This was her city. Her home.

Everything around him was her.

A soft knock pulled him out of his thoughts and Cressida peeked in from the door adjoining their rooms. "You okay?"

Alec didn't respond. She'd been mother-henning him since she helped pick him up off the floor. They were all hovering, sometimes quite literally. If it wasn't Cressida or Declan, then it was Mason who popped by or Shake who wanted to say hello. Alec let them fuss. The few times they had left him alone had been a nightmare.

"It's a beautiful hotel, isn't it?" Cressida asked, coming to stand beside him at the window.

"Aye, it's nice."

Cressida looked up at him, her rich brown eyes filled with concern. "Have you taken your suit out?"

Alec shook his head. He didn't give a shit about his suit. He should. But he just didn't.

Cressida's frown deepened, and she went to his suitcase. She rummaged through and found his garment bag. Alec turned back to the city, unable to stomach looking at the black suit he'd packed for this week.

"You need to shower and trim up that beard," Cressida said from behind him. "We need to be at your cousin's house in an hour and we don't know how the traffic will be."

His cousin.

It wasn't just his cousin who lived there. It was Mercedes's sister. And it wasn't just any house. It was Mercedes's house. Alec had never stepped foot in it, but he knew it well enough.

It had been the backdrop of his long-distance relationship with her.

He'd lost three years with her.

Three fucking years.

Instead, they'd only had a few days. A few days of truly knowing what they meant to each other before those fuckers ripped it away again. Sometimes rage welled in him and he had to force it back before he unloaded it on anything that came near him.

"Alec." Cressida broke through his thoughts again.

"I'm going."

ALEC AND THE OTHERS WAITED ON THE PAVEMENT WHILE Declan rang the bell of the narrow Victorian-style home. That it had once been hers made Alec's pulse thunder. Not the good sort of sped up heart rate that came from love or longing. But the kind that tore through the only defenses he had left.

Charlotte must hate him.

He'd promised her he'd help Mercedes escape the hell she was living in. Instead, he'd turned her over to others. Others who obviously couldn't be trusted.

It was all his fault.

He wouldn't blame Charlotte if she spat on him and slammed the door in his face. He looked around, feeling like he might be sick in the hedges that framed the wrought iron staircase to the house.

The door opened and the bright blue eyes of their younger cousin greeted them.

"Ach, look at you, wee man," Declan said as he tugged Luke into a bear hug. Both of them pounding the others on the back as they greeted each other. Declan introduced Cressida, Shake, and Mason, but Alec barely heard any of it.

She was watching him. While the others talked, Alec's gaze held Charlotte's.

Mercedes and Charlotte shared very few common features. Where Mercedes had been fair with wavy chestnut hair, Charlotte had warm, tawny skin and dark, corkscrew curls that framed her face.

But their eyes. Their eyes were just the same.

When they cried, the vivid green overtook the whisky gold. Charlotte's eyes brimmed with unshed tears, and Alec thought his already devastated heart would fall apart to see her.

She took a tentative step toward him, as if she was unsure of how he would receive her. Alec opened his arms, and she moved to him. He gathered the last thread of Mercedes to him and held her while she sobbed into his chest.

"I'm so sorry, Charlotte. I failed you both," he murmured in her ear, letting his own tears fall.

She drew back and tilted her head. "What? You didn't fail us."

Alec sniffed. "If I'd been stronger . . ."

"Stop it," Charlotte said. "You nearly died for her. There was nothing more you could have done."

There was no one in the world that understood this pain better than Charlotte. Alec nodded and followed her as she welcomed him into her home.

Mercedes's presence was everywhere. She hadn't lived there for nearly a year, having turned it over to Charlotte and Luke when she moved to London.

"It's beautiful. Did you design this?" Cressida asked, her gaze moving around the cozy living room.

"I did, but this is one hundred percent my sister's taste." Charlotte smiled sadly. "She was one of my first interior design jobs. She let me go crazy."

Alec and Charlotte browsed the photo wall she and Mercedes had created together. Some pictures were artistic shots Luke had likely done. Luke was a professional photographer but enjoyed taking shots of nature for fun. But it was the candids that caught Alec's eye. Mercedes's stunning smile glowed from the frames. Pictures of college friends and childhood memories filled the space.

Shake and Mason came to take in the wall as well. "Is that . . ." Mason said, peering in closer to one photo. "Is that Ezra Coulter, the lead singer from Slighted Razor?"

"It is, although he's on his own now," Charlotte said, her lips curled into a smile. She pointed to another photograph. "There's one of us when we were kids."

The photo was taken in the summer. Mercedes and Ezra couldn't have been more than fourteen. The smile on her lips didn't meet her eyes and Ezra carried a similar haunted look. Charlotte, around eight or nine years old, sat between Ezra's knees on the step below. His hand lay protectively on Charlotte's tiny shoulder.

"We grew up with him. He was like a big brother to me."

"No bloody way!" Shake said. "You grew up with Ezra Coulter?"

Charlotte let out a laugh. "Yeah, he was our neighbor. His mom was as messed up as ours. I was too little at the time, but he would help Sadie take care of me when our moms were wrecked. Sadie taught him to play the guitar."

"No shit? That's wild!" Shake said.

"Do you still keep in touch?" Mason was studying the picture.

"I've kept in touch, but he and Sadie had a falling out years ago, and she stopped talking to him."

"Why did they fall out?"

Charlotte's gaze darted to Alec's. "Well . . ."

Alec spoke up. "He and Sadie dated for a while. It didn't end well."

Charlotte looked relieved that she didn't have to be the one to tell Alec that Mercedes had once dated someone as famous as Ezra Coulter, but Alec knew all about him. During the months he and Mercedes carried on a long-distance relationship, she had shared many painful things about her past. Ezra had been a huge part of her life until she let him in, and he destroyed it all.

"Oh, Alec, we were going through some of Luke's photos and found one he snapped at our wedding. I was going to give it to you as a housewarming gift once Sadie could move in with you, but . . ." Charlotte's voice halted, and she walked to the nearby cabinet. "I hope it's not too much for you."

She handed him a frame, and the image made his stomach clench. It had been a stolen moment at the wedding he didn't know anyone had seen.

Mercedes's arms were wrapped around him. One hand gripped the lapel of his Argyll jacket. Alec was dipping his head to kiss her. She had lifted her chin, her lips parted to take the kiss.

Memories flooded his mind.

The garden-scented breeze. The sweet little giggle she gave when she realized why he'd snuck her away from the reception.

She had leaned back against his chest to take in the view. "I think you're trying to ruin me."

Alec laughed and tightened his hold on her. "Ruin you?"

"How can anyone else compare to this?" Her hand came up, and she gestured to the perfect sunset in front of them. Then she'd turned in his arms, her slender body pressing up against him. "I mean, you kiss me by waterfalls and take me out for Scottish sunsets in castle gardens. Not to mention, you look like *this* in a kilt." Her heated gaze roved up his body. "You're ruining me for all other men."

"Aye, good."

Alec kissed her, her lips soft on his. She opened to him, slow and sensual. His tongue stroked hers, languidly. She moaned into his mouth and Alec wanted nothing more than to take her home and love her the way he'd needed to.

They never got that chance.

So many fucking regrets.

Charlie was watching him. Her brow furrowed with worry. He cleared his throat. "Thank you, Charlie," Alec choked out. "It's perfect."

CHAPTER EIGHT

Alec's heart fractured with every beat. That morning, he'd carried the urn onto the flower strewn stage and placed it on the cloth-covered table. Just keeping his legs from buckling under him was a chore.

There were so many people filling the seats. Musicians and lawyers. Bartenders and restaurant owners. Mercedes had an eclectic group of people in her life.

Alec stuck close to Charlotte. She'd asked him to sit next to her during the service. Luke remained next to his wife, anticipating her needs before she could ask. Alec watched his younger cousin's gentleness with his wife and was thankful Charlotte had him. He'd always been the sweeter of the three of them.

There was a buzz in the crowd behind him. Cressida and Shake had leaned in together and were whispering to one another.

Ezra Coulter made his way through the crowd. Broad chested and tall, he would have stood out, even if he wasn't famous. Tattoos peeked out through his sleeves and his long blond hair was neatly tied back. When Ezra spotted Charlotte, he walked toward her, not seeming to notice the whispers of people around him. They weren't just gossiping over a celebrity in their midst. Most of the musical crowd seemed to know him, too. Ezra stopped to shake the hands of several people on his way to Charlotte.

When he reached her, he pulled her into his arms. "Hey kiddo, how are you holding up?"

"I'm doing my best," she said, muffled against his chest. Alec could see Charlotte's resolve was slipping. She clung to Ezra, tears streaming. When Ezra drew away, he dabbed at his eyes.

"I'm glad you're here," Charlotte said, rubbing Ezra's arm.

He laughed ruefully. "I doubt she would have felt the same."

"I don't know about that. I think she'd moved past it."

"I hope so."

Charlotte touched Alec's arm. "Ezra, this is Alec McKinley."

Green eyes rimmed with red turned to Alec. "Oh, damn. You have to be related to Luke." Ezra held out his hand to Alec.

Alec smiled and took it. "Aye, I'm his cousin."

"Ah, did you know Mercy?"

The name threw Alec. He'd never heard her called that before.

Charlotte stepped in. "Alec and Sadie were together. She was planning on joining him in London when the trial was over."

Ezra nodded, studying Alec. There was a little envy and a lot of regret on his face. "You're a lucky man to have had her love you."

"Aye, thank you. I know." Alec managed a smile.

A violinist took to the stage to open the celebration of life. Ezra stiffened and said to Charlotte. "I'll be close by, kiddo."

Alec followed Charlotte and Luke to the front row. The

violinist played a quiet tune, which was agonizing to listen to. Most of the service came and went in a blur. Mercedes hadn't been particularly religious, so they filled the service with music and stories told by the people who knew her.

When Ezra walked to the stage, the room seemed to collectively hold its breath while he struggled to speak.

"Many of you know who I am, but only a handful of you *know* me. The real me." He scanned the audience and smiled and nodded at a few old friends. "Most of you, I met because of Mercy. The music world should have known her name, not mine. She was so much better than most of us. I would be nothing if not for her. Quite literally." The last words came off as a jest and the crowd tittered. "Mercy and I had a special connection. We lived across the hall from each other, and our mothers seemed to be in competition for who could be the worst person in the world. She was my best friend, and I screwed it up. I will live with that regret for the rest of my life."

Alec watched Ezra walk off the stage, knowing he should feel something for this man, but he was too engulfed in his own pain to spare anything.

After the service was over, they moved to the reception in a nearby dining hall. Fatigue was pulling Alec down. He shook hands on autopilot, managing tense smiles and thank yous to guests as they said their farewells.

Mason was suddenly next to him, his considerable weight keeping Alec from passing by him. Alec frowned at his friend. "Everything alright, mate?"

"Eh. We need to head to the car."

"What?" Alec shook his head. "We still have a lot to do before we can leave."

"Dec and I can take care of it." Mason grasped his arm and tried to guide him toward the back door.

"Mason, what the hell?" Alec resisted the hold. "Are you losing your wits, man?"

Charlotte let out a soft gasp and Alec turned his gaze to where she was looking.

Jason fucking Hollis was standing only meters from them.

Luke pulled Charlotte behind him and took a step toward Jason. "What the fuck do you want?"

Jason gave Charlotte a sad smile. "I came by to let Charlie know I'm here if she needs anything."

Alec's exhaustion dropped away like lead, and an overwhelming need to beat the ever-loving fuck out of Jason Hollis rushed through his veins. He moved, ready to unload the rage he'd been storing away.

Mason already had Alec by the waist. "No, no, no, man. Can't do that."

"What the fuck are you doing here?" Alec growled.

"I'm not here to cause problems. I'm just . . . saying good-bye." Jason had peppered his tone with enough anguish to seem sincere.

"You're not welcome here. You need to leave." Charlotte's voice trembled.

Jason took a step toward Charlotte, and Alec lunged against Mason and now Shake's grip. "I will snap your fucking neck," Alec warned.

Declan moved between them and got in Jason's face. "You need to get the fuck out of here before we let him go."

"You don't want to do that now that I'm the one who will be taking down Cooper." Jason smirked.

"What are you on about?" Declan frowned.

"Didn't you hear? Since Alec went and let Sadie die." Jason's taunting smirk roiled Alec's blood. "I'm the key witness now. They begged me to testify." Jason peered past Declan's shoulder at Charlotte, and his eyes softened. "I'm doing this for Sadie."

"Get out of here," she said in disgust. Her gaze shot to the man who appeared to be escorting Jason. "Why has he been allowed here? This is a private service."

The escort stepped toward Jason. "Alright, let's go. Clearly, they don't want to talk to you. They didn't give you permission to come here to cause problems."

Jason shrugged off the grasp, but he turned to walk up the steps. His gaze landed on Ezra, and he stopped.

"You let this fucking guy stay?" Jason said incredulously. "He *literally* fucked another woman in your sister's bed. You're good with that?"

Charlotte gasped. Ezra straightened up to his full height and glared at Jason.

"Un-fucking-believable." Jason looked Ezra up and down. Then he let his escort lead him from the room.

Mason released his hold on Alec. "Sorry, man. Didn't think it would be a good idea for you to get arrested here."

Alec's temper was working back down to a simmer. "Aye. Probably a good call." He straightened out his suit and inhaled a deep breath.

Ezra caught Alec's eye and he could tell he was trying to shake off Jason's words, too. That was Jason's gift. He knew a person's weakness before they did. Then he exploited it.

Alec stepped closer to Ezra. "Hey, mate." Ezra looked up, his expression desolate. "I know for a fact she forgave you, a long time ago."

"You do?" Ezra's brows creased.

"Aye. And she missed having your friendship. I thought you should know."

Relief came to Ezra's face, and he held out his hand. "I appreciate it."

"Anytime." Alec gave him a firm handshake. "We're heading out to Baker Beach to let some of Sadie's ashes out to sea. You should come with us."

Ezra sniffed. "Okay, thank you."

Alec nodded and then made his way back up the stairs to the stage. He inhaled deeply, the scent of the roses and lilies filling his senses. Carefully, he picked up the urn and held what was left of Mercedes to his chest.

The world would never be the same, and Alec was unsure he would ever find his place in it again.

CHAPTER NINE

A dam turned down the lane and took in the sights of the sun-drenched vineyards. It had been a long time since he'd been back, and an ache for home struck him. Sometimes, he wished he could go back to the innocent man that had left here.

This week had been particularly hard. The gruesome death of a target was never something he rejoiced in, but to have played such a role in setting up her demise and then seeing her execution through to completion didn't sit well with him. He needed a recharge. Just something to remember his purpose.

Adam pulled the pickup into the drive and killed the engine. The house looked the same but needed a touch of paint. He wished he could stay and help work on it, but it was better if he didn't stick around too long.

Shannon stood and stepped out of the flower bed. Her short copper hair caught in the breeze. She brushed the dirt from her knees and tugged off her gardening gloves. "Oh, my lord, Timmy! Why didn't you let me know you were coming? I'm a mess!"

He opened his arms, and she grabbed on to him. "I wanted to surprise you."

"I can't believe you came all this way. It's so good to see you."

Adam held her tiny body tight to him, she'd lost more weight since the last time he'd seen her. Fear of what that meant stabbed his heart.

"Well, come on in and have a drink. I made some sun tea."

Adam smiled at the simplicity of Shannon's life. To sit on the porch and drink iced tea was something that young Timmy Barlow had done. The man that had become Adam Wilson had little use for porch sitting.

As he walked through the door, the overwhelming scent of warm, fresh bread filled his senses. He breathed it in, letting the memories assail him.

He followed her through the house to the kitchen, stopping to take in the pictures of two gap-toothed kids on the wall.

"Are these the new ones?"

Shannon smiled. "They are."

"You know I'm going to need some copies." He grinned at her expectantly.

Shannon laughed. "Let me get you some right now." She riffled through her paperwork until she found a large envelope. Then she began cutting out the school pictures.

Adam studied the photos with an ache in his chest. "They're getting so big."

"Yeah, that tends to happen when time passes." She handed him the pictures and went to pour the tea.

Adam grimaced. He was missing so damned much. But he'd known what was expected when he'd taken this job.

Dark circles were heavy under Shannon's eyes, and her fair skin had a tinge of gray shadowing her narrow cheeks.

Maybe it isn't working.

"How have you been feeling?"

"I'm alright. A little run-down. But the doctors think I'm still in remission."

Adam sighed with relief. "That's good. That's really good. You have everything you need? Do you need any money?"

She shot a soft smile at him and shook her head. "We're getting by."

Adam sipped the sun tea to clear the tightness in his throat. "Sorry I can't be here more often. I know it must be hard."

"We manage. But we miss you when you go away for so long."

Shannon had no idea how much safer she was without him around.

Outside, a yellow school bus stopped at the edge of the driveway. The brakes hissed, and the double doors swept open. Two black-haired children ran from the bus and up the length of the driveway, shrieking with delight.

Adam went to the door and waited. His chest warmed when their tiny feet stamped on the porch. Then the door burst open, and they launched themselves at him.

"Daddy! Daddy!" They were both squealing.

"Hey look at you. Look how big you are!" Adam held their perfect little bodies to him. "I've missed you so much." Tears welled in his eyes. He had never had to lie about how he felt with his children. They were his world and his reason for everything.

"Daddy, come and see. I made the honor roll," Maisie said, pulling him to the desk in the living room where they did their homework.

Adam spent the rest of the afternoon cuddling them and looking over art projects and science fair entries. He listened to them squawk on and on about their friends and the plans they had for summer. Jackson was starting T-ball and

Shannon had enrolled Maisie in a music class. They were getting the childhood he'd always wanted for them.

Adam helped Shannon make dinner, and the four of them sat at the table to eat.

"I wish we could do this every night," Maisie said.

"Do what?" Adam asked her.

"Eat like a real family."

Adam's eyes caught Shannon's. His sweet little girl didn't know how much she'd torn apart his heart.

When it was bedtime, he read them stories and tucked them in. Adam was tempted to keep them up for a few more hours, but they had school in the morning.

Shannon had left a glass of wine for him on the counter. Adam grabbed it and joined her on the porch swing, looking out over the sleeping vineyards.

"Are you seeing anyone yet?" she asked.

This was a tricky question to answer. Adam shot her a tight smile. "Nope."

"Why not? You're so sweet. You deserve a good woman."

Adam snorted. Sweet wasn't a word usually used to describe him.

Shannon ignored him. "Not to mention smoking hot. Any woman would be lucky to have you."

"I was seeing someone, but she moved away, and it didn't work out," he said. Shannon gave him a soft, empathetic smile. "What about you, huh? Any man would be lucky to have you, too. But I don't see you getting out there."

"No man's going to take me on when I'm such a mess." Shannon laughed. "Besides, I'd like to see you settled, in case something goes wrong."

"Don't talk like that." Fear and grief swirled through him. "This is working. Right?"

"I don't mean to alarm you. I am feeling better." She sighed and lay her head against the cushion. "I have a lot of time on my own to worry. If something happens, who would I give my babies to if it weren't to their father?"

Adam didn't know the answer to that, because there was no way he could take care of them. The life he led and the things he'd done disqualified him from ever playing a major role in their lives. His children deserved better than the man he was.

When he looked at Shannon, she was still his high school sweetheart. She'd been the homecoming queen and he was the captain of the football team, the cliché American story come to life. The best decision of his life was to ask her to marry him.

He joined the military and somehow made it through BUD/S training and became a Navy SEAL. But Shannon struggled with the demands of the military, especially when the children came along. They had no life together while he was working, and he was always working. Some particularly harrowing deployments left him increasingly bitter and angry when he was home.

When Shannon asked for a divorce, Adam had seen it coming. He wasn't sure he wanted to be married, either.

They separated and found out they were better friends than husband and wife. Neither of them pushed to finalize the divorce and were happy living their own lives. Shannon got a stable home life and the freedom to explore who she was, and Adam could go on missions knowing his children were loved and well cared for.

Until one day, while he was on a mission, The Red Cross contacted him and told him his wife had collapsed at the grocery store. It had taken fifteen hours of flights over two days to get home to her.

When they got the diagnosis, he nearly threw up. Shannon had a rare form of cancer in her right kidney that had spread throughout her body. Adam hunted for specialists and looked for anything he could find to help her.

But there was nothing. She would die within eighteen months.

That was, until Marcus Cooper found him.

Cooper Pharmaceutical offered an experimental treatment that had shown to be incredibly effective against the cancer she had. Unfortunately, it wasn't available except in human trials. But if Adam did a little work for him, just a little job here and there, maybe Cooper could see his way into making sure that his wife was in these trials.

And so, Timmy Barlow sold his soul to the devil himself.

With it, he had bought the life of an irreplaceable woman. As she sipped her wine in the evening twilight, he knew it had been worth every drop of blood.

CHAPTER TEN

SIX MONTHS LATER

Alec pushed open the door and walked out onto the street. Like most of the nights he had a session, it wrung him out. Opening his soul and letting others pick him apart made his head ache.

Tonight was tough. They'd discussed the future and what that would look like. Gerry, the grief counselor, had encouraged them to acknowledge the life they thought they would've had with the person they lost.

Alec was so wrapped up in thought, he barely heard the woman calling his name.

"Alec! Wait! You forgot something!"

Kristin, Gerry's administrative assistant, was hurrying toward him. He smiled politely and walked toward her. They had only spoken a few times, usually as they waited for the group to begin.

Kristin held out a notebook. "I think you left this." Her breaths came out in little puffs from the jog.

"Sorry, that's not mine." He gestured to the notebook under his arm.

"Oh!" She flushed and tucked her ash blonde hair behind her ear. "I could have sworn it was yours."

"No, but I appreciate the effort." He smiled and made to continue on his way. "Have a good night."

"Alec, wait."

He stopped again.

She shifted her feet. "Um, I don't usually do this but . . . I was wondering if you would want to go out for a drink. Maybe tomorrow night?"

Oh shit.

"I uh . . . I'm not sure." Alec ran his hand through his hair. "I thought it was frowned upon to date patients."

"Oh, it is, but today's my last day. I got a better job at another office." She looked down at the pavement. "I thought I would take a chance, since I wouldn't see you every week after this."

"Oh . . . um." *Fuck, this shouldn't be this hard.*

Kristin looked up at him, her eyes hopeful. It wasn't as if he hadn't seen the way she'd glanced at him from time to time. Maybe he should test the waters. He'd spent little time with anyone outside of work, and he was pretty sure Declan would love it if he'd go out with someone other than him.

"You know what? A drink would be nice." As soon as he said it, he regretted it, but he pushed the feeling aside. He needed to break the cycle.

Kristin beamed up at him. "Brilliant. Do you know Sanger's in Notting Hill?" At his nod, she rushed on. "I'll meet you there at six. Maybe we can catch dinner as well."

Alec laughed. "So, not just drinks then?"

Kristin's brown eyes sparked with laughter. "Just seeing what you're up for. Here's my card if you need to get a hold of me."

Alec couldn't help but smile back. "All right then. I'll see you at six."

"Perfect." She grinned at him. "Have a good night."

"You as well," Alec called, watching as she walked away.

Guilt swirled in his gut. He didn't want to go, but it was time to stop pretending he wasn't lonely as hell. Alec pulled his phone from his pocket and dialed. It rang twice before Cressida came on the line.

"Hi Alec, what's up?"

"Hey, Cress, sorry to disturb. I need a favor. I was wondering if you can do a full background for me."

"Sure, new client?"

"No actually. It's personal. I um . . . have a date and I don't want a repeat of Mariah."

Mariah Costa, although no doubt that wasn't her actual name, had been a plant in his company, and in his bed, for months to keep track of his movements. The standard background check hadn't been enough, so the company had upped the way they researched people.

"Aww, good for you. What's her name?" Cressida sounded genuinely happy he was planning a date with someone else. Maybe it was another sign it was time for him to move forward.

He looked at the card she'd given him. "Kristin Mellor. She works in the reception area at my counselor's office. We're having dinner tomorrow night."

"Fab, I'll do a deep dive to make sure she's good enough for you."

"Well, don't get too carried away." Alec laughed.

"I got you, hun. No worries."

Alec hung up with Cressida, his mind still processing all that had happened in the last few hours. By the time he opened the door to his flat, he'd felt like maybe he was making the progress they said he'd make.

THE SPRING DAY WAS BRISK THROUGH THE CITY STREETS AND A chill had settled over him by the time he got to the office the next morning.

Mrs. Downey handed him his files for the day. "The others are getting ready to meet in the conference room. They have some information about the Cooper case."

Alec's gut churned out anytime he heard about Cooper. But he thanked her and headed for the conference room.

His cousin was at the head of the table with a laptop open in front of him, his fingers tapping on the keyboard.

Declan looked up and grinned. "I hear you have a date."

Alec flushed. "Aye, I do. I see Cress doesn't keep secrets."

"Oh, aye. She rang me straight away. I helped with the background check. No red flags there, by the way."

Not for the first time, Alec wondered how often Declan and Cressida spoke after hours and how they felt about each other. There was a time Alec would have disapproved of Declan making a move on Cressida, but not anymore. Life was too damn short to waste it being in love with someone from afar. He certainly wouldn't wish it on two of the most important people in his life.

Declan's teasing smile dropped to seriousness. "You know it's okay, right?"

"Oh, aye. I've heard that a few times. That's what she would have wanted, right?"

"I think so. If you'd have died, what would you have wanted her to do?"

Alec stopped shuffling through his papers and looked at his cousin. He would never have wanted her to live alone forever, but the thought of her falling for another man still turned his stomach.

"I would have wanted her to be happy."

"Aye, and she loved you enough to not want you to be miserable either."

"I know, it doesn't make it easier."

Mason came into the conference room, followed by a bickering Cressida and Shake.

"If you aren't going to read the Manga first, you're losing out," Shake was saying.

Cressida clicked her tongue. "I don't care that much. I like the shows just fine as they are."

"But you're missing *soooo* much."

Cressida pulled her chair out and sighed. "I'm only watching it for you, you numpty. Leave me be."

Mason shot Alec a wide-eyed look and shook his head. Apparently, the twins had been at it for a while.

"Hey, what's this about you having a date tonight?" Mason said, interrupting Shake's rant.

Shake stopped his banter with Cressida. "Oh, that's brilliant, mate."

Cressida leaned toward her brother. "She sounds really nice." Alec tossed a frown at her, and she shrugged. "I mean, at least on paper."

Alec groaned. "Yes, yes. Thank you all. I appreciate the support. Can we get on to business? There's some news on Cooper?"

Shake cleared his throat. "It's more of what we *think* we found. There's a chance Mara Donovan popped up in Ireland."

Mara Donovan had been the catalyst to this entire thing. She had gone to Mercedes with a treasure trove of evidence against Cooper Pharmaceutical and Cooper himself. When another whistleblower ended up dead, Mara took the evidence and ran for it.

Now that Jason Hollis had flipped, he was no doubt giving Whitley plenty of damaging testimony. But Alec would never trust that arsehole to tell the truth. Not to mention, he may not make it to the trial. Cooper's reach hadn't been cut off. Since Mercedes's death, witnesses for the prosecution had dried up. Suddenly they weren't willing to stick their necks out.

"Alright, tell me about Ireland."

"We picked up some activity on an account in County Cork. We know she has family there, so we'll explore the area and see if we can't find something that will lead us to her."

"Aye, good. What about the others in Cooper's employ? Mariah or this Adam that was following Sadie?"

Shake spoke up again. "Haven't heard a peep on Mariah but we might have something on Adam Wilson. Cressida and I caught him on security footage in San Francisco right around the time Sadie was killed."

Alec winced, the reminder never dulling his pain. "How do we know it's him?"

"Well, he's a very careful man," Cressida said. "But the footage of that chase, where he and Jason tried to take Mara Donovan hostage, has a couple of clear shots of his face. Not sure why he didn't take any precautions to hide his identity, but we have enough of his features to use."

"And?"

"Well, any search we could do wouldn't exactly be legal—"

"I don't care if it's legal," Alec interrupted.

"Okay, good, because I already did it." Cressida grinned. "We took the video of the chase and ran him through several facial recognition programs. We found a treasure trove of aliases his face has used. With any luck, Shake and I can narrow them down to his real identity."

Alec studied the grainy photo, an unwelcome ache growing in his gut. "Do you think he was there? That night . . ."

Cressida shook her head. "Not really, but we aren't sure."

"He *looks* like the muscle of the operation, but I don't think he is. I think he's an organizer," Mason chimed in.

"How so?"

Mason leaned forward. "Sadie told us the power dynamic between Adam and the others threw her off. She'd thought Jason was calling the shots, but Adam was the one barking orders at the penthouse. Adam also barred Jason from seeing her and that he only got access to her when Adam left the building."

"You think Adam's the direct line to Cooper then?"

"I do, at least temporarily. Maybe it's me, but I get the impression Jason *did* hold that position before Adam, but then he lost it."

"Not a surprise. Jason's fucking crazy."

"Oh certifiable," Mason agreed. "But we can see a pattern in Cooper's behavior with his people. Think about all the players that have had contact with Cooper. Seth Collins, Mara Donovan and now Jason Hollis. In each of these cases, Cooper demands loyalty, and when they're no longer useful, he tries to have them eliminated. Jason is now in protective custody for that very reason."

It wouldn't particularly break Alec's heart if someone wiped Jason Hollis off the planet.

"This is excellent work. We're finally getting closer to Adam. Let's plunge into those aliases and see what we find. And maybe work on Mariah's face as well. I want to know where she is."

The meeting broke up, and Alec collected his files and laptop.

Declan stopped at the door. "You need anything tonight, you only have to ring me, aye?"

"Thanks, mate, I'll be alright," Alec said.

"I know. But just in case."

Alec followed Declan out of the room and went to his office. He shut the door behind him and took in a deep breath. Telling other people he was moving on was a part of the process he'd been dreading. As much as the team liked to give him shit, he was grateful they were all there to cheer him on.

KRISTIN WAS ALREADY AT THE TABLE WHEN ALEC ARRIVED. SHE gave him a broad smile and waved him over. Alec's nerves were thrumming. Not that Kristin lit a burning need that Mercedes had ignited with just a look. But he worried he was making a massive mistake.

"Hi there," he greeted her awkwardly. He unbuttoned his suit jacket and sat across from her.

"You're even early. That's refreshing," she said, taking a sip of water.

"Is it?" Alec asked, spreading his napkin on his lap. "Do a lot of blokes keep you waiting, then?"

"Yeah, it's been a weird year. Online dating isn't all it's cracked up to be. Have you ever tried it?"

"Ah, no. I only had a few dates here and there. I went a long time not seeing anyone."

"I'm sure someone who looks like you doesn't have to worry about where to meet people." She flashed a look of admiration at him.

Alec flushed. "I appreciate the sentiment, but I haven't dated much lately."

Her brown eyes swam with sympathy. "Is it because of the person you lost?"

Best to get it out of the way up front.

"Aye." Alec's throat tightened. "Partly anyway. It's a complicated story."

Kristin was quiet for a moment before she asked. "What was she like?"

Pain jabbed at his heart, forcing it to skip in his chest. "She was funny, talented and so bloody smart. She used to blow me away."

There was an awkward pause. "Can I ask how she died? Feel free to tell me to bugger off, if you like."

"No, it's fine. Gerry said I shouldn't avoid talking about her." The nightmare that his mind played of her death flashed, and his gut wrenched. "She was murdered." He would not go into the details. Doing that would leave him sick for days.

"Oh, god, I'm sorry. How long ago?"

"Six months." Six agonizing months of misery no one could possibly understand.

The server came to their table and took their orders. Alec was grateful for the reprieve. It certainly wasn't his best first date material. When the server walked away, Alec was quick to switch topics.

"So, tell me, why are you leaving Gerry's office?"

Kristin lit up. "I got this amazing opportunity at another group. I'm going to be managing the entire front office. It's a huge pay increase and I'll have tons more holiday time. I love to travel and just haven't been able to lately."

"Where would you like to go?"

Alec sipped his wine and listened as Kristin launched into her list of must-visit places. For the first time since she'd asked him out, he relaxed. She was quite lovely. Her eyes sparkled when she talked, and her smile was genuine.

This moment he'd been dreading for months had finally happened, and it was going better than expected. Alec exhaled and let himself enjoy the evening.

CHAPTER ELEVEN

THREE MONTHS LATER

Alec shifted in his chair, stretching his arms above his head. This video call with the United States District Attorney's Office in California had been going on for hours and was expected to go a few hours more. They planned to work well into the late evening to accommodate the time difference.

Cressida sat next to him, her quiet yawns becoming contagious. This work was incredibly important, but after the second hour, the questions had become repetitive.

US District Attorney Brenden Whitley was personally prosecuting the case against Marcus Cooper and Cooper Pharmaceutical and had asked to discuss their knowledge of the case. Alec and Cressida were both on the witness list and were expected to be called to give testimony.

Whitley was all business, his pen only pausing when he asked a question. "So, Jason Hollis claims that he is the only reason Mercedes Elliott survived the night the whistleblower was murdered. She was supposed to be killed that night, as well."

Alec ignored the fracturing of his heart and answered, "Mercedes told me he said that to her, but I have no way of confirming it."

"So, you think he may be lying?"

"It's completely possible. Do you actually believe anything that bastard says?"

Whitley offered him a tight smile. "Not all the nonsense about Ms. Elliott wanting to spend forever in the South of France with him. But we've been able to corroborate some of their operations."

Alec nodded, still not convinced Jason Hollis was anything but a deranged opportunist.

"It might be a good time to take a meal break and come back to this. Before we do that, I wanted to address another matter with you, Mr. McKinley." Whitley closed his notebook and looked into the camera. "We've asked you not to get involved with the search for the whistleblower Mara Donovan, Marcus Cooper's former assistant. I know you and your partner have ignored that request."

Alec shrugged. "We're a private security firm, looking to offer security to a private citizen. I don't know what's so wrong with that."

Cressida bit her lip, holding back a laugh. Declan was currently hunting down a few leads on Mara Donovan's whereabouts.

"Just keep us in the loop if you track her down. With her testimony, we wouldn't need to rely on Jason Hollis."

Exactly why we are still on her, mate.

Alec nodded, and they finished the call with a promise to meet again in an hour. The date for the trial was quickly approaching, and they needed all the prep they could get.

Cressida stretched. "I'm starving and I need to get out of here. Want to take the notes across the street for dinner and hash it out there?"

"Are you buying?"

"Of course not."

Alec grinned at her and grabbed his coat.

THE TINY GREEK RESTAURANT ONLY HOSTED A HANDFUL OF seats. Alec paid for their gyros while Cress snagged a lucky seat by the window. He brought their meal to the table, and they both tucked in.

"Mmm-hmm," Cressida murmured after taking a bite. "So freaking good."

"Aye, I love this place," Alec said, popping an olive into his mouth.

"So," she said, wiping her hands on a napkin. "How's it going with Kristin? It's been a couple months, hasn't it?"

"Aye, nearly three months now. It's . . . going well, I think. I'm taking it quite slow."

Cressida quirked her brow. "How slow?"

Alec grimaced. "I kissed her for the first time about a week ago."

"Oh." Her brows shot up. "Well, she's been waiting on that quite a bit, hasn't she?"

"Aye." Alec rubbed at his eyes. "It's not her, really. She's been lovely, *mostly* patient with me. And we've been spending more and more time together, which has been fun. I enjoy hanging out with her."

"But she's not Sadie," Cressida said softly.

Alec shook his head, the swell of grief forming in his chest. "It feels like if I sleep with someone else, I'm being unfaithful to her. Or that I'm letting her go for good."

Cressida set her drink down, her expression filled with sympathy. "There's nothing wrong with that, Alec. I'm mean, it's nice that you're trying, but no one gets to tell you when you're ready."

"I know, but it makes no sense to me either. I keep hearing

people in my group talking about how they were with their partners for fifteen or twenty years. They have children and grandchildren or bought houses and lost pets together. They were such a massive part of their life that it makes sense to be stuck where I am right now.

"I had her, *truly* had her for three days. She was there and gone in a flash. I didn't even have to buy an extra toothbrush or clear a drawer out in my bedroom. I didn't have to accommodate her in my life at all."

Cressida tilted her head. "Maybe that's the problem then. You didn't get memories of buying a house or the promise of children. And you won't get fifteen or twenty years. It's incredibly unfair."

The wave of grief that flooded him every time he thought about Mercedes threatened to spill over his carefully built walls. Tears stung the backs of his eyes. Everything Cressida said rang true.

"Look, it doesn't help that you've been pouring over her story repeatedly for months. Every day this week, we've said her name and talked about what happened to her. In a couple of months, you're going to have to sit on the same side as the man who savagely beat her and left her for dead and confirm everything he says is true." She reached out for his hand. "In truth, you haven't been allowed to let her go."

They sat in silence for a minute. Letting the warmth of her hand soothe him. Cressida was right. The case against Cooper was moving quickly now. The trial was all over the headlines, forcing him to see it every time he turned on the news. Mercedes had been dead for over nine months now, but she was still intertwined in his life.

Alec shook his head. "What do I do?"

"You should talk to Kristin. Tell her you need the closure of the trial before you let yourself take the next step."

"What if I get through the trial and I'm still not ready?"

"Then you should probably cut the lady free."

Alec nodded. It made sense. Kristin deserved more than to be second place to a ghost.

"Alec?" a voice said from across the room.

Kristin standing by the counter, her eyes wide. "Oh, speak of the devil." He waved her over. "Kristin, hey."

She walked to the table, her smile questioning and tight. "I thought you said you couldn't go out tonight because you had to work."

"Aye, we are working." Alec reached out his hand and pulled her into the chair next to him. "This is Cressida. I know I've told you about her."

Cressida shot Kristin a brilliant smile. "Hi Kristin, I've heard a lot about you."

"Hi." Kristin studied Cressida. "Same."

Alec sensed a shift in the air and tilted his head at Kristin, not sure what she was thinking.

Cressida must have picked up on it, as well. She wrapped up her food and stood. "Hey, I have some work I need to finish before our next call with California." Cressida picked up her laptop case and looped it over her shoulder. "Thanks for dinner, boss. I'll see you upstairs."

Alec waved to Cressida, then said to Kristin. "Are you okay?"

Kristin's sunny smile didn't reach her eyes. "I'm okay. I just didn't expect to see you having dinner with another woman."

Alec frowned. "It's Cressida. I've told you about her. We popped down here between calls."

"On a Saturday night?"

"Aye." Alec looked at his watch. "We are working with a team in California, so it's midday there."

"So, you're making calls to Americans on a weekend?"

"This was the best time for all of us to do it."

"I see." She looked down at the table.

A realization hit him. Kristin had no idea what this case

was and how he was connected. He hadn't talked about it. His time with her was a reprieve from the trauma it brought up. Not discussing it kept him from living it all day, every day.

"Why don't you come to my place tomorrow night. There's some things I need to show you. And we should talk."

Kristin deserved to know what he was living with. Maybe it would help relieve some of the anxiety on her face.

Alec's nerves were wound tight when Kristin rang his building the next night. He pushed the button to let her in and went to the door to meet her. She looked lovely. Her fine features rosy from the cold.

"Hey." She smiled and stepped inside, and he closed the door behind them.

Alec leaned in for a kiss and she immediately deepened it, and he let himself enjoy the feel of her. Every kiss was getting easier.

She shrugged out of her coat, her eyes wandering the room. "So, this is the place, huh?"

They'd been seeing each other for months, and he'd never invited her over. He'd never wanted to. "Yeah, not much to see, really. Just a regular flat."

"I like it. It's so tidy," she said as she peered into his bedroom. "What's with the violin? Do you play?"

It hit him like a gut shot. "No, but I had a lesson once."

When she came across the wedding photos, she smiled. "Is that you in a kilt?"

"Oh, aye. That was my cousin's wedding, four years ago."

"Who's the woman?" She touched the frame of the image of Alec leaning down to kiss a smiling Mercedes. Then the one next to it, with the two of them laughing after the last dance.

"That's . . . her." His throat was tight.

"Oh." She turned back to the photos. "She's beautiful."

Alec couldn't speak, so he nodded his agreement.

"Four years ago? I thought you hadn't been together very long before she passed."

Alec had been dreading this for months, but it was impossible to avoid now. Kristin deserved to know all of it.

Kristin accepted a glass of wine and sat on the sofa. Alec slid the laptop across his coffee table and opened it to a news report he'd already laid out. "Yesterday, I realized I never talked to you about this case I've been working on. I thought maybe I would clear that up. It'll go a long way to explaining a few things."

The news report was a rundown of the case against Cooper Pharmaceutical and its CEO. When Marcus Cooper came on the screen, Kristin gasped. He was one famous piece of shit. His face was everywhere, from the tabloids to the business channels.

The image of Mercedes climbing the steps to the courthouse came across the screen. His heart wrenched. "That's her. The last time I spoke to her was a few hours after that."

Her jaw dropped. "I've been following this case. It's insane. How are you involved in this?"

"Sadie . . . that was her name. Mercedes Elliott, was one of the main witnesses." He swallowed hard. "I couldn't protect her, so she had to go back to America into their Witness Protection Program. But, a few days after this hearing, they found her and killed her."

Her fingers flew to her mouth. "Oh, my god. I knew she'd been murdered, but I had no idea."

Alec set his glass on the coffee table and took her hand. "I wanted to show you why this case has consumed my work. It's all I think about all day and it keeps me up at night."

Her eyes softened, and she brushed his hair from his temple.

Alec cleared his throat. "I have to go to San Francisco and

testify. This is the last thing I can give her. She hasn't been allowed to rest yet. And I can't let her go until she can."

"I get it." Kristin nodded, her brows furrowed. "When is the trial?"

"In two months. Cressida and I will fly down together. Then the others will join us right before I testify."

Kristin blinked. "Cressida's going too?"

"Aye. She may have to testify as well." Alec frowned. "Is that a problem?"

"Oh, not at all." She fiddled with her glass. "I didn't expect Cressida to be so . . . pretty."

Alec shrugged. "Aye, she's quite pretty, I guess." Where was she going with this?

"Never mind." She waved it off. "I'm sorry for all you've had to go through."

She set her glass on the table and leaned up to kiss him. It was gentle and warm. Alec let himself go a little, testing his own limits. Kristin's tongue played with his, and he deepened the kiss. He threaded his hand in her hair, pulling her into him.

She shifted herself onto his lap, her legs straddling him. Alec let himself get lost enough to grow hard under her. Kristin ground herself against him, a moan escaping her as she did it. The groan snapped him back to reality like icy water.

Shit.

He broke the kiss. "I have to stop you now."

Kristin's breath had become gentle pants, but she backed up to look him in the eye. "Are you sure?"

"Aye. I'm sorry."

Alec was grateful when she whispered, "It's okay," and crawled off him. "I understand why you need time. I'm just glad you want me enough to have me here."

"I do want you here. This is just . . ."

"I know. Maybe after you come home from San Francisco,

you'll be ready for *our* life to start. Until then, I can wait." She picked up her shoes. "I should go."

Alec walked her to the door, grabbing her jacket from his coat tree and holding it out for her. She leaned up and kissed him. This time she wasn't gentle but demanding. He kissed her back, giving her what he could.

"Good night, Alec."

"'Night."

Alec closed the door behind her and was assailed by a wave of guilt. Kristin was doing everything she could to accommodate him. Making her leave was the right thing to do. She might have given him a night of reprieve, but he'd have regretted it in the morning.

He went to his shower, turned it on and stripped down, his hard-on aching as he moved. After he stepped in and lathered up, he tried to relax as the warm water soothed his tired muscles.

Wrapping his hand around his cock, he gave himself slow and steady strokes. Alec wanted to see if he could keep Mercedes from his mind. Just once, could he find pleasure without her memory?

He thought of Kristin and how hot her kiss had been as she ground herself against him. Warm. Soft. Alive. Alec tightened his hold, turning his wrist to feel that little thrill he got when he hit it just right.

It was so subtle. His controlled mind slipped and wandered away. Alec didn't even try to fight the memory of that morning he thought would be the first day of their life together.

Another shower. Another place.

A shower in which Mercedes waited for him.

Jesus.

She had looked over her shoulder, a soft smile pulling up the corners of her lips. "There you are. All moved in?"

Alec had leaned against the sink to take in this woman who loved him. "Aye."

Water slipped down her shoulders and past her breasts. Mercedes's stunning body left him breathless every time.

She bit her lip and cast him a devilish grin. "Good." Then she leaned back, hissing at the shock of her skin meeting the tile.

With light strokes, she ran her hand down her body and touched herself. She stepped her feet apart, making sure he had a view of her fingers as they dove between her legs.

He let out his breath. "Holy shit."

"Take those pants off."

Alec was quick to dispose of his trousers and stood naked outside the shower door. He braced his hands on the frame to watch her.

Mercedes arched her back against the wall, sliding her middle finger between the soft folds, stroking lightly. She moaned as her hips gently rocked, pressing her fingers over her clit. She opened her eyes to hold his.

It was the hottest fucking thing he'd ever seen.

Alec's strokes were coming faster as the memories became more vivid. The scent of her soap, the way her hair tousled around her face. The way she looked at him as she pleasured herself. All of it filled his mind, driving his hips to thrust into his fist.

"I need you, Alec. Please." That breathless command had been more than he needed. He'd jerked the door open and crossed to her, his mouth savaging hers. The way she'd cried out when he'd pinned her against the wall and taken her hard brought him close to the edge.

He could never get enough of her. The heat of her skin, the way her slick body molded to him perfectly, as if they were made to fit together.

"Jesus, Alec," she'd rasped between whimpers. "Please don't stop. Oh, god Alec."

Whenever she came, she'd cry out his name. It was like a trigger for him. Her pleasure made him shatter. Every time.

He'd come inside her that morning, and he came again now. His body convulsing around his tightened fist, every nerve focused on the intensity of his orgasm. His groans echoed throughout the room.

When the last of the spasms left him, he was alone in his shower, panting. One hand on his cock, the other pressed against the wall. The water ran down his body, and he turned to rinse off.

Every orgasm anchored to Mercedes was mind blowing, whether she was with him or not.

Fuck, he missed her.

Maybe it wasn't that he couldn't move on, it was that he didn't want to.

CHAPTER TWELVE

"I seriously don't understand why Whitley hasn't dropped this case by now. So fucking stupid," Tyler Cooper said, a pissy sneer on his punchable face. "Their witnesses don't know shit and Jason is a fucking liar. What do they even have?"

Like usual, Tyler was pacing the floor of the conference room, the lights of the bay sparkling across the night behind him. Pictures of witnesses and important players were strewn across the table in disarray. Marcus's idea to bring his son up to speed to take over the empire was a joke. The twenty-six-year-old had the attention span of a gnat, especially when it had nothing to do with him. For some reason, Tyler thought griping about it was going to make it all go away.

Adam did his best to mask his annoyance at the little fucker, but even his considerable training was faltering.

Marcus Cooper leaned back in his chair. "We've been over this, Ty. We're going to trial whether we like it or not. They're going to use every tool to make sure they fuck me. We have no choice but to fight."

Tyler's eyes flashed at Adam. "Why can't you do something about it? What do we even pay you for?"

You'd be in prison if it weren't for me, you little fuck. Adam hid his disdain behind a cold stare. "What exactly would you have me do?"

"Take them out."

"Who?"

"I don't know. Every witness they have." Tyler shuffled through some of the papers on the conference table. "The bankers, the accountants, the expert witnesses, that security team from London. You took out the lawyer, are you telling me you can't get to any of these other people?"

Jesus Christ, what an idiot. "So, you think I can manage a major kill operation of twenty to thirty minor targets, all on my own, while the FBI is hunting me?" Adam paused and waited for Tyler to have some sort of realization of how stupid he was.

The little shit only shrugged. "Then let's get them together and spray the place with bullets."

"For fuck's sake, Tyler," Marcus snapped. "This isn't a fucking mafia movie. There are consequences to every move we make. Each person we bribe or witness we silence costs us. We eliminated Seth Collins, and Mara ran for it, taking every document she could with her. We killed Mercedes Elliott and now Jason is taking the stand and the McKinleys are out for my blood."

"Who gives a shit about them?"

Adam scoffed. "That's easy for you to say. Are *you* the one going up against the McKinleys now?"

"No. That's your job." Tyler looked disgusted. "It can't be that hard."

You have no fucking idea.

A raging Alec McKinley would be a nightmare. A nightmare Adam had been expecting over the past few months. He knew what Mercedes Elliott had meant to Alec McKinley. That he hadn't had any visits from the Scotsman meant they still had no idea where Adam was.

Tyler plopped down in a chair. "Nothing a bullet in their heads couldn't fix."

It was the utter confidence in Tyler's expression that pissed Adam off the most. His privileged life was a series of college parties and drunken debauchery. No one had ever told this little shit no, and now Adam had two arrogant fucks to keep under control. At least Marcus seemed to have a grasp of reality. His dumbass of a son seemed to think this was a video game.

Marcus sighed and ran his hand over his eyes. "Adam, tell me what you know about Mara. Have you located her yet?"

"Why do you need to know about her?" Tyler snipped. "You know Mom will have your ass if she finds out you're looking for that little whore."

Adam's jaw clenched until it ached.

"Watch your fucking mouth," Marcus snarled at his son. "I don't need your goddamn opinion about Mara or any other woman I want. Are we clear?"

Tyler glared at his father, but backed off, their little standoff making a nice cover for Adam's brewing anger.

Fuck them both.

Adam cleared his throat. "I have every reason to believe she's alive and living somewhere within the UK. The trial is only weeks away now. We would have heard whispers if the prosecutor had found her. I don't think she's a threat to your case."

"I'm not worried about the case," Marcus said, irritation sharpening his words. "She belongs to me. I want her back. What I can't understand is why she is still out there. When are you going to figure out where she is and who's helping her?"

Marcus had asked this before, but this time he seemed certain she had help.

Fuck.

"I've been in the States for months. I can't be here and there at the same time. If you want me to look for her, you're going to need to let me go back to Britain. Otherwise, I'm doing everything from thousands of miles away."

Marcus was quiet as he thought it over. Adam held his breath.

"No." Marcus shook his head. "As much as I want Mara back, I need you to work on the other avenues we discussed."

Adam exhaled. "Understood."

"Who is this?" Tyler cut in, flipping a photo over from the file.

Adam frowned at the photo. "That's Cressida Bennett. She works for the McKinleys as a computer tech. Why?"

"Look at her. She's fine as fuck, isn't she?"

In a normal man, this sort of talk would be stupid dude banter. But Tyler's appetites were sick as hell. There was no doubt disgusting perversions were playing out in his twisted little mind.

Marcus snapped the picture up and tossed it on the pile. "Jesus, Tyler. You're getting married in a few weeks. You need to stay focused and out of trouble."

"You're one to talk," Tyler sneered. Then he glanced back at the photo on the table. "I just like the look of her."

"It took a hell of a lot of work to get Dahlia to agree to this marriage. Keep your dick in your pants and stay focused on revamping the image of this company."

"Whatever," Tyler murmured, shuffling through the photos again.

Marcus called an end to the meeting and Adam was grateful to get the hell away from both of them. Whenever Marcus brought up Mara, Adam's blood ran cold. He was waiting for the day to come when his boss figured it all out.

Then he'd be fucked.

CHAPTER THIRTEEN

TWO MONTHS LATER

Alec held his niece, Isla, over his shoulder, her shrieks of laughter carrying over the din of the party. His younger sister, Katie, was going through a rough divorce and had come from Scotland to meet with a solicitor in London. A rugby match was on, so he hosted a few friends to cheer Katie up.

Asking Kristin to come over to meet his sister and the baby was a big step, but one that was long overdue.

Alec flipped Isla over and attacked her belly. "Say Al-lec, ya wee monster," he growled.

"Lec!" She giggled. Isla had taken to calling him Uncle Lec and it was getting closer and closer to 'Uncle Lick' every time.

"No! Al-lec."

"No. Lec!" Isla's blue eyes waited for the attack.

Alec's mouth dropped. "You're doing it on purpose now."

Isla's tiny hands and feet kicked out as he went in for the final assault, munching on her belly while she squirmed. When Alec set her down, she scurried away, hiding behind her mother's leg. She peeked out, waiting. Her giggles were addictive.

Kristin was watching him with a soft smile playing on her lips. "You're so good with her."

"Ach, she's easy to get on with."

"It's really sweet."

Alec could almost see Kristin's thoughts as they happened. Best to move off the topic of babies. "So, what are your plans while I'm gone?"

Kristin smiled shyly. "Well, I wanted to talk to you about that. I was thinking . . ."

"Hey, Alec," Cressida said.

"Oh, you made it." Alec stood and gave Cressida a peck on the cheek. "Are you going out?"

Cressida posed, showing off her short cocktail dress, and grinned at him. "Do you like?"

At work, she wore jeans and flannel or comfy dresses. But when she wanted to, she could transform. Caramel high-lighted hair curled past her shoulders and her smoky brown eyes were decorated with gold leaf that shimmered when she moved. The dress was glittery, light pink, contrasting with her warm olive skin. She was stunning.

"You look amazing, but you may be a tad overdressed for this lot."

"Oh, yeah. I have a date tonight." She scanned the flat. "Is Dec back yet?"

"Afraid not."

Cressida's face fell, but she quickly recovered by looking Kristin's way. "And how are you?"

Kristin gave Cressida a tight smile. "I'm good. Thanks. You look good tonight."

"Thanks."

A tiny hand patted at Cressida's leg. "Cress!" Isla said, her head back as far as it would go to gaze up.

"Is that my little Isla bug?" Cress exclaimed, swooping up the little girl and giving her a hug.

"Pretty." Isla patted Cressida's face.

"Well, thank you, my lovely. You're pretty too." Cressida turned to Alec. "I'll chat with you soon." And she walked off, talking in silly voices to the toddler.

When the party wound down, only Kristin, Katie, and Isla remained. Katie was wrangling the baby into her night-clothes, so Alec and Kristin began cleaning up. "That went pretty well, aye? I think you've met everyone now, except Dec."

Kristin gathered up some glasses and placed them in the sink. "Yeah, it was good."

"Is everything okay? You've seemed a little down this evening."

"I'm not down. I'm just being . . . insecure."

Alec wrapped his arms around Kristin. "About what?"

"It's dumb but . . . I didn't know Cressida knew your sister and your niece so well."

Alec shrugged. "When I was in hospital, Cress offered to help watch Isla so Katie could be with me. They became mates." Alec turned Kristin around to face him. "Cress is an important part of my life, as is her brother. I don't know what thoughts you're having about her, but you can put them away. There's never been anything between us and there never will be."

Kristin blinked, looking abashed. "I'm sorry. I just see this intimacy between you and her and it makes me think we might never get there."

Alec pulled her to him. "We will. Just let me get through the trial."

"So, about that. I thought, maybe I could come with you. I have some time off coming up, so I can get away."

Alec grimaced. "I don't know, I'm supposed to stay with my cousin."

"Oh, no. That's totally fine. I totally planned to get my own room and give you space if you needed it."

"It's a long trip just to be on standby for me."

"I told you, I love to travel. It'll be an adventure." Kristin looked down at her hands. "I have a lot of feelings for you, Alec. A lot." She took a deep breath. "I want to show you that I'm all in. That I want this to last. And I don't want you to go through all this alone."

Alec was touched. It was a sweet gesture. "I'll think about it."

A smile spread across her face, and she leaned up to kiss him. His arms went around her waist, and he drew her into him.

AFTER KRISTIN LEFT AND KATIE WENT TO BED, ALEC PICKED up his phone and dialed Charlotte's number. It was afternoon in California, and he wanted to talk to the one person he worried about the most.

"Hey Alec," she answered. "How are you?" Charlotte's American accent always threw him a little.

"I'm doing okay. I wanted to talk to you about something, though. Do you have a second?"

"I do, I just got home. What's up?"

Alec inhaled deeply. "I, um . . . I know I told you I had met someone, right?"

"Yeah, and I'm super happy you're getting out there."

"Aye. The thing is, she would like to come with me to San Francisco. I wanted to talk to you first."

"Oh. Sweetie, you know anyone you brought with you would be welcome in my home."

Alec grimaced. "That would be a little much. We would stay at a hotel. But I hope you don't mind me bringing her over to meet you both."

"I meant it Alec. She is totally welcome here. We plan to have dinner here a few times while everyone's in town. I'd love to meet her."

"Are you sure, Charlie? This isn't too soon?"

"For me or for you?"

Alec huffed out his breath. Charlotte was never one to mince her words.

"We're all having to move on without her. Luke and I had to, too. I want you to do the same. If you're happy, then I'm happy too. And I mean that."

"Aye, thanks Charlie. I'll let you know soon."

If he was going to make it work with Kristin, he needed to treat her as his partner and not keep her on the sidelines.

CHAPTER FOURTEEN

NORTHERN CALIFORNIA

The clean scent of the pine forest infused the afternoon air as Holly Castillo drove through town. Her blonde hair swirled around her head, making her wish she'd thought to bring a hair tie to pile it into a bun. She came to a crosswalk and stopped, allowing some of the festival goers by. Children skipped across the street, passing their parents to meet up with friends. A toddler let go of her father's hand and stopped in the road for a rock. Holly smiled and waved as the dad lifted his hand in apology for holding her up.

She wasn't in a hurry. A spark came off her diamond wedding ring, casting tiny rainbows throughout the car. She wiggled her finger, watching the colors dance across the ceiling.

Deanna, the minister's wife, waved. "Hey, Holly! Are you coming to the dance tonight?"

"We wouldn't miss it," she called back. "I'm on my way home to make my potluck dish."

A truck came up behind her, so she moved the car

forward. "I'll see you there," Holly called as Deanna ran to catch up to her family.

She parked the car in front of her house and cut the engine. Mateo's car was in the drive. Not a surprise. He worked from home, spending most of his time on his computer.

Holly kept herself busy at the community center when Mateo had to work. She'd taken a few culinary classes, and a creative writing class. She and Mateo worked out together daily, sometimes letting their training extend into the evenings.

She was gathering her groceries when she noticed her neighbor struggling to bring a case of bottled water out of her house.

"Hey Joan, can I help you with that?" Holly called, jogging over to take the case.

Joan couldn't possibly weigh more than a hundred pounds and was at least eighty years old. But that didn't stop her from being one of the most active women she'd ever seen.

"Oh, thank you, sweetheart. I need to get a few of these cases to the burger booth. They're running low and I had all these lying around."

She packed all the cases into the trunk of Joan's car. "Do you have someone to take these out for you? I can ask Mateo to go with you."

"No, no," Joan said. "I'll manage." She looked past Holly's shoulder, a spark of interest in her eyes. "Where is that man of yours, anyway?"

Holly laughed. "He'll be out in a second, I'm sure."

"Mmm. I don't know how you keep your hands to yourself with that one around. Especially when the two of you wrestle around in the backyard all day. Whew."

A flush ran up her face. She'd thought no one would pay them any mind when they trained. "It is difficult sometimes, let me say."

Joan had clearly passed the age in which she'd hold her

tongue when it came to finding a man attractive. She flirted shamelessly with Mateo whenever she could. He would glow with a blush under his warm brown skin. It was adorable.

As if on cue, the screen door of their home opened, and Mateo stepped out onto the porch. Joan watched him with appreciation as he came down the stoop and headed their way. He was well over six feet tall, with broad shoulders and a chiseled body. Joan was practically giddy when he grinned at her with his dimpled smile.

"Ah, there you are, *mi cielo.*" Mateo pulled Holly to his side, giving her a toe-curling look. He leaned in and gave her a soft kiss on her forehead.

Joan sighed. "You two are so damn beautiful together. When are you going to give me little rug rats to chase out of my flower bed?"

"Maybe soon." Mateo looked down at Holly. "We've been talking about trying."

Holly smiled up at him. "We have a bit of a trip coming up. Maybe after that."

"To be young and full of love," Joan said wistfully. "I remember those days, hold on to it." She closed her trunk, her keys jangling in her hand as she went around to the driver's side door. "Oh, what are you bringing to the potluck, dear?"

"I'm making a buffalo chicken dip. It shouldn't take long. We'll be there before the music starts."

"Well, come by the booth and say hi."

"We will," Mateo called, waving as Joan drove away.

Mateo turned to Holly and asked skeptically. "What are you making?"

"You mean, what are *we* making? You don't think I'd feed chicken to the entire town all by myself, did you?"

He kept his arm around her as they walked to her car. Mateo hoisted the grocery bag into his arms and closed the trunk. He peeked into the bag.

"You got a rotisserie chicken. It's already cooked."

"So?"

"I doubt even you could poison them with that."

Holly shook her head. "I'm not taking any chances."

Mateo's laugh was rich. "Okay, *mi cielo*. I'll make the dip."

———

THE NIGHT AIR WAS STILL WARM. THE BLANKET-STREWN grass was alive with families and groups of friends gathered around one another. Mateo led her to a bare spot where they could sit. Pine forest, funnel cake and beer scented the air, occasionally accompanied by the rich smell of the barbecue.

Mateo left to get them a couple of drinks while Holly spread out the blanket, slipped off her sandals, and sat down. Deanna called her name and bounced over to her.

"I left Kent with the kids for a little downtime. So, I thought I would make the rounds."

"Have a seat." Holly gestured to the other corner of the blanket. Deanna eagerly sat, tucking her short legs under her.

"Were you the one who brought the buffalo dip?" Deanna asked. At Holly's nod, she gushed, "So good. You'll have to bring it again to church on Sunday."

"Oh, I'm sorry. Mateo and I are leaving town Sunday morning, so we won't be there. But I'll give you the recipe and you can make it."

"Great, thanks," Deanna said, taking a sip of her water. "Where are you two off to?"

"We have some business to take care of down in the Bay Area."

Mateo returned with two cold beers in his hand. He greeted Deanna and handed a beer to Holly.

"Is that a tattoo?" Deanna said, squinting at Holly's outstretched arm.

"Yeah," Holly said, holding her forearm out for Deanna to

look closer. "You haven't seen it before? I got it just before we moved here."

"I haven't. What is it?"

Holly traced the swirling design. "This is a Celtic symbol of strength, which is also a compass rose, pointing me north." Holly pointed to the delicate flowers. "And the symbol is laying atop sprigs of blue heather."

"Isn't heather usually pink?"

Holly's mouth turned up into a smile. "It is, but I liked blue."

"So pretty. I wish I could get a tattoo. Kent would freak." She looked at Mateo. "It's so great you let her get it done."

Holly caught Mateo's gaze and held back a smile. She certainly hadn't needed his permission. In fact, he was her biggest cheerleader when she'd gotten it. Of course, he had his fair share of tattoos as well.

The cries of a fussy baby carried across the air. Deanna perked up, then sighed. "I better go. He's teething, and Kent is probably close to losing his mind. I'll get that recipe from you soon."

The band took to the stage, and Holly relaxed to watch them play. Her fingers tapped along with the music, and she found a contentment wrapping around her.

Bang, bang, bang. The sharp rapports cut through the air.

Mateo jumped next to her, and a few people yelped in surprise. Holly's blood pressure spiked, and dizziness overtook her senses. A feeling of imminent death rushed in. Her gaze darted around, searching for the cause. The other concert goers took it in stride, but her mind was splintering. A full panic attack was working its way through her nerves.

Mateo's voice broke through the thunder of her heart. "*Mi cielo,* it's okay. It was fireworks. Look." He pointed at two teenage boys being chastised by a small elderly woman. They were trading smirks with one another as she berated them for being so inconsiderate.

"Remember what the doctor said when this happens. You are safe. It's just a sensation. Look for the things you can connect to."

Five things she could see, four she could touch, three things she could . . . Holly coached herself until her heart rate settled.

She met Mateo's warm brown eyes and nodded. "I'm okay now."

"You sure?"

Holly took a drink of the beer, a nutty, rich brew, cold on her suddenly parched throat. "I think so. Thank you." She was so grateful he was around when these things happened. Normally they happened at night and not out in public where everyone could see her.

The music of the band returned to her ears as they finished up a rock song. They switched it over to a country ballad.

"Come dance with me." Mateo stood and reached out his arm for her. She let him pull her up and lead her to the wooden dance floor erected under an awning of orbed lights.

Mateo wrapped his strong arms around her, his warmth a comfort to her shaken nerves. A few of their friends from church murmured and shot them looks. No doubt wondering when the two of them would produce a few beautiful babies.

The tattoo on her arm caught her attention, and she focused on it. Although the sheen of a scar could still be seen under the ink, it was the sprig of flowers that held her focus.

Scottish heather.

They had seemed the perfect color when the artist blended it for her. Was it still right? Had she been able to capture that perfect shade of blue? Was she forgetting him?

Glancing around at the perfect little community, her heart ached for reality.

It was too easy to get lost.

She drew back to look up at Mateo, his lips turned up in a smile.

"Remind me," she pleaded.

The smile dropped from his face. He tightened his hold around her waist, and in his soft, rolling accent, he reminded her.

"You are Mercedes."

She took in her name, the words grounding her back to who she was and why she was here.

"And I am Noah. And we—" He looked her in the eye. "Are going home soon."

She smiled through her tears. "We are. Thank you, Noah."

"*Da nada, mi cielo.*"

She smiled and laid her head on his shoulder. A dim spark of hope shimmered in her soul. Just a few more days, and she'd be in the arms of the man she belonged with.

PART II

CHAPTER FIFTEEN

Mercedes opened the door and stepped out onto the balcony. This place was absolutely perfect. Inconspicuously nestled within the Outer Sunset District of San Francisco, the two-story duplex offered a distant view of the open ocean over the rooftops. A single security door between the duplex's units meant Noah would be downstairs, and she would have the privacy she craved for this week.

She took in a deep breath of the sea air, her nerves alive with energy.

Freedom was just within her reach. Freedom and Alec.

It had been eleven months since she'd seen him. Eleven months of loneliness seeping into every inch of her soul. But this week would mark the end of a rough chapter and a new beginning with the man she adored.

Leaving the door open, Mercedes went to her bag and rummaged through it. The cell phone they had assigned her had three numbers on it, Noah's, her therapist, and her lawyer, Lauren Sabino. Lauren had only been her attorney for the last four months, but she seemed to be on the level and had gotten up to speed on Mercedes's unique case quickly.

It didn't stop the cogs of the government machine from

grinding to a snail's pace. The US attorney's office and the federal marshals had been reluctant to share even the prospective timeline of the witness testimony. Most of what Mercedes knew, she'd learned from the news coverage, and that was limited.

Mercedes pressed Lauren's number and was disappointed when voice mail picked up. "Hi Lauren, this is Holly Castillo calling you to discuss that package I'm expecting from the UK. I'm wondering if they finally gave you a time it's expected to arrive. We have other things to discuss as well. Please call me."

Mercedes tossed the phone onto the bed alongside her unpacked suitcase.

Damn it. She exhaled deeply, trying to chill the anxiousness swirling through her.

Noah grunted as he arrived in her bedroom door, his arms laden with a long wardrobe box. "What on earth is in here? Good lord, it's heavy."

"Ooh, those are my clothes." Mercedes ran to help him lug it into the room and prop it against her bed. "Wanna help me pick the best one?"

"Yes, ma'am." Noah's dark eyes gleamed. He knew how to dress her better than she did. More than once, he'd made the modestly dressed Holly Castillo look put together. But now, she would get to dive into a fresh new wardrobe that was all her own.

Mercedes was happy for the distraction as she threw on different outfits for Noah to critique. He sat on the couch, waiting while she changed in her room. When she would come out of the room, he'd grin at her and make comments like; "Definitely a badass bitch in court skirt." Or "That's more for an evening out with friends."

"Okay," she said, coming into the living room. "I'm excited for this one."

It was a signature black dress with a deep neckline, one

shoulder exposed, the other covered with a sheer fabric that swept against her wrists when she moved.

"That is gorgeous. Alec's going to love it or he's a blind man. You should wear the red shoes, though."

"These?" Mercedes quickly switched out the black heels for the red stilettos. Then modeled them for Noah. "What do you think?"

"Ah, *perfecto*. He'll be throwing you on the bed for sure in that one."

"I hope so. Now if only they'd tell me when he's getting here."

Mercedes paused in front of the tall mirror to admire the dress. Her chestnut locks caught her eye and she smiled at her image. The blonde hair of Holly Castillo was gone, and Sadie Elliott had returned.

Noah had flipped on the television and changed it to the trial coverage. The press was going insane. The biggest news channels had sent their top anchors to hunker around the courthouse, each trying to find the best shot for the action inside. *The* Marcus Cooper was expected to appear in person, defiant that he'd ever been anything but a model billionaire.

The way the press fawned over him was horrifying. They simply could not figure out how to separate the philanthropist from the piece of shit that he was. It made no difference that his generosity only poured into his own charities, often used to supplement his own income.

Mercedes paused when the screen switched to a one-on-one interview with Cooper. His overly contrite expression oozed disbelief that anyone could think he was a monster.

"Ugh, that man has such a punchable face," she said as she walked to her room. The less she saw of Marcus Cooper, the better.

Pulling a hanger from the closet, she called out. "Hey, do you want to work out later? Maybe we can go to the beach to practice?"

"Nah, we're going to be a little more locked down here." Noah called back. "You might meet someone you know."

"Yeah, that would be awkward." Mercedes mumbled to herself. Only a few more days and she could be herself again. "How about the little patch of grass out back?"

"Okay, let me know when you're ready."

The helplessness during the attack on her safe house had spiraled her too far into a black hole of anxiety and depression. Once she'd healed enough for exercise, Mercedes's therapist had suggested she take self-defense courses to help her process her trauma. To her relief, Noah offered to train her himself, rather than let a stranger put his hands on her.

What their sweet neighbor thought was a rough foreplay, was Noah teaching her how to escape a trained attacker. Their workouts comprised a little cardio, strength training and then Noah jumping her from different angles.

Knowing that Jason was going to be nearby at the trial made her want to practice even harder.

"Hey Sadie," Noah called out. "Your man's on TV."

"What?" Mercedes dropped the blouse in her hand and ran to the living room. "He's here?"

Her heart soared as Alec moved through the airport. She let out a breath, unsure if she'd get it back again. His hair was longer than it had been and mussed from his journey. Mercedes imagined him running his fingers through it, like he did when he was nervous. That scruffiness on his jaw made him look a little rogue.

Delicious as ever.

"That is one fine man you have there," Noah said, appreciating the full shot as Alec stopped, waiting for someone else.

Why the hell hadn't someone communicated this with her? Would they bring him directly here?

Unease cut through her moment of joy. "How the hell does the press even know who he is?"

"They said his testimony is set to begin in the next two days."

Mercedes frowned. She hadn't realized Alec was playing a role in this.

A blonde woman stepped into the shot, and Alec reached his hand out and pulled her to his side.

"Um . . ." Noah said, alarm in his voice.

Shock slammed through Mercedes's body. "Who the fuck is that?"

The two of them walked together while the camera followed. Alec's expression shifted to annoyance, and he kept the woman close to him. There was no question of the intimacy between them. He wrapped his arm around her, and he rubbed her shoulder. The cameras followed them outside to the curb. The woman gazed up at Alec while they waited, her fingers gripping onto his waist.

Mercedes bit back the nausea crawling up her throat.

Stay in love with me. Tell me you'll be mine through it all.

The reporter shouted his name, but Alec ignored them.

The camera swung to catch Cressida, who came to stand next to them. She picked at her nails with a bored expression on her face. Once the car arrived, Luke jumped out and helped load their luggage while Cressida climbed into the passenger side. Alec wrenched open the door and helped the woman into the back seat.

I won't want anyone else. I love you, Sadie.

Utter betrayal ripped through her. How could Alec do this? Why the fuck would Luke and Cressida go along with it?

Then I'll wait forever, aye?

There was no way . . .

No way.

"He doesn't know," she whispered.

And her fractured heart shattered into a thousand pieces.

CHAPTER SIXTEEN

"Jesus Christ, that was intense," Luke said. "Did you know they were going to be here?"

Alec turned in his seat to watch the small crowd of cameras and microphones shrink behind them. "Not at all. I've no idea why they're interested in me." He cast his gaze at Kristin. "You alright?"

She sent him an unsettled smile. "Just a little shaken, I think."

"Aye, they're a lot to take in." Alec scanned the vehicles behind them. "Luke, we need to take a little drive. I want to make sure we aren't being followed."

"Can't they figure out what hotel we're in and wait there?" Kristin asked.

Cressida popped up with the answer. "We have dummy rooms in our names at a different hotel. Our actual rooms are under aliases, even yours."

"Oh." Kristin cast her gaze away. Alec could tell Kristin didn't like Cressida knowing they weren't sharing a room. He gave her hand a squeeze.

"Cress, can you arrange for Sam and maybe one more of our guys here in town to run security for Luke and Charlie's house? I don't know if we'll need it, but I wasn't expecting the press to know anything about me."

"Mmm-hmm," Cressida said as she put the phone to her ear. "It's almost like they were tipped off by someone inside the circle."

Cressida wasn't wrong. Whoever had leaked Alec's name knew where and when to find him. Only someone from the top had that information.

The trip across the Golden Gate Bridge gave Alec a chance to take in the city from a distance. It looked so peaceful from here. But it held the chaos of the trial in its depths.

A melancholy swept over him. It was familiar. He'd spent the week of Mercedes's funeral gutted by loss. Now he was a little more pieced back together, but it was hard not to slip into the sorrow again. This was hopefully the last barrier to picking those fractured pieces up and becoming whole.

AS THEY PULLED INTO THE DRIVEWAY, CHARLOTTE THREW open the door and came down the steps with a wide grin on her face. The pain of seeing her was as real as it had ever been, but the sight of her growing baby bump gave Alec a jolt of joy.

"Look at you! You're gorgeous." Alec laughed, enveloping her in his arms.

She squeezed him hard and gave him an exaggerated kiss on the cheek. "You're not so bad yourself. I'm glad you shaved that mountain man beard."

"Aye, now you can see my pretty face." He grinned at her, rubbing his stubbled jaw.

Charlotte giggled. "I like your pretty face." Then she looked to Kristin, and back to Alec expectantly.

"Sorry," he said, drawing Kristin to him to make a proper introduction.

"It's so lovely to meet you. I hope you had a nice flight." Charlotte's hazel eyes were soft and warm. No matter how brave a face she'd put on this meeting, it had to remind her of the life her sister had lost. But Charlotte hid it well, smiling broadly to welcome Kristin. Why he'd thought Charlotte would ever do anything different, he couldn't say.

Alec could see Kristin was doing her best to reply with the same warmth, chatting about the beauty of the neighborhood as they climbed the steps.

When she reached the top, Charlotte stopped and turned to him. "Alec, I have a surprise for you."

"Oh, aye?"

"Aye," a voice from inside the door pulled his attention. Declan stood there grinning at him.

"The hell?" Alec said, embracing his cousin. "I thought you weren't coming in for a few more days?"

Declan's shoulder rose and fell. "I had some extra time, so I switched my flight."

"Any luck?"

"Aye, I found Mara Donovan in Ireland. Even managed to meet with her a couple of times. I tried to convince her we'd take care of everything. But she took off on me and her trail went cold again."

"Damn." Alec shook his head. "She has to be getting help from somewhere."

Declan nodded but his gaze shifted past Alec's shoulder. Alec followed it to where Cressida was chatting with Luke. Declan tried to cover a look of longing, but Alec knew that look well. He'd worn it too damn long himself. He wished the two of them would figure things out.

Throughout dinner, Kristin was quiet. When Charlotte tried to talk to her, she gave only a few word answers. Alec hoped she would become more comfortable as the days went on.

After they'd cleaned up, they moved to the living room, where Luke poured whisky and wine for the guests. Declan was in storytelling mode, making them all laugh with tales of growing up in Scotland together.

After the laughter had died down from the latest tale, Charlotte reached out and pulled Luke's hand into her lap and they shared a look that made Alec ache. A conversation took place that only they knew the words to.

Luke cleared his throat. "Speaking of *weans* being unruly, we have some news. Charlotte had her scans this week." There was a baited silence. "And our *daughter* is braw."

"*Slàinte mhath.*" Declan called.

Alec held up his whisky. "*Slàinte.*"

What it would have been to have even half the years with Mercedes as Luke and Charlotte had. Damn, it made him happy to see his wee cousin so enamored with his wife and daughter.

"Alec." Charlotte's voice drew him back to the room. "We're going to name her after both Luke's mom and Sadie. Her name will be Mercedes Clare McKinley."

The name slammed into him, gutting him.

Mercedes McKinley

It was a name he'd hoped would come into existence one day.

Charlotte's eyes were wide with concern. If she thought it hurt him, she was wrong.

He cleared the tightness in his throat away. "She would have loved that."

"Yeah, but are you sure *you're* okay?"

"I'm absolutely sure. It's bloody perfect. I can't wait to meet her."

AFTER THE EVENING WORE DOWN, CHARLOTTE WALKED THEM to the door and gave Alec a kiss on the cheek. Kristin thanked Charlotte for a wonderful dinner and joined Alec outside.

A soft fog had twisted through the quiet neighborhood. Alec breathed in the misty air tinged with the scent of jasmine that hedged the front of the house. A distant foghorn broke through the quiet of the night in a steady call.

Then a black SUV caught his attention. It was sitting across the street with its parking lights on.

Kristin stopped at the base of the stairs and turned to him, straightening the lapel of his jacket. "That was a lovely evening."

"It was. Thank you for fighting off the jet lag for me." Alec agreed and leaned down to kiss her.

"Mmm. Anytime."

They walked to Luke's car, but Alec's attention was on the SUV. As he held the door open for her, he rummaged in his pockets and pulled out his phone and dialed.

"Hey Sam, what do you know about the SUV across the street? Is it the press?"

"No, sir. I spoke to him. It's an FBI agent just checking on the house. Solid ID on him. Three passengers. He said they'd be moving on in a few."

"Did he give his name?"

"Aye, I wrote it down. It's um, Special Agent Nick Kessler."

Alec frowned and studied the vehicle. Nick was an old friend. Why would he sit in his car instead of coming to the door?

"Alright, Declan is staying in the house tonight. Luke is going to drop us off at our hotel and come right back. Anyone else does more than drive by and I want to know about it."

"Aye sir. Call with further directions."

Alec leaned down into the open car door. "I'll be just a tick."

He hadn't even made it across the street when the engine suddenly came to life, the headlights popped on, and it drove away.

What the fuck?

The cold tendrils of distrust worked their way up his spine. He pulled his phone up again, this time dialing Nick's number.

He answered on the second ring.

"Hey Alec, how ya doing?" A fake sunniness filled Nick's voice.

"I'm doing fine. Are you avoiding me, mate?"

"Nah, I just came by for a quick patrol to see how things are. I talked to your boy, and he said everything's been quiet. I have a few analysts in the car, and I need to get them back to their assignments."

Alec gripped the phone until his knuckles ached. *Motherfucker.*

Nick had never lied to him before.

He let the silence coat the air between them for a second. "Is that the story you want to go with?"

"I . . . I don't know what you mean, man."

He wasn't getting anywhere with Nick. "Alright mate. I'll see you tomorrow then?"

Nick exhaled sharply. "Yeah, I'll be there."

Alec strode back to the car and leaned into the window. "Luke, can you take Cressida and Kristin to the hotel for me? I'm going to stay here tonight."

"What?" Kristin said. "Alec, I thought maybe we could have another drink and unwind after all the traveling."

"No, sorry. But something's wrong. I want to stay here in case Charlie needs me. Luke, can you open the boot?"

Kristin popped open her door and followed behind him. "But Declan's here. Can't he handle it."

Alec jerked his luggage out of the car. "Aye, he can. And so can I." He stopped when he saw her crestfallen face. "Look,

I'm sorry. But I was just lied to by an FBI agent, and I don't know why. I won't leave my cousins and Sadie's pregnant sister to deal with it alone."

Irritation flashed in Kristin's eyes. "What are you going to do about it? Hunt them down yourself?"

A choking cough came from Cressida. Kristin shot a glare at her.

Alec stepped toward Kristin. "If someone came for Charlie, I would absolutely hunt them down."

"I see." Her lips tightened. "You sure you don't just want to immerse yourself in the woman you lost and not the one standing right here?"

A flush crept up Alec's cheeks. "It's late, and we've been up for hours. And this is not a great time to have this discussion. Please, go with Luke and Cress. I'll come by for you at eight."

Kristin's face was flushed when she dropped into the seat and jerked the door closed.

Alec caught Cressida's eyes in the light. Her brows were raised, and her lips pursed.

The car pulled away from the curb and Alec watched them leave, then he walked back to the house. Declan was leaning against the railing with his arms crossed.

"I don't know if it was a good idea to bring her or not." Alec said, joining his cousin. "She doesn't seem to understand any of this."

"She will, mate. She'll see what's been happening tomorrow. Maybe it'll open her eyes." Declan smacked his shoulder. "Come on, you need some sleep."

Kristin was right about being keyed up. It was nearly six in the morning at home. As exhausted as he was, his brain thought it was time for breakfast.

Charlotte made up a bed for Alec on the couch in the walkout basement. Like every time he'd been in this house, he felt Mercedes's presence everywhere.

Maybe Kristin was right, and he was still drawn into the ghost. He needed to find a way to live again.

CHAPTER SEVENTEEN

Mercedes paced the room, her stomach roiling. She was trying to right her tilting world ever since she'd seen Alec and his new woman stepped in front of the cameras.

The image of them together tormented her mind. The way he held his body when a reporter got close was one she knew well. He was protecting her, putting himself between them to keep her safe.

All this damn time she'd held on, confident he'd be waiting for her. She'd struggled so much to do it. But she'd pushed aside all her insecurities, believing he would love her through it all.

The idea that he'd shared himself with another was boring a hole in her head, tormenting her. That another woman could have ever taken her place hadn't seemed possible, yet she was living it. And if he'd brought her with him, they were serious. This woman had been with him longer than Mercedes had.

What if he knew she was alive? What if he just didn't love Mercedes anymore?

That was enough. Bile rose in her throat, and she made it

to the bathroom just in time. When she'd finished, she sat on the floor, her elbow on the toilet, struggling to breathe through the heartbreak and nausea. It had been years since she'd let her emotions overrun her this way.

Mercedes finally hauled herself up and was rinsing her mouth when a knock came at the door.

Noah peeked his head in. "Lauren's here and she brought Nick Kessler with her."

Mercedes followed him to the living room, where the FBI agent waited. When Nick's dark eyes landed on her, he stepped back. "Holy fuck! I thought she was kidding."

The grief of the moment was stripped away, and anger filled its place.

"Hi Nick," Mercedes snapped. "Weren't you the one who convinced me to go into the program? Didn't you tell Alec you would take care of us?"

Nick's mouth hung open, his eyes wide.

Rage was working its way to the surface. "So maybe you can explain why Alec arrived for the trial with another woman on his arm?"

"Because . . . you're dead, Sadie."

"Clearly, I'm not dead." The volume of her voice echoed off the wall. "And *you* were the one that was supposed to tell him."

Nick shook his head. "I didn't know until an hour ago. I swear."

"How is that possible?"

Lauren, who had been on the phone, strode into the apartment. "I just got off the phone with Whitley's team. They blew me off. Essentially, he said he is preparing for tomorrow's testimony and can't be distracted by the drama of a witness's love life. He *suggests* you stay hidden until called."

"That son of a bitch," Mercedes growled. She turned back to Nick. "What about my sister? Was she told?"

Nick shook his head. "I don't think so. Both she and Alec have been a mess for months."

Mercedes stalked to her bedroom. She grabbed her running shoes and plopped down on the bed. With a jerk, she opened the laces and crammed her foot into it.

"Wait, Sadie," Lauren said. "What are you going to do?"

With the laces tied, she set to work on the other shoe. "You think I don't know how to get myself to Pacific Heights? It's only about five or six miles from here."

A look passed between Lauren and Nick.

"You can't go to Pacific Heights," Nick said.

"Why not? I'll find my sister and she'll find Alec."

It was Noah that stopped her. "That's not a good idea, Sadie."

Mercedes stared at him. "What are you even saying? They *lied to us*. We trusted you and *you lied to us*!" She was screaming and she didn't care.

Noah held up his hands. "I know, I know. It's a clusterfuck. But give yourself a second to think about this. The sun has gone down, so you'll be out in the city at night. And your leg is going to tire out real quick if you walk more than a mile or two."

Mercedes strode out of the room, grabbing a sweater on her way out the front door. She'd be a limping mess by the time she got there, but who gave a shit. Anger fueled each stride she made.

She hadn't asked for a lot. Considering the shitstorm the marshals let happen on their watch, she'd been ridiculously accommodating.

Two people.

Only two goddamned people had to be told she was still coming home, and she'd play along with the rest. Mercedes had lain there, her body broken from what their own fucking agent had done and listened to their promises.

Twilight had fallen over the western sky, filling it with a mixture of blue and pink on the low horizon and a gentle fog was rolling in, casting a glow around the city lights. Mercedes set out on a quick jog, the muscle around her injury already aching dully.

A car engine rumbled up next to her and the door slammed. She ignored it, making a left-hand turn to cross the street.

"Sadie, wait," Noah called out. The even thumps of his feet as he jogged behind her echoed along the fences.

"Go away, Noah."

"No, get in the car." His usually gentle voice was firm.

Mercedes stopped, her chest heaving. When he caught up to her, she glared at him. "Did you know?" Tears stung her eyes, and she blinked them away. She didn't know what she would do if Noah had betrayed them, too.

Noah shook his head. "I promise you, I didn't. Get in the car. You shouldn't run that far."

Mercedes stopped, cursing that he was right. A deep throb was cutting through her anger-induced adrenaline. She'd probably already hurt herself. If she'd tried to go another five miles, she'd struggle to walk for the rest of the week.

"I can't let this go, Noah. I have to see him tonight."

"Listen to me, *mi cielo*. Seeing him tonight will do him more harm than good." He glanced at the car, slowly following them. "Get in, and I'll make sure Nick takes you to your sister's house. But I want you to listen before you go in, okay?"

"Fine." She wrenched open the door to the back seat and climbed in. As soon as her door was shut, Nick pulled away from the curb.

Lauren was the first to speak. "Sadie, I can't imagine what you must be feeling, but Nick and Noah are right. Telling Alec and Charlotte tonight will do a lot of damage."

Mercedes jaw ached from clenching her teeth. "If I thought either of them was gone, for even a day, it would be agony." She thought of the few hours in London, when she'd convinced herself Alec was dead. She'd wanted to die with him.

Nick looked back at her in the rearview mirror. "Sadie, Alec has to testify tomorrow, in one of the biggest cases in a century. He's primed and ready to go to war for what happened to you. If you show up tonight, it will throw him into absolute chaos. He'll be a mess tomorrow. It might even put the case into jeopardy."

"Maybe I don't care about that anymore."

Noah piped in. "You have spent way too much time hiding because of this. Are you really ready to let it burn for one more day?"

The car turned down a familiar road. The tree-lined streets were quiet in this part of the city. Nick parked across the street from her house. Several lights were on. Alec might be in there right now. She could jump out of the car and be up the stoop before they could stop her.

If you show up tonight, it will throw him into absolute chaos. He'll be a mess tomorrow.

They were right, which is what kept her from wrenching open the door.

"Tell me about her," she croaked.

"Her name is Kristin," Nick said. "I briefly met her on a trip to London a month or so ago. She's a receptionist. They've been seeing each other for about five or six months. They go to sporting events together and hang out on weekends. She seems nice."

Mercedes hadn't had five or six months with him. She'd had three days. "And normal. There isn't an organization of assassins trying to kill her."

"There's someone coming up to the side," Noah said.

Nick rolled down his window and greeted the man who

came to the window. Mercedes didn't listen while Nick spoke to him. Instead, her mind spiraled in and around itself, trying to find a path that brought Alec back to her. No matter how hard she tried, there was no way she could negotiate a different reality.

Once the man left, Nick rolled up the window and looked at her in the rearview mirror.

"When will he be told?" she choked out, her heart breaking to make such a concession.

Nick's words were filled with sympathy. "Once his testimony is over. I'll tell him myself."

She wiped her face with the back of her hand. It could be tomorrow or a week. Mercedes would have to keep silent until then.

"Damn," Noah hissed.

Mercedes looked up to see Alec and the blonde woman walk down the steps. She played with his collar and Alec leaned down to kiss her. It wasn't a long kiss, but it was gentle. When he drew back, he was smiling.

Grief slammed into her chest, suffocating her in its grip. It was already too late.

They walked together to Luke's car, but Alec's attention had turned toward them. After he made a brief call, he walked toward them.

"Shit, he's coming this way."

She could do it. Step out of the car and show herself to him. It was nothing more than a simple tug on the silver knob, and he'd be right there.

"Go," Mercedes said, her very soul shredding in her chest. "Just go."

Nick started the engine and accelerated away from the curb, leaving Alec alone in the fog-laden street.

There was still a chance. He could choose her once he knew. Until he was done with her, there was hope.

Nick's phone rang. "Damn, it's Alec."

Mercedes sucked in her breath while Nick answered it. The call automatically transferred to the car's audio system.

"Hey Alec, how ya doing?" Nick said.

"I'm doing fine. Are you avoiding me, mate?"

Oh, god, that voice.

Mercedes pursed her trembling lips. Every word pierced her battered soul. She leaned forward to keep the sob from escaping. Noah reached over and rubbed her back.

"Nah, I just came by for a quick patrol to see how things are. I talked to your boy, and he said everything's been quiet. I have a couple of analysts in the car, and I need to get them back to their assignments."

There was a heavy pause. "Is that the story you want to go with?"

"I don't know what you mean, man."

Alec's tone was laden with suspicion. "Alright mate. I'll see you tomorrow then?"

"Yeah, I'll be there."

Nick disconnected the call, and Mercedes fell apart.

When they returned to her rental, she didn't say a word to the others. There was nothing more they could do for her, so she was done with them all.

Mercedes thumped up the stairs, the pain radiating up her leg with each step. Her logical mind told her to ice it, but she didn't care. The heaviness in her chest was the only thing she could track.

Opening the door to the lovely room, she let the numbness wash over her. Alec should be here with her now, not in the arms of a stranger.

She dropped onto the bed, her body listless.

What was she going to do now? Alec was supposed to be her haven. Her home.

She was lost without her anchor. The light guiding her to the life she'd dreamed of was gone.

Mercedes kicked off her shoes and crawled into bed, not caring about changing her clothes. Tomorrow, she would fight. But not tonight.

For the first time since the attack, she wished Noah hadn't saved her.

CHAPTER EIGHTEEN

Jason's blood seethed as he watched Alec McKinley from across the reception area. The bastard was in the conference room, deep in conversation, his back to Jason. Every time he moved, Jason wanted to kick his fucking teeth in.

He was eating up Jason's much-needed press coverage. Jason was the one who had brought the most damning information to the table. McKinley was supposed to be the sideshow. The second act, whose only job was to enhance Jason's story of the corruption in Cooper Pharmaceutical.

McKinley hadn't even spent an entire day on the stand and the press fawned all over him, sucking his dick everywhere he went.

The little blonde that followed McKinley around like a puppy caught Jason's attention and he observed her.

Cute enough, but a little plain.

She was another sign that Mercedes had meant nothing to McKinley. If she had, he never would have brought a woman with him.

The woman strolled around the reception area, clearly waiting for the group to finish up. Her eyes followed the ceiling and walls as if she were taking in a museum and not a federal building waiting room.

Little blondie looks bored as hell.

McKinley had no idea how to keep a woman happy.

Jason slid a look at the agent assigned to his detail. "I'm going to stretch my legs."

His agent, Gary, or possibly Terry, shot him a disinterested look and nodded. "Don't leave this corridor."

Go fuck yourself. But Jason gave him a tight nod and got up from his seat.

Jason walked over to a plaque of some politician and put his hands in his pockets disarmingly. He was right in the path of little blondie.

When she came into view, she was gazing up at the wall of picture frames. He watched her with amusement as she caught sight of him and gave a little start.

"Hey there." He smiled, letting his look take on a hopeful quality.

She swept a lock of hair behind her ear. "Hello."

No recognition crossed her face. She hadn't been around for Jason's testimony, and since no cameras were allowed in the courtroom, she didn't seem to know who he was.

Too fucking perfect.

"Are you a part of the big case?" Jason tilted his head, gazing at her with an intensity that had once won over a better woman.

She blushed beautifully. "I'm not, but someone I'm with is."

"Oh, who is that?" He let his gaze fall to her mouth, then trail back to her eyes. "Is it Declan McKinley?"

"Um . . . No." She let out a little laugh. "His cousin, Alec. He just finished his testimony."

"Oh, I know Alec. We're old friends."

Her face lit up. "You are?"

Jason turned his mouth up into a crooked smile and he held out his hand. "Yeah. We go way back. I'm Jace."

"Kristin." She took his hand, her smile broadening. That she didn't immediately back away told him all he needed to know. Alec McKinley hadn't kept her satisfied and now, just like Mercedes, she was aching for someone who would make it all better.

A fucking lamb he could lead off to slaughter.

Jason looked away for a beat, then back to her. She responded immediately, flushing a deeper red and looking away. Oh, she was too fucking easy.

Suddenly, a giant mass was between them, and Alec McKinley glared down at him. "Back the fuck up."

Jason gave a laugh. This was going to make his day.

"Alec, what are you doing?" Alarm and surprise coated Kristin's voice.

"Yeah Alec," Jason taunted. "What are you doing?"

"Stay the fuck away from us, or I'll snap you in half," Alec growled.

Kristin gasped. "Alec!"

Jason's grin widened. "You should use better manners in front of Kristin. What are you thinking?"

McKinley's expression turned deadly, and he stepped in closer. "Fuck you."

Everyone seemed to realize what was going down at the same time. Lazy ass Gary jumped between them, his hand on his gun. "Back off, sir." He pushed back against McKinley's chest.

McKinley stepped back, but murder was still in his eyes.

Jason smirked, making a little shooing motion with his hands. "Back off, Alec."

Kristin stared at him in disbelief, so Jason gave her a sweet smile. "When you're tired of him, sweetheart, look me up." He licked his lips. "McKinley knows he's got nothing on me."

"Fucking Hollis!" Alec's rage was palpable now. "How the hell did he get access to us?"

Cressida spoke up first. "The protection order against him was for Sadie, not for you. And even if she were here, it would have long since expired."

Anxiousness roiled in Alec's chest. "What do I have to do to get one?"

His lawyer answered. "I can draw up the needed paperwork and appeal to the judge. But the trial is winding down so he shouldn't be a problem after this."

Fuck.

Alec inhaled to clear his mind. This was nearly over. He'd given them all he had on the stand. Now he had to be available if they wanted to recall him. After this week, Jason Hollis's smug face would be a distant memory and nothing more.

Kristin touched his arm. "Alec, I'm so sorry. He told me his name was Jace. I didn't know he was the Jason you talked about."

Alec let his breath out. "No, I should have told you more about him. Are you okay?" He reached tugged her to him.

She wrapped her arms around his waist. "Yeah, I've never seen you so angry before. It scared me a little."

He would imagine so. "I'm sorry. That man certainly brings out the worst in me. Please tell me you'll keep your distance from him and stay with either me, Declan or Mason, alright?"

Kristin nodded against him and tightened her hold.

This was his own fault. Alec had done little to bring Kristin into his past, or told her the things he'd done to protect those he cared about. When they returned home, he'd tell her everything. Open himself up and let her see who he really was.

A cough from behind him broke through Alec's thoughts, and he turned to find Nick Kessler standing behind him. Alec narrowed his eyes. "I thought you were hiding from me."

Nick's brow creased. "I know, and I'm sorry. But I need to talk to you. Right now."

Alec scoffed. "You've been avoiding me all day, but now you want to talk?"

"Yeah." The seriousness in his tone cooled Alec's irritation. "But not here. Come on, Charlotte's already waiting for us."

CHAPTER NINETEEN

Alec made sure Kristin was delivered to Declan before following Nick to the small office. Charlotte was leaning against the desk, gazing out the window. When they stepped into the room, she smiled. Alec could see the lines of fatigue on her face. This trial was sapping her energy too.

Nick stepped into the room and closed the door. "I'm sorry for being all mysterious on you. And for last night. That's not usually my style."

Alec glared at Nick. "That's not good enough, Nick. You scared my family last night."

"I know, and I'm sorry for that too. It couldn't be helped." Nick held his hands up. "It's important that you know I didn't know what was happening until yesterday."

"And what *is* happening?"

"People haven't been honest with either of you, and what I'm about to say is going to be hard for you to hear."

Alec tilted his head. "So, you lied to me, then?"

"No . . . I mean . . . Damn it. *I* didn't lie to you, but you were definitely lied to."

Charlotte sighed. "Nick, what's going on?"

"I'm sorry." Nick's brows drew together into a grimace. Then looked Alec directly in the eye. "Sadie's alive."

Alec's brain took in the words but couldn't process them. "What the fuck did you just say?"

Nick pursed his lips. "I said, Sadie is alive. They've had her hidden for the last eleven months, waiting for trial. She's set to testify next."

"I don't understand." Charlotte raised her voice. "Are you sure?"

"Very sure. She and I had quite the conversation last night."

"Last night?" Alec said. None of what Nick was saying made any damn sense.

Nick swallowed. "Sadie was in the car with me. That's why I drove off."

"In the car with you?" Anger flared in Alec's gut. This wasn't funny. "Have you gone mad?"

"No, I'm not mad. I thought they would give you both a few days before they called her, but Whitley wants her now."

Charlotte tilted her head. "Wait. So, you're saying she'll be in the courtroom in a few minutes?"

Nick nodded his head. "That's exactly what I'm saying."

Holy fuck.

"Alec." Charlotte's brow was creased with fear and hope. "Is this real?"

"I don't know." Alec had lost a grip on reality.

He'd had dreams like this before. Grief dreams, his counselor had called them. It had been months since he'd awoken in a cold sweat, fresh agony washing over him, when he realized she hadn't come back to him.

This felt different.

"We can talk more later, but we should get to the courtroom." Nick moved to the door. "Whitley asked for a recess, so I'd at least have a second to tell you."

Their footsteps echoed off the marble floor, mixing with

the thundering of his pulse. Every noise amplified. Inside the courtroom, the murmurs of the waiting reporters and court staff echoed in Alec's head.

Brenden Whitley came into his view and the world suddenly corrected itself.

Bastard.

How many phone calls had they had? How many opportunities had Whitley had to tell him the truth?

If it even is the truth.

Alec didn't believe it. It could be another lie designed to forward the US attorney's agenda. He wasn't exactly sure how, but there was no way this was happening.

A swell of anger broke free, and he crossed the courtroom. "Is this some kind of sick joke?" Alec ground out as he approached Whitley.

Whitley looked him up and down. He didn't have to ask Alec what he meant. "I can assure you it's quite real, Mr. McKinley. And quite necessary."

"So for nearly a year you let us believe this?" Rage was unfurling, Alec moved toward Whitley, his fists clenched.

Brenden Whitley stepped back, warily eyeing him. Then shuffled through a file on the table. He pulled a document out and handed it to Alec. "Mercedes let you believe it."

Alec snatched the paper, blood pumping in his ears. It was a copy of a security and protection plan. Alec scanned it until his eyes landed on his own name. He reread the typed words, hoping he had it wrong.

It stated in no uncertain terms would Alec Ryan McKinley or Charlotte Lisette McKinley be made aware of the arrangement or Mercedes would violate the order and would risk her removal from the program.

At the bottom, Mercedes's name was written in her scrawling script. She had dated it two days after her death.

Mercedes had signed it.

She knew he'd be told she was dead, and she fucking signed it.

"I'm sorry, man. Otherwise, they never would have stopped trying to get to her." Whitley had the look of a man who wanted to have sympathy but didn't.

The strike of the gavel echoed out, dragging Alec back to reality.

"You better take a seat," Whitley said with a smug smile. "This is about to be one hell of a show."

Alec let out a shallow breath. "A show?"

Whitley ignored him, brushing by to take his seat at the table.

Dazed, Alec stepped back, the paper still in his hands.

"Alec, what the bloody hell is going on?" Declan hissed in his ear. "Charlie's as big a wreck as you are."

"Sadie . . ." was all he could get out.

Declan frowned at him as if he'd gone daft. Alec handed the paper to him and sat. Cressida read it over Declan's shoulder, and their jaws dropped as understanding hit them.

"What's going on?" Kristin moved to sit next to him and gripped his hand. "Are you okay?"

"No." was all he could manage.

The judge called the session to order. "Mr. Whitley," the judge was saying, his words muffled. "Do you have any further need for delay?"

"No, Your Honor, that minor detail has been cleared up."

Minor detail.

Alec's gut churned. The roiling emotions were all over the place. Anger. Hope. Grief. Betrayal.

How could this have happened? Why had she let them do this?

"Alright then. Please call your next witness," the judge said.

"The prosecution calls . . ."

This cannot be happening.

". . . Mercedes Elliott, your honor."

Her name struck him like a hammer.

A hum built in the room. Reporters were turning to one another with questioning looks. When the doors opened, the hum turned to a roar.

He couldn't look. It would give him hope. This wasn't something that was possible.

It was Charlotte's gasp of, "Oh, my god," that finally made Alec turn.

Time fell away.

She was as perfect as the night he met her. Her thick, dark hair swept along her shoulders as she walked. Her every movement was filled with a graceful purpose. The tailored suit she wore accentuated every curve of her body. A body he'd craved to touch for far too long.

When Mercedes reached the stand, she turned to face the courtroom, and Alec inhaled as much air as he could. Everything about her delicate features was stunning. That little lift of her chin was back, and her expression was cool and collected.

The judge said something to her Alec couldn't make out, and she gave him a nod. Then she faced forward and lifted her right hand to take her oath.

It never happened.

The defense table was in an uproar. They shouted objections over the calls to order from the judge. The chaos gaining the attention of the reporters who were now talking animatedly to one another.

But Alec was lost in her. She was all he could see.

Mercedes's hazel eyes never lifted to meet his, no matter how much he needed them to. Instead, she focused intently on the back of the room. Her face gave nothing away. Alec's gaze went to her fingers.

Jesus, she still did it.

She was delicately tapping her fingers against her leg. The only tell that showed her genuine emotions.

A sudden shifting in the crowd brought his attention back. The press was scrambling to the doors.

Alec looked at Kristin and shook his head. "What's happening?"

Kristin furrowed her brow. "The judge gave the defense the night to collect themselves. She'll testify tomorrow morning."

A big man he recognized as Noah Ramirez, the agent that was supposed to have died with her, walked up to her and leaned to whisper in her ear. Mercedes nodded to him and stepped down from the stand. The man had his hand on the small of her back as he escorted her down the aisle. She still wouldn't meet Alec's eyes, even after she passed by him.

She couldn't even look at him after what she'd done.

Get ready for the show.

Alec watched her walk away. Mercedes had played her part beautifully.

CHAPTER TWENTY

The panic Mercedes had been stifling down threatened to spill out. Every eye in the room was on her, crawling over her body, igniting every nerve. She'd known it would be bad. The dead coming back to life to take down one of the worst humans on the planet? There was just no way to get out of this unscathed.

But all the prep she'd done to get ready for this moment was out the window the second she'd learned she'd lost Alec. Now she didn't know what the hell she was doing.

Mercedes walked to the front of the room and held up her hand to take her oath. The shouting continued, and she lowered her hand, waiting for any cue that told her what she needed to do.

Just breathe.

Alec's searing gaze was on her, and she fought the urge to look at him. It was hard enough to keep her knees from giving out. One look at his face and she would shatter.

The gavel cracked over and over, but the court was in a frenzy. Mercedes looked around, not able to hear the judge's order. Noah was suddenly at her side.

"He called a recess. We need to find a safe place for you."

Mercedes nodded and focused on the part of the wall that wasn't swimming in her vision. She lifted her chin and walked the way she'd come in. The press followed along, shouting questions. Cameras were restricted here, but she ducked her head against Noah just in case anyone was hoping to snap a picture of her.

"Where have you been?"

"What testimony do you have against Marcus Cooper?"

"Did you know Alec McKinley is with another woman?"

That one caught her attention. Not only because it ripped her soul into tiny shreds, but because it made the media's focus become clear.

Alec had just testified and there was no doubt it was heart wrenching. Mercedes's sudden appearance and Alec's new relationship was just the ticket to make an already spectacular scandal an absolute ratings sensation. Whoever could get the scoop on this little triangle would be king.

This media drama wasn't an accident, it was orchestrated. *Fucking Whitley.*

Noah guided her to a restricted hallway, and she gratefully ducked inside. The shouts became distant as she hurried as fast as the stilettos and her aching thigh would let her. Mercedes entered the small office space and sat in the nearest chair, burying her head in her hands.

She'd been dreading this day for so long. Being dead had its advantages and now she'd just thrown them all away. The momentary peace was going to be eclipsed by reality. And that reality was shittier than she could have ever imagined.

A knock at the door and Lauren came in. She handed Mercedes a bottle of water. "You did really well out there. I know that was tough."

That didn't even begin to cover it. "How long is the recess?" She opened the water and drank deeply, her throat parched.

"He adjourned for the day. Noah's already gone to get

your car." Lauren sat across from her. "Cooper's council is up in arms, trying to suppress anything you might have."

"Of course, we knew that would happen." Mercedes sat up, trying to catch her bearings. "Did Whitley talk to you?"

Lauren scoffed. "No, he brushed me off again. But I did pass along your message. I was told 'they would make arrangements when they could'. Then he and his team jumped right into a meeting down the hall. Probably working out Cooper's defense strategy."

Mercedes sat upright, her gaze falling on Lauren. "Whitley's down the hall?"

"Yeah. In the large meeting room."

Mercedes jumped up and was out the door before Lauren had finished her sentence. If that asshole thought he could hide from her forever, he was dead-ass wrong.

She could see Whitley through the window, grinning from ear to ear. Rage pulsed through her veins. He was collecting congratulations from his minions while they buried her and the people she loved in misery.

Mercedes ripped open the door. "Brenden, you son of a bitch," she growled.

Whitley did a double take, his grin fading from his face. "Ms. Elliott . . ."

"Don't give me that shit, Brenden, we're on a first name basis, remember?" Whitley stepped back. "Or is that only when you need something from me. Shall I call you Mr. Whitley when you won't take my fucking calls?"

A flush appeared across Whitley's cheeks. "There really isn't a need . . ."

Mercedes interrupted him. "What the hell have you done?"

A tic developed under Whitley's eye. "What do you mean? I'm trying to win this case."

"By lying to me and everyone I care about? Or will you

win it by using us to create a media circus? Do you have any idea how dangerous this ploy for attention is?"

"It's not a ploy for attention." Whitley stepped up to her, his own voice raising to match hers.

"Oh, right." Sarcasm thickened each word. "And the over-the-top press coverage isn't being helped along by your office?"

Whitley held up his hands and shook his head. "The press is going to do what the press is going to do. What do you want from me, Sadie?"

"Don't fucking gaslight me. I know what I'm looking at."

"I don't know what you want me to say." Whitley shrugged.

"What about my family?" Mercedes's voice broke. "You and I had an agreement."

"And I kept my end of it," Whitley said. "You have a problem with how it played out, that's on someone else, not me."

Mercedes shot him a look of disgust. "Just answer your goddamn phone."

"Will do." Whitley's smug face looked down on her like he hadn't a care in the world. And he didn't. This was all playing out beautifully for him.

A sudden awareness washed over her. She'd been so pissed she hadn't looked at anyone but Whitley.

But he was here. They all were.

For the first time since she'd made her existence known, she turned her gaze on Alec.

He knocked the breath out of her.

His vivid blue eyes were crestfallen. The pull to him was so strong she nearly crossed to him, longing for the safety of his arms around her. But a slender hand wrapped around Alec's bicep, snapping her back to reality. Mercedes only looked into the woman's brown eyes for a second, but the message was sent loud and clear.

He's mine now.

Mercedes blinked to clear away the sting of tears. She said to Whitley. "My lawyer told me you agreed to help make the arrangements I asked for?"

Whitley sighed, "Yeah, that's what I was told."

"Good. Make sure it happens. *Tonight.* Or tomorrow you're going to have a significantly more hostile witness on your hands than you planned on."

Looking at the gaping onlookers, Mercedes walked to Charlotte, grabbed her arm and tugged. "I'm taking this one now."

Mercedes strode out of the room, Charlotte walking quickly behind her to keep up.

They walked to the office she'd just left. As soon as she'd shut the door, Charlotte launched into her arms, just like she used to do when she was little. Mercedes held her tight, feeling each wrenching sob in her bones. She stroked her hair and murmured softly anything that might comfort her.

"Where have you been?" Charlotte hiccuped.

"I can't tell you."

"You can't tell me?" Charlotte's mouth dropped open. "Jesus, Sadie. Do you have any idea what we've been through?"

Mercedes drew back and wiped her cheek with the back of her hand. "I know, honey. I'm so sorry. Nothing happened the way I was told it would. We don't have a lot of time, but I promise I'll tell you everything when I can."

Mercedes's gaze traveled down to Charlotte's belly. "Oh my god, you're just the sweetest. I'm so happy for you."

Charlotte smiled and swept her hand over her bump. "It's a girl. Her name is Mercedes Clare."

Mercedes covered her mouth with her fingertips, tears streaming down her face. "I don't even know what to say."

"Just say you'll still be around to be an auntie to her."

Mercedes nodded. The danger hadn't passed yet, but the

light was shining through the end of the tunnel. "They told me once my testimony is over, they'll relax my security. I can come over and see you, or maybe you can visit me." When Charlotte nodded, Mercedes added. "Can you pass on a message to Alec?"

"Alec?" Charlotte blinked at her. "Why didn't you bring him with us?"

Mercedes thought of the glare she'd gotten from the woman at his side and choked on the words. "Because he wasn't alone."

"Oh, Sadie." Charlotte's expression turned to sympathy.

Mercedes shook her head, fighting her heart's desire to fall completely apart. "Can you tell him I'm sorry and I swear I didn't know. And warn him we've become the story, so he needs to be careful. He probably knows, but I want to make sure."

A knock sounded at the door, and Noah poked his head in. "I'm so sorry to cut this short, but our transport is here. We need to go now if we are going to keep you out of the press's eye."

Mercedes looked at her sister. "I love you. And I promise I didn't want either of you hurt. Can you tell him, please?" At Charlotte's nod, she walked to the door. Noah and Lauren waited for her in the hall.

Alec stood in the door of the meeting room. She walked past him without looking at him. It hurt too damn much.

CHAPTER TWENTY-ONE

"How the fuck did this happen?" Marcus Cooper's voice carried across the limo. "Not only is Jason Hollis still breathing, but Mercedes Elliot is back from the dead. What the fuck do I pay you for?"

Adam winced. He had to admit, this turn had taken him too. "I told you, I lost my connection on the inside when Larissa King died. She was the one that knew the movements of all the witnesses. Hollis is as well-hidden as Elliott has been."

Marcus growled his frustration into his drink. Straight gin this time, Adam noted. "My lawyers are trying to get her thrown the fuck out of court. It can't be fucking legal to lie to the entire world and fake a witness's death."

The car turned down one of the massive hills and they shifted forward. Adam studied Marcus from under his baseball cap. He already had an unsteady sway to his body as he tossed back another gulp of the clear liquid. Marcus would be sauced in the next ten minutes if he kept up his pace.

"And where the fuck is Mara? Huh?" Marcus shouted, wiping his mouth with the back of his hand. "Are you so fucking useless that you can't even find one little girl?"

Oh, I can find her alright.

But Adam tightened his lips and did his best to look contrite.

Darkness overwhelmed them as the driver maneuvered the limo into the parking garage. Marcus stumbled out and walked to the elevator. Adam followed along with his head down, hoping he wouldn't have to carry Marcus's drunk ass.

They made it to Marcus's penthouse and were greeted by the other Cooper asshole. Tyler's petulant face twisted in disgust.

"How the hell did they pull that off?" Tyler's eyes followed his father as he flopped onto the sofa. Then he glared at Adam. "How is it we have a team of spies on our payroll, and the government could slip right by you?"

"It's not as easy as the movies make it seem," Adam said, doing his best to moderate his tone. "Not everyone has a price."

Tyler stepped up to Adam. "But you do, don't you? Dad told me the price of your work." He tilted his head. "How is your wife these days?"

Ice filtered through Adam's veins. Did this little fuck just threaten him?

"That's enough, Tyler," Marcus said, wiping his hand over his face. "We need to regroup and think of a new way of approaching our problem."

Tyler glared at Adam but backed away. "I think I have a way to at least buy us more time."

Marcus looked at his son and threw up his hands. "Let's hear it then."

Tyler walked to the table and picked up a sheet of paper. "We know all the names of the jurors. We have our people investigate all twelve members and find out what they need. Then, we approach them, one by one and offer them their heart's desire."

Adam scoffed. "You think jury tampering is the best way to win this case?"

"We don't need to win it. At least, it's not looking like we can right now. But we can delay it."

"A mistrial?" Marcus narrowed his eyes. "It would give us another shot at remediating our problems."

Adam had to admit, the little shit had figured out a way to be useful. "There's no saying any of them will take the bribe."

"They don't have to. Even a hint of tampering and the judge may have no choice. Especially if the press were to catch a hint that someone had messed with them."

Adam rubbed his jaw. "They sequestered the jury for the trial. It won't be easy to get to them, but if I know where they are staying, I might leave them a little something in their rooms."

Marcus nodded and stood. "Do what you can. We need something to go our way for once. Come back when you have a plan." He carried the gin bottle with him as he left the room.

Adam stood as well and walked to the door, when Tyler's next words stopped him. "My dad trusts you."

Tyler was studying him.

"I hope so, I've busted my ass to keep this shit together."

"Have you?" Tyler crossed his arms. "It seems like you fucked up more than you've helped."

Adam straightened to his full height. "You have no idea how much of my life I've dedicated to the company and to your father."

"Oh, I know full well." Tyler tilted his head. "Just make sure you remember how much you owe to him, and now to me."

Adam jerked open the door and slammed it on his way out. The nerve of that little fucker questioning him. But a little nugget of doubt formed in his mind. What if they knew?

CHAPTER TWENTY-TWO

A lec sat at the conference table, nausea crawling through his gut. He stared at the paper on the table, his finger running over her signature at the bottom.

"I can't believe she did that to you," Kristin said. "Are you okay?" Her brown eyes were soft and understanding.

He gave a slight nod, knowing it was a fucking lie. How could he be okay?

Mercedes had agreed to let him rot in his grief. He'd been so broken for so long. Not a single word to the ones she claimed to love.

Anger swelled in his chest.

She'd let him suffer.

There was no coming back from that.

Charlotte was glowing when she returned to their meeting room. She jumped into Luke's arms, laughing through her tears. Luke held her tight while she buried her head in his chest.

Alec's conflicted emotions battled inside him. Through his darkest days, he had dreamed of this very thing happening. She would show up, and he'd realize the nightmare wasn't real.

But Alec had done so much work to move past that. He'd allowed himself to live that shell of a life until it seemed to fit. Now she was here, and his fragile world had come apart again.

Mercedes had walked right past him without acknowledging him. Not even a word as they whisked her out of the building. He hadn't even been worth a moment of her time.

Charlotte came to sit next to him. "Alec, she wanted me to tell you she was sorry and that she didn't know. She didn't have time to explain anything, but she wanted you to know you need to be careful of the media. That you both should avoid them the best you can."

Kristin's eyes widened. "Why would I be a part of this?"

Charlotte shrugged, but her gaze never left Alec's.

Alec knew exactly what Charlotte was saying. "We're adding a layer of drama to this circus."

The bastards weren't done using him. Bitterness boiled over. "Nice of Sadie to convey that message since she couldn't even be bothered to talk to me herself."

Charlotte's brow knitted together. "Alec . . ."

"It's alright, Charlie. I get it." He pushed the paper across the table at her. "She's shown us both what we mean to her."

Cressida stepped forward. "I know you're hurting, Alec, but you might be jumping the gun a little."

"I don't think he is," Kristin cut in. "What kind of woman fakes her own death and says nothing to the people grieving for her. It's unforgivable."

"Says someone who's never been on the run from highly skilled assassins," Cressida snapped.

Kristin scoffed and looked away.

"Court's out for the night. Let's go back to our house and take a breath," Luke said, worry creased his eyes. "Charlotte needs to get off her feet and we can all stand to get out of this building."

Alec couldn't agree more. Pushing his chair back, he followed the others as they headed for the parking garage. Kristin walked at his side, and he was grateful she didn't reach for him. His nerves were raw as hell, and her touch irritated his skin.

He didn't miss a look that crossed between Cressida and Declan. It was the same one they'd throw at each other when he was so lost in grief he couldn't think straight.

Maybe he wasn't thinking straight now. It was possible. His nearly healed wounds had been ripped open, dropping him to his knees again. The pain of it was blinding, and he didn't see a way to free himself of it.

AFTER THE INCIDENT WITH NICK AND THE SUV, LUKE AND Charlotte's house had become a fortress. Declan had taken care of the details, calling in several operatives to monitor who came and went from the house.

Kristin hadn't left Alec's side since they had arrived, and she kept shooting him glances. He tried to smile for her, but his mind was far too enveloped in the moment. What he needed was a few minutes alone to process everything. But the house was filled with energy and well-meaning people.

Declan, who had been talking quietly on his mobile, hung up and joined Alec at the counter. "Ezra's here."

Just fucking great. Alec hadn't seen the bloke since the funeral, and he really didn't want to be around Mercedes's ex at the moment.

The door burst open, and Ezra rushed in. "Charlie?" His green eyes searched the room until they spotted her. "Is it true?"

Charlotte's face broke into a grin, and she nodded. Ezra let out a huge breath and pulled Charlotte into his arms. She laughed, and they held each other.

Alec envied their happiness.

Instead, his mind was consumed by a battle between fury and longing. His soul screamed to see her again, to touch her and know she was real. To forgive anything and everything she'd done just to hold her.

But the bite of betrayal was far too deep.

Maybe Charlotte didn't mind that Mercedes had kept her in the dark, but he did. Months of being broken by grief and guilt wouldn't leave him. She was supposed to be his partner. Someone who loved him so completely that she would never do anything to hurt him.

Kristin laid her hand on Alec's shoulder. Her lovely face was creased with worry. No doubt their relationship had taken a huge hit. But the pull to Mercedes was too fucking strong to ignore.

But Kristin didn't deserve that. None of this was her fault, and he'd be damned if he'd treat her like shit because this screwed up situation had blindsided him.

Another knock, and Alec's eyes shot up. Declan moved to the door and seemed to expect whoever it was. Alec cursed himself for not having his head in the game. But he was grateful someone was there to pick up the slack.

Declan opened it, and the tall figure of Noah Ramirez appeared in the entry. He was still in full gear, the same as he was at court.

He gave Charlotte a warm smile. "I'm so sorry for intruding on your evening, Mrs. McKinley."

Charlotte waved him off. "That's okay. Do you have news about my sister?" She peered past him. "Is she here?"

Kristin stiffened on his arm. His pulse picked up.

"I'm afraid not, but she asked me to tell you she's hoping they will let her have dinner with you soon. We'll let you know when that's approved."

Charlotte's shoulders slumped, but she nodded.

Noah scanned the room until his gaze landed on Alec. He

walked to stand in front of him. "I'm Noah. It's a pleasure to meet you."

"Alec," he said, shaking his hand.

"I'm here to offer you the chance to have a private conversation with Mercedes."

The room grew silent, and all the eyes shot to Alec. Kristin's hand tightened on his arm.

"Now she wants to talk to me?"

Noah tilted his head and frowned, clearly puzzled by Alec's tone. "This was a deal she struck with Whitley and my superiors. She was to have a moment to speak with you in exchange for not giving Whitley hell on the stand tomorrow."

Ezra chuckled. "That's awesome."

A flash of anger reared up and Alec stared at Noah. "What if I don't want to meet with her?"

Noah's brows shot up, and Cressida hissed his name.

"Uh, well. That's your choice and she'll have to deal with it. I want to let you know this may be your only opportunity for privacy. I can't guarantee anything past tonight."

"Hell, if you don't want to go, I will," Ezra said. "I have a lot I need to say to her."

Noah looked at Ezra and his eyes narrowed. "Who are you?"

"I'm Ezra. Ezra Coulter."

"Ah." Understanding spread across Noah's face, and Alec wondered how well this man knew Mercedes. "Sorry, but she only wants Alec."

Noah turned back to Alec with an expectant look. Then his gaze trailed to Kristin, and he pursed his lips. "I'll step outside and give you a minute to work it out."

He walked to the door and stepped onto the front stoop, the latch clicking shut behind him.

The warring factions in Alec's mind were spinning him in circles. He was so damn pissed at everything and everyone, but he fucking needed her. There would be no peace for him if he let this chance pass by.

He looked at Kristin and said, "I'll be back soon, aye?"

"Alec . . ." Kristin's eyes were pleading, begging him to stay with her.

A surge of guilt brushed through him. "I have to Kristin. I can't go on without clearing this up with her."

Fear was etched on her face. "What am I supposed to do?"

"I'll make sure you get to your hotel room," Declan chimed in.

Kristin waited.

"I'm sorry, I have to do this."

"Okay." Her face resigned. "But, come to my room when you're done so we can talk."

She raised to her tiptoes and kissed him. Alec made it brief and pulled away. Kristin was doing all she could to hold on to him, but he was already letting go.

CHAPTER TWENTY-THREE

She'd only been six minutes away.

Six bloody minutes.

Alec followed Noah into the house. The main door led to a small foyer. A staircase opened up to the right.

Noah stopped. "We've rented this entire place. Me and one of my guys are in the downstairs unit. You and Sadie have the second story to yourselves. When you're ready to leave, give us a knock and I'll take you wherever you want to go."

"Aye."

Noah gave him a quick salute, opened the door to his unit, and disappeared.

Alec was alone, the world muffled by his racing heartbeat. A thousand questions filled his mind.

How the hell was this supposed to go? What would he say to her?

What the fuck was he waiting for?

Alec took the stairs two at a time, his hand trembling as he reached for the door. He turned the handle and stepped inside, his gaze roaming the flat.

A small entryway lead to a living room and kitchen combo. Wide double doors were open to a balcony, the echoes of the ocean surf reached his ears. Cool sea air filtered through the room, billowing out the curtains with the current.

"Sadie?" Alec called, completely unsure of what he should do.

A movement from the balcony caught his attention, and Mercedes stepped into the room. She was still in the skirt and pressed white shirt she'd worn in court, but the stiff jacket was gone and her feet were bare.

Alec stood frozen in place. She'd stolen his ability to breathe. The green of her hazel eyes overtook the amber, and he felt her drinking him in.

"Alec," she said softly.

Fucking hell.

He strode across the room and pulled her into his arms. Mercedes didn't resist him, molding her body against his. She tightened her arms around his shoulders, nestling her head against his neck.

"You feel so good," she whispered as she ran her fingers through his hair.

The fire he thought had died with her charged to life. Energy surged through him, blinding him with need. He was already losing himself in her touch. He burned for more of her. For all of her.

Alec turned his head into her, his cheek grazing her neck. Her breath caught as he nuzzled her, her fingers tightening in his hair. He trailed his mouth along her jaw, aching to hear that sweet moan she always made when he kissed her. When his lips brushed hers, she leaned away.

Disappointment coursed through him.

Her eyes were dark with desire. "Have you ended it with her?"

Fuck.

The veil of reality dropped over him. The tightness in his throat was suffocating. "No."

Mercedes flinched and stepped out of his arms. "Okay."

"Okay?" Months of depression and pain flooded through him. "Is that all you have to say to me?"

"What do you want me to say, Alec? You're with someone else."

"And why is that?"

Mercedes didn't answer him. She walked a few steps away from him and crossed her arms over her chest.

"I've heard she's nice." Her voice broke.

The heat of anger rose through him. "Aye. She is nice. She wouldn't let the fucking government tell me she was dead for nearly a year, destroying my world and my fucking sanity."

Mercedes winced, her fingers tapping faster. "You're angry and you have every reason to be. I'm so sorry for what they told you."

"Well, they told me exactly what you told them to tell me."

Her brow furrowed, and she shook her head. "I didn't."

Alec ignored the lie. "How could you do that to me?" His voice thickened with emotion. "How could you put me through that?"

"I didn't, Alec. I swear."

"I carried your fucking ashes to your funeral!" He was shouting now.

Tears gathered and slipped down her cheek. She opened her mouth as if she were going to speak but nothing came out. "I've been consumed with guilt and grief for you, so much that Declan and Cressida followed me everywhere for months, so I didn't off myself."

Her tears were flowing freely now, but Alec's pain hadn't finished unleashing. "You did that. You let them do that."

Mercedes shook her head.

"I saw the agreement, Sadie. You gave them permission to fuck us over."

"What?"

The confusion on her face angered him more. "If you loved me, you never would have signed off on that."

"I do love you. And I didn't sign off on anything. I've never lied to you." At his scoff, she said, "Why don't you believe me?"

"Because you're a fucking ghost, Sadie!"

"I'm not," she whispered. "I'm standing right here."

"Are you?" Tears filled his eyes. "I don't think I know who you are."

Mercedes stepped up to him, her gaze holding his. "Yes, you do. You're the only one who does."

Christ, what the hell are you doing?

Mercedes wiped away her tears and pulled in a shaky breath. "I made the mistake of not fighting for us once before. And I told myself that if anything ever got in the way, I would go to war for us, if I had to." She tilted her head and studied his face. "But I look in your eyes, and I can see that you're done."

The finality in her words brought him back to reality. "Sadie . . ."

"No, I get it. Why would you want all this when a normal life is staring you in the face?" Mercedes looked at her dancing hands. "You should have let me go at the hospital. It gave me hope, and I can't rely on hope. I knew then, and I know now. I can't give you the life you deserve."

"Shit, Sadie . . ." Alec reached for her, but she backed away.

"You should leave." Mercedes's voice trembled as she spoke.

Anxiety raced through his body. He couldn't leave her, not when he'd just gotten her back.

"Sadie, I . . ."

"Alec, please just go." Her expression filled with torment, and he could see she was barely holding herself together. "I have court in the morning. And you have someone waiting for you."

Alec fought the urge to beg her to let him stay, to give

them another moment to work it out. But her face had become unreadable and withdrawn. There was nothing more she wanted from him.

"Okay, if that's what you want." At her nod, he moved to draw her into his arms for one last embrace. She stiffened, and he stopped.

As much as it tore him apart, he walked away. He wrenched the door open and looked at her one last time. She wiped her cheeks with the back of her hands, her gaze fixed on the floor.

Shutting the door quietly behind him, Alec walked down the steps in a haze of pain. He barely remembered knocking on Noah's door.

When the big man answered, his deep brown eyes scanned Alec's face. Then he sighed and pulled his keys from his pocket. "Where am I taking you?"

Alec was struggling to hold his composure. "To my hotel, downtown."

The ride was a bit of a blur. Alec replayed their meeting over and over in his head. Misery crawling through each scene. When Noah stopped the car in the hotel drop-off area, Alec nearly asked him to drive him back.

Instead, he thanked him and got out of the car. Once he was alone, he looked up at the skyscraper, his pulse banging in his chest.

Alec pulled out his phone and dialed Declan's number. He answered immediately. "Are you okay?"

"No," Alec choked out.

"Where are you?"

"I'm at the hotel. I can't go in." He didn't need to say anything more.

"Stay where you are. I'm on my way."

After Alec hung up, he texted Kristin, letting her know he wasn't with Mercedes anymore, but that he was going to stay at Luke's again. She responded immediately, asking him to come to her room so they could talk. He knew he should, Kristin had to be worried sick about all of this. But he didn't want to see her, especially not alone in her room. She'd want to kiss and hold him, and the idea of her touching him made his stomach coil.

He sat on a nearby bench and let the gravity of what had happened wash over him.

Mercedes was alive. He had touched her. Her scent lingered on his clothes.

But the pain in her eyes and the tremor in her voice haunted him the most. A stab of regret buried itself in his chest.

Alec had done the one thing he'd never thought he'd do. He'd hurt her.

CHAPTER TWENTY-FOUR

Mercedes was finally wearing herself out. Heavy, choking sobs that coursed through her since Alec left were letting up. The door to the patio was still open. A soft breeze rustled her hair as she lay curled on the couch.

A knock came at the door and hope swirled that maybe Alec had come back. She tried not to be too disappointed when Noah stuck his head in.

"*Mi cielo*? Are you okay?"

"No." She wiped her face and sat up. "Where did you take him?"

Noah grimaced. "A hotel downtown."

Jealousy and pain ripped through her heart. He was with *her*. Images of what they might be doing flooded her mind, and she thought she might be sick.

Noah set a reusable shopping bag on the coffee table. "When I caught Paul in bed with that little slut Aaron, you offered me two things." He reached in the bag and set out a tub of Ben and Jerry's and a bottle of bourbon. "Ice cream and whisky." He set them in front of her. "Choose your poison."

Mercedes smiled through her tears and pointed to the ice cream.

"Wise choice." Noah went to the kitchen and brought out two spoons. He sat next to her and they dug into the ice cream straight from the container.

Noah asked gently, "So, do you want to talk about it?"

Mercedes nodded, hoping the heaviness would ease if she put it out into the world. "When he first got here, he pulled me into his arms and held me. And I thought for a second, maybe we'd be okay." Mercedes closed her eyes, the agony in Alec's words replaying over and over in her mind. "But he's so hurt and angry at me. He said I let them lie to him. That if I loved him, I never would have let it happen."

"I'm sorry, that's rough."

"He's not wrong though. I should have made them prove it to me somehow." Mercedes brought her fingers up to her eyes, trying in vain to stem the flow of tears. "I should have verified they told him."

"Sadie, you were in bad shape for a while. You trusted they'd do what they said they'd do."

"I should know better than to trust anybody."

Noah gave her a sympathetic smile and held out the container of swirled vanilla and chunky fudge ice cream. She dug her spoon in, letting the cool cream soothe her burning throat.

"How did you get over Paul?" she asked.

Noah shrugged. "Well, working with you distracted me. I kind of threw myself into it. And time has helped too. Sometimes I still miss him, or at least the man I wanted him to be."

Alec was every bit the man she wanted him to be.

"I've already had to get over Alec once."

"And how did you do that?"

"I met Jason." She scoffed. "A rebound that turned into a nightmare."

"Yeah, don't do that again."

Her lips turned up into a rueful smile. "It's not like it worked, anyway. I never really got over him."

"Not gonna lie, he looked pretty damn miserable tonight too."

Alec's tear-filled eyes came to mind. She couldn't imagine how the last year had been for him. There was no way to take that pain away.

Something Alec had said struck her as odd. "He kept saying I signed something. That he saw an agreement that let the government lie to him. Do you know what he means?"

Noah shook his head. "No idea, but I don't have a lot to do with that part of things. Maybe Lauren can find out."

"Maybe. I'll talk to her tomorrow."

They ate in silence for a minute, Mercedes drowning in her misery. Suddenly a thought hit her, and she nearly dropped her spoon.

"Oh, shit."

Noah's brow shot up. "What?"

"I don't have anywhere to live." Panic stretched its fingers through her body. "I can't go to London now. What the hell am I going to do?"

Mercedes put the spoon down and buried her face in her hands. All the files she had on London real estate listings were useless. She wouldn't get to show Alec her favorite neighborhoods and see if he'd find them as charming as she did. They wouldn't get to select a real home together. A year of dreaming and planning had come crashing down.

Why hadn't she made backup plans?

Because you knew Alec would be there.

The trial wasn't expected to last much longer than a week. Then she'd be on her own. She had a new life to create in a very short period of time.

After they cleaned up, Noah said good night and went to

the other unit. Even though he and the other agent were close, it was the first time in forever she felt alone.

This was how things were going to be, so she would have to get used to it.

CHAPTER TWENTY-FIVE

Three days.

For three days, Alec had to be near her and not speak to her.

The turmoil of her return hadn't settled in his gut. So, he found himself listening to the exact tone of her American accent, the inflection she gave each word. The formality she was using on the stand was foreign to him. There was no hint of the sweet giggle or the smile that would play on her lips when she teased him.

But her hands gave her away.

The way they moved on her leg or on the armrest of the chair was all her. When the defense started in on her, her emotions were going wild.

Mercedes held her own, repeating answers and going over the evidence in detail. They hashed everything out over and over until Alec had memorized their importance.

When the judge finally excused her, relief was clear in her expression. Mercedes stood and walked from the room with her chin up and shoulders back. The last days had been brutal, but she was as composed as ever.

Noah Ramirez followed closely behind, shooting Jason a glare as they passed.

Alec had to hand it to the agent, he knew his job. More than once, Jason had moved to speak with her. Noah had shut him down before Alec could cross the room. No one came near her except her lawyer and Charlotte.

"Alec," Cressida said. "Whitley wants us to meet in the big conference room."

Kristin sighed. Guilt crawled up Alec's spine. Things between them had been strained since Mercedes returned. He was a horrible companion and more than once, he'd offered to send her home.

"Can I come with you this time?" Kristin asked. "I don't want to be out on my own again in case Jason is still around."

Alec had been so consumed with thoughts of Mercedes; he hadn't even thought about Jason's earlier attempt to talk to Kristin. That distraction was dangerous.

Cressida answered for him. "Yeah, we're wrapping up so Whitley shouldn't have a problem with it."

They followed Cressida to the secure corridor and into the conference room. Mercedes, her lawyer, and Noah were already in the room.

Alec hadn't been expecting her to be in the meeting and his pulse quickened. She met his eyes for a second before she winced and looked away. He sat on the far end of the table. It gave him a chance to take in her face while Whitley said what he needed to say.

"This will be quick," Brenden Whitley said, setting a leather portfolio on the table. "I wanted to touch base with you all and say thank you to Mercedes for her courage on the stand today. I know that was incredibly difficult, especially at the end. We appreciate that."

Mercedes didn't look up and made no acknowledgment that he had spoken.

"Those of you from the UK are free to go now. We won't be recalling you and the defense has stated they don't plan to."

Alec stopped listening to take in Mercedes's fingers tapping on the table. She was a wreck. The hazel green of her eyes drew him in, washing him in the grief radiating off her. He wanted to draw her into his arms and hold her until she quieted. To love her until that haunted look left her.

A sudden gasp caught Alec's attention, and he popped his head up to listen.

Mercedes's lawyer snapped. "Are you serious? Who authorized this?"

"My understanding is that it's coming from the marshal's office. It's time for Agent Ramirez to go back into regular service."

Mercedes's stare darted to the agent, who looked just as alarmed. He gave her a slight shake of his head.

"This is a hell of a time to remove her trusted detail and exchange it with someone new, don't you think?" Mercedes's lawyer said.

Whitley shrugged, looking less than bothered by this. "I don't see a difference. A detail is a detail."

"You know damn well what the difference is in this case. Stop being obtuse. You have the power to fix it and keep Agent Ramirez assigned to her, at least until the jury has the case. You need to do it."

Whitley shook his head. "I don't see the need."

Mercedes spoke for the first time since leaving the stand. "You're going to make that phone call and put Noah back on my detail. Then, you're going to insist any agent that was supposed to take the place of his team be removed from my case. I don't want a single one near me. Are we clear?"

The directness of her tone caught Alec off guard.

Whitley scoffed. "I really don't think you are in a position to be so demanding."

"Oh, that's where you're wrong." Mercedes's glower spit

fire at Whitley as she jerked a file folder from her bag. She flipped it open and pulled out a paper. "I've had a *lot* of unexpected time to research a few things. Let's talk about this document here." She slid it across the table. "Do you recognize it?"

Whitley looked at the paper and shrugged. "It's the protection agreement you signed with the US marshals."

"That's right. I did sign that. It looks like I signed it not even two days after I was injured in the attack. I remember this day. You and the director of the marshal's service came to my room and proposed the deep cover scenario. You couldn't trust your own people, so you said it would be better if I was dead to the world."

"I was right."

"And I said I would do it, as long as two people were told the truth, which you *both* agreed to before you left my room."

"I . . . I don't remember our exact words." The blatant lie fell flat on Alec's ears.

Bloody hell.

"I do. And so did the nurse in charge of my care." Mercedes slid another paper across the table. "This is a signed affidavit from my nurse confirming she administered a large dose of morphine approximately five minutes after you left. Then you unexpectedly returned. She warned you I wouldn't be of sound mind for a few hours, yet somehow, you managed to get this signature from me, right around that same time." Mercedes leaned forward and tapped the paper. "I would have been high as a goddamned kite when I signed that."

Alec stared at Whitley, his breath held as he waited for his response.

Whitley pursed his lips. "What do you want, Sadie?"

The air rushed from Alec's lungs. The bloody bastard had set this up?

Mercedes's icy glare cut into Whitley. "I want you to look me and Alec in the eyes and tell us why you lied to us."

Whitley cleared his throat. "Well, to be honest, we didn't trust him or his team."

"Why?"

"By Mr. McKinley's own admission, one of Cooper's operatives had already infiltrated his organization. He even had an intimate relationship with her. We weren't entirely sure they weren't behind the attack."

"Bullshit. You know damn well they had nothing to do with it." Mercedes shook her head. "It was a US marshal that led him to me, and it was *her* gun to my head. *Your* people, not his."

What the fuck? They hadn't been told an agent had taken part in the attack. What the fuck had happened at that house?

Whitley wasn't relenting. "Letting his entire company in on this would have created too many loose ends."

"And what about my sister?"

"If she knew, then her husband would know." Whitley lifted his shoulders. "And we just couldn't trust him not to share that with his cousin."

Alec let this information wash over him. Whitley had been playing fucking games and destroyed everything they had. Mercedes's tear-streaked face came to his mind, telling him she hadn't lied to him, that she hadn't signed anything.

And he'd called her a liar.

Goddamn it to fucking hell.

There had to be more to this. Whitley wanted them apart for more than just distrusting his team. Alec thought of what Whitley gained by this whole thing, and the last piece of the puzzle snapped into place.

"You wanted Jason," Alec said, glaring at Whitley. "You didn't hide her to protect her, you did it to turn Jason. That's why you lied to us. If there was even a whisper that Sadie was alive and she was with me, he'd blow your case."

Whitley said nothing, tapping the pen on the table.

"You son of a bitch," Mercedes rasped out. "You ruined everything for that piece of shit's sketchy testimony."

"I need to win." Whitley set his jaw.

"I know you do." Mercedes said. "Because rumor is, you're going to run for Governor of California."

Whitley stiffened but didn't deny it. Mercedes had gotten to the heart of it all. This fucker didn't care about defeating Cooper. He'd been using them to make himself a household name.

And he'd tossed a grenade between Alec and Mercedes to do it.

Mercedes pushed one more paper at Whitley. "This is an opinion piece for *The Washington Post* that will go wide this evening. In it, I detail how you lied to me, to my family and took advantage of my incapacitated state to advance your political career. And I discuss how you orchestrated the media frenzy regarding Alec and my relationship, putting us both in jeopardy. I'm sure the California bar and the Department of Justice will be quite interested in the flagrant violations of your oath of office." She sat back, a steely glare still on his face. "Oh, and I've drafted a ten million dollar lawsuit against you for violation of my civil rights and holding me against my will."

Whitley's head snapped up. "We didn't hold you against your will."

"But you did. This agreement is garbage because I wasn't of sound mind when I signed it. And my consent hinged on Alec and Charlotte being told the truth. When you ignored that, my formal consent was relinquished. I doubt I'll win, but it should make for good media drama right before the primaries."

Alec watched her in awe. She was fucking cutthroat, and he loved it.

Whitley pursed his lips. "This is extortion, Mercedes."

"Maybe. But if it keeps you and your fucking people from interfering with my life, I'll risk it."

There wasn't much more than a brief pause. "What else do you want?"

"Well, I got the one thing I wanted, which was for Alec to know the truth." She put her documents into her case. "The rest of my demands are quite simple, really. Make that call to your little conspiracy buddy and get Agent Ramirez back on my detail and tell him to remove anyone new. I don't trust a single one of them. And I want to have protected visits with my family. If he balks, you let him know his name is on my shitlist too."

Whitley nodded, his mouth pressed firm. "Alright, I'll take care of that."

"Good, I'm glad we understand each other." Mercedes stood, hooked her bag onto her shoulder, and walked to the door. "Oh, and Brendan, you ever lie to me or the people I love again and I'll destroy you."

Mercedes jerked the door open and walked out, her heels clicking on the tile floors. Noah Ramirez smirked as he followed her out of the room.

"I fucking love her," Cressida murmured. Declan gave a soft snort in agreement. Kristin shifted in the chair next to him.

Alec pressed his fingers to the bridge of his nose. A numbness had settled over him. How many lies had come between them? And how many more were still unknown.

CHAPTER TWENTY-SIX

"Are you okay?" Kristin's soft voice broke through Alec's thoughts. She slipped her hand into his. The afternoon sunlight cast shadows and light across her worried face as their cab made its way west to Luke and Charlotte's house.

Even before they had left the courthouse, Kristin was watching him warily. Not that he could blame her. Everything was in bloody shambles.

"Aye, I'm fine."

He wasn't fine, nothing was as it should be.

But he couldn't tell Kristin how the revelations from this afternoon meeting shredded him.

Mercedes hadn't signed the document. She'd fought to tell him.

So, they fucking drugged her.

You should have let me go at the hospital. It gave me hope, and I can't rely on hope.

Jesus, this was a disaster.

Kristin's face was filled with worry. "We don't have to go tonight. If she's going to upset you, I'd rather not."

Now that her testimony was over, Mercedes was being allowed visits with Charlotte. Charlotte had practically begged

Alec to come to dinner that evening. He'd declined, not thinking it right to leave Kristin on her own. But Charlotte invited her too, saying she had already talked to Mercedes about it. Charlotte's wide hazel eyes became misty when she talked about having her entire family together and Alec couldn't refuse.

Not that he wanted to. The desire to be around Mercedes was overwhelming.

"She won't upset me."

Kristin sighed. "She could. And then I'm left picking up the pieces."

"I know this can't be easy for you. You don't have to go."

"If you're going, then so am I. I came all this way to help you through this, I'm not going to leave you when you need me."

Alec didn't need her, and that was the problem. Kristin wasn't a pillar of strength holding him together.

"I can't wait to go home tomorrow." She stared out the window, her brow furrowed. "Won't it be nice to get back to normal?"

Normal? Kristin had never known him when things were normal. She'd only had the moments of unrelenting grief.

"I'm not going home tomorrow." Kristin's gaze snap to him. "I need to see this through."

The thought of leaving Mercedes while the trial was ongoing made his stomach churn. Now that he knew she hadn't signed the order to destroy his heart, he was struggling with what he should do. But getting on that plane would be to abandon her completely.

"Alec . . ."

"You should still go."

Kristin's mouth fell open. "Are you ending this with me?"

Alec didn't say anything for a second. "I don't want to hurt you, but I think it might be for the best."

Tears welled in her eyes. "Alec, I'm pretty sure I'm in love with you."

He winced at the words he hadn't wanted her to say. "Kristin . . ."

"I haven't had a problem waiting for you to be ready because I knew you'd be worth it. You and I have been together for months, longer than you ever had with her. I don't think it's unreasonable to ask that you wait for the dust to settle before you send me packing."

Alec nodded. His emotions had been everywhere over the last few days. The joy of knowing Mercedes still existed in this world, the anger in processing what they had taken from them again. He owed Kristin the courtesy of trying to make it work.

"Still, it might be better if you went home."

"If you're staying, then so am I." When he opened his mouth to speak, she interrupted. "Alec, the only way I get on that plane alone is if you tell me you're done. As long as I still have a chance, this is where I belong."

The cab stopped in front of the house, and Alec paid the driver. Once they got out of the car, Alec stopped. "Kristin, I don't know what's going to happen. I can't make any promises to you other than I'll be honest with you." He leaned toward her and cupped her cheek. "I have *never* wanted to hurt you."

"I know, Alec. Just give me a chance. That's all I ask."

At his nod, she leaned up and kissed him. It was light, one they had shared many times before. When she opened to take more, his reflex was to lean back. He tried to cover the reaction, but it was written on her face.

"I'm going to try," he said

CHAOS WAS MOVING THROUGH THE McKINLEY DINING ROOM. Alec and Kristin walked into a flurry of activity. Mason was helping to move chairs, and Declan was opening a bottle of wine in the kitchen.

"Put that glass over there." Charlotte was directing Shake. He shifted the stem of the wineglass on the table again, trying to find the perfect placement until she said, "Yeah, that's it."

"I don't think Sadie needs all of this, my love," Luke said. "She's probably just happy to see you."

"I know," Charlie said, wiping down a plate and placing it on the elegant table. "I need to keep busy."

Alec looked for Mercedes, but there was no sign she'd arrived yet.

Shake saw the look. "They got a little tied up with her lawyer, mate. She went to her place to change, but she should be here soon."

Alec took in the elaborate table setting. "Do you need any help?" He wasn't sure he wanted to touch anything on the table. It looked like a photo shoot.

"Oh, no I think we're just about ready."

A knock came at the front door, and Alec's heart dropped. Charlotte rushed to greet Mercedes as she stepped inside.

Jesus fucking Christ.

Everything about her was perfection. She wore a black V-neck top that lined her body and tight jeans that cuffed at the bottom with a pair of black high-heeled sandals. Her hair piled on top of her head with wisps framing her face. Three sets of necklaces hung at various lengths around her neck. Alec imagined her wearing only those, and his pulse quickened.

After Mercedes had given Charlotte a long hug, she stepped back. "Oh god, don't cry. If you cry, then I will."

"I'm sorry. This baby wants me to sob all the time."

"Well, that's okay then." Mercedes turned to her companion and grabbed his arm. "Charlie, this is Noah. He's saved my life and my sanity a few times."

"We met the other day," Charlotte said, snatching Noah up into a hug.

Mercedes scanned the room until her gaze landed on Alec. He saw when it happened. The shift in her demeanor, the way her shoulders dropped back and her chin lifted. The smile was too perfect.

The veneer was in place.

Except for her fingers. They never lied to him.

She walked to Kristin, the smile never faltering, "You must be Kristin," at Kristin's nod, she held out her hand. "I'm Mercedes. It's nice to meet you."

"You too." Kristin's smile was tight, and her hand immediately went back to Alec's arm.

Mercedes looked up to Alec and smiled. "Alec."

Her greeting cut right through him. Formal and passive, with a touch of hope in her tone. She only acknowledged him because it was expected. He opened his mouth to respond, but nothing came out. Her smile faltered and the veneer almost came crashing down.

"Where the hell have you been, you gorgeous bitch?" Cressida called out.

Another genuine smile spread across her face. "Damn, I've missed you, girl!" She pulled Cressida into a tight hug.

"Look at this fucking outfit." Cressida stepped back and took in Mercedes clothes. "You've been on point all damn week. Where have they been hiding you? Milan? Good Christ!"

"Ha! I wish." Mercedes laughed. Then her eyes caught onto Declan. He grinned at her.

"Dec!" She practically ran into his arms. He held her for longer than Alec expected. Declan was murmuring into her ear, and she was clinging to him.

He'd never envied his cousin more.

"So, she knows everyone," Kristin said under her breath. Alec wasn't sure if he was meant to hear it.

A knock came at the door and Mercedes stepped away from Declan.

"Are we expecting anyone else?" Alec asked Luke.

"Aye, just one more," Luke said. "Charlie invited him."

Mercedes brushed her hand through her hair and smoothed her shirt down. Alec caught the nervous drumming of her fingers. She knew who was coming.

When Ezra Coulter walked in the door, it was like a punch to the gut. Ezra made her nervous. Alec watched them greet each other, jealousy curling through his chest. He hadn't spent a lot of time wrapped in the sensation, but the only woman who had ever invoked it was giving all her affection to a man who didn't deserve her.

"You look incredible. I—" Ezra cleared his throat. He reached out and tugged Mercedes into his arms. She didn't resist when he buried his head against her neck. When she drew away, she gave him a shy smile.

She was studying Ezra and Alec wanted to drag her out of this house and keep her to himself. Ezra had already made it clear he wanted her back in his life. Now she was sending signals that she wasn't opposed to the idea.

Ezra pushed a lock of her hair from her face. "Can we talk? Not now, but soon?"

She nodded. "Maybe after dinner?"

Alec had a sudden and violent desire to beat the ever living fuck out of Ezra Coulter.

"Maybe she's ready to move on too?" Kristin said quietly to him. Alec knew what Kristin was doing, but it didn't make it any less effective.

Charlotte broke the moment, announcing that dinner was all set and ready. The group shifted with people walking to the dining room, but Ezra kept his hand on the small of Mercedes's back. Guiding her to the table. She didn't shrink from his touch. In fact, she seemed to welcome it.

When they settled around the table, Kristin's eyes kept

shifting to him. They stayed rather quiet while the rest of the table moved the conversation forward.

"I don't think I've ever seen eggs be both overcooked and raw until I made breakfast with Sadie one day." Declan teased. Everyone snickered at Mercedes's notoriously terrible cooking.

"Ha! I'll have you know I only burn my eggs about thirty percent of the time now."

Declan's eyes went wide. "Oh, aye? Only thirty percent lass? That's impressive!"

"It is, isn't it? And that's only because Noah is an angel and has patience for days."

Noah grinned at her. "You've made a lot of strides from when we first started out, *mi cielo*. The first time we made enchiladas, I thought you were going to kill me with cumin."

"More is better right," Mercedes said with a laugh.

Noah's grin widened. "Not when it comes to cumin."

Mercedes giggled. Alec was mesmerized by that laugh.

Kristin popped up, her voice carrying across the table. "What does that mean? You call Mercedes, *mi cielo*, what does it mean?"

Noah's dark eyes met with Mercedes's. "It's a term of endearment. It means my sky or my heaven."

"Oh, that's so cute." Kristin's gaze shot between the two of them, clearly implying that Mercedes and Noah were together.

Noah gave Kristin a crooked grin. "Oh, it's adorable, but we did it for practical reasons. Sadie's been my 'wife' for about ten months. Both of us struggled to call each other by our cover names, so we went with endearments to make it easier."

"I called him sweetie, mostly," Mercedes said. "Although one time I called him sugar boo in front of a priest. I thought he was going to throw his shoe at me."

Alec bit back a laugh. Even after all she'd been through, her sense of humor remained as charming as ever.

"You look so natural together." Kristin added. "I thought maybe there was something there."

A flare of irritation ran through Alec. Kristin was reaching on this one. They had none of the tension that drove him crazy when he thought of Mercedes and Ezra.

Mercedes and Noah shared an amused look. "I'm gonna let you handle this one," she snickered.

Noah grinned. "Ah, when it comes to selecting a partner, Sadie and I have very similar . . . tastes, if you know what I mean. We're pretty incompatible."

"Oh sorry! I didn't realize . . ." Kristin stammered.

"No, it's okay. Most people don't look at me and think I'm a gay man." Noah laughed. "And Sadie and I've been through a lot together, so I think it made our fake marriage seem more natural."

Charlotte leaned forward and put her arms on the table. "Can you tell us what happened? They said you were in the hospital for a while. I . . . sort of need to know."

Everyone grew quiet. Alec's heart sped up. He hadn't been able to stop thinking about her revelations, that the US marshal had been responsible.

"I was in the hospital because I had a gunshot wound and I burned my hand pretty badly trying to get out of the house."

Charlotte sucked in her breath and covered her mouth with her hand.

"You were shot?" Alec said. She glanced at him in surprise and he realized it was the first time he'd spoken to her since she arrived. "Where?"

"In the leg."

The room spun a touch. Alec was well aware of how painful a bullet ripping through your body could be. That she'd lived through that on her own made him sick.

Mercedes and Noah revealed all that had happened the night they supposedly died. That Noah wasn't supposed to be there, but a personal matter had driven him to the house.

How his partner lured Mercedes into the open, and when that didn't work, had aimed her own gun at Mercedes to take her out. Mercedes didn't go into detail of the agent's death, but Alec could see it on her face how traumatized she was by it.

Now that he knew what had happened, Alec looked at Noah in a completely different light. This man had killed his own colleague to do his job and protect her. Her fight to keep Noah on her detail made perfect sense.

Mercedes smiled and pushed back her chair. "I'll help with dishes, okay?"

It was clear she wanted to change the subject. She and Charlotte disappeared into the kitchen and of course Ezra followed them, his eyes all for Mercedes. Her laughter coming from the kitchen was more than Alec could take. She could destroy him with her casual flirting with Ezra.

It wasn't the first time Alec had agonized over Mercedes finding another man attractive. The chemistry Alec thought existed between David Kennison and Mercedes wouldn't touch what was happening right now in front of him.

Ezra already knew her. She'd loved him once and had given her heart to him. She was slipping further and further from Alec's reach.

"Hey, I need a word." Declan's voice came from behind him.

His cousin sent him a look and Alec took the hint. He leaned toward Kristin. "I'll be back in a minute."

Kristin looked between the kitchen where Mercedes was and the living room, where Cressida had her phone in her hand. "Can't I come with you?"

"I just need a few minutes of his time," Declan said. "You can hang with Cressida if you like."

Alec didn't miss the flash of distaste that crossed Kristin's face. "I'll be right back." He disentangled his arm from her grasp. It hadn't gone unnoticed how much she had taken to clinging to him since Mercedes had returned.

Alec followed Declan down the stairs to the music room in the walkout basement.

Declan peered up the stairs to see that they were alone. Then he turned to Alec. "I've been trying to figure out a way to say this all week, but what the fuck are you doing?"

"What do you mean?"

"You know exactly what I mean."

Alec blew out a deep exhale. Keeping it all in was tearing him apart. He ran his fingers through his hair. "Fuck, Dec," his throat tightened. "What am I supposed to do?"

"I don't know. Maybe not sit there glowering at her. Meanwhile, Ezra fucking Coulter is ready and willing to be there for her."

So he wasn't imagining the chemistry between Mercedes and Ezra. His chest hurt with the thought of them together.

"Goddamn it. This fucking sucks so bad."

Declan frowned at him in disbelief. "It's quite simple, really. You talk to her and tell her you're sorry for being a total prat. And you let her know how much you're still absolutely mad for her, and then you find a bed to take her to. It's not that hard, Alec."

Alec scoffed. "It's way more complicated than that. What about Kristin? Today she told me she loved me and asked for a little time before I broke it off with her. I think she deserves that."

"Aye, maybe she does. But is Kristin the choice you're making?" Declan's eyes narrowed. "Because if that's the case, you'd better be damned sure. Sadie isn't going to wait for your dumb ass forever."

Jesus, how did he end up here?

Declan's expression softened. "Look, I get you don't want to hurt the lass. They've put you all in a shitty situation." Declan leaned over and put his hand on Alec's shoulder. "But I literally held you while you grieved for Sadie, and it broke my heart. If you think back to where you were then, I know you would have given anything to have her back. And now she's here, you're going to fuck it up?"

A shuffling on the steps drew Declan's attention. He shot his gaze to Alec with a look of 'I told you'.

Ezra was leading Mercedes down the stairs. Her hand was firmly in his. Alec took one look and nausea filled his stomach.

"Oh, sorry, guys. We were looking for a quiet place to talk. We can go up to one of the bedrooms." Ezra's flirty tone was directed at Mercedes.

I could kill him now.

"Nice try." Mercedes bantered back with a laugh. "We'll go out on the patio." She walked to the door to the daylight basement, tugging on Ezra's hand. "Are you guys going to be here for a while." Alec could feel her eyes on him, but he was too lost in the jealousy boiling in his gut.

"Oh, aye. I got the guest room," Declan said.

"I have to take Kristin back to the hotel," Alec ground out. Regret immediately slammed into him.

What a dick thing to say.

"Well, you have a good night then." Alec could hear it in her voice. He'd just fucked up.

Mercedes led Ezra out onto the patio and closed the door behind them.

"What the fuck was that?" Exasperation coated Declan's tone. "Couldn't resist pushing her face into it a little harder?"

"Shit!" Alec buried his face into his hands, his fingers trying to ease the ache across his brow. "I don't know what's wrong with me, Dec."

CHAPTER TWENTY-SEVEN

Mercedes was in hell. Not only did she have to sit and watch that woman latch onto Alec with that smug look on her face, but she had to smile and pretend it didn't bother her. Like her heart hadn't already hit the bottom of the well.

Alec barely spoke to her. Even after she had called out Whitley and his underhanded scheme, he was still so angry. It crushed her to see how much damage they had done to the man she loved.

Declan's all-encompassing hug was a little bit of comfort. It immediately brought back the memories of sitting on a gurney in a London hospital, her arms wrapped around Declan as they both sobbed in relief that Alec was going to live. It seemed a lifetime ago.

"I lost him, Dec," she murmured against him. "I didn't think it could happen again."

He squeezed her tighter. "You haven't. He's just had a hell of a go of it."

"I know. And now he hates me," she choked out.

"Not possible. Give him time." He drew back, his expression filled with sympathy.

"I don't have time." Decisions had to be made, and soon. "I'm so grateful he had you."

Mercedes stepped away, dabbing at her tears. She'd thought the well had dried up when Alec left her. But here she was, flooded with emotions over the love she lost.

Then there was Ezra.

He looked good. Too good.

The years had only added to his features. His striking emerald eyes and dirty blond hair had always been attractive, but the undernourished boy was gone. Instead, Ezra's muscles filled out his tight T-shirt beautifully. The tattoos that decorated his corded forearms added a depth to him that hadn't been there before. Like her own tattoos, they told a story only he understood.

When he pulled her into his arms, she let him hold her for longer than she should have. It was selfish, and she knew it. But it felt good to have Ezra comfort her. Even after all that had happened, she missed her childhood friend.

At dinner, Mercedes tried to focus on the conversation and not on Alec's sharp gaze. He hadn't said much more than a few polite words. Even after she and Noah told them what happened to her during the attack, Alec was stoic. She wished she knew what he was thinking, but he'd erected a wall between them, and she was left in the cold.

Mercedes and Charlotte cleared the table and washed up the dishes. She couldn't get over how sweet her sister looked with her baby bump. Her own life might be shredded into pieces of heartache she couldn't escape, but at least her baby sister had captured the dream. A kind husband who adored her, a career she loved, and now her dream of being a mother was coming true. Her happiness was tinged with a taste of envy. She would never have this chance for herself.

Piano music caught Mercedes's attention as they were finishing up. Someone was playing Beethoven's *Fifth Symphony* on the baby grand. Mercedes thought it might be Shake or

Declan messing around. But when she entered the living room, she was stunned to find Kristin on the bench, tapping on the keys.

Mercedes's heart fell out of her chest as Kristin played as if she owned the place.

And why not. She'd taken the most important thing in her life from her. Why not sit at her piano and play a shitty version of Beethoven?

Annoyance at Alec flushed over her. How could he think letting his woman touch her instruments was acceptable? She searched the room, but he wasn't there. Instead, she caught Cressida's eyes. Cressida's brow was furrowed in a sympathetic frown. Mercedes shook her head and rolled her eyes.

Kristin looked up but didn't acknowledge her.

A large, warm hand laced through hers, and she looked up at Ezra. "Is this a good time to talk?"

Mercedes cast another look at Kristin, who was plunking along as if she were at Carnegie Hall.

"Now would be great."

Mercedes let him keep her hand in his as he led her downstairs. The smell of her old studio hit her. Damn, she missed this place.

Alec and Declan were already sitting on the couch, deep in conversation.

When Alec's stormy gaze met hers, the wall was down. Pain and grief coated his expression, making her ache to wrap herself around him and hold him tight.

His eyes landed on her hand laced with Ezra's, and the wall shot back up. Alec looked away, not acknowledging her presence.

"Oh, sorry, guys. We were looking for a quiet place to talk. We can go up to one of the bedrooms." Ezra was already flirting with her like nothing had changed.

Alec's gaze shot back up, and his face twisted.

"Nice try." Mercedes tried to take away any sting his

joking may have had on Alec. "We can go out on the patio." She walked to the door, pulling on Ezra's hand. "Are you going to be here for a while?" she asked both of them. Maybe Alec would talk with her one more time. She craved a warm word from him.

"Oh, aye. I got the guest room," Declan answered with a grin.

"I have to take Kristin back to the hotel," Alec said, his jaw set.

The flip of her stomach was nauseating. The image of Alec and Kristin kissing and ripping off each other's clothes made her gut revolt.

Mercedes jerked open the slider. "Well, you have a good night then." She choked out before she stepped outside. Ezra followed her, his hand resting on her back.

Once they were outside, she gulped in as much fresh air as she could.

Ezra's sandalwood scent filled the space. She sat on the patio furniture and waited for her heart to slow its pace.

"Hey, are you okay?" Ezra tilted his head at her.

Just breathe. "I—I don't know."

Ezra looked back into the basement, where the light illuminated on Alec and Declan. Their dark heads were pushed together. Whatever the conversation was, it was deep.

"I've spent a little time with him after you were . . . gone. He seemed like a good guy."

Mercedes nodded. "He's the best guy." She couldn't keep the hurt from her voice.

"But he has a girlfriend." Ezra's tone was sympathetic.

She nodded. "Yeah. They lied to him, and he moved on. I'm doing the best I can."

God, it fucking hurt.

Ezra tilted his head, taking another glance through the window. "I can't imagine how hard this is for you."

Mercedes could still see Alec, his head down and his

fingers tented against his forehead. His eyes darted to the window a couple of times, like he was waiting for them to come back.

"It was worse for him." She had to stop looking at him. It hurt too fucking bad. "What did you want to talk about?" She turned her attention to Ezra.

Ezra nodded. "I, um . . . I wanted to apologize."

"Apologize?"

"Yeah, it's long overdue." His voice cracked with emotion. "I—I fucked up with you. So bad. You were my best friend. My only sanctuary during some of the worst times in my life." He stood and walked around the patio furniture to sit next to her. "It was the worst mistake I ever made, and I wanted to tell you how sorry I was that I hurt you."

The warm gaze of her oldest friend met hers. When she'd opened that door and caught him screwing one of her classmates, she thought she would fall apart. Up until then, Ezra had been the only one who had ever loved her for herself, and suddenly he was gone.

That was the pattern, wasn't it?

Ezra.

Alec.

Jason.

Alec.

There had been other men she'd dated, but these were the ones who had leveled her. They loved her enough to give her a taste of normality. Then they pulled the rug, leaving her devastated.

There was no pain that equaled the hell she was living in. Thinking of Alec naked in bed with Kristin would nauseate her forever. The knife would twist every time that woman gazed adoringly at what belonged to her.

Except Alec didn't belong to her.

She looked into Ezra's emerald eyes and tried to judge if

the remorse was real. Years of Jason's false apologies had left her jaded. But he seemed sincere.

"It was a lifetime ago and a different world for both of us."

Ezra's breath let out with a whoosh. "Does that mean you forgive me?"

"Yeah. Life's too short to hold on to grudges like this."

Relief flooded Ezra's face. "Can I see you tomorrow?"

"I'll be here for dinner again. It's not a good idea to be seen with you in public. Your fame would make the press go nuts." She smiled up at him. "I'm proud of you, by the way. You've done some amazing things."

"Thanks." Ezra smiled. "I'm so grateful to have you back."

He pulled her back into his arms and again, she didn't resist him. In the back of her mind, she knew she would need to lay out some boundaries. She wasn't about to fall all over him because she had a broken heart. But at this moment, letting him soothe her soul was irresistible.

When she drew away, he stayed close enough that his breath brushed her cheek. He leaned toward her like he was going to kiss her. She put a hand on his chest. "Ez . . ."

He grimaced and stepped back. "Sorry, I—"

"No, it's okay. I'm not ready for any of that. Like at all."

He nodded. "Because of Alec?"

"Yeah. Because of Alec." She looked down at her hands. "A week ago, I thought I was his everything. That I'd finally found someone who saw me, all of me, and loved me anyway. So, I'm not ready. I'm sorry."

"Don't be sorry. I get it, Mercy. When you're ready, I'll be here. I'm not going to fuck it up again."

"Thank you. We should go in."

Alec and Declan were still on the couch when they stepped inside. This time when Alec looked at her, he held her gaze. It was one of those soul shaking looks that could level her in a second.

God, she missed him so much.

She tore her eyes away and followed Ezra up the stairs.

Alec's voice stopped her. "Sadie, do you have a minute?"

Her heart leaped into her throat. Alec stood, his stare piercing into her very soul. She would give him whatever he asked for. "Of course."

"Alec, are you about ready?" Kristin called, her steps thumping on the stairs. "I was hoping we could get a drink at the bar before bed."

Pain snapped through her like lightning. "It looks like you don't though."

Mercedes brushed by him, passing Kristin on the stairs. The high heels mixed with her trembling, and she nearly fell. She scanned the living room until she found Noah. He and Shake were bent over Shake's phone, laughing at whatever was on the screen. Noah saw her and immediately stood.

Mercedes had reached her limit and needed to get the hell out of there now. She found Charlotte and gave her a quick kiss on the cheek.

"I have to go, lovey. I'll see you in the morning."

"Wait, I thought we could . . ."

"I can't. Tomorrow, okay?" She was already making her way to the door where Noah was waiting.

"Sadie, wait," Alec said behind her.

It was too late. She was going to fall apart, and she'd rather be alone when it happened.

"Good night," she called over her shoulder, jerking the door open. Somehow, she made it down the stoop and was nearly to the car when Alec grabbed her arm. She spun on her heel to face him.

"What?" she snapped.

Concern filled Alec's expression. "Are you okay?"

She scoffed. "I'm *great*. Everything's just perfect. Enjoy your drink."

Mercedes wrenched the door open and slammed it behind her. She kept her composure long enough for Noah to pull down the street, leaving Alec on the curb.

CHAPTER TWENTY-EIGHT

Adam stepped out of the store onto the filth-covered sidewalk. Sirens called out in the night air, a constant reminder of how shitty this area was. A shout from the alleyway filtered to him and he kept his peripherals on the arguing men. Most of these degenerates took one look at him and left him alone, but every once in a while, there was some asshole who thought he could take a chance on him.

Marcus had requested another meeting, and Adam had no choice but to comply. Tyler, that little fuck, was whining about his tennis club friends giving him the cold shoulder. The trial had interfered with baby boy's party time.

Adam couldn't give less fucks if he tried.

But like the dutiful soldier he was, Adam took the dressing down with an exterior calm. Even Marcus had seemed less enthusiastic with Adam's work.

A chill had gone down Adam's spine when Marcus leaned forward in his chair. "I don't need to remind you what you owe me, Adam. Things can change rather rapidly if I don't start seeing results."

He didn't have to be told twice.

Adam stepped over the legs of an unconscious man on the

stoop. He punched in the code for the door, a paltry attempt to secure the building, and entered the dark foyer. The thick, reusable grocery bag crinkled as he climbed the stairs to the third floor. He was pulling out his keys when a shuffling stopped him.

Shit.

The darkness of the hall was hiding someone in the corner. Any number of threats could have found him, Alec McKinley was the first to come to his mind.

Taking a step back from the door, Adam dropped the bag and brought his gun up, aiming at the corner.

"Who are you and what the fuck do you want?"

A soft voice with a British accent came from the shadow, tentative and shaken. "It's me."

Jesus fucking Christ. He dropped his gun and stared at the dark corner. "What the hell are you doing here?"

Mara Donovan stepped into the light, and Adam sucked in his breath. Soft blue-gray eyes searched his as if studying his soul. "I'm sorry, I got so scared and didn't know where to go."

He ripped the key from his pocket and jammed it into the door. Swinging it open, he grabbed her arm and the groceries and yanked them both inside. Once the door was locked, he let himself really take her in.

Damn, she was as beautiful as ever.

Adam crossed the distance and drew her into his arms. The years apart had changed nothing. Her slender body still fit against him like a glove. "Goddamn it, Mara, why the fuck would you risk coming here?"

Mara clung to him, trembling. "Declan McKinley found me." The tearful words hit him hard.

No, no, no.

"When?"

"About a week ago. I think I lost him. I drove around for as long as I could before I used the identification and emergency kit you gave me and got a ticket out of Dublin. I didn't know where else to go."

Adam pulled her to arm's length. "Are you okay? Did he hurt you?"

She shook her head. "No, he just wanted to talk."

Panic welled in Adam's chest. "You didn't meet with him, did you?"

"I had to." Mara's voice quivered.

Adam stepped away from her. "Fuck! Why did you do that?"

"I didn't have a choice. He followed me everywhere. I couldn't get away from him. What was I supposed to do?"

"Not fucking meet with him. I don't know if you remember, but you and I aren't exactly on the best of terms with the McKinleys."

Mara's eyes flashed. "Then maybe I shouldn't have been alone for the last two years. The only time I've seen you was when I was jumping into that bloody, freezing river. If you would have come with me, none of this would have happened."

Adam's teeth gritted. "I didn't have a choice, Mara. Marcus can destroy my family."

Mara looked away. "I know."

"What did he want?" Adam ground out. When her gaze shot to his, he added, "Declan McKinley. What did he want?"

"He said he and his cousin wanted to offer me protection in order to testify against Marcus. And that Jason Hollis is too unreliable."

They weren't wrong about that. "Did you tell him about us?"

"No. He didn't mention you at all. They were focused on taking Marcus down. He asked a lot of questions about Mercedes." She shifted her gaze away. Adam knew she was racked with guilt over the attorney. "I was relieved when I heard she was alive. Did you help her?"

Regret swirled in his gut, like it always did when he

THE LIES THAT SHATTER | 187

thought of Mercedes. "I've helped her when I could. But that last time, my guy worked too quickly and confirmed where she was. I had to order the hit, or Cooper would have known. I'm glad she managed to survive it."

Mara's brow creased. "Maybe we should take the deal. Declan said they would help with my legal team and set me up in a safe house. Now that it turns out she's alive, his cousin might do anything to free her of this."

He narrowed his eyes. "Declan said? How well do you know him?"

Mara huffed out her breath. "Don't be ridiculous."

Adam reigned in his jealousy. "If you side with the McKinleys, you and I can't ever happen again. I've done far too much to ever be in their good graces."

She touched his arm. "If we tell them what Marcus has done to you, or that you helped Mercedes, more than once, maybe they'll understand. Declan seemed a reasonable bloke."

Her expression held just enough hope that Adam might believe it himself. Even after the horrors she'd been put through, she was an optimist. She always wanted to believe the best in people.

But even if the McKinleys could let what he'd done slide, which they wouldn't, he was in too deep with Marcus to ever come up.

"Nothing has changed for me, Mara. If I disappear, Marcus will go after Shannon. It's not like I can hide her and the kids."

Mara nodded, her eyes filling with tears. "I would never do anything to put your family at risk. But maybe I need to be the one to make the call here. If Declan can protect me, I might be able to testify against Marcus and end this all."

Anger slammed into his chest. Mara didn't need Declan McKinley to protect her. Adam had been doing that for two fucking years. And this whole fucking nightmare began when they tried to put Marcus Cooper down. Now that he'd done his most recent job, the trial would soon be derailed. Had he opened the door for Mara to star in the second run of this shitstorm? If she turned to Alec and Declan McKinley for security, she'd be lost to him.

Adam stepped to Mara and slid his fingers into her honey-blonde hair. He jerked it back, tilting her chin up at him. Her eyes widened and then settled into that submissiveness he knew she craved. Not the traumatic shit Marcus had done to her for years. But the kind where she was really the one in control.

"Do you still want me, Mara?" he growled.

"I do," she rasped. "I want you, Adam."

It was all fucking wrong. Adam was an evil ghost. She deserved better than that.

He tugged her hair and slid his thumb across her soft lips. "No. What's my name, baby."

Those lips parted, licking the pad of his thumb. "Timothy," she breathed. Lust went straight to his already hard cock. "I need you, Tim. I've waited for you forever." Her hands were working at his buckle. Once he was free, she stroked his cock in her small fist.

He groaned. "Fuck, Mara."

She was all he needed. Even after years of trying to keep her away, she'd come back to him. It didn't matter what the world wanted. He was going to lose himself in this woman tonight.

CHAPTER TWENTY-NINE

A lec was a fucking mess.

He took a large sip of the coffee, grateful it was strong as hell. Sitting back in the witness room chair, he rubbed his eyes that were gritty from the lack of sleep. He didn't have to be here today, but he wanted the chance to make it right with Mercedes. All night, he'd tossed and turned, thinking about the damage he might have done.

Christ, the look on her face, the way her soft smile fell.

If she never spoke to him again, he wouldn't blame her. His jealousy and anger had eaten at him until he lashed out. He honestly couldn't say why he responded to her question with something about Kristin.

Fuck.

Seeing Mercedes with Ezra was killing him.

He wasn't one to talk. Kristin had firmly planted herself at his arm. And that last statement Kristin had shot off about going to bed was a deliberate blow aimed squarely at Mercedes. Kristin was playing dirty. Not for the first time, Alec questioned why he was letting Kristin play at all.

Guilt, maybe?

Declan was right. Alec wasn't in love with Kristin. Not

anywhere close to it. But abandoning her in San Francisco didn't seem like the right thing to do either.

But damn if he didn't want to.

Mercedes was making him go mad. The scent of her shampoo wafting through the air, the way her hips moved when she walked. That wasn't mentioning the tight dresses and high heels she wore to court. His imagination kept going wild with lust for her. The image of those tight little skirts being pushed up around her thighs, plunging himself into her while she cried out his name.

Last night, Alec had glimpsed a new tattoo on her forearm, and his pants immediately grew tight. Who knew he was that into tattoos? He'd imagined so many ways of taking her that he thought he might be losing his mind.

Alec was used to being in control. He could anticipate how the world around him would move and know what to do. But since Mercedes had returned, he had completely lost all sense of balance.

The large form of Noah Ramirez looming in the doorway dragged him out of his fantasy. Alec's heart picked up its pace and he looked past the agent, hoping to catch a glimpse of Mercedes. He was disappointed to see Noah was alone.

"Is Sadie coming in today?"

Noah gave him a nod. "She's been here."

"Oh, I thought . . . I haven't seen her in the witness rooms."

"She has her own room now. Lots of calls today."

What kind of calls would she be on right now? "Do you think I could see her?"

Noah grimaced with uncertainty.

Kristin was suddenly at his side. She set a tea on the table next to him. "Mercedes asked to be in a separate place, she doesn't want to interact with any of us. Just leave her be."

Annoyance brimmed in Alec's chest. "I have a few things I need to say to her."

Pain crossed Kristin's face, and she looked away.

"If you see her, will you ask her if I can have a word, please?" Alec said to Noah.

"Sure man. If she's too tied up, we'll be at her sister's again this evening. I'll let her know you'd like to talk to her."

Closing arguments were wrapping up in the case and his time was growing short.

THAT EVENING, ALEC WAS DETERMINED TO HAVE A WORD alone with Mercedes. If he could only talk to her, let her know he wasn't trying to hurt her and that he only needed a little time to process everything.

The sound of an electric guitar was coursing throughout the house, and Kristin looked to Luke in surprise. "You guys are playing the music awfully loud," she said, her voice raised to be heard over the music. The song floating up from the stairs wasn't anything Alec recognized.

"Oh, that's Sadie and Ezra." Luke grinned. "They got here a little while ago and decided to jam. You can go down if you like. Everyone else is already downstairs. They're finishing up."

As much as Alec hated seeing Mercedes and Ezra in the same space, he loved watching her play. Everything about her changed when she held an instrument.

But as he made his way downstairs, he found it wasn't Mercedes who was playing. She had a guitar perched on her lap, her slender arms poised on top of it as she sat enraptured by what Ezra was playing on his electric guitar.

She was lost in the moment. Her expression was soft as she focused on Ezra's fingers strumming out the tune. It kept changing from intense and fast to slow, almost a ballad. Each change made Mercedes's grin widen. Ezra would occasionally look up at her, like he was gauging her reactions. It was as if they had done this a thousand times before. And they probably had.

Mercedes leaned forward a little more, the tip of her thumb rested between her teeth. The slight movement sent a shiver through Alec, making his cock twitch.

When the song was over, Ezra looked to Mercedes. "What do you think?"

"I loved it," she said without hesitation.

Ezra's smile widened. "Really?"

"Yeah, it was fantastic." Mercedes held up a finger. "Can I make a suggestion, though?"

"Always." Ezra's gaze was all for Mercedes.

"When you get to that riff in the chorus, you should go up a chord and not down."

Ezra frowned. "Which one?"

Mercedes sat back. "This one." And with little effort, she played back Ezra's song. Ezra's face dropped to a playful annoyance. When she finished, he stared at her. "Did you seriously learn that song after hearing it once?"

Her eyes went wide. "Uh-huh." She nodded. "But did you hear what I meant?"

"I did." Ezra let out a breath in exasperation.

Mercedes frowned. "What? You don't agree that it should go up?"

"No, you're right, it should go up. It's just . . . It took me weeks to write that song. And you learned it like it was nothing."

Mercedes chuckled and stood. Alec's mouth went dry. Those little dresses she wore to court were a strain on his control, but today she had taken off the suit jacket, exposing a dark blue silk tank top. Her arms were toned, much more so than when she'd been in London. The tattoo on her forearm stood out against her pale skin. Jesus, she was sexy as fuck.

Mercedes put her arm around Ezra's waist and grinned up at him. "Thanks for that. So much fun."

"Anytime." Ezra beamed at her.

The twist of jealousy hit Alec again. The connection between them was weighing him down.

"Pizza's here!" Luke called from upstairs, and the party moved up to the main floor. Kristin poured two glasses of wine and brought one to him. They settled around the dining table, much more casual than the night before.

"Oh, good news," Charlotte said to Mercedes. "I was able to get Calvin to close up The Whiskey and Cask for a little private party tomorrow."

Mercedes grinned broadly. "Seriously? Oh, I miss that place."

"What's The Whiskey and Cask?" Shake asked.

"It's an actual speakeasy that's been around since the 1920s," Charlotte said. "The main bar off the street was once a cigar shop. And all these fancy dressed people would visit the shop but not buy any cigars. But if they knew the password, they were allowed into the speakeasy, which is hidden below."

"I worked there in college. It's so cool," Mercedes said. "There are all these hidden rooms behind bookshelves and five different tunnels that take you to various exits all around the block."

"There's a codeword you have to use to get into the place, even today." Charlotte added. "For tomorrow night, it'll be 'symphony'."

Mercedes's gaze darted to Alec and then glanced away. Symphony was the code name Alec had given her when he'd first help her flee Jason in the London hospital.

"Are you ready for this all to be over?" Charlotte asked Mercedes. "I can't wait to have a bit of normal."

Mercedes smiled. "There are so many reasons I'm glad this is almost over. I'm ready to move on with my life."

"Have you decided which job you're going to take?" Cressida said.

Alec's heart dropped. She had job offers lined up? Everyone knew her plans except him.

"I've narrowed it down to New York. The money is good, and I can explore the advocacy portion of the Washington DC job at the same time."

What the hell? New York and Washington?

She was going to be so far away from him again.

Charlotte's face fell. "I was hoping you would want to take the San Francisco job."

"I know, honey." Mercedes frowned. "And I want to be near you guys and the baby. But right now it's better if I start over."

Alec wanted her to take a job in San Francisco, too. It was the next best thing to her being in London. He'd planned to live here for a few months once his company's new office space was ready.

"When are you going to look for a place to stay in New York?" Cressida asked.

Mercedes shot a shy smile at Ezra. "I actually have some time. Ezra is letting me use his apartment in Manhattan."

Alec curled his fist, trying not to be obvious in his pain.

"Oh, that's so sweet. Congratulations, you guys." Kristin gushed.

Mercedes glanced at Alec and flushed. "I don't know if that's necessary. But I appreciate him letting me crash there until I have a place of my own."

Mercedes living with Ezra, even for a day, gnawed at Alec. The way Ezra was looking at Mercedes made it clear he wanted her in his bed.

"What's this?" Ezra murmured. "Is that the scar?"

Ezra was looking down at the space between himself and Mercedes. The only way Ezra would have known there was a scar on her leg was through touch. He'd already been touching Mercedes.

Alec balled his fist and tried to cool his temper. Too much damage had been done by letting his control slip.

Mercedes stood and slid the hem of her skirt up to show the puckered pink scar on the outside edge of her thigh. "Yeah, that's where the bullet entered and then exited on the other side. I want to cover it with a tattoo someday too, but it needs more time to heal."

She sat and gave a tight smile to the group.

"Let's hope you never catch up to Alec in bullet wounds, lass," Declan joked, clearly trying to lighten the mood.

"What do you mean, catch up with him?" Kristin said, her head tilted. "They've both been shot once, and he took *that* bullet for Sadie. Seems they're already equal." She sipped her wine. "I know it's different here in America, but in Britain, we don't have businessmen getting shot all the time."

"Businessmen?" Confusion tainted Mercedes's tone. Her frown deepened, and she leaned forward. "Alec's been shot twice."

"Twice?" Kristin said in alarm. "I thought it was just the one time last year? You were still recovering when we met."

Alec winced, covering it by grabbing his glass of water. They hadn't discussed all his prior wounds. In fact, they had never discussed much related to his work.

"Oh, honey. Alec's been shot and stabbed and all sorts of other body damaging things." Shake popped off. "Didn't you ever wonder where the scars on his chest came from?"

Kristin flushed. "I hadn't really thought to ask."

"You hadn't thought to ask?" Mercedes said. It was more than disbelief in her tone. It was outrage.

Kristin's mouth tightened and her gaze fell on Alec.

He cleared his throat. "I took a bullet in Afghanistan when I was in the military. Most of the other minor injuries came after that."

Mercedes narrowed her eyes and looked at Cressida. Alec didn't miss the little shrug of Cressida's shoulder.

"But you were stabbed too?" Kristin asked.

"I've been . . . stabbed a few times, aye."

Kristin's mouth dropped open. "A few times? Recently?"

"The most recent was last year. Jason stabbed me when he attacked our safe house where we were keeping Sadie."

"*You* were there for another one of these attacks on *her?*" Alec didn't miss the distaste in her tone when she referred to Mercedes.

"Aye." Alec added a warning to his voice.

Declan scoffed. "You could say that. They destroyed that safe house. There were so many bullet holes in it they weren't able to salvage the entire front of it."

Kristin's eyes widened. "It was a gunfight?"

Alec was getting annoyed at the way Kristin was going on about this. He was a security expert. Was this really that shocking?

"And Alec killed one of them," Declan added.

Okay, that's a little much.

"You've killed someone?" Kristin looked up at him in disbelief.

Alec winced. "We should talk about this later." Only Mercedes and Declan knew his kill count. He had no plans to share that with Kristin now.

It was Declan who moved the conversation away. "What are you planning to do between New York and Washington?" he asked Mercedes.

"Oh well, the New York job is at a corporate law firm, much like I was doing here." Her smile widened. "But the Washington DC job will be with a nonprofit who lobby to strengthen domestic violence laws in the US."

"That's amazing, Sadie." Alec couldn't help but say. Knowing she would use her skills to help other survivors like herself warmed his heart.

Mercedes smiled broadly, a flush creeping up her cheeks.

It was the first compliment he'd given her since she came back, and she was glowing.

After dinner, Alec looked for a way to get her alone. An opportunity finally arose when she and Cressida were talking in the kitchen.

Unfortunately, Kristin intervened. She threaded her arm through his. "I'm not feeling well. Can you take me to the hotel?"

"Are you okay?"

"Yeah, I just want to rest."

Torn between wanting to help Kristin and the need to talk to Mercedes alone. Alec didn't want to leave without first talking to Mercedes.

"Alright, give me just a second."

Mercedes was leaning against the counter, her wineglass held delicately in her hand. Alec leaned into her, and her eyes went wide. "I have to step out for a tick, but I'm coming back. Will you be here for a while? I was hoping to talk to you."

Alec was so close to her he could see the whisky-colored flecks hidden in her eyes. They traveled down his face, landing on his mouth. Her exhale was hitched, and she looked away. "Um, actually Ezra and I are leaving too."

A shock of grief and jealousy made him immobile.

He was too fucking late.

He hadn't had a chance to talk to her in days, and now she was leaving with Ezra.

She picked up her purse and slung the strap over her shoulder. "You're going to the party, right?"

"Aye, I'll be there."

"Good. It'll be fun." For the first time, Mercedes's expression sparked with joy.

"Alec? Are you ready?" Kristin called from the arched doorway.

Mercedes's face held a resignation in it, and she gave him

a tight smile. "I'll see you tomorrow then." She brushed past him and joined Ezra at the door.

Ezra's face lit up, his hand smoothing around the curve of her back. It was possessive, intimate. If he thought his heart couldn't shatter anymore, he was wrong.

As Alec got in the car to drive Kristin to the hotel, a heaviness suffocated him. She was really gone. Not because she was dead, but because he'd let her walk right out the fucking door and right into the arms of a man who had already broken her once.

"Well, it looks like Mercedes and Ezra have worked out everything." When Alec didn't respond, she added, "They certainly look good together."

"Really? I hadn't noticed."

"Yes, you did."

"What do you want me to say, Kristin?" An edge had taken over his voice. "I told you I didn't know what was going to happen, and I don't. You want me to make promises to you I can't make. I'm sorry, but that's where we are."

"So even though Mercedes went home with Ezra tonight, you still aren't sure about us?"

The image of Ezra touching Mercedes's body haunted him. "I'm doing the best I can."

"I think it plays out perfectly," she said. "Sadie and Ezra have so much in common. Their music talent, their childhoods. All of it. They're perfectly suited for each other."

No, they fucking aren't.

Alec turned the car into the hotel car park, maneuvering into a space. He knew exactly what needed to happen.

Damn, this was going to be hard.

He killed the engine. "Kristin, we need to talk."

CHAPTER THIRTY

Alec sipped his whisky, enjoying the unique vibe of The Whiskey and Cask. Jazz music swirled softly through the small barroom. Rough brick walls lined the back of the bar, and the ornate copper ceiling reflected the light from the chandeliers.

When Alec finally spotted Mercedes entering the room, his ability to breathe left him. She looked so fucking amazing. The simple black dress reminded him of the first time he'd ever seen her. The neckline plunged between her breasts, revealing just enough curve to draw the eye. One shoulder was exposed with a thin strap holding up the side. The other had a long sleeve that swept around when she moved. The red heels accentuated her supple legs.

Alec's cock stiffened just thinking about running his hands up her soft thighs and plunging his tongue between them. Tasting her again while she arched her hips up to him. A magnetic pulse burned between them, and he couldn't get enough of her. He tried his best not to openly stare, but she was drawing him in like gravity.

Mercedes looked up and held his gaze in her own. He

didn't miss how she looked beyond him, searching to see if he was alone.

When he made his way to her, she eyed him warily. The veneer faltered slightly before she offered him a smile. No warm hugs or kisses on the cheek for him. She held out her hand, and Alec automatically reached for her. Electricity pulsed between them, stealing his ability to see anything but her.

"Thanks for coming," she said, her fingers warm in his.

"You look beautiful," he said.

She blinked at him in surprise. "Thank you. You look pretty dashing yourself."

"Thanks." His gaze was trapped with hers until she looked away. Alec glanced to the corner where a few instrument cases were being stored. "Will I get to hear you play violin tonight?"

Her expression shifted to uncertain. "Maybe. They might drag it out of me. I'll probably make a fool of myself. I haven't played since . . . well, since Scotland."

Scotland crashed into his mind. Mercedes's responsive body arching toward him as he pleasured her. The moans she made echoing in his head.

Alec cleared his throat. "I was hoping I could talk to you tonight, just the two of us. What time is Noah taking you to your safe house?"

Mercedes's brows shot up. "Oh. The case went to the jury this morning so, I don't have a safe house anymore. And Noah's already been reassigned. He left this afternoon to go back to Sacramento."

Shock filtered through Alec's brain. "What?" He scanned the room. "Who's on your detail then?"

A laugh trickled from Mercedes. "I don't have a detail. I moved to a little boutique hotel in Pacific Heights to be closer to Charlie."

What the fuck?

At his expression, she smiled at him. "That's one reason to celebrate tonight. Don't you think?"

Fear crawled up his chest. "I don't understand. Why wouldn't they tell me?"

Mercedes tilted her head. "Why *would* they tell you?"

It hit Alec like a brick. He wasn't in the loop. They had ended her security, and he had played no role whatsoever in her safety. No part in her life at all.

Panic flared and he reached for his phone. "I have a few guys here that I trust. I'll pull them and make sure they're at your hotel."

Mercedes's fingers on his forearm stopped him. "Alec, please don't."

"You need someone to watch out for you." He was finding it hard to breathe.

She shook her head. "No, I don't. My testimony is over. The jury is deliberating. It's time for me to return to my life."

"What about Jason?"

Mercedes's brow creased with worry but she lifted her shoulder. "Jason's always going to be a threat. I can't hide away forever."

"Sadie . . ."

"Alec, this is what my life is. Today, I truly get to start over. To be Sadie Elliott again." She gave a rueful laugh. "Whoever she is."

"I know who she is," Alec said softly. Firelight and laughter filled Alec's memory. The way music would filter through the cottage, the river adding a symphony to their brief haven. It was a moment of perfection he'd been blessed to sample, but not keep forever.

Energy was snapping through his fingertips. He longed to touch her. Mercedes looked at him in a way that opened him up and pulled him in.

Mercedes parted her lips to say something but stopped.

Her attention caught something over his shoulder, and she stiffened.

Fingers wrapped around Alec's arm, and he turned. Shock coursed through him. "Kristin?"

He immediately jerked away, but it was too late.

"Excuse me," Mercedes said with false politeness, and she stepped away from them.

Kristin peered up at him with a tinge of satisfaction in her eyes. Annoyance swirled in Alec's chest. Especially when Mercedes went straight to Ezra's side.

Alec looked at Kristin. "What are you doing here? You should be nearly back to London by now."

"I know. I'm sorry. But I couldn't go." Her voice trembled. "I'm not ready to give up on us yet."

"Kristin, I meant what I said. I'm in love with her and that isn't going to change. You deserve better than to be with someone who loves another. I can't do that to you."

Mercedes's laughter peeled through the room, and Alec's gaze was drawn back to her. Ezra's hand slipped around Mercedes's waist, tugging her into his side. Ezra was clearly sending a message to all around them that they were together. She didn't seem to mind. In fact, she beamed at everyone who was near her.

Jesus, it hurt to look at them.

"They look really happy together." Kristin touched his shoulder. "Isn't that what you want for her? It looks like Ezra makes her happy."

But it didn't. She would never be happy with Ezra. As much as they had in common, Ezra wasn't what she needed. Mercedes had already suffered enough at the hands of undeserving men. It burned him up that she may be walking into more heartache.

"Hey, everyone," Charlotte called, and the murmur of the guests died away. "Thanks so much for coming tonight and celebrating the return of my big sister, Sadie. I don't have to tell you how hard this past year has been without her, and I am so grateful she's come back to us."

Mercedes smiled shyly as the guests all lifted their glass to her.

"So now, we are going to go down into the actual speakeasy," Charlotte said. "We have hors d'oeuvres down there and the cocktails are on us. Please enjoy."

Alec jerked his arm away from her grasp. "You need to leave. Now."

She shook her head. "Alec . . ."

"I mean it, Kristin. Go home."

Alec walked away, leaving Kristin in the bar.

The speakeasy was much larger than the main bar. Books lined the walls, and tables and cushioned chairs were scattered across the ornate carpet. Mercedes stayed on her feet, embracing old friends and smiling as she greeted them.

Alec had an unobstructed view of her face. She wasn't watching him, so he could take her in a little more while still being discreet. He sipped his whisky, hoping it would do its job and mute the misery crawling through him.

After everyone had sampled the food and refilled their cocktails, Ezra stood and clinked his glass. He was so relaxed in front of a crowd, he seemed to draw energy from it. "What kind of party would it be if I didn't stand and make a speech?" The crowd whooped with laughter. When they quieted, he spoke again. "Thank you all for joining us on such short notice. I know all of you are here because at one time in your life you were touched by Mercedes and Charlotte. If you were anything like me, you were beyond happy when Mercy came back to us."

A murmur of agreement rippled through the crowd. Maybe his own reaction would have been different if he hadn't been rocked by betrayal. Fuck Whitley for ripping them apart.

Ezra continued. "I know a lot of you in here were witness

to the mistakes I made years ago and I'm grateful for Mercy's forgiveness, and that she let me come in and be a part of her life again. I can't wait to be a part of your next chapter." Ezra ran his fingers along her jaw, and Mercedes smiled up at him.

Ezra had the look of a man fully gone. Alec knew it well.

"Are you alright?" Cressida said as she sat next to him.

"No," he said honestly. "I fucked this up so much."

Cressida's gaze followed his, taking in Mercedes and Ezra. "There's still time to fix this."

"Is there? Look at them."

"Of course. She thinks she's giving you what you want. She loves you but she's not going to beg you to choose her."

Alec frowned at Cressida's words. Did Mercedes think this was what he wanted? For her to be with Ezra?

"Hey, if Kristin is it for you, that's great. But you should probably stop looking at Sadie that way. Let her move on with her life."

"I broke it off with Kristin. I took her to the airport this morning."

Cressida's jaw dropped. "Then what is she doing here?"

Alec winced. "Trying for one more chance."

"Jesus." Cressida rolled her eyes.

Alec looked back to where Mercedes was smiling and laughing with one of her former colleagues. "Christ. I just need one moment alone with her. Kristin just cocked it up and now Ezra's got his bloody hands on her."

"You'll find the moment," Cressida said. "You two belong together."

CHAPTER THIRTY-ONE

As Mercedes entered the speakeasy, she was overwhelmed by the tearful group of friends and colleagues that banded around her. Ezra brought her an amber-colored cocktail in a martini glass with a sugary cherry on the end of a pick.

Her eyes caught sight of Alec, making her pulse skip.

She could look at him all day. That delicious scruff she loved gave him a dangerous look. He wore a black suit jacket without a tie and his white collared shirt was unbuttoned just enough to expose the V of his neck. Memories of the moans he made when she'd run her tongue over that very spot flooded through her.

Alec's gaze suddenly shifted, and his blue stare pierced into her. His beautiful lips turned up into a soft smile, and her core clenched. She blinked and looked away to cover the flush growing on her cheeks.

Ezra kept putting his arms around her and rubbing her shoulders. It wasn't his touch she minded; it was that Alec could see it. She wasn't sure why that mattered to her, but it did.

Mercedes knew what Ezra wanted from her. He'd made

his intentions clear the night before. But Mercedes had enough of the pain of love to last a lifetime. She wasn't willing to put herself in the way of it again. Once she was in New York, she would move quickly to get out of Ezra's apartment.

An ash blonde head caught her eye and Mercedes wanted to throw her cocktail glass at it. Kristin was standing near the bar, gazing out at the gathered guests.

It didn't matter. Mercedes only had to watch them together for one more night. Then she'd find a way to heal from this screwed up situation. It bothered her that she wouldn't get to say a proper goodbye to Alec. That woman had latched on to him and she'd lost her chance.

"Such a great turnout, don't you think?" Charlotte's voice said in her ear.

Mercedes put her arm around her sister. "It is. You've done such an amazing thing here, Charlie. Thank you so much."

Charlotte beamed at her, glowing with happiness. Luke brought Charlotte a water, his fingers delicately caressing Charlotte's baby bump as he leaned in for a kiss.

Mercedes smiled at them with an ache in her heart. Her own life might be a level ten disaster, but her baby sister was living the fairy tale.

At least fairy tales still existed.

A headache was niggling behind her eyes, and she needed a break. She excused herself and went to the restroom. The ladies' room had a small lounge area with a lighted vanity and a variety of hair products and lotions set out for guests to use.

Mercedes flopped onto the velvet-lined chair with a sigh.

God, this was a mess. The man she didn't know she could ever trust again wanted another chance, and the man she longed for had chosen someone else.

Mercedes opened her purse and pulled out her makeup case.

"You're making this harder for him than it needs to be," a

voice said from behind her. Mercedes looked up in the mirror to see Kristin's tight face in the reflection. "Every time I leave his side, I find you trying to talk to him. Why can't you leave us alone?"

Mercedes frowned. "Well, things are pretty hard all around. And I'll talk to whomever I please. Alec's a grown man, he can speak for himself. Especially to me."

"We talk about you all the time. After we've left your sister's house. When it's just him and I." Kristin smirked. An icy dagger stabbed through Mercedes's heart. "He didn't realize how shallow you were. And he isn't sure he believes you didn't remember signing that form. I don't believe it either. I think you let him suffer and grieve like the self-absorbed bitch you are."

Mercedes could beat this woman's ass. It would feel really good. But the idea of the press reporting for weeks how Mercedes Elliott lost her mind and attacked Alec McKinley's girlfriend was enough to center her.

Mercedes scoffed. "I know Alec well enough to know he'd never say anything of the sort."

Kristin wasn't done. She narrowed her eyes. "He has almost everything he's ever wanted. I'm ready to give him what you're too selfish to give him."

Mercedes swirled the brush against the apple of her cheek. "Oh yeah, what's that?"

"A family." That stopped Mercedes, and she swallowed hard. "He loves children, and you and I both know you aren't going to give him that."

Mercedes loaded her brush with more powder, trying to ignore Kristin's stinging words.

"Can't you just let him go? Leave us be and let him be happy."

Mercedes sighed and packed up her makeup. "See, the difference between you and me is that you want to tell him what makes him happy. I want him to choose for himself."

Mercedes swung her purse over her shoulder. "And if he was as happy with you as you seem to think he is, you and I wouldn't be having this conversation."

"You're a trash person, you know that?" Kristin's eyes flashed at her. "Nothing more than gutter trash, pretending to be sophisticated."

"I don't give a shit what you think of me."

Kristin sneered. "It's not just me. Alec thinks it too. We talk about it every night, after we . . . finish. And he tells me how relieved he is to be with me. And how he now can see how he dodged a bullet with you."

The image of Alec and Kristin snuggled together after sex flashed through her mind. The shield she'd been wearing for days crumbled. Her stomach heaved, and she held the bile down.

"You know what Kristin? You can go fuck yourself."

Mercedes caught sight of Charlotte before she strode from the bathroom. Mercedes dimly wondered how much of that her sister had heard. It didn't matter now. She was done with this shit. She'd get the fuck away from this damn situation and get some clarity. Anything was better than being tortured with the images of Alec's naked body with anyone else. And especially not that nasty bitch.

"Sadie, can I have a word." Mercedes jumped at her name and spun. Alec had been waiting for her. He'd taken off his jacket and rolled up the sleeves of his white dress shirt. He looked even hotter than he had when he first arrived.

Kristin's smug face crossed her mind, and she snapped. "Oh, *now* you want to talk? What is this, a goddamn tag team?"

Confusion crossed Alec's face. "What?"

"I'm sure Kristin will fill you in after you ride her hard tonight. I'm so glad I can fuel your pillow talk." Mercedes spun on her heel and stormed away, needing a moment to cool her temper.

His footsteps followed closely behind. "Stop. What the hell are you talking about?"

"Leave me alone, Alec."

"No." Alec grabbed her arm, pushed open the first door they came to and tugged her in. Mercedes didn't resist, but it added to her rage that was reaching a fevered pitch. He led her down the narrow tunnel and stopped. "Where the hell are we?" Frustration coated his words.

"The tunnels under the bar." Mercedes snapped.

"I know that. Where can we talk? I just want one goddamn word with you in private."

Best to get this over with then.

"Fine. Come on." She stalked down the tunnel to where it forked and went to the right. The door to the storeroom was tucked away in a narrow alcove. Mercedes pushed it open and flipped on the light switch. Edison bulbs hung from the ceiling, casting a dark yellow glow. Shelves lined the walls of the brick room, filled with bottles and casks. The scent of honey, damp oak, and old things permeated the space. She tossed her purse on a cask and closed the door behind them.

Mercedes flipped around to face Alec. "What do you need?"

He suddenly stumbled over his words. "I-I just . . ."

"You've barely said two words to me since you stormed out of my rental the first night. Why do you need to talk to me now?"

"I—" He ran his hand through his hair. "I wanted to make sure you're okay."

"Okay? No, I'm not okay, thanks for asking." She put her hands on her hips. "Now, say what you *really* need to say."

"It's about Ezra."

Mercedes tilted her head and narrowed her eyes. "What about him?"

"Are you back together with him?"

"I don't see how that's your business anymore."

He moved toward her. "Sadie, please." Torment was thick in his voice.

Mercedes stepped back. If she was going to keep her sanity, he had to keep his distance. "You made your choices, Alec. Now I'm making mine."

Alec flinched. "I don't want you to get hurt again."

A laugh jumped from her throat. "Nothing could possibly hurt worse than this last week."

"He cheated on you with your friend."

"Oh, I remember. But he was a kid then. I don't know if you've noticed, but he's all man now."

Alec growled and closed the distance between them. Mercedes backed up against the wall. He stopped inches from her face. She was desperately trying not to be distracted by the scent of his body or the stubble that graced his perfect jaw.

"He's all fucking wrong for you."

Her mouth dropped open, and she stared at him. "I don't think *you're* in any position to give me relationship advice."

"Maybe not, but you need to hear it, anyway." His voice had lowered to a rumble.

"Then so do you." Mercedes snapped. "You haven't told Kristin jack shit about you. She doesn't have a clue who the fuck you are. She looks at you and thinks you're nothing more than a suit who can give her lots of babies. And what kind of person doesn't ask questions about bullet wounds?"

"Sadie . . ."

"And she hates Cressida. *Hates* her. How can you be okay with that?"

"Sadie . . ."

Now that she'd started, Mercedes couldn't stop. "I bet she complains about Cress or anyone else you dare to spend time with. Believe me when I tell you, that's quite a red flag."

"Oh, and Ezra hasn't been a possessive arse?" Alec's breath was coming in pants that brushed her cheek. "He keeps you on a short leash. Always fucking touching you."

"So what? I know where I stand with him. Maybe I need someone to keep my bed from being so goddamn lonely at night."

Alec's eyes darkened. "Are you trying to hurt me?"

"Not at all. You wanted to talk about Ezra, so I'm talking." She tilted her head. "Is hearing about me in bed with another man painful, Alec?"

"You know that it is," he said gruffly.

"Then maybe you have even the slightest taste of what I've been living with since I found out *that woman* had taken my place."

Alec threaded his fingers through her hair. "No one could ever take your place, Sadie."

The warmth of his body pressing her against the wall was more than she could bear. Mercedes put her hand on his chest and tried to push him back.

Alec had other ideas.

He snatched up her wrist and pinned it against the wall, his mouth crashing onto hers. His kiss was rough and demanding, exactly how she needed it. Pure lust burned through her as Alec worked her with his tongue, coaxing her until she was whimpering and panting with every lash.

When he broke away, his eyes were dark with desire. Mercedes studied his face, hoping he wouldn't hate himself for this later.

"We should stop," she whispered, tugging to free her trapped hand.

Alec tightened his grip. "I don't want to." He took her mouth again. There was no fight in her to resist him. He was everything she needed, and she'd let him have anything he wanted.

His kisses trailed along her jaw and down the soft skin of her neck. She put her head back and groaned. He always knew exactly where to kiss her to make her slick as hell.

Reality nagged at her. One of them needed to have good sense. "Alec, you have a girlfriend."

Alec drew back, his heated gaze scorching her with desire. "I ended it yesterday."

Mercedes swallowed. "You did?"

"Aye. There's only you, Sadie." His words a husky murmur. "You're all I see."

The pain of the last week washed over her, reminding her what was at stake. She pushed it aside and kissed him again. Alec moaned into her mouth, dominating her. He released her trapped hand, only to run his fingers along the neckline of her dress. A shiver ran down her spine when he cupped her breast, his thumb circling the hardened bud.

"Christ, Sadie." Alec tugged until the fabric moved aside, exposing her nipple to the humid air. Alec wasted no time. He leaned down and drew it into his mouth.

Mercedes cried out, arching her back, encouraging him for more.

He kissed and sucked on her until she wanted to explode. Then he pulled on the dress, exposing the other side. A fresh wave of lust raged through her as he gave the other nipple the same attention.

A moment of clarity kept invading her mind. Was she really going to let Alec screw her in the dusty storeroom of a speakeasy?

His tongue roved to the side of her nipple, and he sucked in. Mercedes gripped his shoulders and moaned. It was just enough pain to flood her senses. Alec was marking her, and she loved it.

Yeah, she was going to let him do whatever he wanted.

She didn't have any condoms and briefly wondered if he did. They'd never needed them before.

Without warning, the reason they would need a condom now crashed into her.

They say they love you, then they fuck someone else.

Shit. Shit. Shit.

"Alec, stop." Mercedes pushed on his shoulders. "Please stop."

"Darling, what's the matter." Alec cupped her face in his large hands, his labored breath brushing against her cheek.

She was panting as she slipped her neckline back into place. Desire and panic were having a full-scale war inside her head and she knew she was about to be destroyed again.

Mercedes looked into his eyes and wanted to die.

Everything about him had shifted.

Alec, *her Alec*, was standing before her. Not the angry man who'd lashed out or the one who could barely look at her. But the tender lover who would rip the world apart for her.

But she couldn't let him.

"I can't, I'm so sorry. I'm not trying to lead you on, I didn't expect this . . ." she stammered, the tightness in her throat closing her off.

"Hey, it's okay," Alec murmured, leaning in to kiss her. This time it was gentle, like a soothing caress. "It's okay. We can slow down if you need to. There's no rush."

The ache in her heart ripped through her. "No Alec, I can't do this at all. It's too hard."

Alec frowned. "I don't understand."

Mercedes inhaled deeply, steeling herself for the fallout that was sure to come. "Nothing's changed. At least not for me."

Pain shot across his face. "Sadie, I know I fucked up. I hurt you and let you think I didn't want you anymore. That's the furthest from the truth, my love. Please." He lifted her chin with his finger. "Forgive me."

"I do, Alec. But it's too late." She pushed farther out of his arms to give her the space to say what she needed to say. "I'm leaving for New York in the morning. The job's all set, and all my things will arrive at the apartment in a few days."

Anguish pulled Alec's brows together. "Ezra's apartment."

Mercedes nodded. He backed away, running his hands through his hair.

"I'm sorry," she whispered.

"Not good enough." Alec shook his head. "I know you love me. Why won't you try?"

"Alec, I . . ." Mercedes shook her head.

"I need to know."

He deserved to know, but she wasn't sure she could explain it in a way that made sense.

"Every time I think I'm safe loving someone, I let my guard down and then I get destroyed." Mercedes's voice was growing shrill as she tried to hold back the tears. "Every person I have ever loved has utterly broken me. And seeing you with her was the worst."

"Tell me what I need to do, and I'll do it."

"There's nothing either of us can do." Daggers of pain were slicing through her. But it had to be this way. "We have to let each other go."

"No. Jesus, Sadie, please don't do this." The depth of his pain reverberated in her bones.

Mercedes choked back a sob. "I'm sorry. But I can't go through it again."

She swept past him, grabbed her purse, and walked out of the room. Her mind so wrapped in misery that she barely remembered leaving the cold tunnels and entering the speakeasy.

Ezra saw her and frowned. He walked from the group of lawyers he was talking to and met her on the way to the bar. "Hey, where'd you go?"

Mercedes kept her gaze down to hide her red eyes and swollen lips. "I was heading to the bar. Can I get you a drink?"

"No, I'm good," Ezra said. Mercedes knew that tone all too well. She was lying, and he didn't believe her. She chanced a glance up at him. Ezra was tracking something from the direction she'd just come.

Mercedes turned to see Alec come out from the tunnel door. She could tell he was still shaken by their encounter, too.

Ezra watched Alec for a moment. When his gaze fell back on her, understanding written on his face. "Are you okay?"

Mercedes shook her head. "Not really."

Ezra pursed his lips and nodded. "It'll be alright. Go get your drink and step away from the crowd a little. I'll make sure you're covered."

Mercedes smiled up at him. "Thanks." She walked to the small side bar tucked in the corner.

The bartender walked over to her. "Hey, it's the guest of honor. What can I get you?"

She glanced at the cocktail menu, not caring about the drink. "I'll take a Sidecar, I guess."

"You got it."

Her fingers were shaking as she tried to tap out a soothing rhythm on the rich mahogany wood. Alec's scent lingered on her skin, making her ache to run back to his arms. What she wouldn't give to let herself go. To let him love her the way she needed.

It would be a massive mistake.

Tomorrow would change everything. She'd step off the plane into a new life. One that she would build for herself and her alone. It wasn't the life she'd thought she was getting, but she hoped to God it would be enough.

Mercedes looked around the bar, needing a distraction from her turmoil. "Where's Calvin tonight?" she called to the bartender. "I thought he would be here for sure."

"He took a little time off this week before we knew about the party. I know he was bummed to miss it." He slid a glass across the bar.

Mercedes put the thick crystal to her mouth and sipped. She hadn't had a Sidecar in a while, and it was heavy with some sort of mixer. She took in another sip, needing something to calm her nerves. Fatigue was wrapping itself around her, and she just wanted to go to bed.

She sat back against the stool and the room turned ever so slightly. She laid her hand on the bar to steady herself. Her movements were unnatural, weighted.

The bartender was watching her as he poured another set of cocktails out. "You alright?"

His stare was piercing, as if he was waiting for her to do something.

"I'm great. I need to go find my ride." She stepped off the stool, catching onto the bar before she toppled over in her heels. Her legs were heavy too.

"Oh hey, take it easy. Someone might have had a few too many." He came around the bar and took her arm.

Mercedes frowned at him, her pulse racing. He was so close to her. How did he get there so fast?

What the hell?

She cut through the brain fog to realize he was walking her somewhere. To one of the tunnel doors. His fingers digging into her arm.

No, no, no.

This was all wrong. Something was all wrong, but she couldn't focus. It was just like her nightmares. Her body was filled with lead, and she couldn't scream.

Alec.

She scanned the remaining guests.

Where the hell was he?

Mercedes spotted him across the room. He was facing her, but his eyes were on someone else. His features were taut and angry.

She jerked her arm away trying to maneuver out of the man's grasp. She needed just a second to catch his attention.

Alec glanced up and he did a double take. His eyes narrowed when she stumbled.

"Help me," Mercedes mouthed, hoping he would understand her plea.

He did.

Alec sprinted at them, leaping over chairs. Mercedes's foggy mind tried to make sense of everything, but it was all jumbled.

The only thing she could understand in all the sudden chaos was the word. "Fuck," from the man next to her.

Just before Alec got to her, a stabbing pain jammed into her side.

It was then that Mercedes knew death had found her again.

CHAPTER THIRTY-TWO

A lec returned to the bar, his soul sinking in anguish. Mercedes's tearful voice telling him all the ways he'd hurt her was more than he thought he could take. Here he had been worried what Ezra would do to her, but he'd done far worse.

The crowd had thinned considerably. The jovial murmur of the remaining guests didn't match the utter fucking misery stabbing him in the gut.

"Alec . . ." a sharp voice broke through his thoughts. Charlotte was next to him, her flashing eyes taking him aback.

"Hey Charlie . . . what's wrong?"

She stepped up to him, anger making her words quiver. "I love you, Alec. You know I do. But that fucking woman you brought with you is no longer welcome in my home. You keep her away from me, and you keep her away from my sister. Do you understand?"

What the hell?

Charlotte stepped past him, but he stopped her. "Wait! What's going on?"

"Kristin went after Sadie in the bathroom. Told her every night in bed you tell her how grateful you are to have dodged a bullet because Sadie's such a selfish bitch. Then she said Sadie's nothing but trash for trying to talk to you."

Jesus fucking Christ. "I swear, I would never say anything like that about Sadie."

"I'm sure you wouldn't. But Sadie doesn't need any catty bullshit from Kristin or anyone else. She's been through enough."

Fuck. No wonder Mercedes was so pissed.

Alec looked down into those angry hazel eyes, identical to the expression he'd just seen on her sister. "I'm so sorry. I'll take care of it."

He'd start with Mercedes. She had to know the truth.

Alec strode across the room to get to the little sidebar Mercedes perched at.

"Not happening, man," Ezra said as he stood in Alec's way.

Alec bit back a retort. "Excuse me." When he moved to brush past him, Ezra's hand went to his shoulder.

"Mercy doesn't want to talk to you now."

Alec narrowed his eyes and lowered his voice. "Take your hand off me, Ezra."

They were equal in height and nearly the same build. But Alec knew ten different ways to drop him if he needed to.

Ezra lifted his hand from Alec's shoulder, hovering it above his shirt. "You've already upset her enough. You're going to leave her alone."

Anger rippled through Alec's entire body. "Do you actually think you have the ability to stop me?"

"If I have to." Ezra glared back at him.

But Alec was no longer listening.

Mercedes had gotten up from the bar, and Alec could swear she stumbled. Something in her face made his stomach turn to ice.

A man, who was wearing a bar uniform, was at her side. Mercedes's step faltered again, and the bartender leaned in to say something to her. When her gaze landed on Alec, adrenaline rushed through him. She'd been looking for him.

When her mouth formed the words. "Help me." Alec was already moving.

He pushed Ezra aside and bolted to her. The man holding on to her arm was trying to hurry her to a tunnel door. He caught sight of Alec and jerked Mercedes toward him.

Alec leaped around a chair to the bar. He wasn't fast enough.

The bartender had a syringe in his hand.

He jabbed the needle into Mercedes's abdomen and pressed the plunger down. Then he pushed her away and turned to run.

Alec took him down, their bodies crashing onto a table. Empty glasses flew off the top, splintered as they hit the ground. The force of Alec's impact knocked the table over, and the two of them landed on the floor. They wrestled until Alec was straddling the man, his knee pinning down one arm.

The man grabbed a broken wineglass with his free hand and swiped at Alec. Each swing went wild. Alec registered a few hits. His cheek, his left arm. Didn't matter.

Another jab whooshed in front of Alec's face. This time he seized the man's wrist, jerked it straight toward him and struck the crook of his tilted elbow. A sickening crack reverberated, as did the man's scream of pain. The broken glass clattered to the ground.

Alec grasped the mangled arm and twisted. "What the fuck did you give her?"

"Fuck off," the man croaked.

"Wrong answer, arsehole." Tendons snapped away from bone as the man screamed. "Tell me what you gave her!"

"You should let her fucking die." The man's breathing was reduced to a pant. "He's never going to stop."

The man's trapped arm broke free and landed a blow to Alec's cheek.

Fucker.

Alec snatched up the shard of glass, jerked the man's head to the side by his hair, and plunged the edge of the thick crystal into his neck. Alec ignored the glass cutting into his own fingers as he jerked the shard down, carving through the flesh of his throat. The man gagged and jerked, his blood pooling around him.

Frantically, Alec searched through his pockets, hoping to hell to find a clue to what he gave her. He felt a little glass vial with his bloody fingers and jerked it free.

Fucking fentanyl.

Panic swelled as he pushed off the dying man and ran to Mercedes. Vaguely, he could hear Cressida and Shake corralling most of the straggling guests back upstairs to the main bar, until only a few of them remained.

Mason was already kneeling over her, checking her eyes and searching for her pulse.

Mercedes was fighting it, but she was losing. Her pupils were pinpoints, the green and gold stood out against the pallor of her gray skin.

Alec brought her hands into his. "It's fentanyl, Mason."

"Shit! We need a Narcan kit!" Mason shouted to the group of onlookers. "Do you have one here? You! Where's your Narcan kit?"

"Uh, in back." A stunned server answered and ran to fetch the only thing that could save Mercedes. Naloxone was one of the few drugs that could reverse the effects of opioids. They frequently stashed Narcan kits in bars as the first line of defense in saving an overdose victim.

Mason held her wrist, his eyes on his watch. "I was hoping for GHB or some other sedative."

"I think she had that, too. She was stumbling before he injected her."

Mason's dark eyes flicked to his, and the blood rushed from Alec's face.

She's not going to make it.

Mercedes blinked at him. "Alec." Her voice was barely a whisper. She wasn't trying to tell him something, she was just saying his name.

"Sadie, please." The words caught in his throat. "Please don't leave me again. Please."

Her breath was labored and harsh, and her lips were a grayish blue. She was suffocating to death right in front of him.

Alec cupped her face. "Darling, look at me."

Then her eyes rolled back in her head, and her body jerked.

"Fuck, no, no, no."

Alec cradled Mercedes's head in his arms, trying to memorize every little detail of her. The way her hair smelled, the warmth of her skin as he stroked her. Her fragile heartbeat slowing in her veins.

"I got it!" Declan ran to them, unzipping the case and handing it to Mason.

Alec held her tight, her breathing nearly gone. Her soft lips had turned purple.

Mason deftly prepping her leg for the injection, ripping the cap from the auto injector and jammed it into her thigh. He held it there until the needle sprung back with a click.

"Time it!" Mason said to Declan.

"Aye."

Three minutes . . .

Three fucking minutes was what he needed to know if it had worked.

Her breathing stopped. "No! Fuck!"

She needed more time.

Mason's calm direction grounded him. "Start rescue breathing, Alec."

Alec laid her on the floor, pinched her nose, put his mouth to hers, and blew. Her chest rose and fell with each exhale.

He was vaguely aware of Declan holding her wrist, hunting for her pulse with two fingers.

"I got it."

Mason had her other wrist. "I got it too. Keep going, Alec."

Hope filtered through his panic, and he batted it away. It could come crashing down at any moment.

In between breaths, he asked Declan for the time.

"One minute, thirty seconds."

Fuck.

"Is there another one?" Mason said.

Declan said, "Aye."

"Give it to me."

Alec focused on giving Mercedes each lifesaving breath he had in his body. He heard the click of the next injector hitting her thigh.

Within seconds, a rattling exhale came from her. Alec gave her more breaths, filling her struggling lungs with what she needed.

Her eyelids fluttered. Alec stopped, watching her chest rise and fall on its own now.

"Sadie?" He stroked her cheek. "Sadie, darling, can you hear me?"

Her eyes opened, and she blinked. They were green and glassy. The shallowness of her breathing made him think each inhale would be her last.

"Can you speak? What's my name?"

"Alec." It came out in a shuddering whisper.

"Do you know where you are, darling?"

Her gaze shifted to the ceiling above him. "No."

As the counter drug coursed through her body, she was becoming more aware of what was happening to her. Fear clouded her expression, and her thin breaths turned to a panicked pant.

"No, look at me," Alec soothed. "Just breathe. I'm right here."

"Alec, we have a car ready out front," Declan said. "We can wait for the ambulance, but Luke said we are only a couple streets away from a hospital. If you want to stay with her, we should go."

Declan had a point. There was a dead man just feet away. She would get there faster and there was no opportunity for the police to detain him.

"Can you hold on to me, darling?" He scooped Mercedes into his arms. She held him tight around his shoulders, giving him the sense of hope. She had more strength in her body than he thought.

Alec carried her up the steep staircase and into the main bar. Gasps and murmurs were coming from the group of onlookers, but he ignored them. Declan barked instructions to Cressida and Shake.

He followed Luke and Mason to the door and together they got Sadie into the SUV. Alec sat in the back with her and shifted her into his arms the second he crawled in. She leaned into him, stroking his cheek with her hand.

"I'm sorry," she whispered.

"Don't be sorry. Just stay alive."

"I don't think I have a choice."

"I know. But I need you to try." His throat closed up and he choked back a sob. "I can't lose you again."

She nodded and brushed his tear away with her thumb. "Tell me."

Alec knew exactly what she needed. "I love you. Only you."

A smile played on her lips. "I love you, too."

She tilted her head and kissed him. Not like the heated kisses they'd shared minutes ago, but a slow and savory kiss that was meant to stay with him for years. The kind of kiss that held a goodbye.

"Will you be there if I wake up?"

If.

"I'll be there, I'm not going anywhere."

Mercedes sighed and lay her head against his shoulder. "I'm so dizzy."

"Don't go to sleep, Sadie." Alec gave her a little shake. "Sadie, you can't sleep, darling. Please wake up."

Her hand slipped off his shoulder. He'd spoken his last words to her.

Panic and grief tore through him. The only thing he could do was focus on the shallow rise and fall of her chest and pray she kept breathing.

When the SUV pulled up to the emergency room, Luke, Mason and Declan all jumped out. Everything around him happened in a whirl. Mason was barking her stats and before he knew it, they tore her limp body from him.

CHAPTER THIRTY-THREE

The bustle of the waiting room of a San Francisco hospital emergency room was grating on his nerves. Alec paced, his body unable to sit still. He had to keep moving.

Mercedes could be flatlining right now. Needles impaling her delicate skin, tubes breathing for her because her brain was dying.

Dying alone.

It was his nightmare reimagined.

Charlotte broke into the waiting area and ran to Luke. He held her tight while she sobbed into his shoulder. He was making little soothing sounds, her heart wrenching cries matching the ones in his soul.

Cressida followed behind Charlotte. A black T-shirt and a small first aid case were in her hand. "Any update?"

Alec shook his head. "Not a word."

Cressida handed the case and shirt to Alec. "You're a mess. Go to the loo and wash up."

Alec looked down at his blood-smeared clothes. There was a tear in his white dress shirt and the sleeve was soaked. A deep throbbing ache suddenly announced itself.

Shit, he may need stitches.

Mason went with him and the two of them looked rather suspicious in the large stall of a hospital men's room, while Mason examined him. The cuts on his cheek and fingers were closing on their own. But the wound on his arm was another story.

Mason frowned as he examined him. "You need to check yourself in, man. This is deep and I don't have what I need to stitch you up."

"No."

"Alec . . ."

"If I check in, they'll take me somewhere else to wait. I need to be here." He looked up into Mason's dark brown eyes. "I can't leave her. So just bandage me up, and we'll take care of it later."

"Okay." Mason snagged an alcohol wipe from the kit. "Sorry, man, this is all I got. It's gonna sting."

"Aye." Alec braced himself. It hurt like a motherfucker but he tried to keep his grunts and curses to a minimum. The hospital wouldn't look too kindly to someone tending to an open wound in the loo.

Once he was bandaged and cleaned up, he joined the others in the waiting room. Ezra had arrived while they were gone. He was sitting forward in a chair, his tattooed hands steepled against his forehead. When Alec and Mason approach, he sat up. He held Alec's gaze for a moment and then looked away.

Charlotte had her head resting on Luke's shoulder. She stood and walked to him, wrapping her arms around him. A little sniff let him know she was on the verge of breaking down.

"I'm sorry I yelled at you," she said.

"Don't be. I deserved it."

"Yeah, you did."

Alec smiled against her curly head.

She pulled back and looked up at him. "Here we are again."

"Aye. I'm sorry you had to see all of that."

Charlotte shivered at the reminder. "I just hope we get one more shot at this."

"Me too." The way he'd fucked everything up was eating at him.

A woman walked into the waiting room, calling out Mercedes's name.

"I'm Mercedes Elliott's sister," Charlotte said.

The doctor gave her a smile. "You got her here just in time. She's improving, but we are going to keep her to monitor her heart. As the drugs leave her system, her risk of a heart attack or a stroke will decrease, but we want to keep an eye on her. Her breathing is still somewhat labored, and we are watching her oxygen to make sure she doesn't have another dip. She's not out of the woods yet, but she seems to have stabilized for the moment."

The relief that she was still alive was tainted with the threat of her heart giving out. He didn't know if he could survive losing her again.

They would be moving Mercedes into a room, but it would take at least an hour. Charlotte looked dead on her feet. Alec touched her shoulder. "You should go home, Charlie. I'll stay with her tonight."

Charlotte opened her mouth to protest, but Ezra beat her to it. "No, that's alright, man. I'll stay with her."

Anger flared in Alec. *Not happening.*

But it was Luke who spoke. "No, Sadie asked Alec to stay with her."

His cousin's eyes met his. Luke and the others had probably heard what he and Sadie had said to each other in the back seat.

It took some convincing to make Charlotte go home and

get some rest, but she finally relented. After they left, Alec and Declan sat together on the cushioned seat, a silence filling the space. There were no words needed. Alec knew Declan was there. That was all he needed his cousin to do.

Cressida walked in, her eyes on her phone as she sat next to Alec. "I spoke to Nick. He's on site and the FBI is working it since she's still technically a witness in a federal trial that hasn't ended. Tomorrow, he's going to need to talk to you. He said he'll hold them off as long as he can, but, because there are two dead men, they have to talk to you."

"Two?" Alec and Declan said in unison.

Cressida's brows pinched together. "Calvin, the owner of the speakeasy. They found him in the tunnel on the other side of that little bar she was at. That's where he gained access."

Christ. While he was in the storeroom kissing and touching Mercedes, a man was stalking her and killing her friend.

"Also, Shake went with Kristin and made sure she got checked into another hotel."

"Oh, shit. I completely forgot." Alec pulled his phone from his pocket. He'd missed three calls from Kristin. He should call her back, just to let her know he was okay. But if he did, she would beg him to reconsider and ask to see him. All of his focus had to be on Mercedes now.

He shot her a text, letting her know he was fine, and he'd call her the next day.

They sat for a moment in silence until Declan's voice broke through his thoughts. "This feels different, doesn't it?"

"What do you mean?" Alec said.

"With the exception of Jason going batshit crazy and destroying our safe house, all the attacks or threats against Sadie have been covert, hidden where only a few people could intervene. This attack happened right out in the open, with five members of our security team there to witness it."

"It's sloppy as fuck," Alec said.

"Is it? Or is it personal?"

Alec sat back in his chair. "It could be. Let's assume our pal Adam has been in charge since the events in London. Cooper would have been pretty happy that Sadie was dead and let him keep his job. But now that she's back, maybe Cooper's found someone else to do his dirty work."

"Maybe it's not Cooper at all," Cressida offered. "Maybe it's Jason."

Alec frowned. "Could be. But Jason literally gets off on hurting her. And me," he added. "He would have wanted to be there himself."

"He'd never have gotten close to that bar. Not with all of us in it. But he could have watched from the security cameras if he figured out how to hack them. They're all over the place."

"Were they?" Alec said. *Well shit.*

Cressida shrugged. "There were quite a few in the main bar and the sidebar. They should have a good view of what happened to Sadie." She tilted her head. "Why?"

"You may want to avoid any footage from the storeroom off the westside tunnel." Alec grimaced. "I didn't see a camera there, but I was a little . . . distracted."

Declan snorted.

Cressida's mouth dropped open, and her brown eyes sparkled. "Were you and Sadie shagging in the storeroom?"

Alec's cheeks flushed. "Not quite shagging."

"Well, good for you," Cressida said, giving his arm a squeeze. "That place was cool. I'd shag someone in its storeroom if I had the chance."

The echo of Mercedes's whimpers ricocheting around the brick room filled his mind. Was that the last chance they would have?

"I'm heading to a vending machine. Can I get you anything?" Cressida asked. "Water?"

"No thanks, Cress," Alec said.

Declan's face was soft as he smiled at Cressida. "I'm good. Thanks."

As she walked away, Declan's gaze followed her, and Alec could see that what was once a flirtation had become much more. "What's going on with the two of you?"

"What do you mean?"

"I mean, what is going on with you and Cressida?"

Declan shrugged. "Nothing. We're friends."

"Are you sure about that, mate?"

His smile slid away. "There's nothing between us."

"But you'd like there to be?"

Declan's brow furrowed, and he stared at his hands. "Aye, maybe."

Alec nodded. At least he wasn't imagining things. "So what's stopping you?"

"Lots of things."

"Like what?"

"She's too young for me."

Alec scoffed. "She's twenty-six. It's not like she's a teenager. Next."

"You."

"Me?"

"Yeah, you don't like people from the office dating each other."

"Since when did you start listening to me? Try again."

Declan was quiet for a moment. "She's my friend. If I fuck it up, I'll lose her."

"Well, that one is pretty valid." Alec laid his head back. "If she's worth the risk, take it." Declan looked at him in surprise. "Life is too fucking short, mate. Do something about it now. Before she moves on."

"I thought it wasn't a good idea to get involved with someone at work. That was your problem with Mariah, remember?"

"Aye, I remember. And if what you feel for Cressida is

nothing more than I felt for Mariah, then keep your pecker in your pants." Alec sent Declan a warning look. "Or I'll beat your arse."

"You could try," Declan shot back.

"I'd rather see you take a chance rather than watch you lose out on the opportunity. Otherwise, you'd end up fucking miserable like me."

A silence filled the air until Declan broke it. "You talked to Sadie, then? You told her?"

"Aye." Alec stared at the bland beige wall, lost in the pain of the moment.

"I take it, it didn't go well?"

"She walked away from me." Tears pricked the back of Alec's eyes. "She's been hurt too much and doesn't want to try again."

"She'll come around."

"I don't know, she was pretty determined to go to New York with Ezra in the morning."

"Yeah, but she didn't ask Ezra to be here when she woke up. She wanted you."

A nurse came through the double doors. "Ms. Elliott's room is ready. She's sleeping comfortably now. You guys should go home and get some rest."

"We're her security detail," Alec said. "I'll be posted next to her bed tonight."

The nurse looked him up and down, then nodded. "Alright then, come on. I'll show you to her room."

"You go ahead," Declan said. "I'll check on you in a bit."

Alec followed the nurse to Mercedes's room. The sight of her in the bed turned his gut. She was so small and frail. He wanted to gather her up in his arms and hold her, but he was afraid to wake her. Instead, he moved a chair next to her bed and took her warm hand in his. He stroked and kissed it, mesmerized by the rising and falling of her chest. The rhythmic beeping of the monitor letting him know her heart was still working.

Exhaustion overpowered him. Alec lay his head on her bed with her hand resting in his and slept.

CHAPTER THIRTY-FOUR

Mercedes knew she was in a hospital well before she tried to open her eyes. Way too many times she'd awoken to the abrasive scent of medicine and the bustle of the halls.

She was so tired.

Tired of running. Tired of the fear that coursed through her veins every day. Tired of leaving her heart behind.

Mercedes moved her hand to pull the oxygen tube from her nose, but it was captured under something warm and solid. She blinked and opened her eyes to find a dark head resting on the bed next to her. Alec had his face buried in the crook of his arm and his quiet breathing reached her ears.

Mercedes gently tugged her hand free and laced her fingers through his hair. She stroked his temple with her thumb and tried to recall all the words they had said to each other. The memories of the car were fragmented, splintered into a skewed reality.

He'd told her he loved her.

Had that been real? She couldn't be sure.

But the moment in the tunnel was vivid. The way he'd kissed her, raw and desperate, it was seared into her mind. No man had ever done to her what Alec could. One kiss and her body was on fire. He could make her forget the entire world existed.

That was way too reckless. If she was going to keep her sanity, she couldn't let it happen again.

Jesus, Sadie, please don't do this.

The anguish in his voice when he asked her not to leave filtered into her mind, and her heart cracked a little more. She had no choice; they were both safer if she walked.

Kristin might be all wrong for him, but she was right about how much he deserved a normal life. A stable woman who didn't scream with night terrors. One who could give him a family and build a life with him.

Mercedes would have to let him go.

Alec stirred, and she knew she couldn't touch him anymore after this.

His lashes flitted open, and his brow furrowed in confusion. Suddenly, he bolted upright. Those vivid blue eyes searched her face.

"Sadie?" Alec shifted to the edge of her bed. His hand cupped her cheek. "Darling, are you alright?"

God, she missed him so much.

"I'm okay," she rasped. "Did you sleep here all night?"

"Aye, I told you I'd be here when you woke up." His gaze roamed her face. "Can I get you anything?"

"Will you help me sit up?" Alec adjusted the bed and then helped her shift to sitting. Dizziness made the room swim, and she rested her head against his shoulder until it passed, then she sat back.

Alec traced the side of her jaw with his fingers, and she fought the urge to turn into his hand.

Mercedes swallowed, trying to clear the roughness in her throat. "I'm not entirely certain what happened last night. I only remember bits and pieces. But I know I'm alive because of you."

His gaze was soft and unguarded, the way he'd looked at her in Scotland. The kind of look that could burn through all her defenses and leave her clinging to hope.

Alec intertwined his hand with hers. "Do you remember what we said to each other in the car?"

"Not much of it." Mercedes shook her head. "I remember everything up to ordering a drink at the bar. Then it gets fuzzy."

Disappointment raced across his face, but he covered it well.

What had she said last night?

He shifted and Mercedes glimpsed white gauze peeking out under the sleeve of his black T-shirt. She narrowed her eyes and traced the curve of his bicep to the edge of the bandage. "Are you hurt?"

Alec frowned at his arm. "Nah, it's just a wee scratch."

Mercedes lifted his sleeve up and gasped. A slash of deep red was staining through the gauze. She looked at him in alarm. "Just a *wee* scratch?"

"Aye."

She reached up and turned his chin. A darkening bruise accompanied a thin slash on his cheek. Mercedes couldn't remember him fighting anyone. "How bad was it?"

He shrugged. "Only lasted a few seconds."

Ice grew in her gut. "And how did the other guy fair?"

"Not too well, I'm afraid."

"You killed him?" she whispered.

"Aye."

Mercedes's breath caught at the simple word.

He'd killed for her. Again.

There was no remorse. Nothing in his expression showed he regretted doing what he'd done. But he was studying her. Silently asking if it changed anything in her eyes.

How could it? She knew who Alec was. He hadn't asked

for any of this, but he'd respond with whatever force was necessary.

She squeezed his hand and gave a little nod and he exhaled in relief.

"I'm afraid I have rather bad news." He cleared his throat. "About the bar owner, Calvin."

Mercedes's eyes snapped to his. "No . . ."

Alec looked down at their intertwined hands. "I'm sorry, darling. The police found him while they were clearing the tunnels."

No, no, no.

Mercedes covered her face in her hands as the tears pooled and slid down her face. Alec moved closer to her, drawing her into his arms.

Calvin. With his stupid dad jokes and his obsession with Star Wars. He was the kind of man who set up an Angel code system so women could feel safe in his bar. And he was gone. Another innocent life cut short because she'd brought death with her.

She bit back a sob. "I don't know how much longer I can do this."

"This isn't forever, Sadie." Alec moved his hand up and down her back. "We'll make it through."

There was no we. It was just her. Alec just didn't believe it yet.

The tears ran their course, leaving her with a sharp ache in her chest. It didn't matter what she'd said to him in her haze, they were over.

A knock came at the door, and Luke poked his head in. "Hey guys, sorry to disturb, but Charlie's getting antsy and the FBI is here to talk to you, Alec."

"Aye, I'll be right out," Alec said.

Fear knotted inside her. "The FBI? Are you in trouble?"

"Nah, I don't think so. They have some questions for me, I'm sure."

It was so damn unfair. Cooper could kill and maim and destroy lives, but it would probably be Alec that would go to prison.

Her face must have given her away, because Alec cupped her cheek. "Don't worry, darling. I doubt they plan to charge me for it. But I need to speak with them, or they'll think I have something to hide. And we forced Charlie to go home last night for the baby's sake, but she won't be having it today."

Alec leaned in and kissed her forehead. Her body stiffened in surprise, his closeness spreading warmth through her.

"I'll see you soon," he murmured in her ear.

It wasn't the first hospital room he had left her in, and the sense of longing was overwhelming. She wanted him to come back, to hold her and tell her it was going to be okay.

It did no good for either of them. She would ask him one more time to go back to London and move on with his life.

CHARLOTTE AND LUKE ARRIVED WITH FRESH CLOTHES AND A few toiletries to help Mercedes feel a little more human. Charlotte helped Mercedes shower and dress in Luke's oversized football jersey and a pair of yoga pants. All Mercedes wanted to do was sleep, but she allowed Charlotte to fuss over her. The haunted look of fear and grief in her sister's eyes was making her ache.

After she had given a statement to the FBI agents who visited her room, Mercedes racked her brain, trying to figure out why this had happened. None of it made sense. Her testimony was over, she'd played her part.

Why was Cooper still trying to kill her?

Retaliation wasn't a good enough reason. Something else had to be the reason he would take such a risk to have her eliminated.

Scenario after scenario played out in her mind until one possibility finally stood out.

Goddamn it.

If she was right, the move to New York wouldn't be possible. Mercedes clung to the hope she was wrong. She didn't have it in her to do it again.

"Sadie," Luke said softly, breaking into her thoughts. He had a wheelchair set and ready for her. "We're going to take you to our place, aye?"

"You don't have to do that. I'm just going to crash for a few hours, so you can take me to my hotel room."

Luke and Charlotte exchanged a look.

"Alec asked us to take you to our house," Luke said. "He's already increased the security for you."

"Oh, okay." A tinge of warmth climbed up her chest. Alec was still protecting her, even from a distance. After they finished up her discharge papers, Luke wheeled her out into the hall. To her surprise, Declan was waiting for her.

He grinned at her. "How are you feeling, lass?"

"Meh, I've felt better." Mercedes looked past Declan down the hall. "Has Alec been back?"

"Not yet. He's going to be a bit. We'll make sure you get settled."

Fear crawled up her spine. "Has he been arrested?"

Declan shook his head. "Nah. Nick said they aren't going to charge him. The footage clearly shows the attack, he'll be okay. He has some things to take care of before he comes back. I'm going to hang with you until then."

Mercedes tried to be reassured, but worry crept in. She knew it wouldn't leave her until Alec was in front of her.

When they arrived at the house, Ezra was waiting for her in the living room. Anxiety furrowed across his brow. He wrapped his arms around her, and the scent of sandalwood filled her senses.

She sighed, knowing she shouldn't give him any more

hope than she already had. Letting him come back to her flat after leaving Charlotte's the other night had been selfish as hell, and she knew it. Ezra deserved more than to be a rebound. But that's what he was.

"Holy hell, Mercy. You can't do that shit to me. Are you okay?"

"I'm exhausted. I can never sleep very well in hospitals so I'm going to go upstairs and lay down for a bit." She looked up at him. "Can we talk first?"

"Yeah, sure."

Ezra helped her upstairs to the guest room. The bed had a heavy faux fur blanket tossed over its fluffy comforter. She longed to dive into it. As soon as she closed the door, he tugged her hand, and she was once again enveloped in his arms.

"You sure you're alright?" he murmured.

"I'm sure. They said I'll feel terrible for a while, but I'm out of danger."

Ezra cupped her cheek. When he leaned down to kiss her, she put her hand on his chest. Disappointment filled his expression.

But the memory of the last man who kissed her was still imprinted on her, and she didn't want to let it go.

Mercedes stepped out of his arms. "I've been thinking about our plan for me to stay with you in New York. I'm not sure it's possible now. We got a call from the law firm. They want to have a video meeting with me this afternoon. I don't know if the job is going to stick around after this," Mercedes said. Ezra nodded, his brow furrowed. "But even if it were, I don't think my living with you, even short term, is a good idea."

His gaze jumped to hers. "What? Why?"

"After what happened, it's clear I'm not safe. I don't want anything to happen to you."

"There's more to it than that. Are you afraid of where this might be going?" His hand gestured between them.

Mercedes lifted her shoulder and shook her head. "I just don't know if I can give you what you need."

Ezra studied her face. "What happened with Alec last night?"

Damn. She knew Ezra had picked up on the tension between them. Of course, she and Alec hadn't exactly practiced discretion. Mercedes's core clenched at the memory of Alec's mouth teasing her.

Her cheeks grew warm, and she had a hard time meeting his eye. "Ezra . . ." She didn't quite know what to say.

Ezra winced, taking in a deep inhale. "So you're back with him now?"

Mercedes shook her head. "I can't be with him either. He's going home."

His brow lifted. "Does he know that?"

"No, but I'll make sure he does."

"I know you're unsure of being with me and I get that." Ezra took her hands into his, massaging the muscles of her palm. "But, can you think a little more about New York? Even if the job doesn't happen, I can set up whatever kind of security you need."

The hope in his expression wrenched her heart.

The rational part of her mind was no longer in charge. She was running on pure heartache and misery. "Okay, I'll think about it."

He rubbed her shoulders. "Can I see you tonight? I don't care how late it is. I want to come by and make sure you're okay."

The idea of being alone was terrifying. But Noah was gone, and she needed Alec to keep his distance.

"Yeah, that would be nice. I'm not sure where I'll be but I'll call you." Exhaustion weighed on her, making her dizzy. "I'm going to lie down now."

"Need company?" He waggled his brow suggestively.

She chuckled. "Nah, I'm good. I'll see you tonight?"

"I'll bring dinner." She was grateful he didn't kiss her again before he left.

Mercedes flipped off the light and pulled back the heavy blanket, fatigue filtering her movements. She couldn't decide if there was still some of the drugs in her system or if she was just at the end of her energy rope. As she was dozing off, a knock came at the door.

When it opened, she called. "I'm all good, Ezra. Really."

"It's not Ezra."

Alec's voice made her pulse sing. He was standing in the doorframe, still in the tight black T-shirt. His hair was tousled and the weariness on his face gave away his exhaustion.

Mercedes's heart rate quickened even more when he shut and locked the door behind him.

"Are you okay? I was worried," Mercedes said.

"Aye, I had to go to the airport, and it took longer than I expected to get back to you."

"The airport?"

"I wanted to make sure Kristin got on the damn plane this time." A frown creased his brow. "Charlie told me what she said to you last night. I'm so sorry. She won't bother you again."

Mercedes closed her eyes and a deep tension in her muscles eased. She would rest better knowing she would never have to see them together again.

When she opened them, Alec was studying her face. "How are you feeling?"

"I'm all right. Just incredibly tired."

He hesitated for a beat. Then he kicked off his shoes, pulled back the blanket, and laid down next to her. She frowned at him in surprise as he settled the blanket over them both.

"Alec, what are you doing?"

"Something we both need. Come here." The huskiness in his tone sent a shiver through her. When he drew her against his chest, she didn't resist. It felt so damn good, and she was so starved of his touch. He was right. She needed this, too.

"We'll talk later, darling," Alec murmured. "Get some sleep."

Mercedes sighed and wrapped her arms around his waist. He massaged her back gently, soothing her aching muscles.

Her mind was too exhausted to try and fight this. All she knew was his scent was surrounding her, and his heartbeat thumped steadily against her cheek.

She wouldn't question if it was a wise choice. She would just let him hold her one more time.

CHAPTER THIRTY-FIVE

A gentle knock made Alec jump awake.

"Hey guys," Charlotte called softly from behind the door. "Whitley's here. He wants to talk to Sadie."

Alec checked his watch. He and Mercedes had been sleeping for nearly five hours. They were still turned toward one another, her head nestled against his chest.

"Aye, we'll be out in a minute," Alec called softly, hoping not to be too jarring.

Mercedes was waking up, but she made no move to leave his arms. She seemed to sink further into his embrace. Alec stroked her hair and she sighed.

"Did you sleep well?" she murmured.

"Better than I've slept in a year," Alec said honestly. "You?"

"Same." She drew back and looked up into his eyes. "We should go."

"Aye," Alec whispered.

There was a pause, and neither of them made a move to leave.

Alec leaned down and captured her lips with his. Mercedes inhaled sharply, then opened to him, her fingers running through his hair. The kiss was gentle and slow. He savored her tongue stroking his in a soft rhythm. She moaned and heat washed over his body. Alec deepened the kiss, pressing her back against her pillow. His need for her began to fray his control. She must have been feeling it too, because she curled into him, sliding her leg up his and resting it on his hip. When he finally broke the kiss, her breathing was uneven.

He brushed a lock of hair from her cheek. "We really should go."

Mercedes's gaze swept over his face as if she was trying to memorize him. He was drinking her in as well, soaking up every second was able to hold her. After the terror of last night, he wasn't sure he could let her go.

But he had to. For now.

Reluctantly, he released her as she shifted away from him, the absence of her warmth leaving a chill on his skin. She stood and walked to the door. Alec adjusted himself to mask how hard she'd made him.

Mercedes was still a little unsteady, so Alec held her hand as she climbed down the stairs. Charlotte rose from her seat. "We'll give you a chance to talk."

To Alec's surprise, Noah Ramirez was taking up one of the chairs. He gave Mercedes a concerned smile but said nothing. Brenden Whitley was sitting in the living room, his eyes narrowed at Alec.

Mercedes let go of Alec's hand when they got to the base of the steps, and he leaned against the wall. Even in her disheveled state, she held her chin up and glared at Whitley.

"Ms. Elliott," Whitley said as he stood and greeted her formally. "I'm so sorry to hear what happened to you last night. Are you okay?"

"I'm alive." Mercedes didn't smile or return his greeting. She sat on the sofa; her expression unreadable. "I guess I still need security after all."

Whitley nodded and sat as well. "It would appear that you

do." He gestured to Noah. "As you can see, I've asked the marshals to reinstate Noah Ramirez, at least temporarily, while we sort this out. I know you're partial to him."

"I am," Mercedes agreed. "What else did you come here for?"

"We need to have a conversation about why this happened." Whitley shifted in his chair.

"I already know why," she said, before he could speak. "There's about to be a mistrial, isn't there?"

Alec's pulse leaped. "What do you mean?"

The prosecutor's brow lifted, like she'd announced she'd known a secret the entire time.

"That's why they tried to kill me," Mercedes said to answer Alec's question. "Because they know the case is going to have to be retried, and they saw an opportunity."

The truth of it was on the prosecutor's face. Fear snaked to his fingertips. "What would that mean for Sadie's life now?"

"I have to go back into the program," she said, her voice dull. "That's why he's here. To personally request I go." She looked at Whitley. "Am I right?"

"Unfortunately, yes."

Anger knifed down Alec's back. "What the hell happened?"

Whitley pursed his lips. "They compromised some of the jurors."

Mercedes closed her eyes. "How were they compromised? They were sequestered."

"Some of the more honest jurors said they found messages in their rooms. When we spoke to the others, a few of them were a little squirmy. Obviously, it's Cooper. He wasn't even trying to cover it up."

"I thought you had alternate jurors," Alec said.

Whitley shook his head. "Not enough."

Mercedes's fingers drummed on the armrest. "What are you doing about it?"

"An investigation is ongoing, there's not much else we can do. Just having them approached can screw our case. But if it looks as though jurors may have accepted a bribe, the judge will throw it all out and we'll have to start over."

Dammit. He couldn't lose her again.

Mercedes stared at the wall. "How will it work?"

"We'll have to find new accommodations for you. Obviously, you can't go back to where you were before. I'll let the marshals handle that."

Another year. Another fucking year of not knowing where she was. Another year of giving them a chance to kill her.

"I need to talk to my lawyer." Mercedes stood and sighed. "I'm supposed to be in New York right now, getting ready for a morning meeting with my new boss. We have phone calls to make."

"I've already secured your things and set you up at the safe house," Noah said. "I'll take you there when you're ready."

Mercedes nodded and walked to the stairs.

Alec made to leave with her, but Whitley stopped him. "Mr. McKinley, can I have a word?"

He hesitated and looked at Mercedes.

"I'm okay," she said. "I need to get my things and let Charlotte know I'm leaving." She climbed the stairs, holding tight to the rail.

Once she was out of earshot, Whitley said, "I was surprised to see you here."

"Why would that surprise you?"

"I was under the impression the two of you had a falling out."

Rage singed through Alec. "You have some fucking nerve."

Whitley brushed off Alec's heated words. "Are you back in a relationship with Mercedes?"

"That's not your business."

"It *is* my business, I need to know."

"No, you don't. We don't answer to you."

Whitley sighed. "Jason Hollis's testimony is still going to be key to putting Cooper away. If he finds out that you and Mercedes are back together, he'll stop his cooperation, and we'll lose this case."

Alec laughed. "I don't give a fuck what Jason Hollis wants. At all."

"That's an understandable position, Mr. McKinley, but everything rides on whether he testifies."

Alec shook his head. "You should never have made the deal in the first place. He deserves to rot in prison."

"Mr. McKinley . . ."

"I'm not sure where Sadie and I are at the moment, and I don't plan on giving you updates." Alec stepped toward Whitley, his anger boiling to the surface. "If you think that I'm going to let her go because of this case, you're wrong. And I'll be damned if I let you or Jason fucking Hollis decide what we do."

"I understand why you're angry. I know you don't trust me. But this case is everything. It'll save lives. It's already saving lives. I'll do anything to defeat Marcus Cooper."

"Don't pull that shit with me. We all know why you're doing it." Alec looked at him coldly. "And if our relationship is the only thing keeping you from winning, then your case isn't strong enough to begin with." Alec walked to the door and jerked it open. "Now get the fuck out of my cousin's house."

Whitley looked like he might want to say something else. Instead, he snapped his mouth shut and left. Alec slammed the door behind him.

Fuckwit.

Alec went to follow Mercedes upstairs when he caught sight of Noah Ramirez regarding him thoughtfully.

"I saw the video of the takedown last night. It was impressive," Noah said, pulling himself to his feet.

Alec frowned. It was odd to get a compliment for killing someone. "Thanks? I guess."

Noah came to stand in front of him, his dark eyes studying Alec as if he was measuring him up. "We need to talk."

CHAPTER THIRTY-SIX

Mercedes rubbed the bridge of her nose, desperately wanting to go back to bed.

She and Noah had left Charlotte's when he officially took charge of her security again and had returned to the same duplex they'd stayed in before. She honestly couldn't say how safe it was, because nothing was safe. But at least it was familiar.

The benefits of the nap she'd taken with Alec had long since worn off. Checking her watch, she noted she only had five more minutes before the next video call with New York.

Everything was falling apart. Negotiating an indefinite sabbatical for a job she hadn't even started was proving to be a challenge. There were red flags on Mercedes's end as well. That they couldn't even wait twenty-four hours to talk to her after a murder attempt was enough to make her question whether this job was worth it.

When the video call chimed through her computer, she inhaled deeply and answered it with a sunny smile on her face.

An hour later, Mercedes sat back in her chair, rolling her shoulders. That was the last call of the evening, and she was ready to have a cup of herbal tea and go to bed.

Then she remembered Ezra asking to see her, and she sighed. Noah had left a bit ago. She'd have to wait for him to come back before she could arrange to bring Ezra here.

She walked into the kitchen, grabbed the kettle, and took it to the sink.

"It really is a lovely flat," a voice said behind her.

Mercedes yelped and turned.

Alec was casually leaning against the doorframe of the balcony, watching her with a soft smile. "I didn't notice it the other day. Splendid view."

"What did you do? Climb up the balcony?"

Alec's smile curled up in amusement. "No. Noah let me in."

"I didn't even hear you." That wasn't good. Normally her senses were in overdrive, magnifying everything.

"Aye, you were on a call. And I can be quiet." His eyes trailed up her body. "I'm surprised to see you changed into work clothes. I thought I'd find you sleeping."

Mercedes sighed and went about filling the kettle with water. "Trust me, I want to. But I had to try and salvage what I could from the people in New York."

Alec came toward her, and her breath stopped in her chest. "You should set some boundaries. Otherwise, they'll keep taking your time from you."

"It's hard to set boundaries when I have zero control of my life." She sent Alec a tight smile. "What are you doing here?"

The amusement on his face fell away. "We have a problem, darling."

She scoffed. "Just one?"

Alec grimaced. "One that's quite immediate."

Mercedes knew that tone. She shut the water off and stared at him. "What's happening?"

"You were compromised by one of Noah's men."

Cold tendrils of fear poured down her spine. "What?"

"Aye. He's being questioned as we speak."

"What did he give away?"

"So far, I know he gave them the location of the party and your plans to live with Ezra in New York. There may be more."

Jesus, she'd unknowingly put Ezra at risk, just by making plans with him. The number of ways this could have gone down was staggering.

Fear piped through her body. "Am I safe right now?"

"Aye. I won't let anything happen to you," Alec said in a soothing tone. "And Dec and Mason are . . . nearby. But you won't be staying here much longer."

A knock came at the door, and Alec answered it. Noah was with him when he returned.

"I'm sorry Sadie. Things are moving quickly, and I didn't have time to explain." Noah crossed his arms in front of him. "Danny, the agent that's been working with me since we arrived, gave information about you to an outside person. He's in custody now and we'll be transporting him soon."

"Danny?"

Jesus, he'd been the one to stay in the safe house with her the few times Noah left her side. He'd always been so sweet to her. "How did you figure it out?"

"We found some evidence that could only come from the inside. Since I didn't have a lot of time, I asked Alec to have his team check on the three agents under me. Things that would take me a little more time to do properly. They uncovered quite a few red flags, and it wasn't hard to narrow it down."

Mercedes frowned. "Well, the party wasn't exactly a secret. What did he have that led you to believe it was an insider?"

Noah's brow creased. "We found an envelope in the bartender's car. It had a key to a hotel in Pacific Heights, with Holly Castillo, Room 405 written on the front."

Mercedes barely made it to the chair at the table. Her knees gave, and she collapsed onto it.

Alec's eyes narrowed in alarm. "Who's Holly Castillo?"

Mercedes winced. "I am."

"Shit." Alec turned to Noah. "Is he still in the flat downstairs?"

Noah nodded. "My people are on their way. You can ask your questions until they get here. After that, no more."

Alec strode to the door and jerked it open. He was down the stairs at a quick pace and into the downstairs unit.

Mercedes and Noah followed, her legs unsteady on the steps.

When they entered the apartment, Danny was sitting at the kitchen table, his hands cuffed in front of him. To her surprise, Declan and Mason were already there. She had arrived mid-interrogation.

Danny looked like he needed new pants. He clearly understood he was in deep shit, and there was no way out but to cooperate. When he caught sight of Alec striding toward him, his eyes widened, and he gulped in air. Mercedes could understand why. Alec appeared calm, but a deadly violence radiated beneath the surface.

"Do you know who I am?" Alec growled as he sat in front of Danny. The agent nodded. "Good, then you know what I did to your new friend last night." The warning was clear in Alec's voice.

"He wasn't my friend." Danny shifted between Alec and Noah. "I had never seen him before."

"Then who was your contact? What did he look like?"

Danny trembled as he answered. "She . . . it was a woman."

Alec's tilted his head. "A woman? Not a big bloke with black hair and blue eyes. You never saw that guy anywhere?"

"No, just her."

"How did she make contact with you?"

He shifted in his chair. "At a bar downtown. She offered to play a game of pool." He looked up at Noah, his face flaming. "I ended up at her place. And we . . ." He bobbed his head to make his implication clear.

Mercedes made a sound of disgust. "Didn't you tell me your wife just had a baby?"

Danny's eyes widened, and he turned to Mercedes. "I didn't know you were here. I'm so sorry, Ms. Elliott. I didn't want—"

Alec slammed his hand on the table and Danny jumped. "What happened next?"

"The next day, I . . . received a text message," Danny stammered, his gaze dropping to his lap. "It was a video of our night. The message said if I cooperated, they'd give me the only copy and a hundred thousand dollars. If I didn't, they'd send it to my wife."

"A hundred thousand dollars and a sex tape?" Mercedes broke in. Tightness in her throat made her words strained. "That's all my life was worth? A hundred thousand dollars and a sex tape?"

"I swear I didn't know what she was planning."

"Bullshit!" Alec shouted, the anger radiating off him was terrifying.

Danny winced at Alec's words and kept his gaze on the table.

Alec sat forward. "Do they know where she is now?"

"No, I swear. They think she's at the hotel in Pacific Heights."

"You mean, in the room you gave them the key to, you stupid little fuck?" Alec raged. "If we hadn't changed where she was going to be, she'd have been there this morning. And she would have been completely alone."

Danny looked at Mercedes. "I swear, I just thought they—"

"Don't fucking look at her. Look at me." Alec's fists were

clenched. Danny's eyes jumped back to Alec. "What did this woman look like?"

"White, blonde hair, brown eyes, tall, long legs about thirty or thirty-five years old."

Alec stopped short. "Does she have any distinguishing marks?"

Mercedes frowned. He said it like he knew she would.

"Yeah. She had a big red birthmark under her collarbone."

"Fuck." Alec looked to Declan. Something passed silently between them.

"Mason and I will stay with this. You go," Declan said.

Alec took Mercedes's hand. "Come on, we need to talk."

He was taking deep, deliberate breaths as he led her upstairs, softening away the violence in his posture. Once they were in her room, he pulled his phone from his pocket and made a call.

"Artemis. Mariah's in play," he said when Cressida answered.

Oh, that bitch is back.

He paused, his blue stare piercing into Mercedes as he talked. "I'm working on it. We'll keep you updated."

When he hung up, he said, "When are you supposed to leave?"

"Leave?"

"To your next location. They haven't shared that with me." He looked at the carpet, and she knew he was uneasy with being out of the loop. "You're not still trying to go to New York, are you?"

Mercedes gave a rueful laugh. "The New York deal fell through when my soon-to-be employers found out I'd have to go back into WITSEC for another twelve to eighteen months. It turns out being hunted by a billionaire doesn't read well on a résumé."

"I'm sorry, Sadie."

"It's all part of the game. Right?" She gave Alec a shaky smile. "It sounds like I should pack."

Mercedes went to the bedroom and opened her suitcase.

Alec leaned against the doorframe. "It's not a game, is it?"

"It is for them."

"You didn't say when you're supposed to leave."

"I don't know. As soon as I get word from Noah's bosses."

This was an unexpected moment. After everything that had happened, she thought she wouldn't have a chance to say goodbye to him.

"Thank you for everything you've done for me. I know this week's been hard on us both, and I appreciate what you did, all of it." It seemed ridiculously understated after the events of last night, but she wasn't sure if there was a good way to thank your savior that didn't sound underwhelming.

He didn't respond and she hoped he didn't think she was being disingenuous. But he only offered her a soft smile and a nod. Maybe there was no easy way to accept such a statement of gratitude.

She turned back to her packing. "Can I ask you for a favor?"

"You can ask me for anything."

The tenderness in his tone made her falter. This goodbye was getting harder and harder.

"Would you check in on Charlie for me? Just a phone call here and there, especially when the baby gets close." Mercedes's voice broke, and she turned back to her packing to cover up the hurt swirling in her. It was so damn unfair. Marcus Cooper was a free man, doing whatever the hell he wanted, and she was being taken away from everyone she loved again.

"Aye, I can do that."

"Thanks." She could feel his gaze on her as she folded a shirt to put in her bag.

"Mercedes." The warmth in his voice sent a shiver down her spine. Alec never used her whole name. "Come with me."

She paused, taking in his words. He couldn't be asking what she thought he was asking. A steady beat drummed in her ears. "What do you mean?"

His blue eyes held a storm in them. A storm she wanted to get lost in. "Go dark with me."

It was a simple statement that had an entire world of implications to it.

"With you?"

"Aye."

"I can't go with you."

"Why not?"

Mercedes's fingers trembled as she went back to packing her clothes. "Well, you have a business to run and a life to live."

His next words stopped her heart.

"I have this fear—that if you go with them—" Alec was struggling to speak. "You'll be dead in weeks."

The wall he was so good at building had fallen, hollowing out his expression with vulnerability. She wanted to wrap herself into him and make it go away. But she couldn't let him give up his life for her.

"I know. That's always been a risk."

"It's not just a risk to me, Sadie." The quiver in Alec's words sliced into her soul. "It's been my reality for a year."

Mercedes inhaled sharply. The pain radiating from him seeped into her bones, stealing her ability to think straight.

"Besides, it's a greater risk to go with them."

Mercedes swallowed. "Why is that?"

"Because I can't be bought."

She shuddered at his words, knowing it was true. Despite their fractured relationship, there was nothing Alec would take in place of her life. Even in their lowest moments, she could search for him and find safety.

"I have a solid plan in place. All you have to do is finish packing and get in the car."

Some part of her wanted to go, but the other wanted to save him from the wasteland of hiding. "I can't leave with you."

"You've done it before."

"That was different. We thought it was going to be for a week or two while I recovered. Who knows how long this will be."

Alec was nearly to her now. "If I hadn't been injured in London, would you have gone with me then?"

"Yes." She would have walked off the end of the earth with him.

He tilted his head. "Why not now?"

"Because, how I feel about you is much more complicated."

A sad smile played on his lips. "Nah, your feelings are the same. It's the situation that's changed."

He wasn't wrong. Her feelings for him were as strong as ever. But she couldn't get past how hard losing him had hit her. Sometimes she still reeled from the fall.

Alec took her hand into his, the warmth in his palm soothing hers. "After we leave here, I won't touch you unless you ask me to. I need you to be safe, and if I have to keep my bloody hands to myself to do it, I will." He brought her hand up to his lips and kissed it. The simple gesture made her ache. "I'll let you think about it. Finish packing and I'll speak with Noah. Let me know what you decide when I get back."

He was out the door before she could say anything else.

As if in a fog, Mercedes placed her makeup bag into her suitcase and zipped it up.

What on earth was she going to do?

If she stayed with the feds, there was no telling how many people Cooper could turn on her. It had been ridiculously easy to turn the young agent. Not only that, but Whitley was the catalyst for the shitstorm she was in. Their lies had shattered her and Alec both. Why would she ever trust them again?

Alec was always the safer bet.

With her life. Her heart was an entirely different matter.

When he returned, his brow was raised as if he was waiting for her response.

She took a cleansing breath. "I'll go with you, but I have a few conditions."

Hope filled Alec's expression, but his tone was calm. "Alright."

"First, no pretending that we're a couple. I can't do the kissing and the touching, and all of that. I . . . just no."

There was a touch of reluctance in Alec's eyes, but he nodded. "Aye, we won't be a couple."

Mercedes gave a curt nod. "And I want my own bed in my own bedroom. We aren't going to share again either."

"That's already done."

"Oh, you need to have your own bed and bedroom, too. None of this sleeping on the floor crap."

Alec chuckled. "Aye. I have my own room."

"And I'm gonna hold you to that no kissing or touching thing."

Alec narrowed his eyes. "I believe what I said was, once we leave here, I won't touch you unless you ask me to."

"Right." Mercedes nodded, proud that she had established a firm set of lines.

"Since I just agreed to that last one, I have a condition of my own," Alec said, the huskiness in his tone making her cheeks flush. "Well, more of a request, actually. You're free to say no."

Mercedes lifted her brow.

Alec's gaze darkened, turning positively sinful "May I kiss you now?"

The very center of her body clenched.

Tell him no.

But her brain short-circuited, and she nodded.

Alec crossed the room, his mouth crashing into hers before she could rethink it. If she'd thought he might offer up a soft, chaste kiss, she was very fucking wrong.

Alec toyed with her, stroked her, reminded her.

He tangled his fingers in her hair, angling her chin to fit her against his mouth.

And damn it, she was answering him. She should push him away, tell him this was too much. But she couldn't. Instead, she was drawn into him, letting him play with her until he'd pulled every ounce of need up to the surface.

He felt too damn good.

Alec ended the kiss with a tender bite on her lip and Mercedes lost track of the world. Every sensation was him.

She opened her eyes to find him gazing down at her. "You're not going to make this easy on me, are you?"

The corner of his mouth curled up. "No."

Then he kissed the tip of her nose and stepped away. While she was still figuring out what the hell had just happened, he left the room with her suitcase.

She was in so much goddamn trouble.

PART III

CHAPTER THIRTY-SEVEN

Alec held the steering wheel tight, relief coursing through his veins. Mercedes was beside him. Tendrils of her dark hair swirled around her head as the ocean air blew into the open windows.

This was all too familiar. The two of them, traveling down a quiet highway to find a place of refuge. Mercedes quietly strumming her fingers in her lap. Their relationship in tatters.

None of that mattered. After all she'd been through, she still trusted him. It was more than he could ask for.

The radio softened the silence between them. Alec cast a quick glance at Mercedes and his breath caught. The sun was waning in the sky, casting an orange glow across her face.

She was stunning. And she was here, and alive. Considering all that happened the night before, Alec was surprised she was still awake.

"How far until we get to the house?" Mercedes asked.

"About a half an hour."

Her brows went up. "That's closer to the city than the last time."

Alec gave her a nod. "We wanted to have it closer in case we needed to get back quickly."

"Why would we need to get back quickly?"

"For Charlotte. I wanted to make sure you weren't too far away if she needed you."

Mercedes's brows went up. "I'll be able to talk to Charlie?"

"Aye. It's risky, so we can't do it a lot. But we can make it work so you don't have to be cut off. Cressida and I will set up a secure line."

"Can you get me one with Ezra? Tonight?"

Jealousy pulled at Alec's consciousness, and he tightened his grip on the wheel. But the last thing he would ever do was limit Mercedes unnecessarily. She'd spent years trapped by outside forces. He'd be damned if he would become one.

Alec choked on the bitter words. "I might be able to manage. I'll talk to Cressida."

Mercedes nodded in acknowledgment. She settled back into her seat, her face weary from the traumas of the day. When she finally dozed off, her brow was creased with worry.

Damn those meetings she'd had. She should have been allowed to sleep the entire day.

Mercedes jumped awake when the car turned off the highway into a quaint fishing town. The sun dipped below the surface of the water, but it was light enough to see the string of boats tied to the docks.

When Alec pulled into the house, he gave a little smile. He'd asked Cressida to make it as secluded and lovely as possible. She'd certainly delivered. It was tucked away, elevated over the small bay on a sea cliff.

He punched in the code and opened the door for her. The soft creams and yellows of the walls were contrasted with a nautical blue on the pillows and curtains. But it was the wide, white-framed windows that caught the eyes. Filtered through lush pine trees was the darkened expanse of the Pacific Ocean, just visible in the fading light. Mercedes walked to the door and opened it. A steady breeze swirled through the room, and she walked out onto the deck. Alec followed her, taking in the evening air. The light from a small pool and hot tub illuminated the backyard.

"Where does Cress find these places?" Mercedes asked. "And how much are you paying for it?"

Alec furrowed his brow and shrugged. "No bloody clue."

She scoffed. "So you gave Cressida the company card and let her do what she wanted."

"Nah," Alec said, giving her a teasing sideways look. "I gave her my personal card. Well, it's under my alias, but I pay for it."

Mercedes bit back a smile. "I expect to see an invoice."

"An invoice?"

"You think I'm going to let you pay for this?" She gestured out into the night. "I still owe you for Scotland."

Memories of what they'd meant to each other at the river house slammed into him, and he swallowed hard. "You don't owe me anything for Scotland."

Mercedes's eyes jumped to his. The gravity between them arced like electricity. He fought back the urge to reach for her. That deal he'd made was already proving to be tough but he intended to keep it. She had to know there was at least one person in the world that kept their word.

She crossed her arms over her chest and walked back into the house. Alec inhaled the night air before he followed her inside. A baby grand piano was tucked into the corner. She eyed it, but she made no move to touch it.

Alec went to the car and brought in the bags. When he set hers in the master bedroom, he said, "See, just like I promised you, your own bed, in your own room."

Mercedes smiled and nodded. She was twisting her fingers together anxiously. He didn't blame her. His nerves were bubbling to the surface as well. It had been such a long time since they'd been alone like this, and so much had broken them apart.

She checked her watch. "When do you think I might get a

line to talk to Ezra?" Her fingers twitched against her thigh. "I was supposed to see him tonight."

It was like a kick in the gut. Last night, she'd never answered him when he asked if she and Ezra had gotten back together. The two of them had spent evenings alone and those nights had kept Alec from sleeping. The idea of Ezra putting his hands on her made him sick. It taunted him, forcing him into the realization that he might lose Mercedes forever.

Alec cleared his throat. "I'll start working on it straight away."

He went to his room to set up his equipment and secure the network. Then he texted Cressida, hoping she'd tell him she couldn't get the line sorted. Their communications were secure with each other, but Ezra's line could be compromised.

Alec's phone vibrated.

No problem. Will have him reach out ASAP.

Damn it.

Cressida was faster than he thought. It was only a few minutes later that she sent another message.

Incoming, 1 min. Someone is UNHAPPY!

Oh fucking well. Alec wasn't going to cater to Ezra's demands or desires.

He went to the living room, where Mercedes curled up on the sofa, staring out at the night. Even in her exhaustion, she was so bloody beautiful.

"Cressida was able to secure a line for Ezra. He should call in just a few."

Her soft, "Thanks," concerned him.

There was a listlessness in her that made him want to draw her into his arms and make it all better. "Are you okay?"

Mercedes's shoulder lifted, her expression remaining unchanged. "It's been a long day."

It had been, and she should be snuggling down into her bed rather than stroking Ezra's ego. The phone in his hand cut off this thought, and Alec answered it on the first ring. "This is Alec."

"Where the fuck have you taken her?" Ezra's snapped.

Irritation swelled in his chest. "Clearly, I'm not able to tell you that."

"You really orchestrated this to work in your favor, didn't you?"

Alec inhaled deeply before he answered. "I didn't orchestrate anything that wasn't necessary to keep her safe."

"I could have kept her safe, too. You should have let her choose."

"I did. Here's Sadie." He handed the phone to her.

Mercedes stood and headed to the door. "Hey Ez," she said softly. "I know, I know. I'm sorry." She opened the door and went out onto the deck. The breeze through the open window carried her voice inside. Alec couldn't help overhearing a few of her words.

"No, I'm not back together with him. But I had to leave."

Jesus, she was ripping his fucking heart out, and she wasn't even talking to him. Alec stepped away so he couldn't hear her words. If he listened any longer, he might get confirmation that he'd lost her for good.

Mercedes paced on the deck for over ten minutes with the phone to her ear. Alec's nerves were shot, wondering what she and Ezra might be planning together. Maybe Ezra was working on her, convincing her she wasn't any safer with Alec than she would be with him. That was ridiculous, of course. Ezra was highly visible and called attention to himself wherever he went.

When she finally returned inside the house, her eyes were rimmed with red.

Goddamn Ezra for making this harder on her.

"Are you alright?" Alec said, taking the phone from her.

Mercedes shrugged and shook her head. "Tough night."

"Want me to kick his arse for you?"

She chuckled. "No, I'm the asshole today."

"Ah," Alec said, not sure what she meant.

"Ezra's not taking it very well. He's a little frustrated. I don't blame him."

"I'm sorry he feels that way."

Mercedes's gaze jumped to his, gauging whether he was serious. "Are you?"

Meh. But Alec schooled his reaction for her sake. "I've no reason to annoy the bloke."

Mercedes gave a rueful laugh. "Well, he was still hoping for New York. And then I just up and left with my ex so I'd say he's a little more than annoyed."

"Would you rather be with him?" he asked softly.

Her expression shifted and the wall she'd mastered went back up. "Doesn't matter what I want."

"It matters to me."

Mercedes's lips turned up into a smile but she didn't respond to his words. "It's been a long day, Alec. I need sleep. Good night."

"'Night, Sadie."

As she walked away, their fight in the storeroom came to his mind. Just before he kissed her, Mercedes had thrown Ezra in his face. That single dagger she'd launched at him was sticking in his heart. He could imagine a thousand ways Ezra might have touched her.

Every caress she'd given Ezra was one more painful step she'd taken away from him. For the first time, Alec wondered if she'd fallen out of love with him.

CHAPTER THIRTY-EIGHT

The next morning, Mercedes woke to the smell of freshly brewed coffee and knew things were different. Noah didn't drink coffee, so she was the one who made it in the morning.

The divine scent and the unfamiliar bedroom reminded her she wasn't with Noah anymore.

Shit.

She was with Alec. How in the hell was she going to get through this? She could stay in her room all day. If she did, she wouldn't have to speak to him.

But the coffee was too big a draw.

It was quiet in the house as she stepped from her room. The view from the living room in daylight was breathtaking. The Pacific stretched out beyond the tall pine trees. A soft breeze filtered through the air.

Alec wasn't in the kitchen, so she poured herself a cup and added her cream. Outside, a splash of water caught her attention, and she carried her coffee out onto the deck. Her gaze followed the gentle swish of water and instantly her core clenched.

Holy hell.

Alec was swimming.

How could someone look so damn good? He moved gracefully, the strength of his arms gliding him through the water.

Sipping her coffee, she walked down to the pool. She sat on the edge, her feet cooled by the water.

Alec's eyes caught hers and he swam to her. When he rose up, he rubbed his hand through his thick hair. Water cascaded down his chest, following along his muscles. Even with the bruises and cuts, he was stunning.

He grasped the edge of the pool on either side of her, drops rolling from his body onto her knees.

"You should come in, it's lovely."

That would be a mistake. "I would, but I don't have a suit."

Alec's lips turned up mischievously. "You don't need one, darling. It's nothing I've not seen before."

Jesus, he needed to stop looking at her like that.

Mercedes tilted her head, holding in a smile. "Are you flirting with me, Alec?"

"Shamelessly," he said with a grin.

A flutter of butterflies took hold in her stomach, shooting right down into her core. She should tell him to stop. This was hard enough without having to combat his charm.

But damn if she didn't love this side of him. Playful, sweet, and even a little goofy. He could make her forget how hard everything had collapsed around them.

Alec swam to the stairs and pulled himself out. Mercedes shivered and had to look at the water while he toweled himself off.

"I have a little work to do. Then I was thinking we might go into town and pick up a few things. Do you feel up to that?"

Mercedes nodded. "I'll take a little rest in the shade while you work. It's so nice out."

"Aye, it is." Rivulets of water coursed down his neck and

onto his perfect collarbone. The temptation to lick it off him was way too damn strong. Mercedes gulped her coffee, praying her raging libido would knock it off.

". . . try to sleep some more," Alec was saying. "I'll be a couple of hours."

"Oh, mm-hmm." A flush was creeping up her cheeks. She had no idea what he was talking about. Hopefully, he hadn't asked her to do anything important.

Jesus, Sadie. Get it together.

Alec flashed her a brilliant smile before he headed back into the house. Mercedes watched him walk away, the back side looking just as good as the front.

She sighed and flopped onto one of the shaded lounge chairs. Alec was dangerous in more ways than one. If she was going to get through this, she was going to have to do a better job of knocking down her feelings for this man.

AFTER ALEC FINISHED UP HIS WORK FOR THE DAY, THEY DROVE to the little beachside village. Mercedes found a couple of adorable bathing suits and a pullover for the pool.

Their last stop was at a little grocer. Mercedes picked out all she needed to make chicken with a creamy white wine sauce. When she added it to Alec's basket, he stared at it for a moment. Then said, "You know that chicken's raw, right?"

Mercedes scoffed. "Yes, I'm going to make the only chicken dish I'm comfortable making. Noah thought it was delicious."

"Did you kill all of Noah's taste buds when you poisoned him, or just a few?"

She adored that sparkle in his eyes. "Bite your tongue, McKinley," Mercedes shot back. "I'll have you know I've had lots of time on my hands, so I took quite a few culinary lessons."

Alec chuckled. "You? Learned to cook?"

"I did. Only a few of the lessons stuck, though." She took a second bottle of white wine off the shelf and put it in the basket, this one a higher quality.

Alec's gaze was on her.

"What?" she asked.

"Nothing, it's just . . ." Alec's words were suddenly rough. "You haven't called me 'McKinley' in a while." The storm in his eyes told her more than his words. "I rather missed it."

The weight of his pain hit her square in the chest. Thinking he'd never hear her voice or see her face again must have been agonizing.

They returned to the house and put away their groceries. While Mercedes prepped dinner, Alec perched on a barstool, watching with an amused smile on his lips. She wondered if he was watching her to make sure she cooked the chicken properly, or if he just wanted to watch her. Perhaps it was a little of both.

Thankfully, she'd done a great job and Alec was forced to admit he was pleasantly surprised.

Mercedes picked up her wineglass. "Don't seem so shocked. I told you I took classes."

Alec grinned. "Aye, but I was worried about how well they worked." His teasing expression softened. "It was delicious. Thank you."

Mercedes's cheeks warmed under his appreciative gaze.

He stood and picked up both their plates. Mercedes made to clear the table with him, but he shooed her away. "Dinner dishes are mine. You sit down and enjoy your wine."

Mercedes took up the spot on the barstool and watched him clean up the kitchen. It wasn't just the way he moved that held her attention, it was that he was comfortable like this.

This was it. This was part of the life they'd lost.

A simple act of eating a meal and cleaning up was just so normal. And they'd never been allowed normal.

Later that evening, they walked to the beach. A set of stairs led them down the small sea cliff.

As they walked, Mercedes had a hard time remembering not to reach for Alec's hand. It was so easy to forget he didn't belong to her.

Alec was quiet, and he seemed to take it all in. One of the many things she loved about him was this ability to be in silence, not feeling the need to talk unnecessarily.

"Do you mind if we sit for a minute?" Mercedes asked, wanting to take in the ocean breeze on her face.

She wrapped her arms around her knees, breathed in the briny air tinged with the scent of seaweed and fish.

Alec broke the silence between them. "Who were you?"

Mercedes didn't have to ask what he meant. If the roles were reversed, she would want to know where he'd been. And now that she had declined to go back into WITSEC, she didn't see a reason to keep it from him.

"My name was Holly, but you knew that. I had blonde hair, and I drove a sedan. After I had healed from my injury, I volunteered part time at the library. Noah was my husband, Mateo. He worked from home as a 'financial adviser'. We went to community picnics and church every Sunday."

"You went to church?" Alec had a wide grin on his face.

Mercedes laughed. "Yeah, my first time was interesting. I thought they would all figure out real quick that I'd never attended services in my life. They were all really sweet though."

"Doesn't sound so bad."

Her smile faded. "It was exhausting, actually. And lonely." Mercedes found the hem of her sundress and tapped out the waves in her mind. "And I . . . I missed you terribly. I was afraid I was starting to forget you."

Alec winced and looked down at the sand.

"Not forgetting how I felt about you," she said, hoping to reassure him. "But the exact color of your eyes, your hair or the way your scent would linger on me. Sometimes, I thought you were slipping away." Mercedes looked away. She was confessing too much but couldn't stop. "Except for your voice. The way my weird brain works would never allow me to forget your voice. The exact way you rolled your Rs. How you said my name. I can't ever forget it."

Alec's brow was furrowed. She was exposing him to a pain she hadn't meant to give him.

Damn it.

"We should head back to the house."

They made their way up the stairs in silence. Mercedes reflected on all Alec had endured while she went to cooking classes and church potlucks.

Once they were back in the house, Alec poured the last of the wine into their glasses. "Are you disappointed about the job?"

Mercedes shrugged. "A little. I was more excited about the lobbying work, which might still be around when this is over. But the harder part was the whiplash that occurred over the last week. I went from thinking I was moving to London with you, to living in New York with Ezra, who I'm now talking to again. Didn't see that coming. Now, I'm here with you. It's been a bit weird."

Alec's smile faded, and he set his glass down. "Are you disappointed you're not with Ezra?"

Mercedes froze, her pulse thundering at the hurt in his tone. She didn't know how to answer him.

In a way, being in New York with Ezra would be easier. At least with Ezra, she was in control.

Alec was an entirely different story.

But if she had to choose, she knew where her heart lay.

"Damn." Alec must have sensed her thoughts, and he rasped out. "You don't have to ans—"

"No," Mercedes cut him off. "I'd rather be here with you."

Alec exhaled deeply, bracing his hands on the kitchen counter. "I was never a jealous man until I met you, but sometimes it feels like I'm losing my mind." Then he turned back to her. "When you left with him the other night, I thought I might go mad." When she opened her mouth to speak, he cut her off. "I don't know what happened between you and Ezra, and I'm not sure I want to know. I have all sorts of horrific images in my head, and they haunt me, until I can't sleep or think straight."

Mercedes twisted the towel in her hand.

"But I was thinking, if you had a sliver of the same feelings about me and Kristin, then I should tell you about us."

Oh, hell no.

The images of Alec and Kristin in bed took hold again, and she wanted no part in this particular conversation.

Mercedes shook her head. "Alec . . . You don't need to . . ."

"I never slept with her."

Her eyes went wide, and her mouth dropped. "What?"

"I never slept with her," Alec repeated. Mercedes's heart was in her throat. "That's why she didn't know about my scars." He shrugged. "She never saw them."

Disbelief must have been all over her face, because he added, "Even on this trip, Kristin had her own room, but I was sleeping on your sister's couch."

"Why?" was all she could manage.

"She wanted more, but I couldn't give it to her." Alec's brows were creased together. The wall he kept up had crumbled. "Turns out, you're not that easy to get over."

Relief spilled into her veins. All the mental images she'd wept over were nothing more than ugly thoughts and not reality. He hadn't let another love him while she cried alone.

"Alec . . ." She stepped toward him.

He ran his hands through his hair. "Anyway, I figured, if that bothered you, I would put your mind at ease."

Before she could think it through, she crossed the kitchen, jerked him to her by his waistband, and kissed him.

Alec's surprise intake of air turned to a moan as he wrapped his arms around her, clutching her dress in his hands. He cupped her chin, tilting her mouth against his.

Desire tore through her, creating a throb between her thighs. She wanted that sweet release only he could give her.

"I need you," she murmured into his mouth. "Come to my bed tonight?"

"Just tonight?" Alec drew away, his eyes heavy with longing. "Like Scotland?"

That first night they'd made love was magic, everything she needed tonight to be. "Yes."

Regret crossed his face, and he shook his head. "That's not going to be enough this time."

"What?"

"Sadie, I've been burned pretty hard too, and I have my own heart to protect. If I have you tonight, I won't be able to let you go in the morning."

Her breath caught. "What if this is all I have to give?"

"You have so much more to give." Alec kissed her again, his lips teasing hers. Then he ended it and he brushed her hair from her face.

"I want it all back. All of it. The future we'd planned and the life we were supposed to have. If you need time, I'll give you all you need. But tomorrow, I'm not going to pretend I don't love you." Alec stepped back, reluctance on his face. "'Night, Sadie." He turned and walked toward his room.

"Alec," Mercedes called, the ache in her throat growing more painful.

He stopped and met her gaze, the vulnerability in his expression cutting her deep.

"I didn't sleep with Ezra. He came to my room. We talked, and we kissed," she said. Alec's eyes darted to the ground as he took this in. "But I've slept alone since Scotland. You aren't that easy to get over either."

Alec's defenses were down, and the rawness of his pain reverberated off him. He gave her a tight nod to acknowledge what she said. Then he left, the ache he'd seared in her growing with the sound of his footsteps down the hall.

CHAPTER THIRTY-NINE

It had been two days since he'd walked away from her, and Mercedes was still reeling from what he'd said.

Alec still openly flirted with her. At times, she'd catch his sizzling gaze and her face would flush. He wasn't trying to hide how he felt.

But he also didn't touch her. Other than a few brushes of fingertips when he'd hand her something, he'd kept his word. He was giving her space to work things out for herself, but it was hard to look at his perfect body and not hunger for him.

They fell into a routine. Alec would swim every morning and Mercedes would lounge in the sunlight peeking over her book, her eyes hidden behind sunglasses. Then he'd go to his room to work from his secure line.

The quiet that would fall over the house when he was gone gave her time to think. Too much time.

She was in a holding pattern, trapped with the one man she wanted to spend her life with, but was too scared to. And even after all he'd suffered, he loved her. He still hoped for another chance.

I want it all back. All of it . . . Tomorrow, I'm not going to pretend I don't love you.

Mercedes loved him too, there was no doubt about that. When she looked at Alec she could see the future they were supposed to have, too. She craved it so much she ached.

All she had to do was ask.

But whenever she thought about giving in and letting herself fall, the heartbreak of losing him would slam into her, reminding her why she'd ended it.

That evening, they strolled along the beach. The sun was inches above the horizon, beginning its gentle descent into the water. Alec shoved his hands in his pockets, his thick hair tousled by the breeze. The lovely tan he was getting in the California sun was only adding a stunning warmth to his features.

Like most nights, they sat near each other on the sand and took in the beauty of the ocean waves. But tonight her mind was especially heavy. Her past was haunting her, and she didn't know how to make it stop.

"Can I ask you something, Alec?"

"Of course."

She didn't look at him, staring straight out into the water. "Did my mother come to my funeral?"

From the corner of her eye, she saw him wince. "No, darling. She didn't."

Mercedes's stomach knotted, and she inhaled deeply. "I didn't think she had, but I wondered."

"What made you think of her?"

Mercedes shrugged. "I've thought about her a lot lately." The tips of her fingers delicately played out the waves of the ocean. "About her choices. The things she did."

Alec was quiet, as if giving her time to gather her thoughts.

Mercedes's mother had been eighteen when she fell for an older wealthy man, who happened to be married. When he found out his barely legal mistress was pregnant, he cast her aside without a penny.

"She made sure I knew every single day how much she despised me. Until I was old enough to take care of Charlie. Then she could go get wasted and bring home random men."

"None of that was you. You didn't make her a terrible person."

"I know." She was quiet for another minute. When she broke the silence again, it was with another question.

"Do you want children?" When Alec's brows shot up, she added, "It's not a loaded question, I swear. I want your honest answer."

"Honestly, I don't know. Most of my life, I didn't think I'd find anyone I'd want to have children with. Now that I have, I'm perfectly content going either way." He studied her face as if trying to read her thoughts. "If you had wanted them, I'd happily have obliged. If you didn't, then I'd be the best damn Uncle Lick to my niece I could be."

A smile broke across Mercedes's face. "Uncle Lick?"

Alec smirked. "Aye. Isla's a wee little shit."

Mercedes giggled. "That's adorable."

"Aye, I think it's going to stick." Alec chuckled along with Mercedes. When their smiles faded, he gave her a sideways look. "What's bringing all this on?"

Mercedes shrugged and bit her lip. She didn't want to confess the mess that was swirling in her mind. But she'd asked Alec for honesty, she should be honest with him.

"Actually, it was something Kristin said to me."

Alec exhaled sharply. "Shit, Sadie. I'm sorry for anything she might have said. She was jealous and looking for a way to hold on to what she thought we had."

Mercedes gave a reassuring smile. "I know, Alec. I have thick skin and her intentions were clear. But there was one thing she said that stayed with me." Mercedes bit her lip, ready to bare it all for him, just so he could understand why she was so afraid. "She said you loved children, and she was ready to give you the family I was too selfish to give you."

"Fuck," he muttered, the muscle of his jaw working overtime. "We never discussed having kids or anything of the sort. Hell, we hadn't discussed much past the trial."

Another rush of relief worked its way through her. She was so grateful he'd confessed he'd never shared a bed with Kristin. It was becoming clear, they were never as serious as she'd feared. Unchecked, her nightmares could have them planning their wedding and picking out baby names.

"The thing is, I always loved the idea of being a mother." She looked down at her hands twisting against her knees. "But I'm terrified of ending up like mine. Bitter and resentful, hating the idea that my child came into my world and changed it."

"Sadie, you're nothing like your mother. And besides, you've already raised a child. I know for a fact you would move heaven and earth for her." Mercedes turned to him in surprise. "Your mother certainly didn't help Charlie become who she is today."

Mercedes nodded. "I'm so proud of her."

"I know you are."

"I'm on the outskirts now, though. One of these days, I'll get to be the fun auntie to little Mercedes Clare. I'll always carry candy in my purse and teach her to play any instrument she wants." The smile fled from her face. "But that little family is Charlie's. I don't have the same place in it." Mercedes nodded and looked back to the water. "I guess I've just been thinking about family a lot. I don't have much of one."

"I'd be your family, if you'd let me."

His words hit her directly in her heart and she exhaled sharply. Alec's eyes were darkened by the waning sun, but there was a pleading in his expression. He meant every word.

After all the time they'd been apart, he'd wanted to make her his, to love her until she realized he belonged to her.

Her mouth snapped shut, and she looked to the crashing

waves. Tears formed behind her eyes, and she bit her lip to keep it from trembling.

She cleared her throat. "We should go back. The light is nearly gone."

Alec's brow was furrowed but he got up and held out his hand to help her up. As they returned to the house, Mercedes's mind was spiraling.

Her heart had been broken and mended so many times that only a thin tape held it together. With Alec's words, she'd come undone. The shield she'd been using to keep him away was nearly gone, and she didn't know what to do.

The warmth of the house contrasted with the cool night air. She shrugged her sweater off and hung it on the hook by the door.

The piano caught her attention, and she walked to it. For the first time in forever, the fine ivory and ebony keys called to her. She sat on the bench, her pulse quickening. Tentatively, she put her fingers on the keys, and played 'Nuvole Bianche'. Its opening was slow and steady, easing her into playing again.

When the gentle song was over, Mercedes moved right into the next and before she knew it, she was lost in it. For the first time in a year, she could see herself, all that she was.

Alec sat on the bench next to her, his back to the piano. He leaned forward, elbows on knees, occasionally taking a sip from his glass of whisky.

When she'd finished the last song, she let the quiet fill the space between them.

"That was lovely. I was wondering when you might play. I was getting a little worried about it to be honest."

Mercedes nodded, fighting back the tears again. "I just needed to sort out a few things."

"Aye." His tone was one of understanding, but she knew he was concerned about her.

The broken pieces of her belonged to him. Only he knew

how to repair the damage that had devastated her. She had to let him in.

"Alec." She didn't have to look to know he'd turned toward her. "It scares me how much I love you." It wasn't much more than a whisper.

Alec's breath caught, and he straightened up. His cobalt eyes studied her, pain and hope swimming in them. "Don't be afraid, darling. My heart will always be yours."

Jesus, this man.

Mercedes slipped her fingers around his neck, pulled him to her, and kissed him. Alec moaned softly, then wrapped his arm around her waist. His lips were soft and sensual, and the strokes of his tongue sent desire down her body, pooling in her core. His hand trailed up her back, searing her with fire. She needed his hands all over her body, his warm skin on hers.

Alec found her breast and Mercedes let out a soft whimper when his thumb slowly circled the tight nipple. Her body always knew how to respond to him.

He tilted his head and deepened their kiss. What had started out as a slow savoring was becoming desperate and sinful. The gravity that pulled them together had led them to a scorching fire that would consume them.

When he brought his mouth to her neck, she turned into him, moaning as he hit that spot that drove her insane. Her hunger for him had become painful, and she needed him to end it. She cupped his cheek and drew back to look into his eyes. Desire burned in the blue depths, and Mercedes wanted it all.

"Touch me," she whispered.

Alec growled and jerked her knee toward him, parting her. Electricity coursed through her body as he slid his hands under her dress, caressing her sensitive skin.

Mercedes arched her back toward him, encouraging him to ease the ache burning between her thighs. When his fingers finally met the soaked lace, she whimpered, pressing herself into him. He massaged her core, the bliss of orgasm already so close.

With his free hand, he tugged on the strap of her summer dress until it slipped off her shoulder. The fabric pooled under the swell of her breast. He captured the tight bud in his mouth. Mercedes moaned, running her hands through his hair.

Alec's mouth was unrelenting. "My god, you make me crazy," he murmured.

He pushed the lace aside and found her slippery clit. Mercedes groaned as he circled it with his fingertips, setting every nerve on fire.

When he sank his fingers into her, she cried out. "Jesus, Alec."

"Do you like that, Sadie? Is this what you needed?" His gruff murmur making her hotter.

"Oh, god, yes Alec. I need you."

He worked her a deeper, and she whimpered. They were moving together now, his fingers slipping in and out of her, matching the arching of her back.

"I need to hear you, Sadie," he moaned down her throat. "I need to hear you cry my name when you come."

Mercedes gasped. Pleasure coiled through her, tumbling her into a desperation to finish. "I'm going to come. Please, don't stop. Please, Alec, please."

"I won't stop, darling. Come for me," Alec rasped in her ear. "Come for me, my love."

The crest hit her, and she dug her fingers into his shoulders. Each convulsion slammed into her, making her shudder against him.

When the world returned to her, Alec was kissing her softly. Mercedes sighed, the tendrils of pleasure still coursing through her core. She ran her fingers through his hair and kissed him languidly.

When she broke away, Alec was watching her, his lips curled into a gentle smile.

"You are my everything," he whispered.

Mercedes inhaled sharply, his words sparking an inferno deep within her.

All barriers that had come between them lifted. The lies, the heartbreak, the pain they'd both been through. None of it mattered anymore. Even if she walked away right now, he would still belong to her.

But she didn't want to walk away. She had been in love with him for so long, and she was tired of letting him go. For once, she wanted to be what he deserved.

"Come to my bed," she breathed.

A wariness crossed his eyes. "Just for tonight?"

Tears made her vision swim. She shook her head. "For forever." The sob in her throat barely let the words out.

Alec's grip tightened on her back. "Christ, do you mean it?"

Mercedes nodded. "I mean it. I love you, Alec. And tomorrow, I won't pretend I don't."

CHAPTER FORTY

As soon as Alec closed her bedroom door, he had Mercedes in his arms again. He kissed her deeply. Desire raged through his body to the point of pain. The way she had come apart in his hands filled him with such need he was nearly blinded.

He was losing every bit of control he had, and it terrified him she might change her mind.

Mercedes ran her fingers under his shirt, caressing his abs. Her touch laced with fire. She gathered the fabric in her fist. "Take this off. I need to see you." He dragged it over his head and tossed it on the ground.

Mercedes's mouth was on his neck, gently nipping his skin. Alec slid the strap of the dress off her shoulder and down her arm, then he did the same for the other side. The fabric fell, catching around her waist.

He brought his hand to her breast. Their tongues danced while he kneaded her. He trailed kisses down her neck, the heat of her making his nerves burn.

"You feel so goddamn good," Alec moaned and walked her back to the bed. Mercedes sat on the edge, her legs parted.

Alec was about to kneel on the ground before her when

the swirls of ink on her flesh caught his eye. "What's this?" Mercedes smiled shyly as he pressed her back onto her elbows.

How had she kept this one from him?

Delicate music notes twirled across lines, like a sheet of music. Only she was the sheet. Colorful flowers and swirls accented the notes. It started below her breast and ran down her side to her waistline. Alec traced the lines with his fingers. The slight ridge of the scar it covered was the only sign of what she'd been through.

Alec swallowed hard, his throat parched. "Tomorrow, you and I are going to have a conversation about these tattoos."

"You don't like them?" Anxiousness crossed her face.

"I bloody love them," he growled, bending to trail kisses up the design to her taut nipple.

Mercedes sighed, drawing him in closer. He loved the way she moved against him when he took the peak into his mouth. The mark he'd given her the night of the party had faded but was still visible. He pulled in her delicate skin and sucked gently. Mercedes gasped and clung to him.

His heart jumped at her response. "You like that?"

"I do," she breathed.

"Mmm. Tell me if I'm being too rough," he said, deepening the pull on her.

The groan that came out of her was so damn sexy. "I love it, Alec. I want more."

His eyes shot to hers. "Do you?"

Mercedes bit her lip. "Yeah. I won't break."

But I might.

The desire to take his time and savor her fell away. He wanted her to lose herself again, only this time, he wouldn't take it slow.

Alec jerked her legs toward him, bringing her to the edge of the bed. Then he gathered the fabric of her dress up, tugged the lacy knickers off and dove his tongue between her thighs.

Mercedes cried out, her hand fisting his hair. She lay back, giving herself up for him to play with. He toyed with her in an unyielding dance of swirling his tongue and sucking on her clit.

"Holy shit, Alec. Oh, my god," she chanted the whisper over and over.

Alec gripped her hips and brought her in deeper, her arousal coating his tongue. The way he could make her whimper was like a drug. He needed more. He needed her to shatter under him.

Mercedes's body tightened as she was spiraled into her orgasm. She cried his name over and over until she couldn't seem to speak. When it hit her, she groaned, each shudder of her climax pulsing against his tongue.

Once the peak had passed, she lay trembling. Alec tugged on the dress, slipping it off her body. Then he worked on the last of his clothes, tossing his shorts and briefs aside.

He bent over her and kissed her, wanting to offer her a slow recovery. But she wasn't having it. Her fingernails raked his scalp, pulling the kiss in deeper. She wanted nothing to do with gentle.

She grasped his chin, and he opened his eyes to look into hers. "I need you. Now," she rasped. Then she moved, shifting herself onto the bed. "Come here."

Her command pushed his hunger to a peak. As soon as he was between her thighs, he thrust himself inside her. Her cries of pleasure matched his. The tightness of her walls clenched around him, and he savored the sensation.

"Jesus, I've needed you so much, Sadie," he whispered. "I've been so fucking lost without you."

"Then take me, Alec," she said, her fingers stroking his back. "I've always been yours."

Alec groaned, taking her in a deep and steady rhythm. Mercedes lifted her hips, coaxing him until all he knew was her.

"Harder Alec, please. Oh, god, yes right there," Mercedes cried. He increased his cadence, their movements now rough and carnal. He fought to hold back his release, but she was milking it from him.

When her body tightened with her climax, he held back a little longer, savoring her orgasm gripping his cock. She was so bloody perfect, and he was so fucking starved for her.

Mercedes writhed under him. "Come for me, Alec. I need to feel you."

Alec couldn't hold back anymore. His release blazed through him and he cried her name as he emptied himself inside her. The last wave struck him, leaving him panting for air. He kissed her softly, his pulse still hammering in his chest.

She opened her eyes, her expression soft. "Why is it like this with you?"

Alec didn't have to ask what she meant. Every moment they'd spent in each other's arms was unlike anything he'd ever known. She pulled him to the surface and exposed the depth of his heart.

"Because we belong together. And this." He gave her a gentle thrust, which made her sigh. "Is a reflection of how much you love me, and I you."

Mercedes nodded, tears spilling onto her cheeks. "I love you, Alec."

The ice that had formed in his veins over the last year of pain and grief melted, connecting him back to the living. His throat tightened painfully, and he didn't try to hide his own tears. "I love you too."

ALEC AWOKE TO THE BLUE LIGHT OF DAYBREAK FILTERING through the open curtains. He reached his hand out to search for Mercedes, terrified she'd been a dream.

But she wasn't.

She was turned away from him, curled up in sleep. Her chestnut hair spilled all around her. As gently as he could, he shifted himself to curve his body against her, tightening his arms around her. He didn't want to wake her yet. Neither of them had gotten much rest, reaching to love each other twice in the night. She shifted slightly, then settled back to sleep.

The sun was just rising, painting the sky and water in light pinks and blues. He held her, listening to her soft breathing and the crash of the distant waves. A sudden wave of mixed emotions slammed into him.

She was alive. She loved him. This was real.

Last night had been one of the most intense nights of his life. Sex with Mercedes had never just been sex. It was pure energy that sucked him in and wouldn't let go.

Mercedes stirred, and it wasn't long before her fingers tightened around his. When she sighed, he kissed her shoulder. "Good morning, darling."

"Morning," she said, sleep thick in her voice. She flipped over to face him, her legs intertwining with his. "I'm so glad I woke up in your arms. I was afraid you'd disappear on me in the night."

"Aye, I had the same fear."

He brought her knuckles to his lips and kissed them gently. The tattoo on her forearm caught his attention, and he angled it to get a better look.

"Tell me about this one," he said, running his finger along the edge of the compass rose.

"This is a Celtic symbol for strength, guiding me forward."

"And why are the flowers blue? Heather's usually pink or purple."

"Here, let me see." She lifted her forearm and put it next to his cheek. Her gaze shifted between the heather and his eyes. "Nearly perfect."

Warmth spread up his chest, pooling in his heart. "So, tell

me about this one." He said, sliding the sheet down to expose the inked music running down her ribs.

"Well, the one on my arm I did to be practical. I needed to cover up the scar, and a tattoo made sense. But this one." She ran her fingers over the swirls of notes. "I did for me. A little like reclaiming myself from what happened."

"I love that," he murmured. "So, what song is it?"

Mercedes bit her lip. "It's a song I wrote."

"Did you?"

She nodded and peered at her tattoo. "See these higher notes here, they sort of cascade over and over?" At his nod, she said. "Well, long ago, a handsome Scotsman took me on a hike. This is the waterfall that sang to me the first time he kissed me."

Alec's pulse faltered, and he had to force himself to breathe.

"And see these?" She pointed to a pattern of lower notes. "This was the beat of his heart the first time he made love to me. It's quite lovely when you put it all together."

Alec stared at her in utter disbelief that someone could ever love him this much. "Will you play it for me later?" he choked out.

She nodded. The whiskey gold of her eyes had overtaken the moss green. "You're the only one I'd ever play it for."

CHAPTER FORTY-ONE

Jason ignored the sweat dripping down the side of his face. Even the night air was hot as fuck. What pissed him off more was that it was only a short walk back to his motel room. He shouldn't be so goddamned winded. But the humidity in the air added to his lack of breath. He slowed his pace. It wasn't like he was in a hurry to get back to the tiny room.

At least he was free. No one tried to stop him when he bought a bus ticket and got the fuck out of San Francisco. He no longer had access to the technology and resources he'd had working for Cooper, so his cover-up had been sloppy. The FBI probably knew exactly where he was. He hoped they were the only ones who were looking. Mercedes wasn't the only one Cooper wanted dead. Somehow, Jason had skirted around the assassination attempts.

As soon as he could access his overseas accounts, he'd get the fuck out of here. With no money and no access to his connections, he was lucky to get what he had.

Jason couldn't help but wonder what Mercedes had done when she heard the case would have to be retried. Now that

McKinley had chosen the blonde woman, she might find a little comfort in his arms.

He climbed the steps to the second floor and unlocked his room. Just as he closed the door, he caught the faint scent of perfume.

Suddenly, the sound of something being hurled at him came from the dark room. It whizzed past his head and hit the door with a thump.

"Fuck!" He crouched, ready for the next assault to come at him in the dark. Instead, a feminine chuckle rang out.

"You're so fucking out of practice," she said, her British accent filled with amusement.

A switch clicked, and light flooded the room. Mariah Costa stood in the doorframe of his bathroom, from where she had thrown the knife at his head.

This bitch.

The knife was sticking from the door, inches from where he had been standing.

"What the fuck do you want?" She obviously wasn't there to kill him, or she would have done it already.

"Is that any way to greet an old friend?" she purred.

Jason jerked the knife from the door. It was of high quality but smaller than he liked to carry. "What the fuck do you want?" he repeated, glaring at her.

"You've never been any fun." Mariah plopped down on his bed with a sigh. "Cooper needs your help."

"Does he? That's funny."

"I'm not laughing. I'm an effective honeypot and I can handle myself if I have to, but I don't have your skills on the computer."

"Why the fuck would Cooper trust me?"

"He doesn't. I'm pretty sure he'd have my throat slit if he knew I was talking to you instead of ending you." Mariah lifted her shoulder. "But what he doesn't know won't hurt him."

"Why do you need me? Where's Adam?"

"I'm starting to believe Adam may be compromised."

Jason sat at the table, the knife balancing on his fingers. "That seems unlikely. He's one dedicated motherfucker when it comes to sucking Cooper's cock."

"Is he though?" Mariah pursed her lips. "Or does he just play the game better than the both of us?"

"What do you mean?"

"You were there with him when he found Mara Donovan, right? When she was able to get out of his grasp?"

Jason recalled the little village where he and Adam had confronted the lithe blonde and nodded.

Mariah smirked. "You think a man Adam's size couldn't keep hold of a little thing like her?"

"Why would he let her go?"

"Don't know, but I'm pretty sure he was fucking her."

Jason's jaw dropped. "The fuck? Why would you think that?" Marcus Cooper would have had anyone's cock on a stake if they touched her. She was Cooper's personal property.

"Cooper's son, Tyler, reached out to me recently when he began to question Adam's effectiveness in getting this job done. I ran through some of our own security footage over the years to see what he did when Cooper was blindly trusting him. Turns out, he was staying long hours in Mara's room after Cooper ditched her for his wife."

"No shit?" Jason rubbed the hilt of the knife. "That doesn't mean he helped Mara."

"Not by itself, but let me ask you, how did a woman like Mara Donavan, with no training or expertise, evade our team for nearly two years now? It's not like she has an Alec McKinley keeping her company at night."

Hearing that fucker's name hit Jason in the chest, and he glared at Mariah.

She sent him a smirk in return. "I need help. Tyler Cooper wants to be rid of Adam, Marcus Cooper wants me to find and finish off Mercedes and Mara. He can't have them alive for the next trial."

"What do I get out of this?"

"I'll look the other way when Daddy Cooper orders me to kill you, which he already has."

Jason turned his lips up into a smile. "Not enough, sweetheart. I need more than that."

Mariah sighed. "If I find Mercedes alive, I'll let you have her first. Just as long as she's dead when you're finished with her."

Jason's cock stiffened to think of Mercedes at his mercy. But he wouldn't let her die. He didn't care what Cooper wanted.

"She's not going to be easy to find," Mariah said. "My guy blundered our last hit and now she's gone dark. I need your help to try to locate her."

"You already have insiders placed in federal agencies that can help. Why do you need me?"

Mariah tilted her head. "Didn't you hear? Mercedes declined to go into WITSEC again. She and Alec ran off before the judge even announced the mistrial."

A knife in his chest would have been better than learning this.

That fucking whore. After everything McKinley had done to her, Mercedes had gone back to that fucker. When he found her, he was going to tear her throat out.

"I'm in."

CHAPTER FORTY-TWO

"Are you even listening to me?" Cressida snapped into his earpiece.

"Hmm?" Alec mumbled.

No, he hadn't been listening.

Mercedes had on a damn bikini, and she was the only thing he could see. Those bloody tattoos were enough to do him in. The blue fabric barely covered the curves of her breasts.

If Declan and Cressida didn't get to the point, Alec was going to hang up on their arses and go in after her.

Cressida let out an irritated sigh. "For god's sake, Alec. Are you and Sadie in bed right now?"

"What? No. But she's in the pool, and she's a little . . . distracting."

Declan chuckled. "So, things are still going well then?"

"There aren't words, mate. Sometimes I worry this has all been a sick dream and I'll wake to find she's still gone."

"Nah, it's real. She came back to you. You took your head out of your arse. It's been a good month." Declan laughed. "But we got shit to do or the two of you are going to have to stay in hiding forever."

Alec wasn't sure he minded. He and Mercedes had spent the last five days in this beach house. Five days of nothing but talking, laughing, and loving her. Once, he called off work, and they stayed in bed the entire day, only surfacing for food.

For the first time in over a year, he felt truly alive again.

But Declan was right. As amazing as this time together was, Alec wanted a real life with Mercedes. They couldn't do that if they were always on the run.

"Speaking of hiding," Cressida broke through his thoughts. "Whitley is still pissed that Sadie's gone. He's called me more than once this week to threaten to have our American license pulled."

"What a fuckwit," Alec said, rolling his eyes. "I hope you reminded him Sadie still has that op-ed for The Washington Post ready to go if he wants to push his luck."

"Oh, I did. It still makes him squirm."

Alec chuckled. Mercedes surfaced again and the water cascading down her long hair made his cock thicken. Jesus, he'd just had her an hour ago, and he was already hungry for more.

Sighing, he walked into the house. At least inside, the view of her curvy body in that suit was limited.

"Alright, sorry. Back to business. You wanted to tell me something big?"

"Well," Cressida said. "We found Adam Wilson. Like actually found him."

Alec paused his pacing. "Are you serious? How did you do that?"

"Cressida found him because she's bloody brilliant," Declan said.

"I ran facial recognition on him starting in San Francisco and working outward. We got a few hits here and there, he's always careful in the city. Then I got a hit on smart cameras in this tiny town in the Russian River Valley. When he's there, he isn't careful at all. So, I went back as far as I could. He's been there several times over the past year."

Alec frowned. "What was he doing there?"

"We think he's visiting family," Declan said. "Get this. Cressida began a search of the newspapers and databases in the area. And we got his name."

Alec's phone buzzed and Cressida said. "Take a look at Russian River High's former homecoming king." Alec opened the message and the black-and-white photo from an old newspaper stared up at him. "Timothy Jackson Barlow."

"Christ," he hissed. They had spent over a year looking for this man, trying to track his movements and his motivations. And he just showed up in the middle of nowhere?

"Oh, that's just the beginning. Now that I have his name, it led me down a rabbit hole of info on our boy here. I'm sending you my entire file, but this guy was a Navy SEAL. Spent years in and out of war zones and is actually quite decorated."

"Is he still active military?"

"No, he retired five years ago. But see the pretty little homecoming queen with him in the photo? That's Shannon Crosby, aka Shannon Barlow. The two of them were married right out of school. She lives in his last known address and is receiving some of his veteran benefits."

"So, they're still married?"

"Looks like it. She filed for divorce about six years ago, but then withdrew it. As infrequently as he goes there, I would say that they don't live together," Cressida said.

"Aye. Do they have children?"

"I believe so. There are two children with the last name Barlow in the area. One of them is named Jackson. It could be a coincidence . . ."

"Or maybe he gave his son his middle name." Alec stared at the image in front of him. Shannon Barlow's youthful face was fresh and cheery. "The Russian River Valley isn't that far, is it?"

Declan's keystrokes came over the line. "It's about an hour and a half north of your location."

"Send me the address."

"Are you going to pay this woman a visit?" Cressida asked.

"I don't know for sure. I'm not sure what we'll gain by talking to his wife."

"I'll keep looking for more on him, maybe there will be something there."

That was a damn good start.

"What about you, Dec? Where are you off to?" Alec said.

"I just got back to London. I'm going to revisit the gift shop Mara Donovan was working. Her colleagues might be a little more open now that so much time has gone by. If I find her again, maybe I can get her to listen. It's in her best interest to take Cooper down too."

"Aye, let me know how it goes."

Alec hung up and pulled the earpiece from his ear. They had hunted for Adam Wilson for such a long time now, it was hard to believe they finally had a genuine lead.

It wasn't anything they could move on, though. He'd be walking right into Adam Wilson's lair, without much protection. And he couldn't leave Mercedes alone. His primary team had scattered. Cressida and Shake were the only ones left in the area, and while the twins were scrappy, they weren't trained for combat. Declan was back in Britain, and Mason had taken some personal time to fly to Boston to visit his family.

Alec went back out on the deck. Mercedes had gotten out of the pool and had lain out on the cushioned lounge chair. Droplets of water clung to her skin. She had on her dark sunglasses with a wide-brimmed beach hat over her wet hair like she was straight out of Hollywood.

"Enjoy your swim?" He sat at the end of the chair, pulled her feet into his lap and massaged them.

"Mmm-hmm," she sighed.

When he moved his fingers up her calf, working her muscles. Mercedes let out a soft moan. He slipped his hand up her thigh to the edge of her bikini bottoms. "Mmm, make that sound again."

Mercedes giggled. "You're insatiable, you know that?" But she didn't resist when he shifted himself between her thighs, sliding her legs on either side of him.

"Aye, I can't get enough of you." He kissed her lazily, her soft moans captured in his mouth. Mercedes wrapped her legs around him, tightening herself around him, soaking his shirt and shorts. She deepened the kiss, her tongue letting him know she was just as insatiable as he was.

"We should probably stop," she murmured. "If we keep this up, we'll spend the rest of the day in bed again."

"Would that be so bad?"

Mercedes nipped at his throat. "No, but we need to talk about the phone call you just had. From the little I heard, it sounded like they had some news."

Alec groaned and pushed himself off her wet body. He'd vowed not to keep her in the dark, so he would tell her everything. But his brain seemed to malfunction when she was in his arms.

"It was actually big news." He shifted off his knees and sat next to her. "Cressida found Adam Wilson."

"Adam?" Mercedes sat up in alarm. "You've been hunting for him?"

"Aye, we are quite certain he is behind a lot of what happened to you. Cressida found him in a small town north of here. She believes his real name is Timothy Barlow, and he's a former Navy SEAL. She thinks his wife is still living at his last known address."

"He's married?" Mercedes's tone was filled with disbelief.

"We think so. Why does that surprise you?"

"He was one of the few people Jason passed off as a friend. We didn't speak very often, but I would have never known he was married. He liked the ladies. A lot."

"Did they like him back?"

"Yeah, he could turn on the charm when he wanted to. Jason was always jealous of the way women fawned over Adam."

"Did you ever see him go home with anyone?"

Mercedes frowned. "Actually, no. He would get phone numbers, but he never brought a woman around."

He pulled the phone from his pocket. "Cressida sent me a photo of Adam in school. Is this the man you knew?" He handed her the phone, and she studied the screen.

"Oh yeah. That's him."

"We think the woman in this picture is his wife. Did you ever see her around?"

"No, I don't know her." Mercedes handed back his phone. "Do you think she's a part of this?"

"I think she's something. I don't quite know what yet. Cress is going to keep looking."

Mercedes sighed, and a silence fell between them. The waiting game they were playing was exhausting and she was moving into her second year of this.

She perked up. "Oh, hey, this might be a good time to work out. Can you help me?"

Alec hadn't had a decent workout since he'd left London. "Aye, what do you need?"

"I was hoping you could attack me."

"You want me to attack you? Like . . ." He raised his brow.

That earned him a smack on the shoulder. "Get your mind out of the gutter. Noah was teaching me how to escape if I ever needed it."

Gratitude for Noah warmed his chest. Mercedes trusted him. Mostly because he had protected her against his own.

But they had also bonded when they were pretending to be husband and wife. Alec trusted him, because he'd practically begged him to take Mercedes and get the hell out of there.

"It was part of my therapy. I'd like to see how well it works against someone like you."

He stroked her leg with the tips of his fingers. "Someone like me?"

"Yeah, strong and trained. I doubt I stand a chance, but I can always practice."

"Aye, go change and I'll happily attack you down on the beach."

THE TIDE WAS OUT, AND ALEC AND MERCEDES JOGGED SIDE BY side along the damp sand for about a mile. Mercedes kept having to pause to stretch her injured leg, and Alec could tell she was pushing through pain.

"Sorry," she said, bending to touch the sand. "This damn injury makes it hard for me to go too far. My physical therapist said it would take time."

"Don't be sorry, darling. I struggled with that too."

"Aren't we a pair?" Mercedes gave him a rueful smile. She stood to her full height. "Ready to practice?"

Alec held his hands out. "Aye. What do you need me to do?"

"Let's start with you grabbing me from behind." She turned her back to him and waited. Her fingers tapping on her leg.

Alec let out a quick exhale and lunged at her. Mercedes dodged him, avoiding his grasp. Mercedes bit her lip and tilted her head at him. "You're holding back. Don't coddle me. No one else will."

"I'm not coddling you." He was scared as hell to break her.

This time he snapped her up, pinning her arms against her chest. Suddenly, she twisted her body, freed her hand, and cupped him by the balls.

Instinctively, he let her go to protect himself, nearly taking her elbow in the nose. She stopped before she hit him.

"Holy shit, Sadie! You were taught to fondle the man's bollocks?"

Laughter burst from Mercedes. "No, if it were real, I'd have hit you with my fist. I fondled yours because I like 'em."

"You cheeky little minx." Alec stalked toward her and grabbed her again, this time from the front. Mercedes gave out a little yelp and laughed. Instead of trying to wrench herself out of his grasp, she climbed up his body, wrapping herself around him. She locked her long legs around his waist and tucked her head against his shoulder.

Alec tried to pull her off him, but she wasn't budging. He couldn't get any sort of leverage to free her. When he took his hands off her, she clung to him.

He chuckled. "Now what, Sadie? Are you just going to hang on like a monkey?"

Mercedes's hand shot up and gripped his throat. "Now, I choke you out."

"Christ." Alec ran his hands down her back and palmed her ass. "Don't threaten me with a good time."

She drew back and grinned. "You're a very distractible workout partner."

"Only with you. Dec and I don't have this problem."

Mercedes giggled and kissed him. She fit so perfectly against his body, he was already going mad for her. Then she gripped his throat a little tighter and he groaned into her mouth.

Bloody hell.

He broke the kiss and sucked in a deep inhale. As much as he wanted to make out with her on the beach, he needed to see what else she'd been taught.

"You need to stop distracting me, darling. This is quite serious business," he said as she nipped at his lips. "We can continue this part of the workout later."

Mercedes groaned and disentangled herself from him. "Okay," she said reluctantly. "You're right. Let's try something a little less intimate for a while."

They practiced for another half hour, their mood shifting to a more serious tone. Noah had done a nice job of adapting her moves to accommodate her smaller frame against a man of his size. Each technique was designed to stun or incapacitate her attacker, giving her time to get away.

On the way back to the house, Mercedes had developed a slight limp, reminding him of all the traumas she'd already endured. As grateful as he was to Noah for teaching her, he hoped like hell she'd never need the lessons.

CHAPTER FORTY-THREE

M ercedes paced the living room with her phone up to her ear. Alec had arranged a secure line to speak with Charlotte. The poor thing was heading into the last months of her pregnancy and needed some big sister love.

"The baby is lying on my bladder, so I have to pee every five seconds," Charlotte grumped. "Oh, and I'm so hot all the time, I can't sleep. I had to buy a portable air conditioner which I keep cranked up at all times. Luke lays next to me shivering and I sweat like a pig. And I feel like a turtle."

"A turtle?"

"Yeah, a turtle. Like, once I lay on my back, I can't get back up."

Mercedes bit back a smile at her sister's surliness. "Did you go get the pregnancy massage Alec and I gave you?"

"I did, and it was wonderful. Thank you. So good, I paid for another one later this week."

"Oh, nice." A little stab hit her heart. "I wish I could be there to help you."

"Don't you dare try and come here. You're exactly where I need you to be right now, which is safe and with Alec." Charlotte grunted like she'd just eased herself into a chair. "How's everything going with Alec?"

Just thinking about the past few weeks with him sent a shiver down her spine. "Oh my god, Charlie, it's perfect. He's perfect." The world had finally aligned for her, and she wasn't letting go of it this time.

"That's amazing." Charlotte's voice quivered. "You both deserve to be happy."

"Charlie, are you crying?"

"Maybe a little." She sniffed. "Stupid baby hormones. I only cry at happy things for some reason."

"Well, it's nice to have happy things to cry about, right?" Mercedes soothed.

"Uh-huh." Charlotte blew her nose.

Mercedes braced herself for her next question. "Have you spoken to Ezra?"

"Yeah, he came by before he left town."

"How bad does he hate me?"

"He looked a bit miserable, but he could never hate you."

"I screwed up." Lightning in the distant clouds caught her eye. "I sent him a bunch of mixed signals. It gave him hope."

"So, are you saying that you wouldn't have even considered Ezra if things had gone differently with Alec?"

Mercedes didn't even want to think back to what her world without Alec looked like.

"I don't know. I was absolutely wrecked and not thinking straight, but that's not a good enough reason."

"Sadie, it was always going to be you and Alec. Ezra knew that was a possibility. And you shouldn't apologize for being with a man you love."

"I know. And I don't regret choosing Alec. How could I? But I feel terrible Ezra got hurt."

"He'll be okay. If you could forgive him for what he did to you, he can certainly forgive you for choosing the man you were always supposed to be with."

"I guess," Mercedes said, looking at her watch. "I better let you go. If you talk to Ezra again, will you let him know I'm sorry?"

"I will. Love you sister."

"Love you too."

Mercedes hung up the phone and looked out at the stormy skies. Nothing could make her regret loving Alec, but the fallout of her choices was tough to see.

"Sadie!" Alec called, excitement in his voice.

She turned to find him striding toward her, his computer in his hand. "You won't believe what Declan just uncovered in England."

Alec set the computer on the table. Footage from a security camera was frozen on the screen. He pressed a button and a familiar event began to play. Over a year ago, Jason and Adam Wilson had confronted the whistleblower Mercedes had helped hide. They tried to take her hostage. Mara Donavan had gotten free and sent Mercedes the damning evidence against Marcus Cooper on her phone before jumping into a nearby river.

Only this was a different camera angle than they'd ever seen before. The police had released all the security footage from around the square. But this was new. It was lower to the ground, above a neighboring shop's door.

And unlike the others, it had audio.

The video started with Mara striding out of the alleyway and running right into Adam's chest.

"Tim!"

Did she just call him Tim?

Adam grabbed her arm. "Hello, Mara. Been a while, hasn't it?"

Then he leaned down and hissed so quietly, the video barely picked it up. "Send the package, then get the fuck out of here."

She tried to wrench her arm away, but he held on. "Stop

fighting me," Adam growled loudly. "We're going to take a little walk. Don't make a scene, or we'll make sure it hurts."

"Fuck you and fuck Marcus. I'm not going anywhere with you. Help me! Please, my ex is going to kill me!"

Then she wrenched her arm away and ran off camera. Jason followed her, but Adam hung back, watching. The crowd had their attention on Jason and Mara, and Mercedes could tell when Mara had thrown herself into the river by the shouts of the onlookers. Adam let out his breath, then looked up at the buildings.

His gaze caught the camera. "Fuck." Then he walked away.

The footage kept playing, but Mercedes was too stunned to pay attention to it. "What the hell did we just watch?"

Alec's eyes were wide with disbelief. He held up his phone. "Dec? Cress? Are you still there?"

"Aye," Declan said. "I about shite myself when I found this video."

"How did you get it?" Mercedes asked

"Well, I went there to visit the little shop Mara worked at and questioned the owner. He was as tight-lipped as ever, but as I left, I walked the same route she did. I noticed a camera was set above the door of this other tourist shop. I went in and talked to the kid behind the counter, and he was there that day. He said after the woman jumped into the river, the two guys split up. Then a few minutes later, the big bloke came back, offering him two thousand pounds to take the camera down and get rid of any video footage of the incident."

Mercedes looked at Alec. "So, what does this mean?"

"I think it means that Adam Wilson, aka Tim Barlow, let Mara go."

"She called him Tim." Mercedes stared at the screen in shock. "Mara was Marcus Cooper's mistress for years. She told me that he kept her on a tight leash."

"Aye, but Marcus Cooper had people who took care of things for him. One of those people was Adam."

"So, you think they were involved with one another?"

"It's possible. One thing we know for sure is they were in on this together. He told her to send the evidence to you, which means he knew how you and Mara communicated and how the evidence was stored. Then he got her out of there."

All this time, Adam was protecting Mara.

"Think of how long Mara avoided Marcus and his men. How did she have the resources to stay hidden the way she did? We've always thought she might have had help. I just never thought it would be Cooper's own man."

"But that doesn't make sense. Adam killed an FBI agent because he was desperate to get the evidence. He was so pissed when he figured out Alec had kept it."

"That doesn't mean he was trying to get it for Cooper," Cressida said.

"But why tell Mara to send it to me, why wouldn't he just tell her to run."

"Because if Jason took Mara hostage, he would torture her until she gave it up. If she told them she sent it to you, their focus would be off her. Jason wanted to find you anyway."

Mercedes shivered at the thought of what Jason would have done to Mara. "So it was to distract Jason."

"Possibly," Alec said. "So, what do we do with this?"

"If Adam's been thwarting Marcus Cooper all this time, it's clear he's not on the same side. Adam was trying to hang on to that evidence for a reason. If we can figure out his motivations, we'll know how to deal with him."

"You need to pay little wifey a visit," Cressida said.

"Absolutely not," Alec ground out. "I'm not leaving Sadie alone and there's no way I'm taking her anywhere near that man."

Mercedes's gaze shot to Alec. "What do you mean? We

just got our first chance to figure out what's going on. We should talk to her."

"Sadie, he could be there, we wouldn't know."

"Well, actually," Cressida broke in. "I may or may not already have access to a doorbell camera at her residence."

"You can see her doorbell camera?" Mercedes asked.

"Perhaps," Cressida said coyly. Alec pursed his lips and looked away. "Why don't I review the footage and see if he's been there. It goes back two weeks."

"Go ahead and look," Alec said. "But if he's been there, we aren't setting foot in that valley. Understood."

"Gotcha," Cressida said. "I'll call you when it's done."

After Alec hung up, he sat with his fingers tented against his brow.

Mercedes sat next to him and pulled his hand into her lap. "Are you okay?"

"Aye, but I don't like the idea of engaging a dangerous man whose motives are unknown. At least if I knew why he did things, we could anticipate his movements. Not to mention, he's likely responsible for the attempts on your life." His brow creased, and he squeezed her hand. "I'm honestly terrified of what might happen to you."

"I've been scared for so long, Alec. I don't remember what it is like to not be afraid. But I don't want to wait for the next trial. I want to fight back now. And if that means we talk to a woman Adam may or may not be married to, then we should do it."

"I'd feel better if Declan or Mason could come be with you while I take care of it."

"Oh, so one of them can babysit me while you go out alone?"

He shrugged. "Exactly."

Mercedes leaned in to kiss him. "Not happening, McKinley. You're stuck with me."

CHAPTER FORTY-FOUR

Mercedes took in the vineyards, rolling through the green and gold hills of California. Alec's expression was calm, but she knew he was a wreck underneath the surface. They could be walking right into a trap, and Adam Wilson was a scary son of a bitch.

When they finally turned onto the long dirt driveway, Mercedes was struck by how normal it looked. This didn't have the feel of an assassin's home. Not that she had any idea what that might look like.

It was a cozy little place with a large wraparound porch. Poppies and daisies filled the flower beds and clothes were set out on a line.

Alec was approaching the house like Adam might come barreling out. His hand was hovering behind his back, the way he did when he wanted his gun handy.

The front door burst open and two giggling children came scampering out, each with a bright red popsicle in their small hands. Alec straightened, moving his hand to his side.

The dark-haired girl with wide blue eyes stopped when she saw Mercedes and Alec.

Mercedes decided it might be better for her to talk to the little girl first. "Hi sweetie, is your mom home?"

The girl tilted her head and surveyed the two of them.

Oh, that's Adam's kid all right.

"Mom!" the girl shouted through the screen.

"Yeah?" a voice called from inside the house.

"There's some people here."

"Okay."

The girl scampered off, chasing after the boy. They squealed their way out to a small chicken coop on the side of the stable.

A second later, Shannon Barlow stepped out onto the porch. She was definitely the woman from the photo, but she was much thinner. So thin her cheeks were shadowed and gaunt. The space between her collarbone and shoulder was sunken under her oversized tank top. Her eyes and skin had an odd hue to them.

She tilted her head. "Can I help you?"

Alec flashed a brilliant smile and pulled off his sunglasses. "Oh aye, ma'am. My name is Alec, and this is Sadie. I was wondering if Tim Barlow might still be around these parts."

A wariness crossed the woman's face. "How do you know Tim?"

"I met Barlow years ago, when I was in the Royal Air Force. He saved my life."

Her eyes widened. "He did?"

"Aye. We were stationed at Bagram Air Base in Afghanistan. Barlow and I had a few joint maneuvers together and we became mates. This one day, our group was ambushed. The strike was quick and bloody. I lost quite a few mates there that day."

Alec had thickened his accent considerably. He was even drawing Mercedes into his story.

"I was shot just here." Alec tugged on his neckline to expose his scar. "And I was quite out in the open, nearly blacking out from the pain, and pinned down by gunfire. Then Barlow comes out of nowhere, grabs me and drags me behind a vehicle. He helped a couple of others cover our location until backup came." Alec frowned and looked away. "I *dinna ken* what might've happened if Barlow hadn't been there."

Did he say 'dinna ken'? He was laying the accent on really thick now, but Shannon appeared enthralled.

"So, I was in the Bay Area for a bit, visiting my darling's family before we go back to Edinburgh." Alec drew Mercedes to his side. "And I hoped I could catch up with the man who saved my life. Maybe buy him a beer. This is the last address I could find for him."

The lies rolled off his tongue, sweet as honey. If Mercedes didn't know better, she would have thought he was actually trying to connect with his old mate. Of course, the American who had saved Alec was Mason Wright. This story wasn't far off from the truth.

Shannon smiled. "I don't know much about Tim's time in the service. He wasn't allowed to talk about his missions. Unfortunately, Tim hasn't lived here in quite some time. We've been separated for years, although we're still on friendly terms. He occasionally pops in to see the kids, but we don't see him as often as we'd like."

There's no way this woman knows about Adam's full-time gig.

Alec nodded. "Oh, would you happen to know where I might find him?"

Shannon shifted her feet. "I don't have his address. He moves around too much. And no offense, but I don't want to give out his number to strangers."

"Oh aye, that's totally fine. I understand." Alec held his hands out. "But might there be a way you could call him and tell him I'm here? Or maybe I can leave my number and you can pass it along. I'm only in town for another few days though."

She looked between Mercedes and Alec. Mercedes offered her a smile, hoping she set Shannon's mind at ease. "Sure, I can do that," Shannon said, her shoulders relaxing. "Would you like to come in and get out of this heat? I just made a fresh pitcher of sun tea."

"Oh, that sounds lovely. Thank you." Alec once again flashed that sweet smile.

Shannon grinned and beckoned them to follow her. Mercedes squeezed his hand to stop him. He looked at her with his brow furrowed.

She leaned into his ear and whispered, "We are sooo gonna have a conversation about that accent."

His lips turned up into a smile. "Aye?"

Mercedes nodded and turned to follow. This time, Alec stopped her. "Sadie."

"Yeah?"

"What the bloody hell is sun tea?"

Mercedes snorted. "It's iced tea that's made in the sun."

Confusion crossed his face. "How do you make tea in the sun?"

She snickered. "Just drink it. You'll be fine."

YOU CAN TELL A LOT ABOUT A PERSON BY SEEING THEIR HOME. Alec studied the quaint little farmhouse, trying to discern if Adam Wilson had ever been here. All the evidence indicated only Tim Barlow had ever been allowed into this world. School pictures and family candids were everywhere. The fireplace was covered with pictures and knickknacks that mothers collect from their children's art classes.

A few photos of a young Tim Barlow with his children hung on the wall. None of them were recent. Alec figured Tim moved away from the family about five or six years ago.

Shannon brought Alec a glass of her sun tea and he

thanked her. Mercedes was already sipping on hers, an amused look on her face. Alec took a drink. The tea was a touch too cold and sweet for his liking, but he drank politely.

Alec breathed in deeply. "What is that delicious aroma? Are you baking?"

Shannon gave him a broad grin. "I have some banana nut bread I just took out of the oven. It'll be ready in a few."

The door burst open, and two little balls of energy rocketed into the room. Shannon scolded them for being sticky and turned her attention to wiping them down before they touched anything.

"Who are you?" the blue-eyed boy asked.

Shannon nudged her son. "Where are your manners?"

He immediately looked contrite. "Sorry."

Alec laughed and held his hand out to the boy. "That's no problem mate, I'm Alec. I'm a friend of your father's. Nice to meet you."

A smile spread on the little boy's face. "I'm Jackson. Do you know where my dad is?"

"'Fraid not, lad. I'm looking for him myself."

"Oh." Disappointment made his little face drop. This boy loved his father.

The dark-haired girl named Maisie had taken a keen interest in Mercedes. She tugged her by the hand into the living room and was pointing out all her art projects. Mercedes was admiring them the way one would at a gallery.

Shannon had her phone in her hand, and she was swiping her hand on the screen.

"This is a lovely place. Do you own the vineyards?"

"My family does, sort of a generational thing. Our tasting room is off the highway, my great-grandfather built the house behind it. My father runs it now, but when he retires, it'll be up to me and my cousins."

"Do you work for the winery too?"

"I used to. But I had a bit of a health scare a few years ago and my family stepped up to help. I work a few days a week in the office, but mostly I'm home now."

The health scare wasn't over. Shannon's coloring, along with her fragility, told him she was still deep in a crisis.

She offered him a polite smile and put the phone to her ear. "I'll give Tim a quick call now."

Alec's heart rate climbed. Once Adam knew they were here, they would be exposed. He only hoped the man was too far away to do anything about it.

Maisie now had a small violin on her lap, and they were deep in conversation about the workings of the bow. Mercedes was pointing along the fine hair of the bow, and Maisie was watching diligently. She seemed to have found a mate.

Shannon joined him again, tucking her phone in her pocket. "I left a message. He usually gets right back to me. You're welcome to hang out for a bit to see if he calls back."

Alec covered his nerves by taking a sip of the over-sweetened tea.

"Mom," Maisie said. "Sadie knows how to play all kinds of instruments. She used to play in symphonies."

Shannon smiled. "Wow, baby. That's so cool."

"Alright, kiddo," Mercedes said to Maisie. "Let's hear what you got."

The little girl grinned and put the violin to her chin and belted out "Twinkle, Twinkle Little Star". Mercedes watched, her full attention on the little girl's playing.

"It's so good to see Maisie so friendly with your girlfriend. She's usually so shy." Shannon said, her expression soft.

Without warning, Shannon's shoulders slumped, and she reached for the doorway for support.

"Oh, hey," Alec said in alarm, wrapping his arm around Shannon's waist. She was skeletally thin, his fingers able to feel the ridges of her ribs and spine. Her legs were barely holding her up. Alec set his glass on the nearest shelf and pulled her closer to him. "Put your weight on me, lass. I won't let you fall."

Shannon held on to him, but her grasp was so weak. Mercedes had scrambled off the sofa and set a pillow down. Alec helped Shannon to lie down, her body trembling. A thin sheen of sweat had appeared on her forehead and her breathing was labored.

Maisie's wide eyes were on Shannon. "Mom?"

"Sweetie, let's go get a cold cloth for your mom," Mercedes said. "I'm sure she's okay. It's such a hot day and we need to cool her down." Mercedes caught Alec's eye before she let Maisie lead her to the kitchen.

"I'm so sorry," Shannon breathed. "This is pretty embarrassing."

Alec checked her pulse. It was way too slow. "Nonsense, I'm glad we were here."

Mercedes came back with a washcloth and laid it across Shannon's brow.

"Thank you," Shannon said, putting her hand over the cloth.

Mercedes sat next to Alec on the coffee table. "Is there someone we can call for you?"

"No thanks. I just get lightheaded sometimes, but it always passes quickly." Shannon sat up and gave a weary smile. "I had a rare form of cancer a few years ago. I've been receiving treatments ever since. It saved my life but lately I've been struggling. The doctors all swear it hasn't returned, but something doesn't feel right."

"I've heard chemo can really take it out of a person." Mercedes said, studying Shannon's face. "And you've been doing it for years?"

"Oh, I'm not doing chemotherapy. It doesn't work on my type of cancer. I've been a part of a clinical trial for a few years."

Oh, shit.

Mercedes tilted her head. "Oh, I read an article about different trials for cancer recently. Some look really promising. Which company is your trial with?"

"Cooper Pharma." Shannon smiled wryly. "I know they've had a lot of bad press lately, but they gave me these last four years with my kids."

Motherfucker. All the pieces were finally in place.

"That's wonderful," Mercedes said. "How does one even go about getting into a trial like that?"

Alec narrowed his eyes. Mercedes had dealt with medical cases for most of her career as an attorney. She knew bloody well how patients accessed clinical trials.

"I just got a phone call out of the blue one day. They said they had room and wanted me to come in that week."

"Wow, and your doctor didn't have to submit your name or do any preliminary tests to make sure you were eligible?"

Shannon shook her head. "No. They already had everything they needed. It was a brand-new trial and my doctors didn't know about it at the time." Shannon stood, her feet seeming to be sturdier under her. "It was like God was watching out for me."

Mercedes met Alec's gaze, her brow furrowed. She gave a little shake of her head, confirming what he suspected. Clinical trials didn't work that way.

God? Or the Devil himself?

This poor woman had no clue the number of crimes that had been committed in exchange for her life.

Shannon's phone buzzed, and Mercedes's eyes widened. Alec tried to give her a reassuring smile.

"Hey you!" Shannon answered it, with only a subtle quiver in her voice. "Thanks for calling me back."

Alec watched her face, waiting for it to change to alarm, but her grin never faded. "Yeah. I'm fine. His name is Alec." She tilted the phone away from her ear. "What did you say your last name was?"

"McKinley." Alec held his breath.

"Yeah, Alec McKinley. You were at Bagram together. Sure." She held the phone to Alec. "He remembers you. Here you go."

Mercedes's breath hitched, and he gave her hand a quick squeeze. Then he stood and accepted the phone from Shannon. "Bloody hell, Barlow. How many years has it been?"

"Motherfucker, you're playing with fire." A deep voice snarled at him.

"At least seven, I think," Alec replied, ignoring the threat in his tone. He looked at Shannon. "Do you mind if I take your phone outside? I'll just be a few minutes."

"Sure." Shannon waved him on.

Alec stepped out of the house and was nearly to the stables across the dirt driveway before he put the phone to his ear again.

"Hello, Mr. Barlow," Alec growled, dropping the friendliness. "It's high time you and I had a chat, don't you think?"

CHAPTER FORTY-FIVE

A dam stepped out of the shower, his muscles relaxed after getting off. Mara was still in the filthy single stall, washing her hair and humming. She didn't seem to mind, but he needed to get her out of this shithole apartment. He'd never liked bringing her here all those years ago, and he liked it even less now.

Throwing on a pair of briefs, he went to the kitchen for a glass of water. He picked up his phone, realizing he had missed a call from Shannon.

Adam frowned and pulled up the voice mail message. Shannon only called him on holidays, his birthday, or if something had happened to the kids.

Her sunny voice filled the room, and he immediately relaxed. There was no anxiety in her tone at all.

"Hi Timmy, just wanted to let you know an old friend of yours is here. He said you saved his life once in Afghanistan and he wanted to meet up for a beer." Adam frowned, he'd saved a few people in his time in the military. But most would never look for him. Her next words were like a shot in the gut. "His name is Alec. I didn't get his last name but he's Scottish.

He said he's from Edinburgh. Anyway, they'll be here for another few minutes, so call me."

"Fuck!" he shouted, panic lacing through his chest.

It was what he'd dreaded. Alec McKinley figuring out who he was and coming for him.

Only Alec hadn't come for him, he'd gone for his fucking family.

Mara came out of the bathroom, a towel wrapped around her body. "What's going on?"

"Alec fucking McKinley is at my fucking house. He's with my kids." He played Shannon's message again, desperately hoping he was wrong.

Color drained from Mara's face. "She didn't say it was Alec McKinley, maybe it's a different Alec?"

Adam shook his head. "How many men from Edinburgh named Alec do you think are wandering around the Russian River Valley?"

"I don't know. What do we do?"

"I have to call her back and make sure they're okay." He was already dialing, not sure what the hell to say. Clearly Alec had lied to Shannon, making up some bullshit story to gain her trust. The fucker would pay for that one.

The phone only rang twice before Shannon answered. "Hey you! Thanks for calling me back."

"Shannon, are you okay?"

"Yeah, I'm fine."

"The man that's there, what did you say his name was?"

"His name is Alec." There was a pause while she asked for his last name. "Alec McKinley. You were at Bagram together."

The confirmation turned Adam's stomach. Shannon and his children were completely vulnerable, exposed to whatever this man wanted to do to them. And given how much suffering Adam had brought to Alec's life, he had to believe the Scot was there to exact revenge.

He cleared his throat. "Yeah, I remember him. Can I talk to him?"

"Sure." There was a rustling while she handed over the phone.

Then that unmistakable accent came over the line. "Bloody hell, Barlow. How many years has it been?"

Adam gripped the phone. "Motherfucker, you're playing with fire."

Alec ignored him. "At least seven, I think." Then he said to Shannon. "Do you mind if I take your phone outside? I'll just be a few minutes."

Adam heard the squeak of the screen door and the gravel of the driveway crunching under his feet. Anxiety swirled in his gut as he waited for what was to come.

"Hello Mr. Barlow," Alec said smoothly, a threat of violence concealed below his calm tone. "It's high time you and I had a chat, don't you think?"

"You've got a lot of balls going near my family."

"Oh, aye. My balls are quite adequate, thank you very much." Alec had the fucking nerve to sound amused.

"If you touch Shannon or my kids, I swear I will hunt down everyone you love, starting with that pretty little sister of yours."

Alec scoffed. "Let's get one thing straight here, Timmy boy. I don't execute lovely, sun tea–drinking women or harm little children. I have a conscience, unlike the man you work for."

"Oh, so I'm supposed to believe you're there for the tea? Fuck you, McKinley. I know your file."

"Aye, and now I know yours. A former Navy SEAL who was awarded the Navy Cross for valor. Well done. An all-American hero, as they say. So, I couldn't figure out why a *hero* would do the bidding of a piece of shit like Marcus Cooper."

Holy fuck, he knows too damn much.

But Alec wasn't done. "But now that I've met your lovely wife, I get it. That experimental cancer treatment she's receiving is an absolute miracle. Does she know the bargain you struck?"

Anger and panic curled in his gut.

"I didn't think so," Alec said at his silence. "All you have to do is keep the murdering you've done a secret, and the rest will all work out. Right?"

So that was it. Alec had access and the ability to destroy everything, just by telling Shannon the truth. She would stop the treatments if she knew what it cost.

"What the fuck do you want?"

"What I ultimately want is for you fucking people to leave Mercedes alone. But for now, I'll settle for a meeting. Face to face, you and me in a public place. I'd tell you to come alone but you and I both know you're tapped out of resources, so you have no choice but to be alone."

"What do you mean? Cooper has unlimited resources."

"Cooper does, aye. You don't."

Adam's gut dropped. "What do you know?"

"Oh, I know a lot. Like I know you weren't responsible for the speakeasy hit on Mercedes. Cooper left you out in the cold on that one, didn't he?"

A cold tendril of fear worked its way up his chest. "That wasn't us. That was Jason." Adam said this with more confidence than he felt. He had no fucking clue who had worked that hit.

Alec gave a low chuckle. "The fact that you say it's Jason, tells me either you're lying or you're well on the outside of Cooper's circle of trust. I think it's the latter."

Fuck.

"And I'm sure you weren't the blonde who fucked one of Mercedes's agents and filmed it to blackmail him."

Shit. Cooper had pulled in Mariah without a word.

"There are so many lies, Tim. So many secrets have

destroyed lives. And I know a few secrets Cooper doesn't know. And if he did, he would certainly kill you for it."

Adam's heart leaped, and his eyes shot to Mara. She trusted him to protect her, but they were far from safe.

There was no way. No way they could figure it all out like that. He could call Alec's bluff. But what if he was wrong?

Goddamn it.

Adam had tried to warn that fucker Hollis that McKinley needed to stay in the dark. He was too fucking dangerous to trifle with. But Hollis had been an arrogant shithead, with one thing on his mind.

Now here he fucking was. Hollis was in the wind and Adam was outmanned, having to face Alec McKinley on his own.

Perhaps it was better to try a fresh approach. He had needs of his own he was tired of ignoring.

"Alright. I'll meet with you, but I want Mercedes to be there too. I have a few things I need to say to her."

"Not fucking happening," Alec spit out.

"But it has to. I know you won't gun me down right in front of her, at least not unprovoked. And I don't plan on provoking you. She'll be safe from me. Besides, I know you don't want to leave her vulnerable without you. The size of the boner Hollis has for that woman is fucking ridiculous. So, that's my deal."

McKinley was quiet for a moment, and Adam was sure he was going to tell him to go fuck himself.

"Fine, but if anything happens to her, I'll kill you slowly. Do you get me, mate?"

"I don't doubt you'll try, Scottie."

"Cute," Alec said curtly. "There's a winery called Divinity Vineyards just outside of Santa Rosa. Do you know it?"

"I can find it."

"We'll meet you there at two o'clock tomorrow for a sit-down tasting in the gardens. The reservation will be under the name Ryan. You try anything, and the FBI will pay your lovely wife a visit within thirty minutes. Now I better go. Shannon has banana nut bread I'm dying to try out."

The line went dead, and Adam nearly threw his phone against the wall. Alec was putting him in an impossible position. He couldn't go against Cooper. Not out in the open.

Not ever.

If there was even a whisper to him of what Adam had been doing, he would pay.

CHAPTER FORTY-SIX

A lec made sure he and Mercedes were seated twenty minutes before the meeting time. The vineyard's large garden was sprinkled with tables, allowing visitors to enjoy their tastings in the shade of the oak and maple trees. Staff brought out trays of wine in stemless glasses and charcuterie plates to snack on.

They selected a table near a gate to the parking lot in case they needed to get the hell out of there fast. The wine and food were delivered by the personal host. Alec informed them they were expecting one more person to join and asked they be allowed privacy for their meeting.

Not for the first time, Alec wondered if he'd lost his damn mind. Meeting a man like Adam could be disastrous, especially with Mercedes with him. But his team was scattered, and he couldn't leave her on her own. She was safer with him than without.

Mercedes was pale, her fingers tapping on her skirt. Alec took her hand into his lap. This man had ordered her death, and she had witnessed him slaughter others. Yet she was here, wanting to face him herself. Her strength never failed to amaze him.

Alec saw him coming well before Mercedes did and she dug her fingers into his hand when Adam came into view. He was a hulking man with a constant, brooding glare on his face. He pulled his chair out with a jerk and sat, veins bulging in his arms. Alec released the safety switch on the gun he had rested on his thigh. The fucker moved wrong, and Alec would put him down.

He turned his glare on Mercedes. "Nice to see you again."

Mercedes shifted, her fingers tightening on Alec's.

"Well, you wanted this meeting," Adam said. "What the fuck do you want?"

"I want access to Mara Donovan," Alec said.

The tic in Adam's eye told him all he needed to know.

"If I had any idea where that bitch was, she'd be dead by now."

"Oh, I don't necessarily know if that's true." Alec picked up his phone, swiped a few times, then pushed it across the table.

Alec could see when Adam made the connection. The video was only a few seconds long, but the words he'd hissed to Mara were clear before he let her go.

"Funny thing," Alec said, sliding the phone back. "When you pay a clerk to destroy a recording before police show up, you should make sure he actually destroys it."

Adam's jaw tensed. "I was in a bit of a hurry. I had a dipshit with me who wouldn't shut the fuck up."

"What do you think Marcus Cooper would do to you if he knew you were sleeping with his mistress?"

Adam's glare shot up. "Motherfucker." He didn't even try to deny it. The truth of it was all over his face. "I knew you'd be the one to figure this shit out."

Alec tilted his head. "Did you?"

"I used to tell Jason he was underestimating you. I was right."

"How long were you and Mara together?" Mercedes asked, her voice quiet.

Adams's scowl shifted to Mercedes. "For three years. It would be five, but I don't count the last two."

"Five years." Mercedes whispered under her breath. "And all that time, she was his mistress too?"

"She was never his fucking mistress." Adam ground out behind his clenched jaw. "She was his slave."

This was an unexpected turn. "When was Mara brought into the trade?"

"When she was seventeen. Tell me, how many billionaires have executive assistants who are barely out of high school?" Adam's expression shifted to one of loathing. "Cooper figures out ways to get what he wants. Things you can't say no to. For me, it was a lifesaving treatment for Shannon. For others, it was real estate or a shitload of money."

"And for Mara?

"A full-ride scholarship to any school she wanted to go to, including Stanford. Only when she got to California, the scholarship required frequent blow jobs for all the grantors. Just a little something of a thank you for all they'd done to make her 'dreams come true'. When she refused, they would beat the fuck out of her. Didn't take long before they were outright raping her at parties."

Mercedes gasped.

"What Mercedes? Little too close to home for you?" Adam snarled. "I know about your mother and how fucked up she was. It's good you had music to keep you out of the grasps of rich fuckers who wanted to gang bang you and film it. Do you have any idea how many videos there are of Mara? Most of them when she was underage. All of them without her consent." Anger was radiating off Adam. "When I met her, Cooper had just made her his *personal servant,* as he called it. She was fucking grateful, because she'd only have to screw one nasty old man."

Mercedes shook her head. "I find it hard to believe Whitley wouldn't have gone after sex trafficking charges along with all the others."

"You have to prove it, right? And they would never believe her word alone. Cooper no longer brings in his girls the same way. Now, he prefers well paid and very willing escorts in whatever city he happens to be in."

"And he expected you to be his personal servant as well?" Alec asked.

"I had a part to play. Someone to keep his wife from knowing what he was doing and take Mara home after spending hours in his bed. Then there was the dirty work he likes me to do." Adam's jaw clenched tight, and he ground out his next words through clenched teeth. "He waits, you know. He waits until you're good and hooked, unable to betray him before he lays out the *real* cost."

Alec sat forward. "So help take him down. We both know Hollis is a shit witness. He could change his testimony in a second if it served his purpose. We need to get Mara on board to make a difference."

"We already tried that. It was a clusterfuck."

Alec frowned. "What do you mean?"

"Who do you think convinced Mara to go to Mercedes in the first place? I thought we had a shot at bringing him down then. And we failed. Hard."

Mercedes's eyes went wide. "You were a part of that?"

"I knew all about the first whistleblower, so we thought we could add Mara's knowledge to the deal. Then, out of the blue, Cooper ordered the kid's death and for us to destroy everything. There was nothing I could do to stop it. Then Mara panicked and begged me to get her out of there."

"So, you helped to hide her in England," Alec said.

"I did. She was upset I wouldn't go with her. But I couldn't leave, or Cooper would go after Shannon and the kids."

"Then you put yourself in charge of hunting Mara down. Brilliant."

Adam's lips twisted into a smile. "She could have stayed hidden forever if Jason hadn't figured out she was a whistle-blower too." He looked at Mercedes. "He thinks he saved your life by taking you to London, but it saved Mara's, too. If he'd found Mara, we'd have no use for you. So, he only half-assed looked for her until you ran off on him."

"I have to admit, I'm a little surprised you're so talkative," Alec said, taking a sip of wine.

Adam looked down at the table, his brows clinched. "I don't like the man I've become, and I know I can never fully redeem myself. Some things I've done are unforgivable. But when I can, I try to be the man I used to be." His gaze shifted to Mercedes. "Mara said I should tell you the ways I helped you. But I honestly don't think it would matter."

Mercedes frowned. "How did you help me?"

"Well for one, I let Alec take you."

What is he on about?

Mercedes gasped. "What do you mean, take me?"

"I fucked up. Back in London. I was the reason Jason knew you met with Alec in secret. I wanted to rub it in his smug face. I didn't think he'd do what he did. How bad . . ." Adam cleared his throat. "So, when I spotted one of Alec's men wheeling you out of your hospital room, I knew what was going down. And I let it happen."

"You got on the elevator with us and stared at me for an entire floor."

"I let you go, Mercedes. I never said I wasn't an asshole. Besides, Jason was coming in, so I was on the move, anyway."

"Why was he there that day? He never came to the hospital before that," Mercedes said.

Adam scoffed. "Yes, he did. He tried to come see you all the time. We were babysitting you to make sure you didn't run for it, but we also tried to keep Jason off you for a bit."

"Am I supposed to thank you for that?" Mercedes's trembling words were coated with anger. "You knew what he was, and you helped him cover it up over and over."

"I did." Real remorse shot across his face. "But I didn't know how bad until London. That last time he beat you . . . Fucking hell. He didn't know if he'd killed you or not, so I ran up to check. What I saw stuck with me. You were half naked, all sliced up, and lay in a fucking river of blood. I didn't think there was a chance in hell you'd make it."

Alec's stomach turned. He was well aware of how brutalized Mercedes had been by Jason but hearing a firsthand account of it was revolting.

"So, when I saw what was happening at the hospital, I looked the other way. Call it absolution if you want, or don't." He shrugged.

Mercedes leaned forward. "You want absolution? Convince Mara to testify. Or better yet, testify yourself. Whitley might make a bargain with you. Trust me when I tell you he'll do anything for a win."

"Not going to happen. Shannon won't survive without the treatment. Cooper and his fucknut son, Tyler, are already threatening to cut her off. My kids can't live without her."

"Your kids are probably going to live without her soon anyway, mate," Alec said.

Adams's stare became piercing. "The fuck you mean by that?"

"Have you seen her recently? She's incredibly ill. Blue lips, thin as hell, and her skin and eyes were yellow. I think her liver might be in bad shape. She would've collapsed had I not caught her." The color drained from Adam's face. Alec tilted his head. "Are you quite certain Cooper is still treating her?"

Realization dawned in Adam's eyes, and Alec gave him a moment to let the information settle. Then he slid a business card across the table. "This is the number to my office in London. If either you or Mara call, you'll be given access to either myself or my cousin Declan. I can offer her protection. I would offer it to Shannon as well, but I don't have the resources to help her."

Alec pulled Mercedes to her feet; her hand clasped in his. "I told you, I would never hurt your wife or your children, and I meant it. But you know as well as I there are people in this world who wouldn't have a problem with it. Think about it and call me."

Alec guided Mercedes toward the gate that opened to the parking lot, leaving Adam rigid in his seat.

CHAPTER FORTY-SEVEN

J ason sat typing at the little table, sweating his fucking balls off. Now that he had access to some of Cooper's money, he'd wanted to find a different place to stay. But Mariah had nixed the idea. This place was one of the few that took cash, and she didn't want any chance that Adam or Cooper himself would figure out she was using Jason to find their targets.

The acrid scent of smoke filtered through the dirty screens. This fucking state was an inferno. The skies were brown with a thick haze that never seemed to go away. And since they didn't have a functioning air conditioner in this shit-hole, Jason was forced to breathe in the toxic air from the distant wildfires.

Mariah was lounging naked on the bed, fanning herself with a camping guide. Since she'd appeared in his room and made her offer, she'd been staying in this dump with him.

Jason let her suck him off most mornings, but he wouldn't fuck her. God only knew what kind of nasty shit she had going on down there. Besides, Mercedes was the last woman who had taken his cock, and there was no competing with that.

He tried to focus on the task at hand. Adam had suddenly

fallen off the radar, and arrangements had been made to pull him out of the dark. Mariah was certain Adam knew where Mara Donovan was. She hadn't shared her thoughts with Cooper quite yet, but even Jason wondered what Adam was up to.

Not only that, but Cooper's idiot kid, Tyler, had taken up some of the reins. This plot to draw out Adam had been the little turd's plan. It would be effective, but dangerous as hell. Adam wasn't one to fuck with.

"Are you trying to get through Cressida's firewalls?" Mariah said.

"I told you," Jason snapped. "Cressida has skill, so it's a waste of time. We're better off figuring out where Adam is and working on the others later."

Adam was a smart man, and he certainly knew how to stay in the shadows, but he didn't know current trends in technology.

"I found him," Jason said.

"Really?" She swung her legs off the bed and joined him.

"Yeah, If I go back through Cooper's secure lines, I can find a bunch of numbers for all of Cooper's shitty associates that call in. But only one of those numbers has ever gotten a call from Shannon Barlow. Her last call was a few days before he went quiet."

"His wife called him? On a phone he uses to talk to Cooper?"

Mariah's tits were right at his eyeline. He grunted in annoyance at them and looked at the computer. "It's sloppy as hell, but only we know about this line. Adam wouldn't have thought he was going to be our target. I'm still not sure I understand why he *is* a target."

"I told you, Tyler Cooper's got a small dick complex when it comes to Adam. He wants all of daddy's love and thinks he needs to prove Adam's dirty to get it." Mariah shrugged. "What does this all mean?" She gestured at the computer.

"It means I can start tracing that number. The next time it's used, I can track where it is and who he's talking to. Now we just have to wait for the bad news to come in."

"Damn, that could take a while." Mariah went back to fanning herself. "I can't do another few days in this place. Let's call around for rooms."

"Thank fuck. This heat is killing me." He looked back at her. "How much longer do they think it'll be?"

She shrugged. "It could be any day now."

"Let's make the next place closer to that valley. We're going to need to be nearby if shit goes down." Jason wiped the sweat from his brow. "And let's make it a place with air conditioning."

CHAPTER FORTY-EIGHT

TWO WEEKS LATER

Before Alec even opened his eyes, he could feel her. He inhaled deeply, savoring Mercedes's mouth caressing his skin. She moved down his chest and onto his stomach, the bedsheet slipping from his naked body. He was hard as hell and aching for whatever she had in mind.

"Mmm, good morning, darling."

"'Morning, love," she murmured against him.

He ran his hand through her silky hair, gathering it up. "I'm rather enjoying this wake-up call."

"I hoped you would." She continued, her trail of kisses burning down his body. "I've spent the last ten minutes debating on letting you sleep."

Alec moaned. "You made the right choice."

Her tongue ran over a ticklish spot on his side. He bit his lip to hold still, not wanting to disrupt her trajectory. She grinned up at him. "I love that if I kiss you there, you squirm around and try not to laugh. But if I kiss you here . . ." Her mouth sucked in the apex of his thigh and pelvis.

A groan escaped as the burn of desire coursed through his veins. Arching up, he gripped her hair tighter.

"I love to hear you moan like that," she whispered and assailed the same spot again, this time not letting up while she tortured him.

"Christ, Sadie. Please."

Her gaze was on him. "Please what, Alec?"

"Please, stop teasing me."

She gave him a devilish smile before she pulled his cock into her mouth. Alec groaned and within seconds lost all sense of himself. Her mouth and the fire it brought were all he could feel, all he needed. She worked him, taking him to the back of her throat. Soft moans escaping her as she pleasured him.

As his release built, his hip thrusting up to meet her. "Christ. Holy shit, Sadie. You're going to make me come."

She moaned, but her mouth was unrelenting.

"God, Sadie. Oh god."

When Mercedes tightened her lips around him, he hit the peak. He cried out as his climax ripped through him, spilling onto her waiting tongue. When the last wave left him, he was gasping for air. She eased her grip, sucking him gently until she'd taken every drop.

"Bloody fucking hell. Can you wake me up like that every day?"

Mercedes chuckled and shifted to his side, curling up against him with a satisfied sigh. Alec needed a moment to recover before he turned his attention to her. His phone buzzed, but he ignored it. His focus was on how many ways he could pleasure her.

"You should answer that," Mercedes murmured. "It rang once before."

"It did?"

She chuckled. "Yeah, we were a little preoccupied."

Alec stretched, fumbling for the phone on the bedside table. Cressida's irritated text glared up at him.

Dammit Alec, pick up your phone.

"Shit," he said, scrambling out of bed. "I missed four calls from Cress."

"Is everything okay?"

"I don't know, but something's happening." He tossed on his shorts while he rang Cressida back on speaker.

Mercedes sat up; her naked body wrapped in the white linen.

"Bloody hell," Cressida snapped when she answered. "Where have you been?"

Alec checked his watch. "It's only five in the morning. We were sleeping. What's going on?"

"I got a call from Adam. I'm not sure what's happened. He said he'd only talk to you. But whatever it is, it's fucked up."

Mercedes's fingers drummed on her knee. Adam terrified her.

It had been two weeks since their terse meeting. They hadn't heard from him, although Cressida confirmed the doorbell camera had caught him paying Shannon and his children a visit later that same day.

"Did he leave a number?"

"He did. I'm working on patching you through."

They waited in silence, his pulse thumping hard in his ears. When Cressida came back, she said, "We have a connection, the line is yours."

"This is Alec."

"She's dead." Adam's deep voice was flat.

"What? Who's dead?"

"Shannon."

Mercedes winced, and Alec reached for her hand.

Damn. Shannon had been in terrible shape, but he'd hoped there was time to get her help.

"She collapsed yesterday while making dinner. The kids came in from playing outside and found her unconscious. My daughter," Adam's voice broke, and he cleared his throat. "My daughter was the one that called the ambulance. Shannon never woke up. She died just after midnight this morning."

"I'm sorry to hear that. She was a kind woman. And she didn't deserve any of this."

"She was." Adam's words were thick. "You were right. Cooper wasn't treating her anymore. Not only that, I think they were poisoning her. They were poisoning all of them."

"How?"

"I don't know, but I looked in on Shannon right after you and I met. She'd declined fast, but the symptoms weren't the same as when she had cancer. And now, my son . . ." Adam paused again to clear his throat. "Now my son is showing signs of it, too. It's likely a heavy metal like cadmium or arsenic. Shannon's family is going to have the well tested."

Jesus Christ.

The thin woman who had welcomed him into her home came to Alec's mind. Adam could very well be right. Her weakened body wouldn't have stood a chance against a large dose of poison.

"I want you to talk to your guy and set up a meeting," Adam said.

"My guy?"

"Yeah, the FBI, the federal marshals, the US attorney. I don't fucking care," Adam snapped. "The gloves are off. Mara and I are ready to make a deal."

Alec bit back the sharp exhale, not wanting to show his hand. It was what they'd always needed. Mara coming forward was the best scenario to free Mercedes from testifying. If Adam was serious about adding in his knowledge, Cooper would be fully exposed.

"Aye," Alec said. "I'll make some calls."

"Good. Mara seems to believe if she can tell them everything first, they won't come for me. I keep telling her my days of freedom are numbered but—" Adam's breath came out in a frustrated huff. "Anyway, she's not going into that fucking lion's den alone. You set up the meeting and you and Mercedes escort her there."

Alec's pulse kicked up. "Fuck that. I'll make phone calls, but we're not getting involved with this."

"You have to. Clearly, *I* can't take her there."

"Well, you'll have to see another way around this. I have my own interests to secure."

"Then you and Sadie should get ready to be on the run forever."

"We can manage until the retrial."

Adam scoffed. "It's cute you think there's ever going to be a retrial without Mara. If crazy-ass Jason hasn't already dropped off the face of the earth, he will. Especially when he hears how you're shacked up with Sadie. And without Mara or Jason, Sadie is it. And you and I both know her testimony only touches the surface of what Cooper's done. I doubt Whitley will even ask for a new trial if he can't get the others."

Alec's gaze shot to Mercedes. Her brows were knitted together and he could see she'd already considered this as a possibility. Whitley needed a slam dunk and the information Mara offered eclipsed what Mercedes brought to the table.

"Goddamn it. We don't want any part of this."

"Well, too fucking bad, Scottie, you're already a part of it. If you can't help me with this, then Mara and I will be in South America by the end of the week." After a second, Adam's sharp tone softened. "Look, I get it. You think I want to turn Mara over to you or to the fucking feds? None of this is ideal. But you have almost as much to lose as I do. So you're it."

Alec ran his hand through his hair. "Aye, I'll have arrangements made. Call me in a few days."

The line clicked off without a goodbye. Alec tossed the phone on the bed and rubbed his eyes.

"Those poor kids," Mercedes whispered.

"Aye." He thought of the little black-haired children who'd just been dealt a lifetime of pain to bear. If Adam testified, there would be more trauma to come. "Do you think Whitley will make a deal with Adam?"

"I do. He wants to take down Marcus Cooper so much, he'll probably give Adam a slap on the wrist. The only thing I doubt he'll forgive is the murder of the FBI agent and the embassy employee. Politically, that would be a disaster. But he might try for a reduced sentence."

Alec frowned. "He may not get justice for the things he did to you."

Mercedes shook her head. "I want to take Cooper down, too. And if everything Adam told us is true and he let me leave with you, then I can live with it." Mercedes had a glimmer of hope in her eyes. "Besides, if they both testify, there's a chance they'll remove me from the witness list. With what I have on Whitley, he might cut me free, just so I don't expose the shit he did to us."

It was too easy, and nothing had ever been easy for them. But he nodded and drew her into his arms. Hope was a dangerous thing, but he'd hang on to this feeling a little longer.

CHAPTER FORTY-NINE

The windshield wipers squelched over the window as they drove through the darkened countryside. Rain moved across California's parched valleys, providing relief to the thirsty landscape. Alec gripped Mercedes's hand, stroking it with his thumb.

It felt as if they were heading into an abyss. Would they resurface, free and whole? Or would they find themselves trapped, walking right into a fresh hellscape?

It had taken a couple of days, but the arrangements with the FBI were set. Alec would pick Mara up and take her to a secure facility in San Jose. There, Nick Kessler would take custody of her care. Once Mara was settled, Adam would turn himself in to be formally charged.

Alec didn't want to do the transfer during the day. So he and Mercedes left the haven of their beach house to pick up Mara the night of Shannon Barlow's funeral.

It had been a private affair. No announcements were made, no community members were let in on the services. It would only be Shannon's family and Adam. A large public service had been scheduled for the following week.

Alec turned off the highway and onto a well-groomed

driveway. Unlike the dirt road to Shannon's small home, the public used this lane to access the tasting room of the family's winery. It was meticulously landscaped, with rose and lavender bushes skirting the edges of the darkened driveway. They drove past the tasting room to the large farmhouse owned by Shannon's family.

Alec kept his hand on his gun as he got out of the car and walked to the house. The wind swept through the sleeping vineyards next to the house, blowing the rain all around them.

The front door opened as he and Mercedes walked up the steps.

Mara Donovan stepped out onto the wood porch. Her blonde hair curled in waves on her shoulders, gray eyes wide as she studied him. "You must be Alec. You look like your cousin."

"Aye, we hear that a lot." Alec held out his hand in greeting. "I've wanted to meet you for quite some time."

Mara took it and offered him a timid smile. "I know. Thank you for helping me."

Then she looked past his shoulder to Mercedes. Regret crossed her expression. "Hi, Sadie," she murmured.

Mercedes's face was hard to read in the dim light. This woman was the catalyst for all Mercedes had endured. The one who brought collateral damage to both their lives.

But Mara had been a victim longer than any of them could even imagine. Alec couldn't fault her for fighting to get out of her situation.

Mercedes stepped to the shorter woman and drew her into a hug.

"I'm sorry," Mara whispered, clinging to Mercedes. "I'm so sorry."

"I know. It's okay."

Mara stepped back to let them enter and said in a hushed tone. "Come on in. Tim's with his kids."

They followed her into the dimly lit living room. Adam sat

on the sofa, the small bodies of his sleeping children wrapped around him. Adam turned and pressed his lips to each of their foreheads before he slid out from under them.

Alec kept Mercedes behind him, still not trusting a single thing this man did. When Adam brushed past them, they followed him into the foyer.

"There's been a change of plans. Shannon's family has made a few arrangements, so my kids are going to stay here with them. I'm going in tonight."

Alec narrowed his eyes. "My people are only expecting Mara."

"Well, they're getting both of us."

"If I'd known that, we wouldn't be here."

"Which is exactly why I didn't tell you."

"Listen, fucker—" Alec growled.

"Gentlemen," Mara broke in. She turned her pleading look onto Alec. "We know this is an unexpected change, but I feel better having Adam with me. Can you please take us where we need to go?"

Alec snapped his mouth shut, glaring at Adam. "Aye, but he sits in the front seat next to me. I don't want a bullet in my brain at the first stoplight."

"I'm not even fucking armed, Scottie. You can check." Adam lifted his arms.

Alec didn't waste the chance. He patted Adam down. When he was satisfied Adam wasn't packing, he stood to his full height. "We should get going. We have a bit of a drive to the location."

Alec stalked out to the car, holding the back seat door open for Mercedes. Adam got into the passenger seat, shooting Alec a hostile glare while he buckled in. Mara situated herself behind him, latching in next to Mercedes.

Once they were on the highway, a quiet conversation between the two women came from the back seat. Mara described how she escaped Cooper and how for a time, even Adam didn't know where to find her.

"I swear, I didn't know how bad it would be for you," Mara said.

"I understand, really," Mercedes responded. "I'm just glad you are coming forward now."

They fell silent, the thrumming of the rain the only sound.

Alec didn't see what hit them.

There'd been no lights. No warning of what was to come.

The front side of the SUV had collapsed in on itself.

Alec's head hit the side window before the airbags exploded in his face. The car spun, coming to rest in the middle of the highway.

Disoriented, Alec pushed the airbags down, his heart thundering in his ears and his head felt like a drill was going through it. Blood trickled down his face and into his eyes.

Adam's door was already open, and the big man was gone. Alec reached for his gun, but it was gone, too.

What the fuck?

Alec pushed his door open and swept his gaze around the dark. Blood and rain pooled in his vision, blurring out the surrounding landscape. He could barely make out the pickup that had slammed into them steaming in the street. Wiping to clear his eyes, he stumbled and grasped the handle to Mercedes's door.

She was conscious but clearly dazed. Unbuckling her seat belt, she shifted to get out of the car. "Alec, what the hell hap—"

Footsteps on the wet asphalt came to his ears and Alec blocked the first hit. Another punch came at him swiftly, hitting him in the gut. Alec doubled over, struggling to catch his breath.

"Alec!" Mercedes screamed.

A heavy thump of a fist hitting skin broke through the night and she fell silent.

"Sadie!"

But it was the last thing he would hear from her.

He was nearly to his feet when the barbs of the Taser cut into his skin. Then an agonizing voltage struck like a jack-hammer through every nerve. His muscles convulsed painfully, paralyzing him. Even his screams were trapped in his chest.

When the device ran through its cycle, Alec fell to the pavement, gasping for air. He tried to grasp the wires to pull out the barbs, but it hit him again. The impact slamming into his body until he was sure his muscles might snap. When it relented again, his heart raced, unable to keep up with the currents being shot into him.

"How's that feel, you fuck?" an unexpected voice screamed at him.

Fucking hell.

He hadn't been fighting Adam.

Car lights illuminated the dark highway and Jason Hollis's murderous eyes came into his view. Jason sneered as electricity crashed into him again, pulsing over and over throughout his system. When it ended, Alec was certain his heart would give out.

"I need him alive, you stupid fuck," Adam shouted out. "You're fucking everything up again."

Alec registered Adam's words as he struggled to regain his strength. The lights were brighter now. A third car had arrived.

"I'm not leaving this bastard alive," Jason ground out. "We're taking Sadie and Mara to Cooper, but I want to end McKinley now."

"Back the fuck up," Adam growled. "This fucker poisoned my kids. I'm taking him in for myself."

Poisoned his kids? What the fuck was he on about? Dizziness overtook Alec as he tried once more to stand. Another punch to the face brought him down again.

"Guys, we can't bloody well stay out here," Mariah

chimed in. "Knock him the fuck out and bring them all. We can sort it at the estate."

Mariah handed Adam a syringe.

Fuck!

"Hold him down, he's a big fucker."

Alec reared up, taking a swing before Jason's weight brought him down again. Alec landed one solid punch across Jason's cheek before his arms were restrained, and Adam plunged the needle into his neck.

CHAPTER FIFTY

Mercedes woke with a pounding headache. She blinked, straining to recognize anything in the darkened room. There was a soft, linen-covered mattress. Her eyes were like sandpaper, and she tried to rub them, but her arms wouldn't move.

Panic clawed through her. Mercedes twisted against the rope binding her wrists, pins and needles numbing her limbs.

"Don't struggle, babe."

A cry escaped her when she heard his voice. The same one that haunted every nightmare she'd ever had.

The strike of a match echoed in the room as Jason lit a tall wax candle. Firelight flickered off his chiseled face, the scars of the bullets he'd taken in his chest last year shone in the light.

Then he slid his hand down his unzipped khakis, massaging his erection slowly.

Mercedes bit back another sob. There was no way she could survive this. Jason would get what he wanted.

For a second Alec came to her mind, and she shoved him away. The last thing she wanted was to associate this moment with him. She had to stay focused, control her breathing.

"Jason. You have to untie my hands." She was failing at keeping the trembling from her voice. "Please. They hurt."

"But I like you like this." He sat next to her. On the surface, he was as gentle as a lover approaching his virgin bride. But he was stalking her, ready to strike when she least expected it.

The bed shifted as Jason laid against the pillow, his fingers still stroking the bulge of his exposed briefs. "I've missed you so much, Sadie. I don't think you have any idea how much I've needed you."

Think Sadie. What had Noah taught her?

Her training hadn't gone over what to do when her arms were restrained behind her back. She had to get her hands free.

"Jason, please. I think I'm going to throw up," she cried, tears streaming down her face. "Please . . ." She worked up a gag, and Jason was off the bed like lightning.

"Goddammit, Sadie. You'd better not puke."

He flipped her over roughly, her face pushed into the pillows, stealing her breath. The full-on anxiety attack was taking hold, and she wasn't sure she could control it.

When he freed her hand, Mercedes worked herself to a sitting position, inhaling deeply and rubbing her arms as her circulation painfully returned.

Jason was next to her again. He reached out a hand and rubbed her back. "Better?"

Stay focused, Sadie. "Yeah. Just, give me a sec." Gulping air, her gaze moved around the dark room.

It was a residence. The bedroom they were in was large, with a king-size bed. It looked professionally decorated and not lived in at all.

The door had a keyhole instead of a lock. *Damn it.*

Then she caught sight of a tall dresser next to the door. She only looked at it for a fraction of a second, but she could swear Jason's gun was on top of it.

Now that he was certain she wouldn't throw up on him, he moved closer. The gentle rubbing on her back had become a caress, one that found its way under her shirt. Unless she could produce some real vomit, he was going forward with his plan.

"Your skin is so smooth," he said, sliding her blouse up even higher.

Mercedes fought the urge to wrench herself away. Nothing pissed Jason off more than to have his advances turned down.

His fingers worked the clasp of her bra. When it fell away, he shifted on the bed, slipping his hands under her shirt to cup her breasts.

Don't think about it. Think about what you need to do.

Her gaze shot back to the dresser. Jason was too preoccupied to notice her squinting at it, trying to see if the shadow was a gun.

Too risky. Even if it were, it was too far away.

"Do you ever miss us, Sadie? Do you miss what we were?" Jason was kissing her neck now, his fingers digging into her breasts.

He always expected an answer when he asked a question like that. Without thinking, she responded with a little noise of agreement. Just like she always had.

Mercedes scanned the room, but there were no other potential weapons. Even the candle he'd lit was only a flimsy taper. They had likely swept away anything solid she could use against him. An elegant prison for Jason to rape her in.

When he tugged her shirt over her head, her control slipped. She hated the touch of his bare skin on hers, his mouth roaming her body. Maybe she should let her mind go away, separate from herself. Let him take what he came for, so he'd leave her alone.

But when he was done, he wouldn't leave. He'd either kill her or keep her.

"Do you feel it, babe?" Jason groaned. "This connection we have?" He sucked painfully on her neck.

He really fucking believes it. He believes I'm choosing him.

Then it hit her.

The only weapon in the room was Jason's deranged obsession.

To fight, she would need to comply.

Mercedes turned her head and kissed him. Jason moaned and yanked her in closer, his fingers digging into the back of her neck. When he plunged his tongue into her mouth, she pushed down the urge to scream.

He was panting when he drew away, his hands still groping her. She licked his neck. "I've missed you, Jason. I've thought about you so much since we've been apart."

Jason gave out a laugh. "I fucking knew it. I knew you'd come back to me again."

Mercedes moved off the bed and pulled Jason to his feet. Bile churned in her gut, but she jerked his head down and kissed him hard. Holding on to his shoulders, she slid one leg up his body to his hips. Mercedes remembered what he liked and how he would respond.

She was right. He slipped his hands down her ass and picked her up. Mercedes locked her legs around his waist, kissing him deeply.

Jason groaned. "Holy fuck, Sadie. I can feel how much you want me."

"Can you?" she murmured between deep kisses. "I do, Jace. I want this so much."

She caressed his throat, searching for the ridge on either side of his Adam's apple. There were no do-overs, she had to get this right the first time. Mercedes took a deep breath.

Then she squeezed.

He didn't seem to register it at first.

Then he gagged and jerked. His fingers flew to his neck, and she lifted her shoulder to protect her hand from his grasp.

Mercedes's pulse raced in her ears as she tried counting, but she kept messing up. Jason thrashed about, clawing at her over and over. She whimpered when he dug his fingernails into her, tearing apart the naked flesh of her back.

Shit. Maybe she had the wrong spot.

She adjusted her grip, searching for the artery that should shut him down. Jason staggered toward the dresser and slammed her into it. The pain of it nearly made her lose her hold on his waist. She tightened her legs around him, locking her feet together.

Finally, he swayed and sank to his knees. Even after his head knocked against the wood floors, she held on, gripping his throat until he stopped moving. He could be dead, but her brain was too fractured to stop and figure it out.

Mercedes untangled herself from Jason's limp body and raced toward the door. The knob wouldn't turn.

Fuck!

She was right. It was locked from the outside. No matter how much she jerked and tugged, it was solid. She was trapped in this damn room with him.

"No, no, no. Shit!"

Mercedes ran to the window. She had to be at least three stories up, with a straight drop onto a stone patio. She'd never make it.

Jason had to have a key. How else was he going to get out of here? She didn't want to touch him, but she needed the damn thing. Scrambling to him, she patted his pockets until she found a small ring with a single key. She jerked it from his pocket.

A soft moan was her only warning that he was regaining consciousness, and it came too late.

Jason's hand snaked out and grabbed her wrist. Mercedes landed on her ass next to him.

"You fucking bitch!" He crawled onto his knees. "I'm gonna fucking kill you." Jason reared back and punched her in the face. The blow reverberated across her cheek, and she fell to the ground.

She screamed and scrambled away. But he was already on her, jerking her head back by her hair. "I was gonna make it easy on you. I was gonna take my time and be gentle," he said, jamming his hand down the waistband of her jeans. "But now I'm going to make it rough, and it's gonna fucking hurt."

His fingers dug into her flesh, and she cried out, the lace of her panties giving way.

Don't think about it. Fight.

Mercedes twisted, releasing her hand from his grip, and struck him in the crotch.

The air came out of him all at once, and he doubled over. When her elbow connected to his face, it gave a sickening crack.

"Fuck!" Jason shouted. Blood poured from his twisted nose.

Mercedes hurried to her feet and ran across the room, even knowing the door would never open for her. The key had fallen out of her hand, and Jason was already getting off his knees.

Then the dresser came into her view. The dark shadow *was* a gun. Mercedes grabbed it, aimed wildly, and pulled the trigger. The sound pierced her ears, an echo pulsing through the room. Her hands were trembling so hard she wasn't sure if she'd even hit him.

Jason staggered. A small round patch of red opened up on his bare chest.

He blinked at her in disbelief. "Sadie?" Then the rage returned, and he stumbled toward her. "I'm gonna gut you, you fucking whore—"

Mercedes fired again.

This time, she hit him in the head.

CHAPTER FIFTY-ONE

Classical music was the first thing that hit Alec's consciousness. Was Mercedes playing while he slept?

Then agony in every part of his body struck him, and he remembered.

The car. Mercedes screaming his name. And fucking Jason tasing the fuck out of him.

Alec took stock of himself. They had bound his hands behind his back. His rain-soaked shirt was smeared with blood and dirt.

"Good, he's finally coming around," a feminine voice said. Mariah's face came into his view. "Hello, Alec sweetie. It's been a while, hasn't it?"

"Fuck off," he muttered.

"Oh, I was hoping we'd have a little fun together." Mariah gave a pout.

They were in a study. The decor reeked of new money desperate to fit into old. The large mahogany desk was oversized and ornately carved with lions. Gold seemed to be the theme of the room. It was fucking everywhere.

"Where's Sadie?"

"I'm afraid she's rather busy at the moment." Mariah's

mouth turned up into a sneer. "Jason took her upstairs a bit ago. He's making a snack of her as we speak."

Panic reared up, and he thought he'd go mad. Instead, he pulled in air and cleared his mind. He was no good to her where he was. In order to get to her, he had to survive.

And to survive, he would kill them all.

Adam's deep voice cut in. "They wanted to be here for this. Go get them."

Mariah's footsteps echoed on the marble as she left, leaving Alec alone with Adam.

"You're a real piece of work, you know." Alec spat on the floor. "You had me convinced you did all this for your family. To protect the people you loved. But it looks like you're just a loyal soldier out for the money."

Adam smiled coldly. "We all make sacrifices Alec. Cooper helped me keep Shannon alive for as long as he could. I'm grateful to him."

"How grateful will you be when he puts your pretty daughter into his scholarship program?"

Adam's solid fist landed on his cheek, reverberating through his head. Adam gripped Alec's chin, forcing him to look up. "Don't fucking talk about my daughter."

But there was something in Adam's expression that didn't connect to his words. The anger wasn't there. He stared down at Alec, his glare piercing into him.

Adam let him go and backed away, holding his eyes. Then he leaned against the desk and crossed his arms. His gaze shifted down and up, ever so slowly. Using his peripherals, he could see what Adam was indicating. A small camera, no bigger than a ballpoint pen, was on the desk, aimed at him.

They were being watched. And Adam wanted Alec to know that.

"You're lucky I'm not armed anymore. Mariah made me give up your gun and Jason has the only other one."

Alec stared at him. Why would he give that info up?

What the bloody hell is going on?

"Cooper will be here soon," Adam said menacingly. "And then there will be *hell* to pay."

Heels tapped on marble and a young man followed Mariah into the room. He looked vaguely familiar, but Alec couldn't place him.

"I apologize my father isn't here to greet you. He'll be joining us in a moment." He bent down in front of Alec, his hands on his knees. "So this is one of the McKinleys you were so worried about. He doesn't look like all that much." He said to Adam and Mariah. Then he turned back to Alec. "I'm Tyler."

There was an awkward pause, and Alec frowned at him. "Is that supposed to mean something to me?"

Tyler flushed. "I'm the heir to all this."

"Bully for you." Alec looked past the boy's shoulder to Adam and Mariah. "Is Daddy Cooper around?"

Tyler's openhanded slap connected with Alec's cheek, and he grunted.

"I'm running this show tonight."

This little fuck had no clue how to establish proper authority. Alec glared up at him. "Do *you* know where Sadie is?"

Tyler gave a dismissive shrug. "Not at the moment."

"Then piss off."

The second punch wasn't any stronger. "You want to play with me, asshole?"

A chuckle erupted from Alec's chest. "Aye, I like a little love tap before I fuck someone up."

Then Alec lurched forward, as if he were about to take the younger man out. He tested the bindings on his wrists to see if there was any give. There wasn't.

Tyler yelped and scrambled back, knocking a table over.

Adam chuckled. "Don't worry, Tyler. He's bound pretty tight." Adam shifted his gaze to Alec. "I tied the ropes myself."

Something in the way Adam stared at him made him feel the length of binding his hands. A series of knots tightened against his wrists. There was a piece of the rope sticking forward, easy to grab. He gave a test pull and the first knot came free.

Bloody hell.

All he had to do was pull.

Tyler's face had turned a deep red, and he walked to Mariah. "Give me your gun."

Mariah raised her brow but handed the gun to the kid.

Tyler strode back to Alec, holding the gun sideways in his hand. When the cold barrel met his temple, Alec flinched.

"What were you saying, bitch?" At Alec's silence, Tyler laughed. "Yeah, that's what I thought, you piece of shit. Your girl's off with that other guy, isn't she? I saw her when they brought her in. She's a fine piece of ass. Maybe when he's done with her, I'll take a turn." He pressed the gun harder against Alec's head. "Do you think you'll still want her after we've all fucked her?"

Alec's control was already about to snap. He inhaled in the oxygen he needed to clear this new threat away from him.

Tyler looked triumphant as he straightened up.

Alec focused on his hands. He caught the tail of the rope with his fingertips and tugged until he felt a little give. Then the knots melted away, one after the other. Adam had done his job in making them appear sturdy, but the knots were useless. He gathered the rope in his hand as it came unraveled.

Footsteps approached the study, and Marcus Cooper came into the room. "Adam, what the hell is this?"

"I brought you Alec McKinley."

Tyler flushed. "No, he didn't. I'm the one who pulled Mariah in. *I'm* the one that got your dirty little whore back, and I brought you one of your witnesses." He pointed at Adam. "He didn't do shit."

"Actually," Adam piped in. "You brought him two witnesses."

Marcus Cooper tilted his head. "What do you mean?"

"Jason's upstairs with Mercedes Elliot."

Cooper spun on Mariah. "What the fuck is Jason Hollis doing in my house?"

Mariah stammered. "I needed his help to find what we were looking for. And it worked."

"Don't worry boss, he's not making it out of here alive." Adam's eyes once again shifted to Alec.

Cooper waved it off. "Fine. Just make sure everything is cleaned up and can't be tied back to me or the company."

Cooper looked at Alec. "I honestly have no idea why you're here, other than you've been a pain in my ass for years."

Another knot came free and Alec was starting to get a good idea why he was here.

Cooper sighed. "Just get rid of them all and tell me when it's done. I'll be with Mara, so knock first."

Before he could turn away, a sharp report of gunfire echoed through the house. Alec felt it in his soul.

Sadie.

And then another.

The last of the knots came free in his hand. He leaped from his chair, gripped the rope in both hands, and wrapped it around Tyler's neck.

Tyler cried out in surprise and grasped at the rope. Alec jerked it tighter. The kid gagged and fell silent, still struggling against Alec.

Marcus Cooper stammered. "Jesus, do something!"

Mariah shifted, slipping a knife from her belt. She was gifted with a blade and would need to be eliminated.

Waiting for this little fucker to die was taking too long.

Alec dropped the rope, wrapped his hands around Tyler's

head, and twisted. The thick crack of his neck made him go limp. Alec shoved him aside and picked up the fallen gun.

He swung up, aimed at Mariah, and fired. She didn't have time to cry out before two bullets entered her brain.

Dimly, he was aware of Marcus Cooper's shout of anguish. "You fucker!"

Cooper was nothing. The next threat in the room was Adam. He shifted his aim, anger and distrust battling in his mind.

"Give me the gun, Alec." Adam held his hand out.

There would be nothing to stop Adam from turning the gun on him and killing him. Mercedes needed him.

Adam took a step forward and cast a glance at Cooper. "Give me the fucking gun, Alec."

Cooper had slid to his knees, choking sobs as he stared at his dead son at Alec's feet.

"For Shannon." Adam's voice was thick with emotion. "And Mara."

There was now a desperation in Adam's eyes, a need to seek his own brand of justice.

Alec turned the gun in his hand and offered it to Adam. Then he stepped back and waited.

Adam snatched it and turned to Marcus Cooper.

The old man's jaw dropped when he realized Adam had the gun trained on his head. "Adam?"

Adam unloaded. The gunshots echoing through the room. Each shot hit Cooper in the head. Blood and skull splattered up the wall until nothing was left but bone and pulp.

An eerie silence fell over the room, punctuated only by soft music and the breathing of the two men left alive.

Adam spat on the remains of his former boss, his former warden.

Good riddance.

Alec ran to the door. This place was fucking huge. He'd

have to search for an hour to find where Jason might have taken Mercedes.

"Alec." Adam said, stopping him. "I swear I didn't set that crash up. But an opportunity presented itself, and I took it."

"Where is Sadie?"

"Take the stairs. Third story. Go right at the top of the landing to the last door on the left. That's where he's got her. There's no one else here." Adam tossed the empty gun on the ground and moved to the doorway. "I'm going to find Mara. When she's secure, I'll help you hunt him down."

Alec nodded and sprinted up the stairs until he got to the third floor. He cursed that he didn't have a weapon. Jason did. He would have to be quiet as he moved through the corridor.

Everything was dark, the only light was coming in from the last door. His eyes adjusted as he hid in the shadow, easing his way down the hall.

The silence of the rooms sent terror through him. There was no murmur of voices, no sign of the living.

Alec didn't know if he could live if he lost her again. Dread swirled in his gut. Each silent step brought him closer to learning what that bastard had done to her. If it was anything close to the horrors in his head, his mind would snap to see her like that.

Soft rustling caught his attention, and he stopped.

A dark figure lay crumpled against the wall.

Then it let out a soft whimper.

"Sadie!" he cried.

"Alec?" Her head snapped up.

Relief washed over him, and he ran to her.

"Oh my god, you're alive." Mercedes tried to stand, a gun still in her hand. She was in his arms before she got to her knees. She collapsed against him, her body racked in sobs. He held her as tight as he could without hurting her. Her shirt was gone, and the delicate skin of her back was torn and bleeding. Alec bit back his rage and focused on her.

"I heard a bunch of gunshots and I thought they'd killed you. I couldn't—I couldn't make it down the hall."

"I'm okay, darling. I'm alright." Alec slid the gun next to him. Then he looked through the darkened corridor but there was no other sign of life. "Where's Jason?"

"He's in there." She pointed to the opened bedroom door. "I-I think I killed him, Alec." Panic made her voice shrill. "I fought back, and I shot him twice."

"Did you hit him?"

She nodded. "I got him in the chest with the first one and the head with the second."

The tightness in Alec's chest loosened. *Oh, thank fuck for that.*

"Aye, okay. It's okay." He stroked her hair and murmured gentle words, but she was inconsolable.

"I never thought I would ever kill anyone."

Her cries were tearing his heart apart. Alec understood her meaning. Most people are never put in a situation where they would have to.

"Aye, I know. You did what you had to do." He kissed her head and held her as tight as he could, trying to soothe her increasing panic.

"Darling, look at me." Her wide hazel eyes blinked up at him. "Are you injured?"

"A little. But I . . . I think . . . it's okay," she said between gulps of air.

Mercedes sat back, and the dim light flickered on her face.

Alec sucked in his breath. She was covered in blood and tears. A dark bruise was swelling across her cheek and jaw.

The light must have shone on his battered face too, because she cried. "Jesus, what did they do to you?"

"It's nothing, darling. I'll be fine." He wasn't feeling any of it at the moment. All his thoughts were on her.

Unbuttoning the top buttons of his damp shirt, he tugged it over his head. He helped her put it on, covering her trembling body. As soon as that was done, she was back in his arms. She inhaled deeply, the tears slowing as he rocked her.

A groan broke through the silence. Alec snapped up the gun and trained it on the door.

Mercedes gasped and clawed at his shoulders. "Oh, my god. He's still alive. We have to go."

That was not the sound of a man that could chase them down.

She made to stand, but he held her with his free hand. "No, no, no. I've got you. I've got you. Look at me."

Her eyes were wild with fear, her breathing coming in soft pants. "Alec, we have to run."

"Listen to me, darling. We're done running. Do you understand me?"

Alec could see her fear shifting away and the rational part of her brain was returning.

She inhaled deeply and nodded.

He kept his attention on the door, waiting for a sign of movement. "I want you to stay right here and cover your ears if you need to. I won't be long."

"Okay," she whispered.

Alec stood and approached the room cautiously. A single candle lit the space, and his stomach churned to think of what this fucker had done to her here. He trained his gun on Jason's sprawled form.

Mercedes wasn't wrong. She'd shot Jason twice. Blood streamed across his bare chest, and the side of his head was opened up. Her bullet had taken a chunk of his skull, but hadn't entered it. This wound was likely survivable.

But Jason wouldn't be surviving anything.

"I figured they would have done you in," Jason rasped. "I was hoping to do it myself."

"Aye, I know you were. But it looks like that's not going to happen."

"So, you gonna kill me?"

"I am."

"I thought a guy like you would let me suffer. You know, as payback."

Alec crouched down out of Jason's reach. "Nah, I don't care if you suffer. I just want you out of our lives. Besides, if I let you die on your own, your death will be on her. And even your worthless life would weigh on her conscience. She doesn't need to struggle with that. So, I'll take it on for her."

Jason tried to drag himself to his feet but swayed and slipped back. "Fuck," he growled. He sneered at Alec, blood dripping down his chin. "You know, everything I did to her she wanted. She was begging for it."

"Mm-hmm. That's why she put a bullet in your brain."

"You did that to her," Jason spat. "You got in her head and fucked it up. Without you, we would've been happy."

Alec stood, wanting nothing more than to finish this and get back to Mercedes.

"She chose me long before she ever met you. And she's chosen me over and over ever since. After I end you, I'm taking her home and making a life with her. One that she deserves."

Jason shifted and tried to stand one more time.

Alec brought the gun up and pulled the trigger.

CHAPTER FIFTY-TWO

TWO MONTHS LATER

Mercedes ignored the lightheadedness being in the hospital gave her, focusing instead on the happy reason they were there. Luke called her at one in the morning to tell her the hospital had admitted Charlotte. Excitement buzzed through her body. She hadn't missed one of the most important moments in her sister's life.

Alec tightened his grasp on her hand as they waited for the elevator to stop on the maternity floor.

"Are you sure you don't want to go back to the hotel and sleep? It could be a while." she asked him.

He scrunched up his face and shook his head. "Nah. Sleep's overrated."

Mercedes giggled and leaned against his shoulder.

Alec hadn't left her side since carrying her down the stairs at Marcus Cooper's estate. Jason's death wasn't the last of her traumas that night. Even though Alec had done his best to shield her from the carnage in the study, she'd seen more than she knew what to do with.

Then at the hospital, the kind nurses and physicians

encouraged her to have a rape kit performed. Although she didn't think Jason raped her, she'd been unconscious in his custody for hours. Unfortunately, it wasn't the first one she'd ever endured. She suffered through one in London the last night she and Jason were together.

He stayed by her side, holding her hand while they gave her a pelvic exam and keeping her water steady as she swallowed down the Plan B pills. It was only a precaution. Her IUD was still in place, but she wasn't taking any chances. Alec supported her through every decision. When her doctor called to tell her that they'd found no evidence Jason had violated her more than she knew, Alec held her while she sobbed.

Alec had been her rock through it all and she realized this was what happened when two people loved each other. It wasn't just the beautiful times that mattered, it was the broken times, too.

The last few weeks had been filled with healing and rediscovering freedom. Alec was so gentle with her, keeping her at the beach house until she felt strong enough to reemerge into the world. For a time, she wasn't sure she ever wanted to leave the safety of the little haven they'd carved out. But after a week or so, she was ready to reclaim herself, to work on getting on her feet again.

The elevator stopped on the maternity floor. Just before the door slid open, Alec placed a soft kiss on the top of her head. Mercedes sighed, her heart full.

They walked to the waiting area, and Luke called out to them.

"Hey, there's the Da to be." Alec grinned at his younger cousin and hauled him into a bear hug, slapping his back.

"Jesus, can you believe it?" Luke was a bit of a wreck. He pulled Mercedes into him next. "I'm so grateful you're here. I need backup in there."

Mercedes scoffed. "I have no idea what I'm doing either. I'm sure the nurses will help us manage."

Before she followed Luke to their room, she drew Alec into her arms. "Last chance for you to go catch some sleep."

"Aye, I'll be fine. Maybe I'll charm the nurses into turning on the rugby game for me." He leaned down and kissed her. "I'll be right here."

Mercedes followed Luke to the security doors, pushing back the fear for her sister. Charlotte and the baby would be okay. They had to be.

ALEC SAT, HIS ARSE GROWING MORE AND MORE uncomfortable as time went on. The smells of the hospital permeated his clothes and he hoped being here wouldn't be too triggering for Mercedes. After everything that had happened in the last year, the scent sometimes made him queasy, too.

But when Mercedes popped out to give him an update, she glowed with excitement. So maybe he was overthinking it.

Every day, her bravery astonished him.

The last three weeks had been an unraveling of trauma. Not just from the events at Cooper's estate, but for Mercedes, of the last four years. She still struggled with anxiety, especially at night. Her therapist had been in contact with her, which helped some. Once they settled on a place to live, they would both seek help to put this all behind them. Each day, they took new steps to come back into the light.

The first time Alec took her on an actual date showed they both had a lot of unlearning to do. They'd chosen a popular restaurant that Mercedes used to love. Their table wasn't quite ready, and they waited at the packed bar. Both of them tried to appear relaxed around the crowd of bar guests, but her fingers danced, and every sharp noise made Alec want to pull her out of there and take her home. Mercedes, determined to conquer her fears, made them reservations at different restaurants nearly every night.

Alec's phone rang.

Disgust coated Declan's words. "Oi, you watchin' this shite?"

Alec scoffed. "No, the hospital will only put on news stations. They apparently don't have channels that'll play rugby games in Scotland and their Wi-Fi is weak as hell."

"Ach, you aren't missing out, mate," Declan said. "Any updates on the wee lassie?"

"Not in a while. Sadie came out once and said it would be hours and told me to go home. But I'm fine here."

"Still can't leave her?"

It always surprised him how Declan knew his thoughts. "Not yet. I'm working on it."

"Give it time," Declan said reassuringly.

"We are." His need to know exactly where she was at all times hadn't let up. Alec shifted in the uncomfortable chair. "How is Noah settling in?"

"He's doing great. Only been here a week and already hit the ground running."

Noah visited a few times and confessed to Mercedes he wanted to leave the US marshals. His disgust with his superiors over their handling of Mercedes's case left a nasty taste in his mouth and he was ready for a change.

Alec offered him a job on the spot, knowing he would make a hell of an addition to his team. Even though the new San Francisco office needed to be staffed, Noah asked if it would be possible to take a spot in London instead. For everything Noah had done for Mercedes, Alec would give him whatever the hell he wanted.

Declan chuckled. "I think Shake's a bit smitten, to be honest. You might have to have one of your thrilling chats about workplace romances."

"Nah, they're grown men, they can handle themselves."

Alec laughed. "Speaking of which, how have things progressed with Cress?"

Declan was silent for a beat. "No progress there. I don't think it's going to happen."

Alec sighed. "You're a moron, you know that?"

"Don't toss my words back at me, aye."

"It was true then, and it's true now."

Declan muttered something and Alec was pretty sure the word 'prick' was thrown in there.

"Any word on Tim Barlow?" Declan said, clearly wanting to talk about something else.

Alec let the subject drop for now. "Nothing new. I figure he'll show up wherever Mara is, but who knows."

Barlow had been in the wind since the night at Cooper's estate. With Cooper dead, his coming forward would only incriminate himself. He left Mara in Alec's care with the promise he and Mercedes would help her ease into the WITSEC program.

Mara wasn't only a good record keeper when it came to Cooper's criminal dealings, she'd created records of all the men taking part in the sex trade and bribery schemes, as well as names of the other young victims she'd met over the years. Her testimony would be wide reaching, bringing down corporate CEOs and celebrities alike.

The deaths of Marcus and Tyler Cooper and Jason Hollis, along with a mystery woman at the Cooper's country estate, drove the press wild. They competed to be the first with breaking news about the drama. So many key players in such a major criminal trial mysteriously died together and, for once, not a word had broken through the firewall Whitley and the FBI created.

Thankfully, Alec's name faded in the press and Mercedes's name wasn't widely published during the trial due to her protected status. They knew of her dramatic return, but few revealed her identity. And since Whitley didn't want to be exposed for what he'd done to Mercedes and Alec, he worked extra hard to keep their name out of everything related to the new investigation.

"I best go," Declan said. "Mrs. Downey's wanting to feed me some sort of cardboard protein bar. Call me when our new cousin arrives, aye?"

Alec hung up and watched the news repeat for another cycle, catching some updates on the investigation into the deaths. He'd started to doze off when the elevator doors opened, and Ezra Coulter stepped off the lift. They hadn't seen each other since the night at the speakeasy.

Alec lifted his brow in greeting. "Ezra."

"Hey Alec. How's it going in there?"

"At the last update, Charlotte's doing well, and they think it should be anytime." He checked his watch. "That was an hour ago."

Ezra sat next to Alec. The silence was thick between them.

Finally, Ezra cleared his throat. "I'm grateful you were there that night at the party and when everything else went down. As much as I hate losing her. I know she's safe and happy with you."

Alec nodded. "Thank you for saying that. But you didn't completely lose her. She still very much cares for you and wants you in our life." When Ezra nodded, Alec added, "Just keep the touching to a minimum, aye?"

"I'll do my best." Ezra chuckled. "Do you know where you're planning to settle yet? I doubt she is still thinking about that New York firm."

He shook his head. "She's not sure what she wants right now. There's no rush. So, we're going to stay here for a while to be near Charlie and the baby. Then we want to spend a month or two in Scotland. We can sort it out from there."

"Is that where all your family is?"

"Aye, my family lives in Edinburgh. But Mercedes and I have a little river cottage in the Scottish Borders we've been wanting to go back to." Alec tilted his head. "What about you? Aren't you touring soon?"

"Yeah, eighty-six shows over the next six months. It'll end in Europe, so I hope you and Mercy can come one night."

"Aye, she'll love that."

The security door buzzed open, and Mercedes came skipping out, a huge grin graced her face.

"She's here!"

Alec stood and she threw herself into his arms.

"Charlie did so well. It was insane! The baby weighs seven pounds, eight ounces and she's just the cutest. Well, she's pretty gross too, but she's amazing!"

Alec laughed. "Congratulations, darling. You're an auntie!"

"Thanks, Uncle Lick." She shot him a mischievous smile.

"Aye, bloody hell. I never should have told you that."

Then her attention caught over his shoulder. "Ezra! Hi."

"Hey Mercy! Damn good day, isn't it?" Ezra opened his arms, and she strode into them, laughing and going on about the baby girl who had just entered the world.

For the first time, seeing Ezra's arms around her didn't bother him. Ezra may still want her, but it was clear where her heart lay.

Mercedes stepped back and took Alec's hand. His soul leaped when she gave him a tug and said, "Come on, let's go see our niece."

Our niece.

Our family.

EPILOGUE

"Sadie," Alec said, breaking through Mercedes's sleep. "Sadie, darling. Time to wake up."

The soft rumble of the river outside was the first thing Mercedes recognized other than Alec's soft voice. He gently stroked her cheek with his thumb. Then, he bent down to rain little kisses on her face.

She opened one eye and got a feel for the climate of the room. It was dark and cold. Mercedes grumbled and gathered the blanket tighter to her chest.

"Darling, can you wake up for me?"

"Alec, it's not even light out yet."

"I know, but I want to take you on a hike."

"A hike?" She stared at his dark form. "Are you serious?"

"Quite serious," he said, slipping the blanket down to her waist. "The skies are perfect today. It's going to rain the rest of the week."

Cool air hit her naked skin, and she shivered. "Clearly, jet lag is hitting you differently than it's hitting me," she grumped.

He chuckled and caressed her breasts, the heat of his hands radiating to her skin. Mercedes arched her back and sighed, letting Alec's gentle strokes coax her awake. She didn't think there would ever be a time she would turn away from his touch.

When his mouth captured her nipple in his mouth, she gasped and moaned. "What are you doing to me?"

Alec chuckled and sucked her in deeper. "I'm trying to get you up. This is the only thing that seems to work."

He moved, and the sheet slid away from her a little farther, chilling her skin. Mercedes blinked and took in Alec's tall form in the dark move to the end of the bed. The weight of him joining her on the bed made her shift in front of him. He brought her legs on either side of him and covered her with his clothed body. His kiss was slow, taking his time with her.

"You know, if you won't wake up, I'll have to take drastic measures," he murmured in between his assault on her lips.

Mercedes giggled. "Oh yeah, what's that?"

In a smooth motion, Alec dipped between her thighs, the warmth of his tongue searing into her growing need for him. He stroked her clit, caressing every ounce of pleasure to the surface. Mercedes moaned, her orgasm building quickly. Alec always knew exactly how to drive her mad.

She tangled her fingers through his thick hair and pulled him into her. "This is the exact opposite way to get me out of bed."

"Aye, I know. I just love to listen to you."

Mercedes gripped the mattress while her hips gently thrust up to meet his mouth. When he added his fingers, she writhed against him. No matter how many times he did this to her, it would always feel like his first touch.

"Oh, god, that feels so good. Don't stop," she whispered, nearing the edge of her climax.

When her release struck, she cried out his name, tightening her hold on his head as each wave coursed through her core and out to every part of her body.

Once the world came back into focus, she sat up and drew him onto her. He kissed her deeply, and she tasted herself on his lips. The length of his hard shaft pressed against her, and she slipped her hands down the waistband of his sweats. Alec moaned when she tightened her fingers around him, but he drew away without warning.

"No, no, love. We really have to go."

Mercedes kissed him. "Are you sure you don't want to get naked and stay in this nice warm bed with me?"

"Aye, it's very tempting." He let out a deep exhale as he stood. "But there's something I want you to see. Come on, darling." Then he left the room.

As much as she would love to spend the rest of the morning wrapped in his arms, his excitement for whatever he wanted to show her was infectious. She climbed out of the bed and turned on the light. Still bleary-eyed, she rummaged through her dresser, searching for clothes that would work for a chilly hike in the woods.

When she emerged from their bedroom, Alec was in the sunroom packing items into the backpack that rested on the window seat. The view of the rushing river was barely visible, silhouetting him in the predawn light. Mercedes inhaled sharply at the sight of him. He was as beautiful as the day she'd met him.

He held out a travel cup of coffee and Mercedes took it gratefully.

"Mmm, a man after my own heart,"

"Aye, I already have that, darling. I'm smart enough to keep it by giving you orgasms and coffee."

His crooked grin made her pulse quicken, and a flush ran up her cheeks. She loved how his flirting still made her giddy as hell. "Orgasms and coffee *are* the main reasons I keep you around, McKinley."

"Look at you. All cheeky before the sun's even up." Alec chuckled, strapping his backpack onto his shoulders. "Come on, darling. Don't want to miss it."

They stepped out into the cool Scottish air, the fresh scent of late summer giving way to the crispness of the coming autumn. The river and the breeze in the trees made a rushing symphony in the night.

The light of his flashlight illuminated their path. She had never taken this part of the trail before. During her last visit, they'd mostly stuck to the main path between the river cottage and the main inn. It grew a little steeper as they walked, a growing ache in her leg reminding her she had a ways to go to regain her mobility.

Daylight had brightened the landscape enough that Alec tucked the flashlight away in his bag. Mercedes stretched, trying to relieve the tension in her injured leg.

"Are you okay?" Alec asked.

"Yep, I'm doing great. A little sore," she said reassuringly.

"Are you sure? It's just a wee bit farther."

She hated that worried look. "I'm fine, I promise. This exercise is good for me."

They walked the trail for about five minutes more before Alec turned onto a much smaller path into the brush. An over-look came into view and Mercedes inhaled sharply. The dawn had washed the valley below in deep blues and greens of the lightening sky.

"Ah, here we are." Alec led her to a grassy flat, a perfect vista to take in the sunrise. He pulled his bag off his shoulders and unzipped it. Rummaging through, he brought out a thick plaid blanket and spread it on the ground. Then he brought out a few containers of berries, soft cheese, and bread.

Mercedes bit back a smile. He'd even made her breakfast. How on earth had she gotten so lucky?

Alec sat on the blanket and held his hand out for her to join him.

Mercedes set her coffee down and settled in front of him, her back resting against his chest. "Where did you learn to do things like this?"

"Like what?"

"Like this." She waved her hand around to the impending sunrise over the Scottish hills. "You can be quite romantic when you want to be."

"Aye, I have my moments. My father does stuff like this for my mum all the time. It used to gross us out when we were kids. But he knew what he was about." A smile played on his lips. "Maybe someday, I'll gross out our children with how much I love their mother."

Mercedes's breath caught at his words, and she stroked his cheek with her thumb. "I hope so. Being grossed out by love sounds like a wonderful way to grow up."

The thought of having children no longer scared the hell out of her. In fact, she wanted nothing more than blue-eyed *bairn* to fill her arms.

Someday.

They both wanted time to be Alec and Sadie for a while.

He wrapped her in his warmth, and they snacked on the fruit in silence, taking in the view around them. When the sun finally peaked over the hills, the sky above them turned into a stunning array of pink and orange clouds.

"Ah, we got here just in time," Alec said, nuzzling her neck.

"It's beautiful," she breathed. "Totally worth going on a hike in the dark."

The serenity of the moment filled her chest. Love, commitment, security, hope. All the things she thought she'd have to live without had come back to her, and she didn't think she could be more grateful.

Mercedes sighed and snuggled in tighter, lightly stroking the back of his hand with her fingertips. She might just fall asleep, right here in the safety of his arms.

"Sadie, darling. Can I ask you something?" Alec's husky tone broke through her drowsy thoughts.

"Mm-hm."

"Will you marry me?"

Mercedes's heart came to a halt, then plunged back to life, hammering out a fiery new rhythm. She gazed into his beautiful eyes. "Do you mean it?"

Why she'd asked him that, she couldn't be sure. There was no reason to doubt his sincerity. But sometimes, his love for her seemed too good to be true.

"Aye, I knew long ago I wanted to marry you." Alec studied her with a soft smile on his face, then he held out a silver ring resting on the end of his little finger. The diamonds sparkled in the newly risen sunlight. "I bought this right after you left London, just as soon as I could manage the shops. After I lost you I . . . I couldn't part with it. But I never even dared to dream I'd be given another chance." Alec's voice was thick with emotion, and he cleared his throat. "I want to be your family, and I want you to be mine. Marry me?"

"Yes," Mercedes choked out, tears spilling onto her cheeks. "I love you so much."

Alec captured her lips with his and kissed her slowly. When he drew away, he slipped the ring onto her finger and interlaced his hand with hers.

"I love you, too," Alec whispered. "You are my everything."

THANKS FOR READING

Thank you so much for reading Alec and Sadie's journey together. I truly hope you enjoyed it.

Want to know when the next book comes out? (Can you guess who will star in that one?) Sign up so you never miss out on new releases, book news, giveaways, and ARC opportunities!

Find the link on my website: www.avasher.com.

Love you!
Avie

ACKNOWLEDGMENTS

Sometimes, I still can't believe I accomplished my publishing goal, not just once, but twice now. I have to say that I'm quite hooked on it and can't wait to publish book three.

For my readers, thank you so much from the bottom of my heart for your kind words and encouragement over this past year. Even before I published the first book, I found one of the most supportive communities in the world. From the private emails and DMs, to finding a place on social media, you have welcomed me into your book filled world and I am ever grateful to you.

To my gorgeous Alpha Readers, I love you all so much! There's really nothing like having another author you can panic DM to bounce ideas off of or to soothe a bout of crippling imposter syndrome. If you haven't already, please check out these wonderful authors.

Greer Rivers- Girl, I have no idea what I would have done without your steady friendship and vast legal knowledge. I know I probably still took quite a few liberties with the story, but I can't tell you how much your support means to me.

Nerys McCabe- I can't thank you enough for our private DMs and your friendship. Your guidance led me to feeling more comfortable when writing my British characters. Not going to lie, our conversation about sun tea was absolutely hilarious. Yes, I promise, it's a real thing in America.

Garnet Christie- Your feed back really helped me focus on what I needed to do to remove and what was really working. Your patience with my overwriting is amazing and I can't thank you enough for your help and your friendship.

Renee des Lauriers- Your love for my story was so freaking heartwarming! I loved reading every thought you had as you worked though the rough copy!

Hope Parker- You are amazing at writing spicy scenes and I can't thank you enough for you input to make Alec and Sadie sizzle!

For my beta and ARC readers, thank you for taking the time to read not only one, but two long books and leaving amazing reviews. You are all so wonderful and I am grateful you gave a new writer a chance.

Thank you to My Brother's Editor for letting me push back my deadline a touch to make more story better! Also thank you to Robynne and Damon at Damonza for the beautiful covers. They look so pretty together.

To my kiddos- I know that I had to be working a lot on this one with my tight deadline. I appreciate you waiting for me to finish before we could start a new show together. I love you all so much.

To my husband, Dominic- More than twenty years later and you still make my heartbeat quicken. I love you.

ABOUT THE AUTHOR

AV Asher (Avie) was one of those kids who always got in trouble for reading in class. She has been creating stories since childhood, but only recently began writing them down. Currently, she is working on her third romantic suspense novel. Avie lives in Northern Nevada, USA, with her husband and three children.

[a] amazon.com/~/e/B08Y64CX66

[f] facebook.com/av.asher.author

[y] twitter.com/av_asher_author

[o] instagram.com/av.asher.author

WHERE TO FIND ME!

Want exclusive updates? Sign up for my newsletter at
www.avasher.com.

Purchase Signed Copies on my website. www.avasher.com

Instagram: @av.asher.author

Facebook: @av.asher.author

Twitter: @av_asher_author

Goodreads: @A_V_Asher

Tik Tok: @author_av_asher